THE LIGHT OF SEVEN DAYS

Also by River Adams

There Must be YOU

THE LIGHT OF SEVEN DAYS

A NOVEL

RIVER ADAMS

Delphinium Books

THE LIGHT OF SEVEN DAYS

Library of Congress Cataloguing-in-Publication Data is available on request.
ISBN 978-1-953002-25-9
23 24 25 26 27 LBC 5 4 3 2 1

Jacket and interior design by Colin Dockrill

To my mother, to whom I dedicate everything I do. She lived to see all but the last chapter of this book. Never my best critic, she was always my best reader.

By the rivers of Babylon,
We sat down and wept
When we remembered Zion.
On the willows there
We hung up our harps.

—Psalm 137

I wonder if I shall fall right through the earth!
How funny it'll seem to come out among the people that
walk with their heads downward! The Antipathies, I
think—

—Lewis Carroll, *Alice's Adventures in Wonderland*

CONTENTS

CHAPTER 1
December 1997

I spent only half an hour on the train, but in that time the fog has lifted, and the air is clear and shiny and wet as a G-sharp. Constellations are visible overhead, and out of habit I look for Orion, my loyal celestial companion. When I was a child, I could see him in the evenings from my bedroom window: the warrior-protector with his bow and arrows and his starry belt. I studied his picture in *The Greek Myths for Children* and pretended he was there to look in on me.

It'll soon be seven years since I came to America, but I still search for Orion in the sky when I'm falling asleep. When I'm feeling desperate and alone. Like today.

The new moon is out, too—the freakish American moon that lounges on its back. I cannot get used to this lazy crescent with its horns pointing up, snobby and indifferent. In the Russian Northwest, the crescent gazes down on humanity. It watches over us. It cares.

You would think it's the big things that make me lonely and immigrant in a sky-scraping American city—the language barrier, the capitalism, the view upon the ruins of my civilization—but it's not. Those were the nightmares of my early years of refugeeism, when every night I lay in bed into the morning hours, feeling infinity crawl on my skin and the dark waters unspool between my body and the real world. Feeling homeless and loveless and burned to ash. Now it's mostly the little things, like that moon. It's the buses without heat and the restaurants without cloakrooms.

It's the damn faucets, all designed in some different, ingeniously evil ways to stump a foreigner, and the glances of the bystanders who watch me do battle with the faucets. Poor girl. Stupid girl. Foreign girl. It's hearing people say "We'll call you back" and waiting for them to call back, stubbornly, stupidly, again and again. Because, where I come from, words mean what they mean.

It's the new acquaintances. "Where are you from?"—"Russia."—"Welcome to America! You must be so happy to be here!" And they smile—broad, surface smiles that wrinkle their skins.

Am I happy to be here?

I wouldn't rather be there.

And they ask: "Do you like America?"

"It's a complicated question," I've learned to say.

It's the clouds. They are exactly like they're supposed to be, like they were back home. That's the worst thing about them. Because sometimes I tilt my head back and look at the sky and forget everything that happened and where I am. Almost everything that happened. Then it hits me: These clouds are on the wrong side of the world.

Without the fog, there's a taut, unlikely serenity over the Schuylkill River. I wouldn't have come here on purpose, to this utilitarian sidewalk overhanging I-76. Below it is an Orwellian pit of networks: cement, steel bars, and barreling metal, down into the dark. There's always construction along the river, too: more metal and cement barriers. Choking, thunderous din. This is not a corner of Philadelphia where I go for serenity, but running up from the 30th Street Station a few minutes ago, I found myself thrashing between a boil and a simmer of the exits. The crowd carried me off, pushed through the graying, winterish twilight, this way and that,

a crosswalk and another, and burst out onto the riverfront—
and suddenly, there, on one side of me was space.

It's just after six; the construction crews must have left.
I have thirty-five minutes till I must be at the hospital, so I
stand. Breathe. I can feel the vibration of a hundred trains
and a thousand cars underneath me assuaged by a million
tons of water. It's a calming sensation, like I am touching the
Great Turtle with my feet as it bears the earth and dreams
its rolling, time-burdened dreams. All around, Philly hurries and honks into the evening. I've forgotten how much I
miss a river, even a dark and dirty one, caged so far beneath
the highway that it is barely alive and nearly voiceless. I
can hear it whisper something indiscernible. I should visit
Penn's Landing soon, look at the tall ships. In the whole of
Philadelphia, I think, I like the tall ships best of all.

I suppose I've been nervous today. The name of the department I'm going to at the U Penn medical center has
that effect on people. Changing into my street clothes at
the studio, I couldn't get my feet into my pant legs, and
even now my fingers are shaking, but it's purely physical.
If there's panic somewhere inside, I am not feeling it. Orion
looks down from the sky: "Do you need me to come down
there, Dinah?"

I don't.

I don't know.

What's the worst that could happen? I die?

Twenty minutes to the appointment, and I begin to
walk. A gray mouse runs down Orion's bowstring to my
shoulder and nestles there. She smells like Leningrad: wet
granite, lilac, cabbage soup, the crease of Matthew's neck,
and Babby's perfume.

"No squeaking," I shush her in Russian and catch a star-
tled glance from a passerby.

University City is a noisy place, swarming and sleepless. Two universities, three or four medical centers, campuses, dorms, high-rises, research buildings, cafés and fast foods galore, and international houses of anything you like: cinema, students, pancakes. Day and night the streets are bottle-necked to the bridges across the Schuylkill that lead into Center City, and pedestrians hoof it to the station or duck out for sandwiches and smokes, or sprint from one building to another. Sophomores from a feminist film class mix with orthopedic surgeons in a Wawa line. Ambulances splash colors and cries into the air.

The hospital at U Penn towers over the corner of Spruce and 34th—cement and glass and monochrome corners, sooty from exhaust. A sheer cliff of brutalist architecture, but it's different inside. I remember: The first time I wrote to Lisa Ushevich about American healthcare, I might have called it a "palace"—not this place, a place like it. A temple of Western medicine. I marvel every time I enter.

Inside, the foyer is the world of healing, confidence, and ficus trees. The world where science meets sales. The world of promise. Faux leather armchairs promise comfort, and sparkling windows promise clean hands for when you go upstairs. Smiling faces on the posters assure you quietly that, when you go upstairs, all your problems will be fixed.

My elevator whirrs and lets me out—upstairs, on a high floor. *Monkey in the elevator* stirs in my head. It's a scene from some old Soviet comedy, everybody's enduring favorite, though the movie itself is lost to me: A monkey is forgotten in an elevator, and the poor thing panics and spins around like a dreidel, climbs all over the windowless box, screams and bangs on the walls, not knowing that all it has to do is push a single button, of which there are a dozen in front of it. For five minutes it goes on like that until it hits a button by pure chance, and the machinery comes to life, and the doors open. It became in Russia a household phrase for a nincompoop just off the turnip truck.

Six years ago, on my second night in my own apartment, I couldn't turn on the overhead light. I fiddled with the round knob, back and forth and back and forth, finally decided it was broken, and—a trembling voice spitting out five pre-rehearsed words of barely comprehensible English—called maintenance. He came in the next day, a tall, burly guy in jean overalls, with a tool box in hand and gloves tucked under his belt, exactly as I'd pictured an American handyman. He walked over to the light switch and pushed on it, and the light came on. "It's a dimmer," he said and shook his head as if he'd known this would be a waste of time. Stupid girl. Foreign girl. Monkey in an elevator. And left me standing by the door as I'd been when I let him in, stewing in my own blood. At least I haven't felt this way in a couple of years, and the elevators here are more or less the same as everywhere else.

I make a left and another left to Oncology. I know the route now; it is my second visit. Check in. Wait in a faux leather chair. I've been doing a lot of waiting lately. When I was seventeen, I thought it was the hardest thing: to wait, not to know. And then I knew, and since then I don't mind waiting, knowing only so much.

I read somewhere once (a philosopher who comes to mind without a name) that there is no such thing as the present: By the time we become aware of the moment, it's already passed, and so, really, all that exists is the past and the future. And us, in perpetual flight between the two. Do you have that feeling sometimes? My feeling is that time's a porous thing, a thing of fragile structure like a ball of spiderwebs or a termite-eaten piece of wood that crumbles in the hand. And my mind in it like water, pouring through its nooks into the past and future, filling its passages, destroying the thing in the process. Or petrifying it.

A woman in blue scrubs smiles at me from one of the waiting room doors. "Dinah? Come on in." She smiles like a friend who hasn't seen me in weeks, but I don't remember her: A nurse from last time? An assistant? It's easy to smile back, and I follow her through the hallway. "Hi, Dinah," she says, repeating my name. There's intimacy in that, which I'm powerless to return. "How've you been doing?"

"About the same."

"Any pain at the site?"

"It's sore."

"It'll take a bit of time to heal. As long as it's not getting worse." She gestures into a room.

This isn't the typical exam room I expected but an office: a spacious, grainy desk; two wooden chairs in front and one behind; bookshelves along the walls. An enormous window looks out onto the river and farther, toward Center City, and I want to go over and see, but the woman is studying my face. Her gaze hits me with the anxiety that's been hiding just under the surface of my mind. Suddenly I am acutely aware of where I am.

She is petite, with a supple waist and raven hair to her shoulders and olive skin. Gigantic, almond-shaped eyes.

"Did anybody come with you today?" she asks. "We do recommend you bring someone: a friend or a family member."

"I...don't have any family."

"It's all right. Dr. Ming will be right with you." And she goes. She says it as if Dr. Ming were to be my family for today. It should be laughable, but it sounds comforting, and she must be exhausted from all the death working here, but her smile is real. It's for me.

I am standing before the window at the top of the Penn Tower. There's Philadelphia below me, vast and full of plans and memories and lights and movement, empty of certainty, and strange. With no ledges on the tower wall, the air is right under my feet. I can envision easily falling into the evening, into the rush of it, or veering up and flying off and high with Orion by my side. He shakes his head: "What are you doing, Dinah?"

"What do you know?" I say.

The door opens, and Dr. Ming walks through it, trailed by a nurse and a social worker. A burst of introductions, and she settles behind the desk. She is just as petite and willowy as the almond-eyed nurse, but her eyes are hidden by a pair of glasses, and she wears her hair in a bun.

"I'm going to get right to it, Dinah," she says and leans toward me. "We have the results of your biopsy, and I'm afraid it's what we thought: You have non–small cell adenocarcinoma of the left lung."

The social worker's voice is smooth, gentle, laced with just enough reality to keep the dose non-lethal. Her hand is resting on my forearm. It is wrinkly and veiny and has a slight tremor to it—she may be the oldest person I've encountered since stepping foot inside the Penn Tower.

"Yes, thank you," I answer her last question and realize that I've nodded through several minutes of explanations I haven't heard. The doctor was talking; the social worker was talking. Something about types of cancer, types of support services. The nurse adds another brochure to the stack on the desk in front of me—they must have everything in writing for us. Because they know, don't they? How many people keep their wits after the word "adenocarcinoma"? Not that I should be surprised: It is "what she thought."

The phrase creeps into my brain and begins to repeat, rolling, becoming rhythmic, setting itself to melody. I can feel a twitching mouse tail on my neck: downbeat, down-beat, downbeat. Barabashka is bobbing his head and drumming on his angular knees that are sticking up above his ears. He likes drumming, this one. Barabarshkas are known in Russia as house spirits who are fond of tapping on walls, which is where the name comes from: *baraban* is Russian for "drum."

I can't put my finger on the music at first, but it's bouncy, perversely playful just now yet unshakable, a mix of staccato and sticky quarter notes—*it i-is what we tho-o-ought; it i-is what we tho-o-ought*—and then I recognize it. Schubert. Allegretto from "The Shepherd on the Rock." It was my first ballet teacher's favorite piece of music, and she choreographed a number to it. Was it my first ever recital? Momentarily I remember the movements that went with the melody: pas de couru, jeté, plié—*it i-is what she tho-o-ought*...The simplest sequence there is. For children.

Dr. Ming waits for the door to click shut, and we are alone across the desk from each other. Her hands with interlocked fingers sit heavily atop my closed medical file like a little headstone. "Let's talk about the next steps," she says.

What next steps? Not dance steps, that's for sure.

"Why lung cancer?" I ask.

Her lips tense up. I don't think she understands the question.

"Out of all the cancers I could have gotten, why this? Why not lymphoma or leukemia? I don't smoke."

She nods and loosens her fingers. They scrape the surface of the binder as they slide off it into her lap. "Have you ever smoked?"

She'd already asked me that, last time. All the answers are in the chart in front of her.

"I'm a dancer," I say.

"That's right, I'm sorry. Ballet."

"Yes."

"Exposure to secondhand smoke?"

Well, there was that. The ghost of Lesha's room coalesces around me: polaroids of a faraway war crowding the walls, blood-speckled towels soaking in a bucket. For an instant I am washed in its abiding odor of harsh tobacco and vodka and salted cabbage on black bread, and dirty socks. I can hear Kot's voice, slippery like velvet in fish oil. *"No problem,"* *he said, "you're our yid," and I said nothing.* How can I miss that place? It's where I lost the last of my hope.

"There was secondhand smoke," I say. "A lot for a couple of years. Is that what did it?"

"I doubt it, though it's almost impossible in most cases to tell what causes a particular tumor." Dr. Ming raps her fingertips briefly on my chart and catches herself. Her skin is wrinkleless, her hair ink-black, and I cannot tell her age, but it occurs to me she might be older than I first thought. Maybe she's done this many times, enough to know what I need: information, not consolation. I'm not afraid. I'm suspicious. "It's true," she says, "you are very young for this. Lung cancer patients on average are about seventy, and at twenty-nine it is very unusual to develop a neoplasm in a lung—because lung cancer is so strongly associated with environmental pollutants. But it happens."

"Environmental? But not just smoking?"

"That's true. Smoking is the most common."

"What about radiation?"

"Have you had radiation exposure?" She is back to bending over the desk and leafing through my file, her whole body a whirr of attention. "Have you had radiation treatments for breast cancer? It's not in here."

"No," I say, and she stops. "No." Across the open binder, across her desk we stare at each other through the thin barrier of her glasses. She didn't understand the question. Again. "No," I say. "I mean Chernobyl."

We halt. Dr. Ming puts down the binder and leans back in her chair, then slowly takes off her glasses, and I can finally see her eyes, shallow-set and triangular, with tight eyelids and thin grayish shadows underneath. She is still trying to sound professional, but her voice has changed. There's no humoring and no hurry, no more veneer in it. It's not just for me. We're really talking now.

"You were in Chernobyl when it happened?"

"I was in Leningrad. In the path of the Chernobyl raincloud. It was a holiday, and we didn't know it happened then, so everyone was outside in the rain, celebrating——"

"That's right, I read about that." She's folded her glasses and now twirls them in her hands, round and round. "The Soviet government didn't announce the explosion until some scientists in Finland detected unsafe radiation levels."

"It was Sweden actually," I say. "It was a nuclear station in Sweden. But Gorbachev never really announced anything. A one-liner on the evening news about a minor accident. The West knew, and we still didn't."

She seems to be thinking: About my cancer? About politics? About her cat? Or is she just playing with her glasses? "How did you find out?" she asks.

I peek at Orion, who is propping up a wall in the corner, but he only shrugs. "You know, I don't remember." *The absurdity of it.* "Most of us don't remember. Somehow eventually everybody just knew: from a friend, who knew from a friend, who listened to the Voice of America. Or something."

The ludicrous senselessness of it. "Could it be Chernobyl? My cancer?"

She twirls her glasses over the desk. Their lenses catch the ceiling lights, pull them in, and release them as sparkles from the corners—catch, release, catch, release—and we both watch them flash.

"It's very difficult to tell for sure what may have caused the type of malignancy you have," she finally says. "With the rarest exceptions, impossible. Sometimes there are no identifiable reasons. Then there's radiation. A solid tumor could manifest ten, fifteen years after exposure; blood cancers usually sooner. There's pollution. Smoke. Do you have any family history of cancer?"

My guffaw bursts out unseemly, intrusive, possibly indecent. Her eyebrows jump, and I choke a foul laugh. I keep expecting her to understand, but why would she? Why would anyone here?

Still. If she is going to be my doctor, she must understand, at least a little. At least a hint. At least for those who will come after me.

"You don't understand," I say. "Where I come from, everybody has a family history of cancer. Leukemia, lymphoma, thyroid. And then breast cancer or colon or lung. Pancreatic, multiple myeloma, brain tumors, or a few of those at once. One from column A, one from column B. There isn't anyone I know, in Leningrad, who hasn't lost family to cancer. There's cancer. It's everywhere."

It's the downslope of rush hour at the 30th Street Station: The stairs are packed, a train's already boarding, but I let it go. There will be another soon. The platform grows roomy around me, and I slip onto a bench and watch the space fill

11

with a spreading mass of people from the stairs like a blood spill from a vein.

My support network is in full complement, but they're being subdued. The mouse is hiding under my collar; Orion is shifting awkwardly from one foot to the other, his bow over the shoulder, both thumbs hooked behind his belt, eyes sideways; Barabashka is squatting on the next bench, squashing his floppy ears between his knees and knocking out some intricate rhythm on the benchtop with his semi-transparent fingers.

"Cut it out," I say. "I'm fine."

I *am* fine. I'm still not feeling it. Maybe, there's nothing to feel.

I'm a little dazed, I admit, but that's mostly the bits and pieces of Dr. Ming floating in my possibly cancer-ridden brain, my near future reordering itself. PET scan, CAT scan—that's all tomorrow and the day after. MRI of the head separately.

"We need to see how far the cancer has spread," she told me, "and we need to start right away." My cancer can metastasize to the brain, she said. Had I experienced any symptoms? Headaches, seizures, hallucinations? Barabashka wilted on the chair next to me, his angular head sinking to his ankles, sniffling and murmuring something resentful from down there.

"I don't think so," I said. "I mean, headaches, for sure. But I've been coughing."

Do they do it on purpose, give the scans those furry names: PET-scan, CAT-scan? So they wouldn't be scary? SCARY-scan. FURRY-scan.

She kept me in her office another half hour maybe, longer than I thought she would, but I am glad. I am grateful. I wasn't ready to go home just then. I'm not sure I am now.

The train rolls into place at the platform like a sliding wall, completing the space, and I step through the door as though from one room to another.

The car is just full enough to give each passenger a row. I find a place by the window, my favorite, but it's too dark to make out the details of the city swimming backwards beyond the dirty pane, only outlines. I scan them with unfocused, untethered eyes: roofs at first, chains of raw homes, then stout, right-angled, one- and two-storied warehouses, parking lots, storage containers, something piled, something stacked, something sprawling.

To think of it, that doesn't look right.

We pull to a halt. "Lansdowne. Next stop, Gladstone."

It figures: I boarded a train in the wrong direction, south instead of north. In the empty seat by the aisle, Barabashka is blinking apologetically. I should get off now and cross the tracks to wait for an inbound train. Better do it fast, before they shut the doors. There is an unlit parking lot beside the railroad, and I cannot tell through the window what color the cars are. In the dark, green is like blue is like black. White is like yellow. Everything is gray.

I missed my moment: My outbound train shudders and begins to move, hitting the seams faster and faster, reminding me of the metronome. Shouldn't I be terrified? I may be dying.

It's like I rehearsed this too many times, and now it's my turn, and there's no juice left in me.

Every big loss is a small death, don't you think? You fall apart, and then you scrape yourself together and rise again, changed, and you begin to live—a new life, because what else is there to do. You just hope this new life is worth it. But how much can you lose and keep rising?

My parents died when I was three years old, and I don't

know much about their deaths except it was an accident. They left for work one day, together, as always, and never came back. I don't remember those first three years, but I've always imagined them as this paradisiacal time of childhood joys. A string of nuclear family clichés. If I exist in that time at all, it is beneath consciousness, through the irony of its first and greatest finds, which I cannot recall, and its first and greatest loss, which brought it to a crushing end and made me who I am. It is, of course, ground zero for all things to come. My "life zero."

My life as I know it began in Leningrad, with Babby. My grandmother and me—two boots a pair, as the saying goes. I think of it as my first life. My real childhood. Because, if I'd ever been young enough to believe that things last forever, I don't remember myself that way.

"Last stop, Media. Last stop." The conductor passes through the car grasping the headrests and making eye contact with the few of us still tucked into our seats. I unfold myself and trudge down the steps, where I merge with the small crowd that crosses the tracks in front of the engine, trickles up to a street, and divides: left and right. I linger a moment and turn left, uphill. The empty inbound train thunders through underneath, sending vibrations up my feet as I step off the overpass onto the road. There's an apartment complex on both sides, and it eats most of the group that came up from the station with me. I pass lawyers' offices, a hair salon, an intersection with a bank and a municipal parking lot—and I'm in town, on something that looks like a main street.

It's pretty here: a small suburban town with a spark to it. In early December they've already put up Christmas decorations. Multicolored garlands run continuously to contour every building and create a townscape with flat and pitched roofs, balconies, and clock towers. A block away, a street performer is playing the viola over his open case, his back against one of the sidewalk lights, which imitate gas lamps—it's all as though a page had turned from Pushkin, Dumas, or Dickens and swept me along into a smaller world, where things are still simple and within reach.

I've come to accept the misery of Pennsylvania winters, snowless, featureless, always on the brink of freezing that turns mud into puddles and back into mud, biding time between life and life. Winter is a sad, waiting time in Philadelphia, but this town doesn't look sad. Storefronts are flooded with warm light; sidewalks are full, but nobody's hurrying. Across the intersection, a gaunt man in jeans and a chunky knit sweater is holding the leash of an enormous, equally gaunt greyhound. The dog stands in zen-like calm while two children drape themselves over him. Red changes to green, and I move in the direction of the dog and the violist.

I pass by restaurants with couples seated near the windows and see their interlocked fingers brushing the glass. One couple smiles at me in unison. I stop at a lighted vitrine, where an office scene is constructed from everyday hardware: nuts, bolts, screws, staples and paper clips and nails and things I don't know what to call, little smooth metal things and curled metal things and buttons. It is extraordinary. There's a little boss behind his little desk, swooping his bent-nail glasses arrogantly in the air. He is quietly hated by the employees in their cubicles as they type and talk and don't look at him, and one is sneaking a curled-paperclip smoke into his pocket. There's a secretary steaming outside the boss's door and a couple smooching their screw heads shamelessly in the bathroom. Each little person is so animated, so moody—I find myself grinning into the pane, steaming it up, then read the sign on the door: TURNING

POINT GALLERY. I wave a tiny good-bye to the metal people before moving on.

I am not reading street signs. This is just walking, down this main street for now, past a pedestrian promenade where two grizzled men are playing chess on a special chessboard table, a frozen yogurt place with a tiny mob outside, a theatre with three musicals on the marquee, away from downtown. It is murky and muted here, and I turn right, then turn again, wandering, keeping the violist just on the margin of earshot.

I should make my way back to the station and take a train home before it's too late.

If loss is a kind of death, then death must be a kind of loss, mustn't it? Loss of life. I don't mean for others; I don't mean grief. I mean here, now, for me. The social worker thought I was frozen with fear—because we are afraid to lose the things that matter. The things that are worth keeping. At least we're supposed to be.

I've been standing still, I realize, near a building on a narrow downhill street. The building draws attention because it's a squarish gray-stone construction amid single-family homes, but that's not why I stopped. For a second I have to focus on the reason, then I hear it: There's music. The door is wide open, and a song is streaming from inside, a simple melody in a male voice wrapped around guitar chords, in a sultry, ethereal language warped with age—plush and ringing and guttural at once. Have you ever heard a song you recognize, even though you've never heard it before? A song that seeps into your bones? This song is like that. It is about something elemental, below words. It is filling my veins and my eyes, and answering questions I've always known I needed to have answered and never known to ask. It has brought me here. It knows me.

If only I could decipher the words...

I go up to the door and step inside, slow motion, feeling my way through a small lobby and up a staircase. The music leads me down a hallway, to a rectangle of light falling on the floor from another open door, where the melody becomes a living voice. I have arrived.

On the other side of the doorway is a room that looks like an academic's office: floor-to-ceiling shelves stuffed with books, some modern, others medieval-looking multivolume collections, unbound manuscripts spilling over the top and off the desk that's pushed against an open window. In a far corner, a mess of musical instruments makes me think of a school band. There's a trumpet, a clarinet, a violin in a case, a tambourine, and judging by its agonized shape, a broken drum set. Three simple chairs, one of which is piled up with books and another occupied by a contraption I wouldn't dare name. On the third, the singer is resting his foot.

In my twenty-nine years I'd never walked into a place un-invited. We don't do that. I definitely wouldn't do that in America. But just now it doesn't seem to be important. Only the song is important. Not losing the song.

He is sitting on top of the desk with his guitar, tapping his foot on the chair and engrossed in what is probably a re-hearsal, because he goes back a phrase, repeats and goes on, then repeats again. When I start coughing, he raises his head. The song cuts out with a whine and leaves the air orphaned. He hushes the strings with a flat palm.

"The door was open," I say.

"Uh...yes, our heat's gone crazy." He leans the guitar vertically against the desk and slides off, extending his hand. "Hi. Simon Levi. May I help you?"

Of course, it was Hebrew. I should have known. But I don't remember Hebrew sounding like this. Like blood. And if that means anything, I couldn't tell you—here, in a small American town, where Hebrew flows from open doors, recognizable, I imagine, to real Jews. Whatever that means, too.

Simon Levi's hand is dry and warm, and his face is working muscles near the ears and eyebrows—I must be an oddity at best. He has a good face. Kind. Wrinkles of excessive thinking about the eyes. He's surprisingly short, narrow in the shoulders but with a paunch that's weighing down his white cotton shirt and stressing the lower buttons above the belt. He has a head of dark wavy hair and a prickly salt-and-pepper beard, which he scratches with both hands, each on its own cheek, like he's fluffing it, then flashes a short smile and asks pointedly, "What?"

With his unabashedly Semitic nose, and his beard and bookish build and mannerisms, he's such a defining stereotype of an Ashkenazi Jew that when I open my mouth to answer, it slips out: "You're Jewish."

"Ah."

Who says that? What will he think of me?

Simon Levi has turned his head a bit to the side and is watching me out of the corner of his narrowing eye, and for a sweep of a second I wonder if he can't see the gray mouse on my shoulder. But that squint appears to be amusement.

"I am, indeed," he drawls out. "This is a synagogue, and I am, after all, a rabbi."

This doesn't look like a synagogue to me. But then, it's better.

"Your song. What does it mean?"

"What, that?" He picks up the page of sheet music from the desk. "It's a new '*Lecha dodi*' for tomorrow's Kabbalat Shabbat."

There's a pause, like the answer was self-explanatory, and I imagine what he sees: a short, scrawny foreign woman with a clipped nest of kinky hair, too pale, too skinny, two brown-ish bags under her eyes, standing in his doorway in a coat too bulky for the weather, with bamboo legs in faded jeans sticking out from under it, lost in the jungle of tongues and continents and circumstances, comprehending nothing of the simple thing he said. The thing a real Jew would comprehend.

"It's a prayer," he explains. "'Come, My Beloved.' You like it?"

And then I cry.

This isn't the place—not here, not like this—so I try to stop. I blink and swallow, stuff down the sobs, but I'm wet and burning and twisted in the mouth, out of control, spilling, and I shake my head and keep saying "I'm sorry, I'm sorry" as tear droplets fly off my chin.

It shouldn't be like this. It should be at home with Babby and Matthew, tangled in four strong arms and two warm bodies on my own bed, crying myself dry and pretending to fall asleep and hearing them whisper over me. It should be in Lisa's apartment, or in Cleo's, or in anybody's apartment, to think of it, where it would be real. One of the guys' places even (somebody from the Kirov Theatre), where Lisa would hold my head in her lap, and I would let it out, loud and self-ish and careless. There'd be ten dancers crowding the rooms, bringing tea and blankets; someone would yell at me—"Don't you get hopeless!"—and someone would shush him. There'd be an argument about how to handle what's next: Who would stay with me and who would take me to treatments. Who lived on which side of the Neva. Because they raise bridges in Leningrad, and if you need someone in the middle of the night, they can't always get to you across the river.

Except there is no more Leningrad. St. Petersburg now, there, on the right side of the world. They renamed it after I left, and I've never been to that other town.

And there is no more Kirov. They've renamed the theatre, too, everything, as if, by relabeling the maps, you could erase the past. As if you could write over what shamed you, and the old lines wouldn't bleed through.

The rabbi is holding my shoulders and asking something, his brow a dancing plicate leaf: now horizontal, now vertical. They always ask if you're okay. Especially when it's clear that you are not, they ask if you're okay. And you have to say you are. This is American English.

"—like to sit down?" he says. "Hey. Come here and sit." He leads me by the shoulders to the chair that used to hold his foot, carefully, like I'm an unglued pyramid, and turns to lift the contraption from the other chair. "Let me just move the shofar." He enthrones the giant spiral that looks as though it were made of bone on top of his papers and pulls the chair up in front of me. We are almost knee to knee. "Were you looking for a rabbi?" he asks.

"No."

I realize that he doesn't know my name. Most Americans, I've found, cannot tell a Jewish face when they're looking at one, but I bet American Jews still can.

"Can I get you something?" He reaches for nothing in particular, waves his hand in the air. "A tissue or some water?"

"I have cancer," I say, and he freezes. We hold still for a while.

"You just found out...?" It's a half question. His arm comes down slowly into his lap.

Something's changed. It dawns on me in increments that Orion isn't here. Barabashka. The mouse. None of them; they're gone. It's me and Simon Levi, and reality filling the place, airy and thick and fibrous as cotton candy.

"I have cancer," I say. I want to add something. I want to tell him about the fear, or no fear, but it sounds wrong in my head, like I'm being brave, and I can't find the words. He won't understand. Who *wants* to be afraid of death? "I should go," I offer.

"No, you should stay." He scrambles to his feet and fishes a plastic water bottle from behind his desk, unscrews the top, and hands it to me. "Stay a little bit. We can talk about something else. Or that, if you want."

The bottle is warmer than my hand. It must have been sitting near a heating vent.

Have you ever felt so tired, you thought it wasn't possible: to be so tired and live? I felt that way waiting for Matthew, saying good-bye to Babby. Flying to New York. Leila Kahn's funeral. But I am more tired now. I cannot move.

Life keeps you going on adrenaline most of the time: No one will get you to the watering hole; no one will watch your back while you drink. Not many places where you can rest.

If I could spend what's left of my life without moving from this chair...

"Your prayer," I say. "Can you sing it again?"

CHAPTER 2
1971–1978

In my first life, Leningrad is spacious and infallible and full of light. This place, which made me and killed me. This time, before I think of myself, of home, and of innocence as things that can be lost.

I live in a residential part of the city, one of those "bedroom areas" that over the twentieth century replaced the villages that used to encircle old Petersburg. The avenues here are grand, lined with ash trees and maples and sparkling movie houses. Linden alleys run into playgrounds surrounded by straight-walled, straitlaced apartment buildings. Everything is airy, safe, and rectangular.

Some buildings are long and slender like revolutionary battleships. In early June, their gray-bricked hulls float amid the waves of lilac that inundate their corners: purple waters, white foam. One of these is on my way to school, and when I run past it, holding on to the straps of my backpack, I turn up my face and squint and imagine it's the legendary cruiser *Aurora*. I saw it moored on the Neva when we went to the Hermitage on a class trip. The ship was gray and long, cold as steel, enormous and graceful, guarding the place where it had started the Revolution with the loudest shot in the world. I ran up the gangway and touched my hand to its sleeping hide, but it was dreaming of flint-faced sailors in black peacoats, of smoke-filled glories and cannonades, and it didn't wake up.

Other buildings are like the one I live in, magical square

towers rising from the earth, so tall that I can only see to the tops if I bend backward. I like to do that, feel the dizziness of it and watch the clouds sweep the roofs.

I like to walk through the grove between my school and my house. In the winter, the morning after a fresh snowfall, even the tiniest branches of the trees are coated in white fluff, and just then I live in a great underwater kingdom, where wondrous fish are sleeping among the limbs of my coral garden. In the spring, kids make whistles out of maple pods and earrings out of birch blossoms, and girls braid dandelions into circlets and crown each other.

Tanya Ladina is the master circlet weaver. She puts one on me and teaches me how to weave until Babby calls me in for supper. An artist with her hands, she will become a hairdresser and marry a boy two years ahead of us in school, a bus driver, and have two sons with him. She will die of thyroid cancer when her children are six and three, but I'll be then in the throes of my first American year and will not make it to her funeral. I wave to her as I run to my house, pressing the golden circlet she's made down on my hair, and she waves back with a bunch of dandelions. Their long, limp stems dangle from her fist like noodles.

My favorite chore is picking up groceries with my little "what-if" bag, a net of fine rope with handles that fits into my pocket. Everyone carries one of these bags around in case they see some "deficit" item when passing by a store, like oranges or bananas or smoked salami, or toilet paper or pantyhose. With Babby's list and a couple of rubles folded into a tight fist, I run, wind in my hair, the four-minute run to the supermarket, then walk a careful ten-minute walk back. It's satisfying to feel the what-if bag's pull on my arm and fingers, hearing the brittle clink of milk bottles or the rustle of eggshells. I step solemnly, like a grown-up.

I like the supermarket more than the grocery store at the convenience center because there I must talk to the clerks. They loom behind the counters, aproned, giant, and impatient in the haze of mixing odors of pastries and raw meat. I rehearse what I must say while I wait in the queue, but when I step up, I lose my words, and they prompt me in booming, reverberating voices, so loud that I'm convinced every single soul in the building must notice me and know me to be inept, and puny, and lost, and forgetful. "What do you need, girl? How much do you need? Have you paid at the register yet?"

My consolation comes from the bread kvass vendor. He sits by the convenience center with his two-wheeled yellow cistern, a tap in its side, two men and a lady with a stroller standing around, drinking their kvass. A small mug, which is still too big for me to hold in one hand, costs four kopecks. He throws my coins into a saucer, accepts an empty glass mug from the lady and rinses it over his water fountain, then opens the tap, and the hissing, foaming brown liquid fills it to the brim with chilling freshness.

There is nothing like cold-barrel kvass anywhere. Many years later, I will read an interview with a Soviet spy who spent decades under deep cover in the West. He will say that kvass is like blood, like the native tongue, like folk tales and lullabies—a drink uniquely Russian and inescapable, brewed from bread, from the heart of the land. All Russians love it and none others do. By how people drank kvass he could tell who was of Russia and who was not.

At home, on the twelfth floor of the fantastic tower, it's almost two o'clock, and Babby is cooking dinner. Our two-room apartment smells like cabbage soup and chicken rissoles and sour, spongy black bread with butter. Sometimes it smells like cold, lumpy kefir, blindingly white and jiggling in my sweating glass, or dried fruit compote. On New Year's and Revolution Day and Victory Day and on my birthday, it smells like yeasty, golden, heat-radiating apple pies. It smells like beet soup and soft, creamy sautéed squash and plum juice. The juice is so thick with pulp that I can see currents in the opaque, burgundy suspension when I turn the glass around on its axis again and again, and I watch little shreds of plum do their mysterious dignified churning: up, right, down, left, the way galactic dust drifted in that film in the planetarium.

"Are you playing with your glass again, kitten?"

Babby is at the stove. Her hands are busy, one with a potato, the other with a knife, so she wipes her forehead on her sleeve. Her hair bun is coming loose, and long, thin white strands stick to her cheek and get caught in the wrinkles. When Babby makes home fries, she holds a spud over the pan, and perfect slices fall into the spitting, bubbling butter. The knife whirrs like sparrow wings—*vzzzhik, vzzzhik, vzzzhik*—and a darkening crust sizzles into existence around the tender potato flesh that will melt on my tongue.

My first life is full of Babby, delineated, guided, and protected by her, though I am not yet conscious of this. I don't question how she manages to support us on our two government pensions: the one she earned after forty years of teaching literature to middle schoolers and the one I get for my parents. My grandmother is my only family, my adult world, and the reason Siberian dumplings will always have the power to lift me out of a funk. She is the safety net I still take entirely for granted. Her smell, her voice, her clothes are my only sense of home. One day, years from now, on a television screen I will see Queen Elizabeth wear a headscarf tied the Russian way, under the chin, a flowery headscarf like my Babby's, and I will love her instantly—a woman separated from me by distance, by class and circumstance as far as humanly possible. But in that moment I will know her, and I will forgive her everything.

Babby and I live in the magic tower most of the year, but we spend our summers in a Ukrainian village, at the house of her childhood friend, Aunt Grippa. Babby's face always takes on a strange foggy expression when she mentions Aunt Grippa, and I never know why. We ride to Ukraine in a long, green sleeper train, where the conductor comes through the cars with glasses of tea and sugar cubes. The tea is so hot that even the handles of the ornate metal glass holders are warm to the touch. We drink tea and eat sandwiches of black bread with butter and sweaty cheese, and I spend many hours lying prone on the top bunk so I can watch farms and forests roll back past the window. I read a book, lifting my eyes from the pages to watch more of the forest, and tap my toes in time with the clacking of the rail seams.

Babby chats with the neighbors or reads at the little table below, sitting on the lower bunk, underneath which our bags are stowed: one suitcase with clothes and two bags of food. We don't bring books (the village library is to die for), but the food is a gift for Aunt Grippa. It is mostly nonperishables—condensed milk, cookies, and candy—plus whatever perishables Babby could hunt down and save in the weeks before. Maybe smoked salami. Maybe *shpik*—salty, smoked pork fat. Maybe cheese or Aunt Grippa's favorite sweetened yogurts.

I know how it will be: As soon as the first hugs are done, Aunt Grippa will plunge her hands into the bags and rummage through them, hungrily, then take out each item and lay everything out on the table and admire it, as if preparing an exhibition. Then she will pick something out—a cookie or a candy or a stick of salami—and take a single bite, blissful and a little teary. Still chewing, she will say, "Thank you, Freeda." And Babby will watch it all standing up, clutching my head to her belly, and never smile.

I asked her once why we couldn't just buy all these gifts for Aunt Grippa right there in the village, and she got that foggy expression again and said, "They don't have that in the country, kitten." She hugged me to herself the way she does sometimes when the news is on, and said, "Don't you worry about it. Not yet."

The summers of my childhood smell like a pine forest: warm, viscid amber and fresh needles and August wind. The pines are straight and tall as clipper masts, with golden flaky bark and faraway crowns that tangle together in the sky. I splash in the lazy Desna River with the local children, whose game is to whip the surface with long, pliant willow switches, and our din shatters against the steep shore across the water.

I look for mushrooms with Babby. She has a big basket, and I have a little one.

"The best mushrooms are white mushrooms, good for drying. They hide under spruce trees," she says, and shows me the sticky brown top of a penny bun peeking out from under the blanket of caked forest bed.

"Why are they called 'white' if they're brown?" I demand.

"I don't know," she says, laughing, and I am pouty for the rest of the outing.

In the afternoons, I wander barefoot among the pines. I sink supine into the silky mix of fine sand and dry needles and listen to the roots click beneath the earth. The cuckoos count out the years of my life (however many times the cuckoo calls without pausing, that's how many years you will live), but I always lose count around fifty. The sun is prickly through the foliage overhead, and I squint and hum whatever melody is rolling around my brain.

Beyond the pines is a leafy wood of aspen, birch, and oak, where I find clearings full of blueberry bushes, heavy with the black that hides underneath green curls. I lie on my stomach and eat from around me, as far as my arms will reach, until I am full and my face and my fingers and knees are brilliant purple. Then I roll over a body's width and eat again and gather the rest of the berries into an enameled milk jug. Babby loves blueberries, and Aunt Grippa likes them mashed with sugar: our summer preserves.

I pick the berries and hum my no-word made-up songs, letting the melody take me to the next handful, and that, to the next bush. On my way home the music in my head grows louder, bounces off the tree trunks, takes over my thoughts, and I begin to stomp my heels into the earth. There's the beat. I sing without thinking, to myself and to the woods, and I dance my way down the trail and through the soft dust of the village street until I hear laughter and stop. The neighborhood women are warming themselves on the sunny bench nailed to our fence: flowery headscarves and skirts, crossed arms and ankles—they could be sisters.

"Oh, kitten, kitten!" Babby shakes her head and shakes with laughter, glances sideways at Aunt Grippa. "She does that at home, too, just bursts into song and dance, you know?"

Aunt Grippa shakes her head and shakes with laughter, too, and shares Babby's conspiratorial look. "I know, so musical, so musical!"

"We've got to get you into a music school. Or something," Babby says and grows pensive.

I hand over the jug of blueberries, and it makes its way along the bench, accompanied by murmurs of "Good girl, good girl."

"Thank you, Dinush." Babby plants a ringing kiss on the bridge of my nose. "Why don't you wash up? You're awfully purple."

The streets in the village are dust on dry days and mud when it rains. With the other children I chase a wheel from an old cart down the road, where it rolls a hundred meters before crashing into a puddle to an explosion of cheers, showering us with dirt. "Dinah, is it true in Leningrad you can't play in the street, or you'll get run over by a car?" they ask.

The oldest boy, Thomas, likes me. He wears chic corduroy trousers that are too big and are gathered under his belt like an accordion, and he leads our little pack as his personal retinue to go swimming or to race to the next village or to hop the fence at the nearby summer camp. When I come near the group, he looks down and blows his nose into the street, masterfully, like an adult. He gives me a poplar rod he's hewn himself with a pocket knife so I can carry it when I go to the outhouse. Aunt Grippa's angry rooster won't attack if I have a weapon.

My last summer in the village, he is thirteen and I am ten. Three days after the poplar rod gift, I run into him outside the village store. It's not a place I've expected to see him, so when a sprouting boy with knobby knees in shorts and a T-shirt waves from his bike and draws a wide curve in the dust to brake in front of me, it takes me a moment to recognize who he is.

"Hey, Dinah," he says, panting, and wipes the sweat off his forehead with the underside of a dusty elbow, creating a broad smudge of mud. "Is it working?"

"I don't know," I answer honestly and then realize: He must mean the rod. Yes, it's working. Now the rooster keeps along the fence when I pass.

Thomas frowns but doesn't give up. "Do you want to ride to the Desna? You can hop on the back."

I try to be cool. "Sure," I throw out as if the offer were nothing more than pleasant, but a glowing grin betrays me.

Thomas will die four years later, at the age of seventeen, putting out a silo fire. He will have kissed three girls by then, and I'll have been the first.

It's already August. I spend the rest of the summer holding hands with Thomas, and together we watch the bees fuss with the sunflowers in our front yard and a harvesting combine crawl in the wheat over at the collective farm. When Thomas is busy with chores, I climb up on the old retired collective farm horse named Agni. He grazes, grumbling through his lips about flies and clover and a pebble in his shoe, and I fall asleep astride his back, breathing in his thick odor of skin, heat, meadows, and manure. Each morning I run across the road still yawny and sandy-eyed and look on as a neighbor milks her ginger, delicately horned cow and pours the steaming whiteness into my jug. Aunt Grippa and Babby have just taken bread out of the hearth. For the rest of my days, when I am alone and far from the world of hearths and of anything real, every moment of happiness will taste like crusty, breathing, freshly baked bread and silky-sweet milk still warm from the body that made it.

In my first life, magic is still nearby and easy to share. Babby and I come home to Leningrad, where, from September to May, it all fits into my daily world of seven apartment buildings, a school, a supermarket, a convenience center with groceries, shoe repair and a militia station, and a football field that turns into a skating rink in the winter. A ski path snakes around the football field, the birch grove, and the playground, comes back to the daycare center, and winds through the alleys, through the nooks and crannies full of myths and fairy life. We play hide-and-seek in this mini-world of ours. We play Headless Horseman, the Three Musketeers, and the Labors of Hercules. And we play war.

We are growing up in a city that dreams every night of the Blockade and can fall asleep to no music but the slow beat of the air-raid warning metronome. Sometimes I hear it in my head—slow and steady, the skies are clear—and I see a frame from the iconic documentary series that runs on TV every couple of years, *The Great Homeland War*. The frame shows a stretch of Nevsky Prospect, empty as death, only here and there corpses are frozen into the snow, nothing but bumps in the white. A little girl, bundled up like a bump herself, is fussing over her mother or grandmother, who had just fallen, too starved to move again. This girl seems little, my age. I'll never know the names of these people, but I know this spot on the Nevsky: a thronged intersection between the Duma and the Gostiny Dvor, the axis mundi of my city. Sometimes, when Babby and I come out of the metro there, I have a jolting sensation that I'm walking on flesh.

More than a million bodies were laid in Leningrad's ground during its 900-day siege in the Second World War, and now the city's soil is three parts earth and two parts blood and one part ash. More than twenty years after the war, my generation is born with the knowledge of it and the sorrow of it, intrinsic and inextricable. The war inhabits our books and films, the stories of our parents, who were children of the war, and of our grandparents, who were soldiers of the war. It still hovers over the granite of Leningrad's embankments, chipped by German bombs, and its boundless cemeteries. We have medals that state we are born citizens of a hero city.

We hunt Nazis as we play. We are the Soviet Army, the liberators, the scouts, the pilots, the sappers. The brave among us lie in wait atop a concrete defense bunker built in 1941. It sits between the playground and the convenience center, grown into the earth, squat, scarred, and brownish gray, with narrow steps going down to a heavy metal door, and something dark stares from within through the squinting eye of the machine-gun embrasure. The city has grown up around it, but legends travel among the kids that you can get locked inside the massive walls and die of starvation. No one will find you; no one will hear you scream. They say there are bones of the last Soviet soldier inside the bunker, still sloped over his machine gun, and the skeleton of a child who went in many years ago and never came out. We dare each other to go down the steps, colorless from age, and put our hands on the door.

Our commanding officer is Dennis Luzhin, a big-boned and ruddy-cheeked dark blond two years older than me. There's always a damp, gentle curl stuck to each of his temples. I know they must be salty, and I secretly want to lick them. Dennis is the fastest runner, the bravest climber, the most devious strategist. He used to send messengers up to our apartments, knocking on doors to gather the troops for a campaign, but after a little boy accidentally locked himself in a basement, the adults installed security doors in every stairwell in the neighborhood. Now Dennis buzzes from downstairs, and the intercom screeches and sputters: "Dinah, you coming?" He will become a renowned neuroscientist and move to Australia, where he'll lay the foundation for finding a cure for Alzheimer's. He will marry and divorce three wives and father five children, all of whom, along with eleven grandchildren, will mourn him together when his time comes.

But the best friend of my childhood will not play war or Magellan or Gagarin or Tom Sawyer and Huck. She will not build snow castles or tear pale, sugared petals from daisy hearts and chant, "He loves, he loves not, he will kill, he will kiss." Cleo Ivanidis is an odd, addictive presence in my early life, a lanky, heavy-headed stick figure with devouring round eyes and sparse, dangling brown hair. Yet attached to a pencil, she is grace. She is muse. She puts the point of soft graphite to paper, moving it without pause the way a conductor wields her baton, and there comes to life a nervous eagle with a twitch in his eye, or a confused giraffe sniffing a cactus, or two teenage rabbits carrying a colossal carrot. The back rabbit is eating from the carrot so much that his tummy is dragging on the ground. When Cleo draws, magic condenses into the point of her pencil.

She lives in the tower, one floor beneath Babby and me, with her Greek mother, who believed she could bestow strength upon her daughter by calling her Cleopatra, and with her grandfather, and with a fat, glossy white cat she named Horror, whom she walks on a leash around the green before our building. The cat will run from her one day, and the passersby will be swept aside by the inimitable image of a gangly, unthinkable girl-child dashing through the alley, long, thin, angular arms and legs waving about with such abandon that they threaten to break in every wrong place, crying out in a voice of pity and doom: "Horror! Horror!"

For Cleo's sake, I miss the snowman roll and the storming of the Reichstag and, regularly, our still-awkward collective learning of football, volleyball, and badminton. She will play only with me, and only cats, rabbits, monkeys, and monster families. For weeks we develop plot twists of high drama and slapstick comedy, each assuming several characters, intertwining relationships, attending to the daily minutiae of their lives, reaching grand achievements and resolutions, and starting anew. The lilac bushes are a wild, impassable jungle; the defense bunker is a desert plateau; the birch grove is a magic forest; the bench by the front door is a boat on a white-watered mountain river. The fence of the daycare center is an unscalable precipice.

In the year before we turn seven, we blow fragile, hoary manes off dandelions and hurriedly, time and again, repeat our wish before the tiny parachutes touch the ground: *Please let us be in the same class together!*

This is not a prayer because, as atheist children in an atheist world, we don't know to whom we would pray. We don't know what powers we are imploring for protection and for help, and I have not yet begun to ask myself this question. All I know, in some deeper caverns of my being, without analysis or critique, is that everyone wishes on a falling star and on a dandelion's flight. Everyone spits over the left shoulder to avoid tempting fate and knocks on wood. Everyone looks in the mirror upon returning home for a forgotten item, and no one celebrates a birthday before its date or touches hands across a threshold. The Invisible that guides us may be taboo, we don't mention its name, but we all know that it is there. It imposes its unspoken higher order upon the universe, and we obey.

CHAPTER 3
1975

On September 1, 1975, Cleo Ivanidis and I are together in first grade, class "A." September 1 is a celebration in the USSR: first day of class. Every school in the nation opens its doors to a flood of chaos and commotion, over-stuffed cloakrooms, and scarlet Young Pioneer neckerchiefs flying through the hallways behind their zipping, running, jumping owners.

My school is a typical Brezhnev-era four-story build-ing with large windows that run together and, near sunset, blind innocent bystanders with reflected sunlight. Its mas-sive main porch under a cement awning is flanked by the ubiquitous giant posters done up with slogans in a ubiq-uitous block font. On the left, Lenin stands surrounded by a group of kids, his hand on a boy's head. His face, besides Babby's, is the safest, most comforting face on the planet. At the bottom, square red lettering reads THE MOST HUMANE HUMAN. To the right of the door, an identically sized poster shines with the golden words of a quote I've known, I think, from birth: LEARN, LEARN, ALWAYS LEARN. Lenin said this, too.

In front of the school today is a sea of autumn flowers, asters and gladiolas, quivering in the first-graders' nervous hands, almost hiding the uniform colors underneath—the boys' navy blue suits, the girls' brown dresses under white aprons. Babby has woven an enormous lavender bow into my curls, which at their least frizzy best resemble black steel wool. The bow nearly makes my stubborn bird's nest of a head look groomed, but that won't last for long.

Cleo and I stand in formation, trembling elbow to trembling elbow, coquettish brand-new apron wings ironed to a solar shine, with all the parents behind us in a hushed crowd and a line of tenth graders before us. The senior students are glamorously tall and wise, beautiful, immeasurable and untouchable, except today, for one day, for one moment. The principal's welcoming speech is done (I couldn't tell you what he said), the music starts, and each graduating senior takes a newcomer by the hand so the oldest can lead the youngest into the school for the first time. I tip my head back to see my tenth grader. He is skinny, with shadowy scruff on his chin and skeptical squinty eyes over round cheeks. He hangs my shoe bag on the hook in the cloakroom and leads me upstairs to my classroom. At the door, he taps me on the back, says, "Here you go, kid, good luck," and vanishes into his mysterious grown-up realm.

The teacher is assigning seats in our room. I am in the second row by the window, behind Tanya Ladina, who keeps twisting around and craning her neck until she knocks my ruler off the desk with her chestnut ponytail.

I kick her chair and hiss, "Quit fidgeting!"

"Dinah Ash, sit properly and leave your classmate alone!" The teacher has a viscous contralto that fills the air from wall to wall.

There are thirty-two of us seven-year-olds in class "A." Quiet, rowdy, tall, short. Forty-five minutes of class, then fifteen minutes of break, and the girls, beaming and giggling, elbow each other for the right to promenade about the recreational area arm in arm with our teacher, who is soft-curved and soft-laughed, easy to adore. She emanates a faint smell of baby powder. Some girls trade secrets in the corners; others fold up their candy wrappers into shapes and play candy wrapper leapfrog, flicking little squares and pyramids over each other on the wide windowsills. Boys dash through the hallways, knocking into us with pathetic thuds, and we roll our eyes at their shenanigans like the elegant ladies we are.

Katie Pasiuk is a stout figure even at our tender age, not much taller than average but robust and sort of square in the jaw and shoulders and in her whole unmistakable waistless outline. Greasy brownish hair and short eyelashes make her eyes appear naked. Intellectually dim, for eight years she will insist on not being bothered inside the classroom. Outside of it, however, she will be a powerhouse. Always flanked by two of her best cohorts—one tall and leggy; the other copper-haired, with a shaky pigtail above each ear—even on her first day she strolls through the hallway as though it were her private avenue.

In the break before the last period, Cleo and I are running to the restroom, holding hands fast against the sheer of student currents, when Katie Pasiuk stops us cold with all the movability of an iceberg. With her feet wide and arms akimbo in the middle of the hallway, she looks me up and down.

"Jew!" she says. Her voice is dripping with disdain.

I know vaguely that it is true. I know also that it's somehow offensive, but I don't know why, so I stand before her lost and searching for defense, precious seconds ticking away. Leggy and Pigtails register the scene like mounted cameras, still and hungry-eyed, and Leggy's jaw is hanging down slowly, as if her brain couldn't handle being fascinated and keeping her mouth shut at the same time. Cleo tugs on my sleeve.

"You're a Jew!" Pasiuk restates the undeniable fact and

clarifies: "You look like a Jew, and you talk like a Jew, and Jews sold out Russia. Jew!"

Control is getting away from me, something has to be done, my lip begins to quiver, and desperate and helpless, I shout back *"You're* a Jew!" and run off, tears streaking my flushing face and Cleo in pursuit. The trio don't holler after me. For all I know, they stand there triumphantly as I run down the stairs, out the door, and past the football field, losing Cleo along the way, through the birches, past the day care fence, through the security doors and into the elevator, home. Red, swollen, and snuffling, I push on the bell until Babby opens the door and dig my face into her side under the fluffy cardigan. She sweeps me up into her arms right there in the foyer and shuts the door behind us with her foot. She smells of baking, old wool, and Red Moscow perfume.

"What's the matter, kitten?" she asks. "Who's hurt you?"

Katie Pasiuk will make it through eighth grade and go to VoTech, from which she will graduate in 1986, the spring of the Chernobyl disaster. After several miscarriages and starter jobs, she will settle into a quiet life of a janitor at our old school and spend her mornings mopping the floors and her afternoons wagging her finger at the unruly hoodlums in muddy shoes.

I had not fully realized before that I was Jewish. I knew the fact of my Jewishness, yet the concept had been an abstraction until now, and I arrived at my first day of my first grade not having thought deliberately about it. There'd never been a reason for me to give form to that thought: Like most Soviet Jews, my family is secular, Russian-speaking, and entirely assimilated.

My being Russian is a better-crystallized idea. Leningrad is in Russia. Living in a vastly diverse federation,

I've read enough books and watched enough cartoons, seen enough folk dancing, and heard enough songs to figure out that, among the multitude of peoples making up the Soviet Union—Uzbek and Buriat and Armenian and Ukrainian—I am of the Russian.

But the clearest identity I have formed by the time I turn seven is Soviet. I am in awe of the undeserved and precious luck of having been born in the USSR. I had a greater chance to be born elsewhere, I calculate, and shudder at the thought. At the same time, I calculate, I had a greater chance to be born here than in any other particular country, and I caress the world map with grateful eyes. On the map, my country's ideologically prominent pink takes up a full one-sixth of the planet's land mass.

My favorite moment of the day is just before three o'clock, when an announcer's voice comes on the radio to give the exact time. Our radios are smallish hardwired boxes, each with a single switch that controls power and volume, and they broadcast a single state-controlled station across the Union. In Lviv or Kamchatka, the same familiar voices cheer us on to morning exercise, bring to life plays and Sunday comedy, deliver the news, and introduce concerts and sports and my favorite children's program, *Radio Nanny*, hosted by two burly-sounding clowns. But just before three o'clock all goes quiet for a moment, and the announcer steps in:

We are broadcasting exact time.
The sixth beep corresponds to fifteen hundred hours.

Until the day I die, I will recite this formula by heart, and on all sides of the earth, this woman's voice will be soaked into the membranes of my being. I will know to say it as I will know to breathe, as I will know the Young Pioneers' pledge, Babby's favorite lullaby, "Dance of the Little Swans," and, one day, the Pledge of Allegiance and Shema Israel.

Beep-beep-beep-beep-beep-beeeeep:
This is the voice of Moscow. It is fifteen hundred hours in the capital. Seventeen hundred in Ashkhabad, eighteen hundred in Karaganda, nineteen hundred in Krasnoyarsk, twenty hundred in Irkutsk, twenty-one hundred in Chita, twenty-two hundred in Khabarovsk and Vladivostok, twenty-three hundred in Yuzhno-sakhalinsk. In Petropavlovsk-Kamchatsky, it's midnight.

With the last phrase, I feel the shiver of a miracle, of belonging and gratitude go through me—that quaking of the heart we experience in the face of the loving divine, dwarfed by its infinity and stirred by its intimacy. Someone across ten time zones recognizes these same words and loves the same books that I love: the one about Bukhara's irreverent folk hero Hodja Nasreddin, the one about Chukotka's sledding dogs, the one about a Georgian boy-monk who prefers death, free in the mountains, to subsistence in a monastic cell. Someone across ten time zones loves the same movies about Ivan the Terrible lost in modern Moscow and about a kindergarten principal mistaken for a thief. Together with this person we know the same truths and quote the same quotes and are building the same incredible future for all. I don't know this person, but I love them.

Babby holds me until my sobs turn into slurps and those into sniffles, and sends me into the bathroom. Washing up, I hear her calling the school, dishes clanking in the kitchen, and the heavenly chirping of butter in a frying pan; I smell mushroom soup heating up on the stove. Life cannot be terribly bad when Babby is setting up for dinner, and I emerge from the bathroom ready to be consoled by the gastronomic wiles of love.

After I'm done clearing the table, she pulls a cardboard box from a high shelf in the foyer closet and nods toward the living room sofa: "Come sit with me, Dinush." She unwinds several loops of paper twine and nestles the box in her lap, takes off the lid.

On the top is an ancient-looking photograph. It's sepia-toned and stiff, with an intricately cut border and a faint odor of old age. It reminds me of the illustrations from the pages of my historical books: a woman on a high-backed chair, in a floor-length ruffled skirt and a blouse buttoned up to her chin; a man standing behind her in a vaguely military coat; five children, girls in long dresses and boys in suits that appear to choke the life out of them. They all wear identical expressions of somber boredom, except for the littlest girl with a sour face, who looks like she is about to burst into furious tears.

"See, kitten?" Babby plants a finger on the sour girl. "That's me."

"That's you?" No way! What century was this?

"Yup. That's my parents—your great-grandparents—and me with my brothers and sisters. In 1914."

"But there's only five of you."

"Your uncle Samuel wasn't born yet. I'm only seven years old here, see? Like you are now."

I am glued to the picture. "Did you always wear dresses like that?"

"This was a special occasion, but we always wore long skirts. See, my father was a shoemaker, and we lived in a small town in the Pale. That's the place where Jews were allowed to live before the Revolution. In Ukraine and Belarus, but not in Russia proper."

"Why not?"

She shifts in her seat, puts the picture aside. "There isn't a good answer to that, kitten." Her voice is hoarse and slow. *Did I ask something wrong?* "It's a primal drive to fear difference, and all through human history blood's been spilled on the altar of homogeneity. Death and pogrom and exile."

Babby seems to have forgotten I am here, and I try to wait but last only a few seconds. I didn't understand "the altar of homogeneity," or frankly, much of anything she just said. The questions that burn my tongue are smaller and more immediate. "Babby, how come we live in Leningrad now?"

"Hmm?" She snaps back from some distant thought. "After the Revolution, the Pale was eliminated. Many people came up to Moscow and Petersburg to work and to go to school."

"Did you go to school?"

"I did. That's how I became a teacher. Look at this." She rummages through the box and pulls out a small black-and-white picture with a group of smiling young people in raincoats. Some girls have scarves on their heads, tied in the back, and all the guys, flat caps. They link arms and push into each other, sparkling teeth and shining eyes. "This is me." Babby points to a laughing figure on the end. "In 1927, with my Komsomol group—'young communists.' And this is your grandfather."

My grandfather stands next to Babby in the picture—a little stiff, I judge—smiling shyly from under the visor of his cap. He looks nothing like the portrait of a dignified man in an army uniform, beginning to bald, with a hint of sadness on his face, that sits atop our bookcase. Babby brushes the picture with her fingertips. "We were teaching the workers who couldn't read," she says. "And painting public hygiene

posters at night: *Being clean is wise; Typhus comes from lice!*"
She giggles the way she does when we watch cartoons together, but before I have a chance to ask what the joke is and
what typhus is, she resumes rearranging the muddle inside
the box. "We were young. And happy." She murmurs as she's
riffling in there, and her voice is velvety. "Now look at this."

Another group photo, but this is different, newer. Nine
people dressed in winter gear are in a silly heap on an enormous pile of snow, some sitting, others reclining, two tip-
ping over the top as though falling into it, with their skis
sticking out all around. They are waving and clutching each
other's wrists and ankles in some comical meme of unbal-
anced interconnectedness. Behind them, a landscape of primordial, rounded mountains rolls into the distance, covered
with the stubble of hibernating trees like a sleeping giant's
unshaven double chin.

"That's your parents on a ski trip to the Urals with their
friends."

I only remember a few scenes from my life with my parents,
and even then I wonder if they are real memories or if I have
imbued my grandmother's tales with sights and sounds and
a sense of experience that has come to life. My mother and
father were caught in an explosion at the military-industrial
installation where they worked, but I don't know any details
of what had happened to them, nor even exactly where it
happened: We lived in a restricted zone somewhere on the
Kola Peninsula, near Murmansk, and they did some restricted engineering work there for some top-secret project.

I remember, I think, sledding with Papa. It's polar night.
Lights are on everywhere, in all the windows and along the
streets, shining, pushing the leaden midday twilight to the
edges of human space, dispelling the paradox. I am so bun-

dled up in several layers of clothing—mittens, sweaters, a fur coat with a hood over an ear-flap hat, and a scarf around the hood—that my arms stick out like tree branches from a snowman, and I can't turn my head beyond a few degrees. I sit on the sled staring straight ahead, waiting for the whoosh of the downhill rush. Papa pushes the sled off the hill, jumps on, and wraps his arms around me. The wind stings my face with prickly ice pellets, and I laugh, and I hear Papa laughing in my ear.

It is possible I remember berry picking. I am sitting on the ground in the middle of a lingonberry patch, nestled between my mother's knees, tearing smooth crimson berries from their miniature bushes. Mama holds her large hand under mine and catches the berries that slip through my awkward toddler fingers. Papa descends from on high next to us and opens his palm before my face. "Look what I found," he says. He has a husky voice and brings with him a trace of tobacco smoke. "Ripe cloudberries. Here, Dinah. Take this yellow one. Cloudberries are funny berries: They go from red to yellow. That's when you know they're ripe."

There is one memory that's even shorter than these: Mama is lifting me out of bed. It's dark beyond the window and early. I don't want to wake up, I don't want to go to day care, and I am unhappy about the whole situation. I believe this is my earliest memory. It's neither pleasant nor significant, but I cherish it more than the others. Because I know for sure it's really mine.

When I lost my parents, my mother's mother became my only family. Both of my father's parents had been caught in Ukraine at the start of the war and died in a Nazi concentration camp. Mother's father was killed in the battle of Stalingrad in '42. There used to be other relatives, but most of them were gone in different ways, and a few had lost touch.

Babby had been close with her youngest brother, Samuel, the only one of her siblings to survive the Leningrad Blockade with her and my then-toddler mother, but he, too, had died by the time I was born. Babby tells me stories of their Revolution-swept childhood and tumultuous youth, but she is always reluctant to talk about Uncle Samuel's time after the war, and I live that reluctance as a habitual mystery.

She never will tell me what happened exactly, and only later, as an adult, through hints and tones of colloquy, will I be able to puzzle out that Samuel was arrested in one of the dark years of post-war repressions. I will gather from Babby that he survived long enough in a prison camp to see the 20th Party Assembly of 1956, which spelled the end of Stalinism. He returned home, probably, like most of them: ecstatic and hopeful, and bitterly angry, and forever damaged. I will never know what killed him only a couple of years after that, but I am not surprised something did. After slowly dying of starvation in the Blockade, then slowly dying of despair in the camps, his body and his heart had both been broken. All I really know of Uncle Samuel is a gravestone in a cemetery crowded to untidiness, Russian style, squeezed between the neighboring plots but with a bench at the foot for a proper visit. A name on the stone and two dates:

SAMUEL ISAAKIEVICH FUKS, 1915–1959

I had barely turned three on the day of the explosion, too young to remember Babby's coming to pick me up in Murmansk. Our moving. Whether she cried or not. The anguish and the terror that must have been emanating from her. My occasional longing for parents has always been a kind of abstraction, a concept more than a lack. With the exception of a few whiffs of recollection (some images, some noises), my life with Babby is the only life I can imagine, and she does just fine being everything to me. Now and then there comes a question to the tip of my tongue, something to do with Mama or Papa, but I figured out rather early that Babby found it hard to talk about them, or didn't know how, so most of my questions remained in the back nooks of my mind, lying in wait for their time, until I came home from school sobbing because Katie Pasiuk had called me a Jew.

"That's your parents on a ski trip to the Urals with their friends," Babby says, repositions the picture and waves a finger over the primordial, rounded mountains, the black of spruce trees on the snowy slopes like stubble on a giant's double chin. In the merry pile in the foreground, I find my father pinned under two bodies, thrusting both hands up and making an exaggerated expression of horror. "This was in 1964."

"Where's Mama?"

"Right there, upside down, honey." Babby puts the box to the side, gets up, and fetches the other framed portrait from the bookcase. I know this one well: My parents stand hand in hand on a beach in swimming suits, Papa squinting against the sun and shielding his eyes, Mama grinning from the shade of a wide-rimmed panama hat. I am hanging between them, holding on to their index fingers, face up with my mouth wide open and my eyes squeezed shut. It isn't entirely clear whether I am laughing or wailing like a beluga, but Babby says she's choosing to think the better. She's told me I was two in this picture, on a summer vacation to the Black Sea. My mother was partial to the Georgian coast. Babby puts both pictures down before us. "I want you to look carefully, Dinush. What do you see?"

I strain my guessing powers. "They're pretty?"

"Ha! That, they are. Anything else?"

My brain is turning so fast, I think it will overheat and ooze out of my ears, but I still don't know what she wants.

Babby laughs and tousles my hair. "Stop biting your tongue, you'll bite it off one day! God, you even do that just like your father." She leans closer. "Do you realize how much like your parents you look?"

This is not a thought that has ever occurred to me. My parents' faces have not been much more in my mind than a portrait on a bookcase. *Do I look like them? How can I look like* both *of them?*

"You have your father's hair," Babby says. "See? Look at those curls, impossible, a swallow nest. And his brown eyes and thick eyebrows. But you have your mother's lips—see how full they are? She got them from her father. And you have her curved nose, and the shape of her face. And you laugh just like her, but you bite your tongue the way your father did when you're thinking hard. See?"

I don't really see, but the possibility that it is true is a discovery of proportions I have not previously fathomed.

"Babby, do I have anything of yours?"

"You do actually. You have my hands, I think." We put our hands one next to the other: her sizable, bumpy, wrinkly palm with protruding joints, and my smooth, puffy palm, sixty years in difference. Two longish hands, thin wrists, identical ring fingers, curved inward. Babby stirs and puts the pictures away, then reaches for me and pulls me into her lap. "Let's talk about what happened in school today."

I can feel my voice getting wet again. "I didn't know what to say."

"I know, kitten, and it's all right this time. It'll happen to you again."

"It will?"

"Probably many times. Your classmate—her parents, really, are called 'antisemites.' You'll learn to recognize these people plenty. And you'll make enough friends and enough enemies to tell very early who is good and who is no good."

I will always remember this speech. Maybe because it's our first adult conversation, or maybe because for the rest of my life I will steer by what she says next. I also remember vividly the bright idea that occurs to me just then: "Babby! What if I don't tell them I am Jewish?"

She laughs again, but I can hear wrongness in that laughter. It cuts out too abruptly. "Did you tell Katie Pasiuk you were Jewish?" she asks.

"No."

"But she still knew, didn't she?"

"Yes."

"People are going to know you're Jewish, Dinush. It'll say so in your passport." She picks up my parents' picture again and holds it in front of us. "You have a Jewish name, kitten. And you have a Jewish face. You see? You look like your parents, who looked like their parents and their parents' parents." She traces the curve of my nose with her index finger, then does the same to my mother's face on the photo paper, and then to herself. "For the rest of your life people will know what you are. But you know what?"

"What?"

She presses her lips against my ear and whispers, and hot air tickles my skin: "It's a good thing." I can feel her smile pushing her cheek against mine, and I smile unwittingly in response. "What we are is written on our faces like a sign you wear," she says, "like a litmus test for the world. There's nothing you can do about that. So you might as well wear it with dignity."

That night I am awake late after my bedtime. Babby is asleep on her couch in the living room, snoring deeply and reassuringly, but I stand before the mirror in my room and study my seven-year-old face by the light of a night lamp, trying to see my parents' features in it. I try to see Jewishness, but all I see is what I've always seen in any face: two eyes, a nose, two lips, two eyebrows. I don't see ethnicity or family, not yet. All I really see is that people look like people.

Babby says I look like my parents. She says the world will look at me and see more than eyes and a chin and a nose. It will see a Jewish nose and, in that seeing, reveal itself.

From beyond the window, Orion is watching in silent solidarity, my guardian constellation. His bow is poised to ward off any threat, his quiver is heavy, his belt is tight and full of sparkle. I've never thought of the kind of face Orion has. Must be Greek. Cleo is Greek. Does that mean she has a Greek face?

Orion smiles and nods toward the bed: *Get in, Dinah. I'm here.*

CHAPTER 4
1978

When Babby wakes me up in the morning, I keep my eyes closed for a minute or two. It is a habit I will retain into adulthood, long past the time when the screeching of alarm clocks replaces Babby's voice. That first slide into consciousness—I'm not yet ready to let the day look me in the eye. The blanket is warm and the darkness is safe, and I can take a while to brace myself against what's coming. Every morning is a birth from some hazy, unremembered comfort into the light and loud of daily life.

"I'n wanna," I murmur into the thick, gentle folds, and hear Babby giggle.

"You're such a lazy butt," she says. "Smell something?"

I smell millet. Hot millet porridge sweating with butter and sprinkled with sugar crystals, which melt into viscous glistening puddles over its surface. And a glass of ice-cold milk. I could get up for that. When I stop by Cleo's on the way to school, I could scoop up the giant, apathetic cat from the indentation he's made in the couch, settle him in my lap, and stroke him and feel him purr—tiny vibrations all through my body, in and out with his breaths. Cleo would click her tongue and complain, "He is such a horror!" and we'd both snigger. Then she and I would dash through the grove for the school, through the mud and puddles, her long legs zipping in front of me, splattering our boots and hems, blowing into the cloakroom with the ringing of the bell. I could get up for that.

Then all other thoughts are gone, and I'm upright as a tilting doll. How could I forget? Today is Friday! Today is a dance day.

Twice a week, on Tuesdays and Fridays, I come home from school and change into my leotard, stuff my soft slippers into the backpack, and go to ballet class. I have been taking it for two years at the local children's center, and besides Babby's dumplings, it's my favorite thing in the universe.

There is a major street to cross between home and the club, so all through second grade Babby insisted on going with me. At the intersection, she took me dutifully by the hand and held it till we reached the other side, where I tore out of her grip and darted for the center, visible across the playground in the middle of the block. I'd hurricane through the doors and up the steps into the studio; Babby would plod behind. She is already in her seventies. Now I'm finishing third grade, and she lets me go alone. I haven't been this proud since I learned to fire up the gas stove with a match.

I remember the last time Babby took me to ballet. It was late May in second grade, almost a year ago—the kind of spring day in the North when the baking power of the sun finally cancels out the cooling power of the wind, and it's bright, breezy, and warm. Lilac bushes had started to bloom around our tower, pillowy as clouds, ready to fly. I'd been sick through the winter on and off with strep, but that day we stopped at the supermarket to buy an ice cream in a waffle cup, and as we walked, Babby licked it, peeled off the waffle soaked in white, sticky sweetness, and handed it to me piece by piece. The sun skipped in and out of our eyes; I smudged her cheek with my ice-creamy finger and jumped for joy: "You're It!"

"Don't you smudge my sweater," she said.

*　　*　　*

Today this all will change. Three weeks after my tenth birthday. One night after an ordinary dance class. My childhood will end, and a magic new life will begin.

They are a man and a woman, middle-aged, he in the usual spruce-pattern suit, she in a somberly shaped, gray high-neck dress accenting a slim figure. I see them watching the class but pay little attention. With the other children I stand at the barre before our grand floor-to-ceiling mirror and drill the usual exercises. The teacher's voice sounds metric: "First position, second, fourth position, fifth, second position, fifth. Plié, relevé, sauté. Plié, relevé, piqué. Annie, higher! Point that toe! Dinah, watch the neck! Plié, relevé, piqué. Hold it. Good." We strain our backs into what is supposed to be a fluid curve. A few grandparents along the wall are elated. The teacher throws a glance at the pair sitting in the corner and turns to the accompanist: "Let's run through our performance piece. Schubert, please? Children, places. Remember your parts? Hold your elbows, point your toes, chins up. Let's go."

I live for this. For the moment when the music starts, when all the little steps flow together into movements, and the mechanics of the dance come to life and turn into dance itself—swirling, irrepressible, curving, stretching, soaring, blurring, breathing dance. When the music stops, I feel as if the silence slapped me out of a wonderland. Every time.

The class is over, our chirping flock scatters to the chairs to change shoes, and that's when they come and stand over me. "What is your name, girl?"

"Dinah Ash."

My teacher looms near us on the other side.

"Ash," the woman repeats and glances at the man, then

sits down and pats the adjacent chair with her hand. "Do you know about the Vaganova School of Ballet?"

"Sure."

"Well, we are from there. We've been watching you dance, and we think you might have potential in ballet." The woman looks up at my teacher and shifts into business tone. "We are going to need to talk to her parents."

I didn't exactly lie when I said I knew what the Vaganova School was—I'd heard the name, and in my ten-year-old mind, it belonged to some unattainable fairyland of legendary prima ballerinas, sweeping movements, and mystical, sparkling vestments. It is the world of the sorcery of dance, into which only the chosen apprentices are allowed through the jealously guarded gates, and it had been far above my aspirations until two ordinary-looking sprites coalesced at my and Babby's door. They sit at the table in our living room, sipping tea. Babby spoons out homemade plum preserves into our best, crystal jam dish. I nuzzle my nose between my elbow and the tablecloth, dangle my feet off the chair, and listen ravenously to every word.

They're on a recruiting tour, they say. As fierce as the competition into the school is, every year some of the faculty cruise amateur ballet classes, looking for talent that doesn't realize its potential, encouraging those children to apply. I swallow and feel the edge of the table against my throat. *Am I "talent"?*

The Vaganova School is the premier ballet college in the world, they say. It was founded in the eighteenth century by the Empress Anna. It created the standards of classical dance practiced around the globe. It was named after the great ballerina Vaganova, who taught there and invented the Vaganova method: the signature grace, athleticism, and beauty of the Russian ballet adopted now universally on every continent. I listen to their words as if to incantations, rolling them like tiny bells inside my head. *Ballerina. Grace. Épaulement.* Breathless, I watch my grandmother with pleading eyes. *Please, Babby, don't say "No." Say "Yes." Say "Yes!"*

The entrance exams to the Vaganova School are not exactly exams; they are a combination of auditions, a physical, and aptitude assessments. On the day of my first round, Babby and I take the metro from our sprawling bedroom district to the Gostiny Dvor station, located under the Gostiny Dvor itself, the greatest and oldest eighteenth-century shopping mall in the heart of the city. The escalator brings us up through a bowel cut from the depth of the earth. It is so long that it narrows into a point if one looks from one end to the other—the Leningrad metro is the deepest in the world. It burrows through the ancient ground below the Neva, below the rivers that divide the city into islands, below the drained swamps upon which it was founded by a young and rebellious Czar Peter the Great, below the moisture that still soaks the surface soils and slowly swallows the work of careless builders. The escalator spits us out into the enormous, churning crowd, and we take the exit onto Nevsky Prospect and turn right.

A typical Baltic June strokes our faces with a chilly breeze; tattered clouds overhead seem to have threatened a drizzle but lost their resolve. The Nevsky (Leningrad's main artery) roils about us vast, noisy, and swarming, and I twist around in Babby's hand to look behind me, but the moving forest of adults is blocking most of the view. I can see the peach-colored tower of the old Duma marking the intersection where thirty-seven years ago a little girl crouched over her mother's frozen body, but the spot itself is behind a dense mob. Across the Nevsky, a dark globe encircled by a ribbon reigns over the House of Books. It is my favorite: the Singer emblem. Once upon a time Singer was the most famous sewing machine maker in the world, with this building as their headquarters in pre-revolutionary Russia—and now, still crowned by the somehow appropriate symbol of universal reach, it houses the city's largest bookstore. I'm counting on Babby to stop by there on the way home: Celebration or consolation, there'll be an excuse to buy a book.

We veer to the right between the chiseled gray stone of the National Public Library and Cathy's Garden—that's what everyone calls the little park in front of the Alexandrinsky Theatre. The monument to Catherine the Great rises here above the fray with her nine most loyal citizens at her feet—commanders, educators, explorers. It is surrounded by loitering bohemians and chess players, plus tourists on the hunt for urban landscapes and nesting dolls. The tourists get a few folk tales with purchase, because the monument is subject to quite a number of stories. People say Cathy arranged for her royal spouse to be assassinated in the course of the coup d'état that made her empress and then took lovers for the rest of her long life. It is they, the story goes, who are bound to her pedestal even after death, though on occasion, under the cover of Stygian winter blizzards, Catherine's favorites run off from their posts to find new conquests, and then she abandons her vigil over Russia and tromps after them with earth-quaking bronze steps until the wayward paramours are returned to order.

The bohemians wink and smirk and point for the tourists: "How fitting that she stands with her back to the Theatre and her face to the Nevsky! See, there used to be a grand brothel right across the Prospect in the very old days."

Cathy stands still and smiles her flirty half smile. *Let them talk*. She watches over Russia.

The Vaganova School is close, on the other side of the Theatre, at the far end of Architect Rossi Street. It's the most perfect street in the world. I've never been here before, but now Babby and I stand at the door of 2 Architect Rossi, looking along the cream-colored facades, and I know it's real: the fairyland.

Rossi designed this street as a single, perfectly proportional geometric figure: 22 meters wide, 22 meters high, 220 meters long. Each facade is identical; each building dissolves into its neighbors, so the impression is that the street only has a single long palace on the left and one like it on the right, extending their colonnades like warm arms toward the grandeur of the Theatre. It draws, it reigns, it invites. It smiles.

Babby hugs me to herself, and I smell her unique scent through the raincoat and the cardigan she wears over her dress: chamomile tea, Red Moscow perfume, something else, warm, inexplicable. The ends of her paisley headscarf, tied under the chin, bother in the wind and tickle my forehead. Babby. For a few seconds we stand together, taking in the Architect Rossi, then she says, "You could be coming here every day. Let's go see about that."

The door feels massive to me, wooden and weighty, and it turns on its hinges with a substantial *whoosh*. It is entirely appropriate for an entrance gate that separates the ordinary world from the magic kingdom.

"You look nervous, Dinush."

There is no word to express the woefulness of that understatement. I shrug noncommittally.

*　　*　　*

It takes three rounds to be admitted to the Vaganova School, if you get called back. I remember it a bit like a dream, without pauses or transitions—trancelike highlights of a stretch when I don't yet know.

Standing by the wall in the hallway, waiting for my name to be called. Every few seconds I pull on Babby's sleeve. "Babby, did they forget me?"

"I'm sure they didn't, kitten. Just wait."

Standing at the barre in a queue of several girls, in underpants and undershirt, shivering. A man with a white mane strolls up along the queue, touches me on the elbow, and says, "This one looks good."

Adults mill about and ask me to move, to turn out my toes and knees, to jump, to bend forward and back and sideways. They clap intricate rhythmic patterns with their hands and ask me to repeat. I sing a song. I dance, sinking into cold sweat again and again because my back isn't straight, my chin isn't up, my toes aren't pointed; I know it, and I know I have exiled myself from the pixie world with my clumsiness.

I answer questions that seem bizarre in their irrelevance. *What does it matter how many kids were in the room with me, or their names?* I want to scream, but I don't. They know better what would set or ruin a spell. A doctor traces my spine with his finger, listens to my heart. A momentary shock of cold into my ear, and he tells me to get dressed. The woman sprite who came to my home is there; she smiles. She is wearing her gray high-neck dress, and her fluid body curves over me like an enchanted forest's canopy.

All new people, all new faces, all new things, and waiting for results in the large, colonnaded hall after the third round, I cozy under Babby's arm and let my eyes loose around

the room. The hall is teeming with families—sitting, standing, pacing. Two girls are skipping around each other by the
coatroom. In the corner across from our bench, a boy seems
familiar. I cannot place him in a context. The ballet class?
That would make sense. I smile, wave and nod, worm out
of Babby's embrace, and walk over to where he is squeezed
between his mother and father on an overcrowded bench.
His shoulders are pushed in by the adults so much that both
of his arms are jutting out straight to his knees. He is all
limp everywhere, watching his index finger rub a shiny spot
on the knee of his blue uniform pants, and he raises his head
only when I come close.

"Hey," I say. I skip the name. Names are overrated. "Did
you get the big white-haired man? Did he pick you up on
his shoulders and make you balance?"

The boy is looking, but not to me—*at* me, up and down
me, like I am naked in front of him, like I have green, scaly
skin or a sign across my chest that reads EXPLANATION
PENDING. His eyes rest on the sign, his lips purse, and in
that moment a horrid wave of cold sweat takes away my
recognition. I don't know him. I was wrong. I am standing in front of a stranger with a strange face, and I've just
made of myself the most unforgivable, ridiculous fool in the
history of mortification, and I did it in full view of those
who might become my classmates—and their parents. Cold
sweat burns. *Help me...* "I'm sorry..." My lips won't open—
they can't hear me, can they? "Sorry..."

I dash back to Babby and slip into my spot next to her,
bury my head between her bosom and her arm. Maybe time
can stop now, when there's still hope for me, before a willowy sprite comes out to announce that unforgivable and
ridiculous fools are not allowed in the enchanted lands to
become prima ballerinas.

"What's the matter, kitten?"

"Nn-thm." Just let me suffocate.

Something pokes me in the back, and I free one eye from Babby's folds. A girl on my other side seems unaware of my untouchable status.

"Hey," she says. She smiles. She damns herself by acknowledging me.

"Hey."

She is a redhead but not copper-red—rather, a blushing-peach-red, with a thick braid in a crown around her head and myriad little hairs sticking out from it, creating a halo the way sunrise does. Her grin is missing a tooth on the side, and she keeps probing the hole with her tongue. It must be new.

"My name's Lisa," she says and extends her hand like adults do on TV: stiff and straight, shoved right in my chest. "Ushevich. Elizabeth. Were you scared in there? I was a little. Especially when that teacher threw me in the air."

"I'm Dinah Ash." I take her palm in mine and let her shake our clasped hands up and down.

The door on the other side of the hall opens, and everyone rises at once, as if the room had gasped.

I don't know why I imagined the sprite woman coming out to announce my name and to guide me inside with her hand stroking my head, then peeling back a heavy curtain and leading me onto a stage, where other newcomers were already dancing in tutus and pointe shoes, flying through the air to the sounds of an invisible orchestra. It's not what happens.

Someone comes out to the hall and posts an initial list of rejected names on the wall. I can't see who it is because the adults immediately surge to the spot. The first group is allowed to leave, then the second. To my relief and shame, the boy I falsely recognized disappears after the second list. Lisa Ushevich and I play candy wrapper leapfrog and grow drowsy and gloomy. Babby is becoming restless. I can see it by her fidgeting with her scarf and her coat and her book, retying and unbuttoning and rebuttoning, leafing back and forth, tightening and loosening things about herself. It's getting late. Then the door opens again, and the third list of rejections is posted. The rest of us must be staying.

Acceptances are called in by name. Lisa gets the big man with the mane, and I can see her white-knuckling her father's hand as they go inside. Babby and I get an older woman in a flowery skirt and silky white blouse. She has bright, peroxide-dyed hair cut to the middle of the neck and styled with a slow wave, and she has a thickly lipsticked mouth and comforting eyes, one of which winks at me after she orders me to sit in the corner of the classroom. She and Babby take chairs at the teacher's desk. It smells like dust and fresh paint where I'm sitting, and fleetingly I wonder if dust sticks to the paint before it dries, but pretending to count bumps in the wall, I am mostly listening to what Flowery Skirt is saying to Babby.

"She's very musical and has an outstanding sense of rhythm. Her flexibility is all right, I've seen better turn-out, but those are the things we can develop. She is petite, perfect height-to-weight ratio, good stability, great memory, obvious enthusiasm. Unless she has a growth spurt..." The woman casts a brief, doubtful glance on me, then turns again to Babby. "How tall are her parents?"

Babby clears her throat. She always does that if she has to talk about Mama. "Her parents...were both just under average height. Her mother, a bit shorter." She checks on me with her eyes.

"Were?"

"They were killed seven years ago."

"I'm sorry." Now they both are looking at me, and I am afraid they may be waiting for me to do something, but the woman turns back and puts her hand on top of Babby's. "I think your girl has the gift," she says, "although only time can tell. I'll work with her."

"Thank you, Anna Ivanovna." Babby's voice is barely audible. I can't tell what she is feeling.

The ballet pixie who will be my teacher comes over and sits on a splintered wooden chair across from me. *The Kirov sucks!* is carved into its seat.

"Are you going to work very hard?" she asks and scrutinizes something in my face. *Is this the last test?*

"Yes." My throat is so dry, I am amazed she can hear my croaking. I lick my lips.

"Are you going to follow instructions and learn well and work very hard?"

"Yes."

"Are you going to be a good girl?"

"Yes?" I raise my eyes at Babby, who is standing to the side of the teacher's desk, but she has folded her hands over her belly and doesn't appear about to contradict me. A proud smile has taken over her face.

"Then, you can become a ballerina someday." Flowery Skirt winks again. She exudes some sort of promise, some wisdom I cannot yet decipher, so I'm content just basking in the glory of the moment. "You are a professional from now on," she says, "and it'll be a difficult life, but it'll be a beautiful life. Welcome to the Vaganova School, Dinah."

CHAPTER 5
1982

There is a legend of the Wandering Jew. It was born in the Dark Ages of Europe, in the time of short, pestilential lives and blood libel, serfdom, and illiteracy. The only charity then was to be found in the Church, and the only hope, in Heaven, so the Wandering Jew gets neither hope nor charity, not until the end of time. He is immortal, cursed to roam the earth until the second coming of Christ. Many claim to have met him throughout the centuries under different names, but no one knows for sure. Some say he is Cain, doomed to pay for the first murder in human history. Others say he is Simon, who shooed away the Nazarene from his doorstep when the Son of Man sat down for a rest on his way to Golgotha. What's important is that he is restless, homeless, repentant, and waiting for God. What's more important is that he is a Jew.

I discovered the legend two years ago, once I turned twelve and finally decided to wade out of my childhood library—three shelves at the head of my bed filled with Greek myths and Twain and Milne and Carroll and Aitmatov and Panteleev, stories about dolphins and the *Encyclopedia of the Night Sky* I'd worn out with my fingers. This was well-traveled territory, so two years ago I stood before Babby's bookcases, which take up three walls of our living room, and I was antsy as a rookie burglar because Babby had said I was still too young to choose my own reading.

As I slid open the glass door, my eyes scattered. *The Li-*

brary of Soviet Science Fiction. The Library of Western Science Fiction and Fantasy. Complete Works of Pushkin, Dostoevsky, Shakespeare, Hemingway, Voynich, the Strugatsky Brothers. Selected Works of Dumas, Poe, Maupassant. Márquez. Lorca. Yuri German. Lermontov. My hands were shaking, and I silently thanked a hypothetical God that Babby had gone to the department store—far, on Glory Avenue. It took a while for my hand to float up and pull out an unprepossessing brown tome in a creased dust jacket, from the Russian side of the shelves.

This novel stirred all things together, fantasy and dystopia and social satire, and the Wandering Jew in it gathered several myths unto one: He is the slave who got his ear chopped off by the apostle Peter; he is Christ's beloved disciple. He is dwarfed and empowered by the immensity of time he's been walking the earth—an obsequious little man with a saddening sense of humor who becomes terrifying at the glimpse of his intimate priviness to the mysteries of existence. He is every Jew. He is Demiurge's confidant. By hobby, he is a collector of souls. In the modern Soviet Union, he sells insurance.

I read the novel and thought, *What a unique character...* And then I read *One Hundred Years of Solitude.*

I came to Babby with the open Márquez in my hands, the passage showing. I asked, "Is this a real thing? This legend? This inhuman creature they call the Wandering Jew?"

She pursed her lips in a way that told me she was annoyed, but I couldn't parse if her annoyance was with me or with the book. "You shouldn't be reading this," she said, bending over my wool sock, which she was darning with thick thread, not quite of the same color. She didn't elucidate but didn't take the book away.

I am fourteen now, and Babby has acknowledged my

right to read what I will. We still have never discussed the legend of the Wandering Jew, but I can see it everywhere, in music and literature West to East. O. Henry has him show up in a small American town coveting death, exhausted, dropping his *g*'s to try to convince the world he isn't Jewish. In a Soviet romp set in 1919, the White Guard find the immortal geezer on the shores of the Dnieper and shoot him dead. They're bored, and what else would you do with an old yid?

One thing I always ponder is that Russians don't call the Wandering Jew "the Wandering Jew." They call him "the Eternal Jew." It seems that here, in Russia, what's most important is not that he is homeless but that he is immortal. The Jew is always around. He will wait for God until the end of time, come pogrom or apocalypse, and civilizations may collapse, and all calamity may plummet unceasingly upon his wretched head, but he is the Eternal Jew. Don't worry. He will always be around.

Within my Soviet lifetime, Soviet anti-Semitism will fall mainly into two categories: institutional—unofficial though it is—and popular, that is, the type exuded spontaneously by the masses in the streets, on buses, and in supermarkets. Institutional anti-Semitism delimits in thinly veiled terms how high we can be promoted or how many of us a university can accept per year, and more often than not, people know in advance what to expect from it. I will have a series of career-defining encounters with it once I'm a member of a dance troupe, but in 1982, it still doesn't concern me much.

As for popular bigotry, as a Soviet Jew, I live it in a habitual daily manner I've learned from Babby and somehow by osmosis from every other Jew in the Union. I scan any room I enter for safe faces; I evaluate new people by veiled, key phrases; I don't allow explicit Jew-related words (like the Yiddish expressions Babby drops at home now and again) to leak into my conversations with strangers. I earn myself a few but well-chosen scraped knuckles. Still, anti-Semitism punctuates our lives as no more than a counterpoint to their real melodies, occasionally swelling out of subliminal background. We don't think about it until we have to.

Three months before leaving my first school for the Vaganova Ballet, I finally get into a fight with Katie Pasiuk, from which I emerge with a fat lip, and she, with a broken finger. Babby is called to the principal's office, where she describes what happened and is told indignantly that it is, of course, impossible to have had an antisemitic incident at the school because anti-Semitism does not exist in the USSR. As a phenomenon. Then I leave to begin a new, preternatural life on Architect Rossi Street, and Katie Pasiuk becomes but a memory.

At the Vaganova, ethnic dynamics turn out to be rather complex. The bulk of the students are local and Russian, but a number have traveled from a distance: Central Asia, Armenia, Siberia, Ukraine, the Baltics, and a whole tight group from Georgia. Our schedule is not like that of a normal school. We no longer finish classes at one or two o'clock. Instead, we spend the whole day on Rossi until five in the evening, when Leningraders, who don't live in the dorm, go home for the night. Boys and girls come together for general education and separate for dance classes; we eat dinner in shifts, between one and three o'clock, in the cafeteria; we change together in locker rooms. We come to know each other quickly and well. And when we started classes together, out of the sixty of us in my year, there were three Jews and eight identifiable antisemites—a determination I made in steps over the course of the first several months.

My first Jewish classmate was a boy named Eugene Ovin, though everybody called him Genie. Genie had a head of straight chestnut hair, a pink bulbous nose, a blessedly purposeless family name, which at least in children did not arouse suspicion of any accursed lineage, and enough brains to keep his ancestry on the down-low. Genie was walking a tightrope, but Genie was passing.

The other Jew was Alex Klempowitz, a gangly kid who would have been in a bind if not for the unfaltering protection coming from our best and, incidentally, most muscular dancer, who happened to live on Alex's block. Klempowitz was such an awkward thing that everybody wondered how he'd gotten in—quietly wondered, for usually such incongruencies involved a phone call from the orbit of someone very highly positioned in the Party. Indeed, he washed out after two years, which made me the only workable target for our one truly rabid chauvinist and leader of the pack: Nicholas Yanowski.

Obviously, Yanowski had always had it in for me, and Klempowitz's departure didn't help, but the tension revved up and settled into its constant level about our second year, when I was picked to dance the part of Masha in the Kirov's annual production of *The Nutcracker*. Girls and boys don't generally compete for parts. I think it just stuck in Yanowski's craw that it was me, the Jew, and not somebody else who got the coveted performance.

Most of our school days, Yanowski and I circumnavigated each other around an axis of muffled hatred, tethered by sporadic comments of a hissing nature. I ignored them with what I could only hope presented itself as the dignity Babby always reminded me to wear on my face. I've never been sure quite how it works.

Yanowski and friends were bolder outside, when we

were leaving the school, and every so often I'd hear them shout some obscenity after me. One time, a man passing on Architect Rossi stopped and tried to catch one of the boys by the sleeve. I watched the tiny horde of them take off like a quarrel of sparrows while the adult in a coat and fedora berated their scattering, bobbing backpacks. That was a good day.

Lisa Ushevich once asked why I didn't complain to the teacher, our class curator, and I told her about my fistfight with Katie Pasiuk in a school where there could be no anti-Semitism because anti-Semitism didn't exist. I thought she'd be amused, but she batted her eyes, soulful, like a cow's, then asked again: "So why don't you tell the teacher?"

I left it alone.

This precarious status quo finally crumbles in the spring of '82, as we are finishing our fourth grade, which would have been seventh in a normal school. It is a marked day for me, because this is the day I learn how to be afraid. But it is also the day I meet Matthew.

Nicholas Yanowski must be in an atrocious mood because he starts with me right there, in Biology. I sit in second row center with one of the Georgian boys; Yanowski with his buddy right behind us. The teacher is writing something on the blackboard, and we are copying in our notebooks when I hear Yanowski's pronounced mutter: "You write like a freaking kike, man!"

Here we go.

"What's with the world?" Yanowski continues still quietly but a notch up. "Can't spit without hitting a damn Jew."

I feel his feet pushing on the back of my chair. This is more aggressive than usual. I look up at the teacher, but she persists in pretending she can't hear anything. The feet kick my chair, and I smudge the ink in my notes. *I should just move.* I raise my hand, but the teacher is set on ignoring the whole scene behind her. She is young and thin, always in formfitting dresses and heels, with heavy earrings and a high-sitting blond ponytail, which now bobbles nervously while she moves along the blackboard, demonstratively engrossed in her writing.

Another mutter from behind me, this one loud enough for the whole room to hear: "Don't know what we're gonna do about all those Jews..." Another, stronger kick to my chair. I look over at my deskmate, and he shrugs, his unibrow inching up in a questioning move. He is nothing but nice, this boy, but feeble anywhere except on a dance floor. He has no will of his own. He cannot help me.

I give up, gather my belongings, and rise. Changing desks without permission is strictly forbidden, so either Ponytail will confront me and I'll tell her loudly why I was moving, or she'll keep ignoring me and I'll make my escape. I turn and begin to walk along the aisle toward the back of the class. The bell rings just as Yanowski sticks out his foot, and I crash to the floor on top of my books.

By the time I scramble back up, Ponytail has removed herself, and Yanowski stands over my pile of papers, shuffling them with his shoe. His posse is gathering about him, and I turn around looking for mine.

I don't have a posse. I've never made a lot of friends, not in my first school, not here. Lisa once let slip that my slow coming to trust people and my humming to myself make an ambiguous impression, and I carry a mixed reputation of a shy girl and a priss. But I thought (too optimistically, it occurs to me now) I had enough goodwill to back me up when it's all for one. Against a scoundrel.

They aren't gathering about me, that is clear. The four or

five kids I've spent time with (practiced and studied together) are hanging back behind the others, who are clearing a circle, of which Yanowski and I are the center. Even the girl I've tutored in Russian Lit on the metro. Even the boy who lives a bus stop away from me, with whom I've spent many a weekend doing homework, eating each other's sandwiches, holding each other's legs up, pretending we were dancing pas de deux on the Kirov stage. I can see them behind other faces. Are they just going to watch?

I catch a glimpse of Lisa Ushevich—my best forever inseparable friend—in the closing door. That, I did not expect. *What's the feminine of Brutus?* Her signature peach braid swings left and disappears, and I stand alone in a crowd in front of Nicholas Yanowski and three flunkies by his side, the Rubicon of crumpled notebooks between us. My knee and my forehead both hurt. I want to bend my leg to check that nothing is damaged but don't dare. For the first time, I am really scared.

Yanowski crosses first. He steps onto my books and off on my side, spits on the floor, and declares, breathing the odor of pickles into my face, "You goddam yids are everywhere, taking everything from us. You killed Lenin!"

"What do you know!" I fire back. "It's not even true!"

"It is true too!"

"You're scum," I say, and then he hits me.

On August 30, 1918, a woman named Fanny Kaplan is thought to have fired three bullets into Vladimir Lenin and wounded him. It isn't positively proven—because he survived, but she was executed without a trial four days later, and her body was burned in a barrel by the Kremlin wall—but the fact of it is not yet disputed in 1982. To a Jewish Soviet child, all this story brings is pain, and a fierce desire to defend herself and her kind, and a fiercer longing that this never had happened. Years later my wish will be partially granted, as historical truth is shaken by the earthquake of shifting narratives, but I will by then be older and sadder and more careful about making wishes.

Narratives are unreliable pillars of history. In Russia's revolutionary culture, the narrative was clear: A Jewish woman tried to ruin the Revolution by shooting its Russian leader. But almost a century later, standing on the ruins of that Revolution, the culture will have a drastic change of heart and abhor everything revolutionary. Its narrators will discover that the leader himself might have had a Jewish grandfather—and yes, it will matter. Because those Jews. They did it to us. They always do it.

Of course, I'm not thinking anything like that while tussling with Nicholas Yanowski on the floor of a Vaganova classroom. He is bigger than me—all the boys in ballet are bigger than the wispy girls, whom they have to lift and toss—so only my rage keeps the fight going for a little while. I remember thinking that any second either one of us could get an injury that would end our careers forever. Somebody is already bleeding, and I can feel sharp pain but cannot tell where. And then things get worse, and just for a moment I forget losing ballet and contemplate losing my life.

Two of Yanowski's minions pick me up off the ground and hold my twisting and kicking body in the air. Their grip is a vise on my upper arms. He gets up and adjusts his dusty uniform jacket with bloody smears on the sleeve. It gets quiet. I wonder if no one will really stop him, and then wonder what is about to happen, and then close my eyes. Then the door slams, tables screech, and my feet are on the floor. When I open my eyes, Matthew Kivi is holding my disheveled enemy by the collar, sliding him up the wall. "What do you think you're doing, you idiotic little ass?"

The words ooze through Matthew's teeth, the room is filling with upperclassmen, and my glance falls on Lisa, who is slumped on a desk in the corner, wiping sweat off her brow and breathing noisily with her whole body. Our eyes meet, and exhausted, she beams.

"Dinah! Dinah? Come back!" Matthew is shaking my shoulders and peering into my face. He is a year ahead of me, but even though years rarely mix, everybody knows Matthew Kivi. He doesn't rank high in dance and, the rumor is, will probably end up in corps de ballet, but among students, Matthew is famous for two things: He is beautiful, and he is noble. It is a foregone conclusion around the school that, if Kivi has taken a position on a matter, it is the right side to be on. Because Kivi has an unmistakable, freely accessible conscience, which he carries through the halls in a body of gentle and nimble strength, behind immaculate, soft Baltic features, under a mound of flighty blond hair. There's one more thing: Kivi is known never to lose his temper and never to say any bad words. Everything about him is light, and good, and pretty. Half the girls (and probably a boy or two, without advertising it) are in love with him, and first graders, still anxious in a new place and unaccustomed to the heavy workload, run to him between periods like they would to a parent and hug his legs as though they were tree trunks, pressing their cheeks into him and exhaling their worries.

"Dinah! Looks like Ushevich got us just in time. Are you injured?"

"You said 'ass.'"

"I think you are." Matthew touches the bridge of my nose with a finger, and I flinch.

Ah, so that's what's broken. Well, thank god it's not a limb. I dab bloody snot from under my nose, look down, and discover the condition of my uniform.

"Come on." He grabs me by the elbows and pulls me to my feet. "We're going to the nurse's office, and then to Anna-Vanna's."

Anna Ivanovna Fedorova, the ballet pixie who told Babby on the day of my acceptance that she would "work with me," teaches Classical Ballet, and she took me into the class of which she was the curator. That means not only that she teaches us Classical but that she is responsible for us overall: our academic troubles and achievements, our extracurriculars, our "behavior." What they call our "development." She is the one to whom parents go to complain; she is the one who complains to our parents about us. Not that it happens much. Ballet dancers are a driven lot. The work is so much and so hard that at twelve–thirteen years old, once we started practicing on pointe, we woke up screaming at night from the stress and the pain, yet we dreamt of nothing but the big stage at the Kirov, the world's premier ballet troupe. We dreamt of the floodlights. The unique aroma of powder and naphthalene coming from the tutus. The swell of the orchestra before the cue. The feel of the air underneath in a long, soaring jeté. And the applause. The applause...

I am rather good in Modern, I have fun in Character, but I love Classical best of all, and the teacher has something to do with it. It's simple: I love *her*. We address our teachers by name and patronymic, but no one ever enunciates both fully, so Anna Ivanovna becomes Anna-Vanna.

By the time Matthew and I, bandaged and cleaned up, sit in Anna-Vanna's office, there is no doubt the incident will have to be a thing. Blood was spilled, we missed class, and there were enough witnesses to make the school explode. We press our backs into the chairs along the wall and watch the fumes rise from Anna-Vanna's ears.

"Fisticuffs? Have you lost your minds? You're dancers! How can you even think of getting physical when you know your body is a temple? A temple!" She draws a figure in the air with her hands, ostensibly conjuring up the shape of a temple. "You ought to be thrown out for this behavior! Both of you!"

"But Anna-Vanna, he——"

"I don't care who did what or who started it. You should never have allowed it to progress to a fight. Dinah, you know better!"

"I care who did what." Tiana-Sanna (Tatiana Alexandrovna Sinelchik) walks into the office with the boyish gait of a piano player among dancers. She teaches Accompaniment and serves as the chair of the school's Party committee, so any ideological disturbance is rightly her purview. She is my second favorite adult at the Vaganova. Always clad in a pantsuit that matches her closely cropped raven-black hair, she stays with us late in the piano room playing tunes from Glinka to Gershwin. At dinnertime she joins us in the cafeteria and tells us stories about her ancient Uzbek hometown of Samarkand. Its minarets kiss the sky, she says, and its heavenly melons, full of the nectar of the gods, wait inside their rinds to be tasted, to turn the lucky chosen loose on a divine journey. I can't wait to go there one day.

Tiana-Sanna props her butt on Anna-Vanna's desk and crosses her arms. "Looks like we've had a pretty ugly incident."

"Outrageous!" Anna-Vanna interjects.

"Yes, well. I've asked for Nicholas Yanowski and Lisa

Ushevich to be sent up here, if you don't mind, Anna-Vanna, but if I'm hearing it right, Matthew is the hero here, and Dinah...If it happened the way you kids have told the nurse, there will definitely be consequences. I assure you, we won't leave this unattended. Anti-Semitism will not be tolerated at this school, all right? And let me tell you right now how sorry I am for what happened."

Anna-Vanna sits back in her chair, covering her mouth, and I cannot tell if she is happy with the outcome or upset that she's been contradicted, but just now I don't care.

Tiana-Sanna reaches down and lifts my face by the chin. "How're you doing?" Her voice is soft and gooey and sweet, like fresh apple pie filling, and all of her is homey, kind, and safe. I finally begin to cry, as if some switch had been waiting for her hand to turn it, and she moves down to the chair next to me and wraps me in her arms the way Babby would do. "All right, all right," she purrs. "It's over now."

Matthew and I walk out of the building onto Architect Rossi close to seven-thirty. After the classes, the whole bunch of us involved in the "incident" were held over in the principal's office with Tiana-Sanna, Anna-Vanna, and the Ponytail teacher, who was innocent and ignorant of the whole sordid affair. Now it's all done and done with. Babby's been called, reported to, assured of my safety, and informed I would be late, and the same was done for the other students, except Matthew and my unibrow deskmate, who live in the dorm, and Yanowski's buddy, whose apartment doesn't have a phone yet. Two days later, Nicholas Yanowski will be made to stand in front of everyone at the morning lineup and apologize to me, with Tiana-Sanna's formidable figure hovering behind him.

Yanowski will snap his meniscus three years into his dancing career and be forced to retire, teach at a regional children's center. After the collapse of the Union, he will join a monarchist movement, run a racket for a local mafia in order to finance the return of the Romanov line to the throne, and spend a year in prison. Disillusioned eventually by movements and politics, he will embark on a soul-searching journey and in 1998 shock his family by marrying a woman named Sara Finkelstein-Rabinowitz. The two of them will move to Israel, where they will live blissfully happy in a kibbutz, picking kiwis. For now, however, Nicholas Yanowski stays at the Vaganova, and he and I avoid each other from this moment on.

I step out of my school's doorway mildly battered—my nose throbs, my head aches, my left knee burns—but I feel airy, as if the world had been lit up and swept with a fresh breeze.

Matthew shuts the door behind us and says, "I'd better see you home. Which way are you going?"

"Won't the dorm master worry? I'm taking the metro all the way to the Lomonosov station, and then a bus."

"No, I told them."

We begin to walk toward the Alexandrinsky Theatre, through Cathy's Garden to the Gostiny Dvor. Our hands hang close together but don't touch. It's eight o'clock, light as midday—the white nights are only a month away—and the sun is playing on roofs and trees and streetlamps. The green is young, shiny, and juicy on the branches, looking freshly lacquered, and I want to stop and touch the leaves in the Garden. I would, if not for Matthew walking next to me.

"That Yanowski's always been a creep," he says.

"I know. With a face like mine, it's easy to know who is good and who is no good."

He looks over and chortles, startlingly loud. "Should I be envious? With a face like mine, it can be pretty hard."

CHAPTER 6
1984

Matthew graduated from the Vaganova but didn't do very well. Male dancers are tall, yet he'd grown too tall in his last three years and found it hard to balance the length of his body. He is a good dancer but not spectacular, and after graduation he has no offers except to corps de ballet from provincial companies, where he doesn't envision his future going. It's really just as well, because Matthew wasn't born for the stage. He was born to be a teacher. At the graduation ceremony, our little ones soaked in their own tears like sponges hanging on to his suit jacket.

It is June twenty-third, the Scarlet Sails Night. Mellowed by fatigue and excitement and swathed in the lace of a white night, we are lounging on a bench behind St. Isaac's Cathedral when Matthew tells me he knows what he is going to do with his life.

Leningrad lies on that magical sixtieth parallel, skirting the Arctic Circle and playing with the idea of the Great North. For two weeks in late June, though only for two weeks, the sun never quite sets into the bay, and it is shadowy and dreamy in the deepest hours, at two, three in the morning, but never dark. One of the bards (our guitar-wielding singer-songwriters) has called the white night "a gray mouse that runs through the day," and the image is stuck in my head: The gray mouse sweeps her gray tail from horizon to horizon—out with the old day, in with the new—and scurries away to hide from the sun.

The Scarlet Sails Night happens every year on a Saturday that falls closest to the summer solstice. The night belongs to this year's high school graduates, who have their proms that evening. They dance and drink sparkling lemonade and hug their favorite teachers good-bye, then make their way to the Neva, right in the heart of the city. By midnight, girls in chintz dresses and boys in pressed shirts, seventeen years old, hold hands and gather along the river from the Senate Square to the Winter Palace. They mill by the Peter-and-Paul's Fortress and fill the spit of Basil Island between the immense pedestals of the Rostral Columns, on the tops of which the flames are lit that day as in the days of old, when they guided tall ships safely toward the sea. Other crowds, too, come up behind the kids in the summer twilight, because on that night the drawbridges over the Neva will rise early, and until the end of the ceremony, no ship will dare occupy the steely waters but one special ship. Up the stream from the bay, a white galiot with silk scarlet sails will glide into the vast space at the mouth of the Neva's delta, as though it had slipped straight off the pages of Alexander Grin's romantic féerie.

Every Russian-speaking child has grown up with this book. It is the story of being true to yourself, of daring to dream and making the miracle happen for the one you love. Once the Scarlet Sails reaches the midstream, the music will soar to the steeple of the Admiralty, and astonishing, kaleidoscopic fireworks will burst into the air all around—from bridges and embankments, from under the Fortress wall, from the water itself—to light up the symbol of indomitable hope in a triumphant blaze. It is tradition, a send-off into life for the youth of St. Petersburg.

Couples in love will linger afterwards, until morning, and the metro will keep running for the occasion—but then, couples in love always dawdle by the Neva about the time of white nights. They look on as the boats draw figures on the water and watch the pale rays of undying dusk play with the golden domes; they whisper sweet nonsense to each other and drift off on linden-shielded benches. Here Pushkin once caressed his muse, and Dostoevsky wept in the arms of his.

This year, after his Scarlet Sails Night, Matthew and I amble down to the Senate Square and tuck ourselves onto a bench at the feet of the Bronze Horseman. The chill from the river is raising goose bumps on my bare arms. I fold my legs under, and Matthew throws his jacket over me like a blanket. I feel his solid shoulder rise and fall under my cheek. Other couples, just the same as us, are scattered on other benches and hushed by the enduring dawn.

"Dandelion?" His half whisper fits the mood.

"Hmm?"

"I'm not going to move for corps de ballet."

"I didn't think you would."

He shifts next to me, intertwining his fingers with mine. "I don't have the passion, you know? Plus you still have a year to go till graduation, and then you'll be at the Kirov here."

"From your lips…"

"C'mon, of course you will. Listen, I've applied to the Pedagogical Institute. Do you think it's stupid?"

"I think it's perfect."

"I want to teach the little ones, elementary school. You think I'll get in?"

"You see a shred of doubt anywhere on me? We've all been telling you this since your neck got too long to hear us!"

"But the entrance exams—"

"You have a red diploma: top grades in everything Gen Ed. What are you talking about? You barely have to take any exams." A thought strikes me, and I sit up and search his face, softened by the lighting. "The Pedagogical is kind of a skirt fest, though. You'll have the whole institute swooning over you."

He tilts toward me and touches his forehead to mine, whispers, "They'll be swooning of disappointment, for I am taken."

Through the veil of eyelashes I see his eyes closing, too, and feel the first, unsure touch of his lips. They are thin and warm, and we become still like this together and don't move. Slow breaths from his nostrils tickle my upper lip, and I am afraid it will end. The dome of St. Isaac's, standing its ever-protective guard, peeks over the foliage. Peter the Great on his rearing stallion tramples a serpent into the titanic rock, which carries him up like a petrified wave. He stretches out his hand above us, pointing somewhere—probably, toward the brighter future. I wonder how many silly kissing children the Horseman has tolerated in his bronze calm.

We spend the summer in the city, roam the enfilades of the Hermitage and the Russian Museum, weave our way through the intimate nooks by the sphynxes, braid trembling fingers, and kiss, forgetting the nature of time, under the cozy humps of the bridges. Matthew sits for his exams and is admitted to the Pedagogical, second on the list; I spend the time on endurance and lung capacity: swimming long distances and running sprints. He leaves for Tallinn in August to visit his parents while I wait breathlessly for September and watch the autumn come.

It descends upon the Russian Northwest softly and right on time, covers the Neva Bay with morning mists, breathes cool air into the city, paints the first branches with a light peach brush. The metro smells like asters, and the streets, like mud. Drizzly days will grow more frequent now, and demi-season boots and coats will be pulled out of closets. Every day I walk to the bus stop past a brighter-burning palette of the maples, lindens, and ash trees lining our alley, through the grove of filigreed birches. Soon their wind-blown manes will be emptied into a thickening, springy, motley sponge under my feet.

We are graduating seniors now and take regular part in the Kirov's corps de ballet. The work revs up to a final sprint—the last push before getting offers from dance troupes. I know Anna-Vanna is grooming me for the Kirov. Ever since the second-grade *Nutcracker*, she has never let up: "Straighter! Higher! More! Can't you feel it? Why aren't you sweating?"

In the early grades she had a way of measuring the quality of our effort by how much fluid we exuded from our pores. Passing by the queue of girls working at the barre, she slid her hand along our backs. "Dinah, you're barely even moist!"

I pouted. "I just don't sweat, Anna-Vanna."

"Right. Dinah Ash is a unique and unheard-of phenomenon 'the dry dancer.' Work harder!"

On a winter day in third grade, I sneaked into the bathroom and smeared water from the faucet onto my back, dripped some into my leotard. Five minutes later in the classroom, Anna-Vanna brushed her palm between my shoulder blades and shuddered. "What is this? You're all wet and freezing!"

I still shrink when I recall the verbal pummeling that followed.

Now in my last year, in every class I am soaking my leotards from neck to thigh, nowhere more than in Classical. Anna-Vanna always gets her way. Usually because she is right.

"Dinah. You did well today." My personal ballet pixie pats me on the shoulder and moves on to scold Lisa Ushevich for faltering on her last series of fouetté turns. Lisa never seems to keep her spot from drifting and, after seven or eight turns, ends up facing some corner or another. It would be funny if our time for mistakes weren't growing so short. Stuffing my pointe shoes into the bag, I watch as she receives Anna-Vanna's reprimand with a hung head and throws agonized glances of a drowning puppy in my direction. I shrug with the most reassuring expression I can muster. Nothing I can do but let her cry it out later. Tomorrow. Today I must attend to something special. I leave them to it and walk out.

It is a rare half day for us (done at dinnertime), but I told Babby I might not be home until supper. I didn't tell her why. I didn't know exactly myself, but I had a feeling that it was going to be interesting.

At one o'clock Matthew is waiting for me outside, sitting on our stone steps and tapping out some sort of rhythm with the heels of his shoes. Seeing me in the doorway, he rises, and his face shines with the light that pushes my heart into a momentary somersault, every time as it did that first time, when he stood tall and unruffled in the midst of chaos, and the enemy dangled his feet in my hero's mighty hands.

"Dandelion," my hero says. "Shall we go?"

I slip my fingers into his big, comfortable palm and try to match his step. Tall people's legs are too long. "Where are we going?"

"Let's walk a little."

"Walk where? You said it'll take all day, and you won't say what it is! Matty, what's the mystery?"

"It's not! I...Can you not be so paranoid for one day and just go with it?" If I didn't know better, I'd almost think he could be ruffled, my king of poise.

"Should I be worried?"

"Not as long as I breathe."

He is so tall that I have to do a little sauté to peck him on the chin. "I don't know if I can 'go with it,' but I'll go with *you*. Satisfactory?"

"Overwhelmingly."

We saunter along the Fontanka River and turn right on the Kryukov Canal. For the middle of September, the afternoon is warm. In the sky, topsy-turvy clouds twirl in the wind like tutus, but down here, gentle gusts only push our jackets closer to our bodies, tucking us in. Matthew feels subdued, so I listen to the water slosh against the granite beneath us and hum something from *The Bronze Horseman*—the last melody stuck in my mind, which accompanied Lisa's unfortunate fouettés. It rolls perfectly in time with the splash of the waves: *pe-tee-e-e, pe-tee-ri-tee, pee-tee-e-e, pe-tee-ri-tee.*

By the Nicholas Garden, we stop. We both love this place, have come here time and again the past two years—studied, talked, lost ourselves in a trance on the wide benches under the high maple canopy. Thrown volleys of strictly taboo snowballs, which can inflict dislocations and concussions upon our nationally treasured bodies. Gazed at the delicate azure-and-white of St. Nicholas Cathedral, the intricate wrought iron of the railings, the shine of its onion domes.

I'm about to aim for the benches, but Matthew pulls me toward the cathedral gates.

"Matthew, what are you doing?"

"Come on. Come with me."

"You want to go in the church?"

"It'll be all right."

That Matthew is Christian is about all I know on the subject. We've never talked about it; I've certainly never seen him pray nor heard him use any specific terminology, and he's never before attempted to bring me into the world of his religion. I come from the mass-produced mold of an atheist society, and I comfortably presume secularism everywhere around me—a presumption that had never let me down until I met Matthew. But even his Christianity, once he made it known to me, has always remained largely unspoken, largely unimportant, a little mysterious, and a little embarrassing—a foreign kind of thing. A bit of alien knowledge that has made its way into my mind and needn't be disturbed again. It just hasn't been part of our lives. Until this moment.

He pulls the heavy wooden door open and waits for me to walk in. I step over the threshold as if onto the ground of another planet, uncertain what it would feel like under my feet, in my lungs, upon my eyes. *Thank God I'm wearing a skirt. 'Thank God...'. That's funny. What if anyone who knows me has seen me go in? Damn it. Doesn't matter. Should I think 'damn it' in a church?*

I am not entirely wrong. The door of St. Nicholas separates the mundanity of urban life from something else. Something other. An art museum infused with Dante's limbo. I gaze into its depths from a safe vantage point near the entrance. It is enormous, tenebrous, and heavy with frankincense, and it rustles in a haunting, uneven mix of shuffling feet and wordless groans, which well matches the lighting: shadowy, lambent, diffuse. The sound and the light both fill the air like dust, in floating bits. The vast center space dissolves into the dome, from which a giant Jesus looks down upon his prayerful flock, and every millimeter of wall beneath him is covered with icons. Huge and tiny saints walk, sit, stand, suffer, and hover on the ceiling, on the walls, and in frames that hang on every side of every square column supporting the many arches of the transepts, separated only by the gold trim. Even the floor is somehow ornate, but I cannot make out the pattern. It would all have been dazzling, I'm sure, if bathed in brighter light, but still, there is a gloomy beauty to this world—muted in reverence and frozen in time, with ever-moving shadows cast by an unseen source, keeping a cache of the old and precious in some secret, solemn state of readiness.

Matthew touches me on the wrist, and I realize that he's just come back from a small kiosk on the other side of the door, where he bought two thin candles, and is handing one to me. I accept it and screw up my face in question. He nods toward a twilit space in the left transept. As we pass by the kiosk, the woman behind the counter in a dark woolen cardigan and black headscarf glowers at me and chews her lips. *Am I doing something wrong? Or wearing something wrong? Should I have my hair covered? Does it show I'm an atheist?*

Matthew leads me to a smallish icon on one of the columns deep within the church. In front of it, a round candle rack holds a few burning candles, and in their flickering light I can see Madonna and Child in a classic pose. Between its age and the dimness of the space, the icon is colorless, little more than an outline, almost lost against the golden shine of its heavyset frame yet graceful in the bend of a mother's head over her son.

"This is Mary and Jesus," Matthew whispers into my ear.

"I know," I hiss back.

He lifts his candle, inviting me to do the same, lights it from another, which is already in the rack, and lowers his into one of the glass holders, then closes his eyes, and his lips move silently. Before an icon to our right, an old woman, covered by a flowery shawl from her head to the floor, prays on her knees. She crosses herself and bows earnestly, almost hitting the floor with her forehead, then rises with a groan, sees us and beams, nodding several tiny nods, and shuffles away. From the back, she looks ancient. Matthew opens his eyes and looks at me. "Come on," he whispers. "It's all right. Light your candle and put it in."

I light my candle from his and slide it into a neighboring

holder. *Should I be saying something?* "Thanks," I mouth to the icon. It feels silly.

I watch Matthew while he crosses himself and takes my hand. "Let's go."

Where the old woman was kneeling, a priest now towers, observing us like a sentry of religious order. Clad in a black frock and tall black hat, with a bushy beard and an elaborate, hefty cross hanging off a thick silver chain, he folds his hands on his barrel-like belly and glowers with the exact same expression as the woman in the kiosk. Matthew leads me by him without a glance, out of the cathedral, into sunlight and fresh air.

Back on the street, we slow down.

"You all right? Do you need to sit for a while?" Matthew asks.

"I'm fine." *Are you going to decipher for me what just happened?* "Then, let's go."

We continue quietly for a minute or two; I don't register the direction. Matthew watches his feet. I wait. Then I can wait no more. "So, is this what today is all about? Your taking me to church?"

"No. I just wanted you to see." He stops to face me. "I just need you to accept that I do that sometimes. Go to church. I like this icon of the Holy Mother. I feel she watches over me. Like a mother, you know? I put up a candle if something important is happening. I'll go to Mass from time to time—not as often as I should actually. Don't tell my mother." He smirks in a strange way that's unlike him, and I can't catch his eye. Flat jokes aren't Matthew's thing.

"Couldn't if I wanted to. I've never met your mother."

"Mmm." He frowns at his feet again, and again without a prompt we begin to walk.

"Matty?"

"What?"

"Why were they looking at us like that? That priest and the saleswoman? Was it that I had my head uncovered?"

He shakes his head as if he were throwing off a bug. "Don't pay any attention."

"Seriously. They looked at me like they were chewing my face."

"I mean it, don't you mind them."

"Matthew! Do you know what I did wrong or not?"

"God...You didn't do anything, all right?" He stops abruptly, picks up my other hand, and squeezes them both. "They're just not used to...uh...non-Russians walking in."

"Ah." Matthew is looking down at me, and I, up at him. "You mean Jews. Because Estonians don't seem to be a problem."

"Dandelion—"

"Did you know your church was an antisemitic snake pit when you brought me into it?"

"Dandelion..." He sighs. "It's not exactly my church."

"What does that mean?"

"I'm Catholic, actually. But, you know, I'm used to the Orthodox church now, after all these years here."

"Matthew, *why* did we go in there? You know I don't believe in God!"

"I don't need you to! And you don't ever have to go again! But just once, just today, I need you to—"

"What?"

He is fidgeting and unsure, and lost for words. Not the tall hero Matthew. A chastised boy Matthew.

"Matty. What?"

He draws and lets out a deep breath. "I need you to know who I am."

Relief, like air from a balloon, comes out of me with a whistling giggle. "Is that it?" I step up to him, all twenty of our fingers together, can't tell which is which, and poke my chin into his chest. "I know who you are. I don't care about the God stuff."

"God stuff?" I can hear him restraining a smile above me.

"You know what I mean."

"I really don't sometimes." He leaves a kiss on my hair and frees one hand from mine. "Keep walking, curly, or we'll never make it."

A flower bed along the sidewalk sports a new contraption of red three-dimensional block letters that spell out one of Brezhnev's recent pearls: THE ECONOMY MUST BE ECONOMICAL.

Slogans have been an inexorable part of Soviet life from the beginning, and we accept them on the par with every other thing we take for granted: free universal healthcare, panic-inducing crowds on public transportation, casual access to the best of the high arts, free daycare and education and guaranteed employment, hours-long lines for cheese and pantyhose, the life-threatening rudeness of store clerks, and an absolute assurance of a brighter future.

Slogans accompany our collective journey and formulate the concern and spirit of their times. The hair-raising anti-typhus slogans of the 1920s long passed into oblivion with the achievement of basic hygiene; the dark "Be vigilant!" slogans of the 1930s were taken down with the death of the Stalinist paranoia. The wartime slogans of the '40s yielded to those of victory, and they still endure. One of my favorite billboards has always been the one on Moscow Avenue, with a World War II soldier on it. He is wearing a battle-green tunic and helmet, spreading his arms wide, holding a red banner in each hand. His face is beaming with joy so uncontainable that it spills from the billboard like sunlight, like freedom. Like salvation. Large golden letters above his head shout: WE WON!

Slogans are here and there, everywhere. We breathe them in like air, much of the time without noticing. Sometimes we exhale them, mostly with a wink and a nudge, occasionally outright sarcasm. By the time I enter the world of Soviet slogans, it is the Brezhnev era, the years of calm and predictability, the years when normalcy is being slowly but finally redefined after Stalin's repressions and Khruschev's "the Thaw." They call this time "Stagnation." It is my time, and for what it's worth, I grew up in it telling jokes without fear. The slogans of Stagnation are about peace and about economy, about internationalism and culture. Slogans of the good times.

For a minute we loiter before the new monument to Brezhnev's economic policy without registering its meaning. The crimson of the letters is deep; the cut of the font projects conviction.

"Pretty." I bump Matthew with my shoulder: "Hey, I liked that icon, though."

"Yeah, me too."

"But I like Madonna Litta better."

He grins and bumps me back. "Yeah. Me too."

"Matthew. Where are we going?"

"It's a surprise."

I stop. "No more surprises. Where are we going?"

"You'll see. Soon, I promise."

"Matthew Kivi, I'm not taking another step until you tell me where we are going!"

"Yeah? You forget I don't require you to, little miss."

"Aaaawiiii! Put me down right now!"

Matthew's lifted me high above his head in both hands,

and I automatically tense up to help him hold. He lowers me into a cradle hold. "You sure? You gonna do what you're told?"

"Ha! Fine, I'm perfectly comfortable right here, thank you."

I adjust in his embrace and drape my arms around his neck. "How far do you intend to carry me like this?" His face is so close that I fight the urge to press my cheek to his.

"Suddenly, I don't really know," he says.

"Children!" A woman in a tall hairdo shakes a predatory-looking umbrella in our direction. "Behave like decent people! Immediately!"

I slide off Matthew's arms, and we run, hand in hand, snorting with laughter and peeking over our shoulders, until we find ourselves, spent and breathless, by the Institute of Technology.

"Well?" My breathing is still loud and choppy. "We went to church. We had a spat. We got a scolding. Now what? You going to tell me anything?"

He points. "Right there."

"The train station? That's better. All right, then."

Our mid-afternoon suburban train pulls away from the platform at 14:49. We slide onto the smooth wooden benches inside the car, facing each other by the window, and watch as the city floats away and is replaced by the blur of autumn foliage. I don't ask any more questions. I know that, whatever it is, I am going to find out when we get to Pavlovsk.

This is another of our special places. Just outside St. Petersburg, these had been Catherine the Great's favorite hunting grounds before she gifted six hundred hectares of the land to her son Pavel (the future emperor Paul I) in 1777. It is for him and his wife and three generations of his progeny that local serfs and soldiers were brought in to clear the dense forest, to build and plant and lay down roads. The best names in architecture, sculpture, and landscape artistry combined their designs, and for a hundred years finishing touches were being put on the Pavlovsky Park. It spread out from Pavel's palace with an elaborate network of paths, pavilions, ponds, and landmarks. These radiated along a river valley, reaching the boundary of the woods, toward the first-in-the-country railway that would open in 1836, with receiving and entertaining stations. After the Revolution, once the Great Princes had gone and the great throngs poured in, the palaces were turned into museums, but the Park remains mainly a park. It offers more plebeian entertainments now, like boating, tennis, and skiing, yet in its essence it is the same: a place so magnificently peaceful, so beautiful and vast, that no matter how many souls come in at once, each one can breathe a sigh of serenity and melt into nature's bosom in complete and undisturbed rest.

It was nearly destroyed when Pavlovsk fell under Nazi occupation during the Blockade. The museum staff had managed to evacuate maybe five thousand exhibits and to bury and hide some more, but almost twenty thousand others were ruined or stolen by Hitler's troops. They chopped down the woods and used the land for an endless cemetery, knocked down pavilions and sculptures, and set fire to the main palace as they retreated. It burned for two days. Little by little, spot by spot, Pavlovsk is being restored to its glory. The last few spots will finally open to the public long into the future, in the twenty-first century, but on this autumn day in 1984, we are going to an old corner of it, undamaged by time, cared for but unchanged from centuries past—Matthew's and my favorite spot.

The train stops right by the Park's main entrance. It's getting late in the day for starting a walk, and the broad main alley is occupied mostly by outgoing foot traffic. Nobody hurries. Children scoop nuts out of their grandparents' pockets and run to the sides of the walkway, where the park squirrels, for generations too spoiled to forage for their own food, wait to be treated. Gorgeous rodents with shiny coats jump onto human hands to choose the most desirable pieces and sit there, stuffing their cheeks and shaking nimble, rounded tails, while the children squeal in ecstasy.

"Do you think their nails are manicured, too?" I ask.

"Eh...who?"

"The squirrels. They just look so groomed. What are you thinking?"

"Oh, yeah, nothing."

He is distracted, not that my joke was particularly funny, and I suspect this whole day's preparation is about to come to a head.

The Pavlovsky Park caresses the eye, never more than in mid-September, when the leaves have already turned but have not yet fallen. It is splendid in the manner of northern nature—soft colors, flowing lines—and it becomes apparent that every tree is growing just where it was meant to stand, and every stone has been lovingly put down in its proper place. Classic sculptures line the pathways, overhung by the smoldering carmine awnings of the red maples' branches. Meadows run up the hills to the evergreen backdrops of spruces punctuated by white pavilions. Weeping willows sweep the surface of the ponds with their lemony locks.

We walk downhill and over a tiny bridge to a bench by the languorous, narrow stream. This is our bench. We often come here in early mornings, when the Park is almost empty, to have breakfast: sandwiches of bread with butter and soft cheese (I like black bread, and Matthew, white crusty loaves). Fresh cucumber crunches between our teeth. We throw clumps of bread into the water for the ducks, which gather in front of us from up and down the stream. Across the river, up on a hill, an old, lone spruce stands dark and tall before a group of birches with feathery, canary-yellow crowns—like a grandmother with her blond girls in white dresses. An impressionist painting.

We sit for a while just inhaling the aromas of the fall: mushrooms, wet bark, the beginning rot of the leaves. It seems I should give Matthew time to gather his thoughts. *Do I want to know? Whatever it is?*

Finally, he speaks. "Dandelion?"

"At your service."

He smiles. "I love you."

"I love you, too."

We kiss, a warm, short kiss.

"Do you really?"

"Matty...more than anything in the world."

He keeps looking at me, our faces close but not touching.

"Matthew, what's wrong?"

"Nothing!" He stands up, sits down again. "Nothing, really, everything's great. It's getting late, though. Maybe we should get back."

"Back! Have you lost what's left of your tiny little mind? You didn't drag me around Leningrad all day so we could sit on a bench for five minutes and go home, did you?"

He stands up again and sits down. Blows out a force of air. Sucks in and lets go of his upper lip.

"Matty." I try to gather my flailing nerves into a semblance of order. *No matter what, we'll get through it together.* "You can tell me anything. It's going to be all right. You *were* going to tell me something, so *what is it?*"

"Yeah." He clears his throat. "I was...going to ask...if you would marry me." There is a pause. "I love you so much.

We love each other—don't we?—and I'll never love anybody else." Another pause. Another breath. "So will you marry me?"

I should speak, but the link between my brain and my lips has not yet reestablished itself.

Matthew's features become momentarily distorted, like on TV when it malfunctions, reassembles the picture, and drifts again. "I knew it," he mutters. "I didn't ask it right. I mean, you don't have to—"

"Wait. Matthew, wait!" I cover his mouth, but it feels weird, and I jerk away. He blinks, dumbfounded.

"No?" he says. I can barely hear the word.

"What are you talking about? Of course! Of course I'll marry you! I just thought it was...you know. Always the plan."

"Oh." He begins to grin, wider and wider, so for an instant I worry how far his lips can stretch. I can sense his relief with the whole surface of my body. "Thank God," he says.

"Thank God? Wait a minute, what did you think we've been doing all this time? Just whiling away?"

He laughs, sweeps me up into a hug, and we kiss long and deeply until I disentangle my lips from his enough to protest, only in part comprehensibly, "You didn't...mmm...answer my question!"

"Shut up, kid," he says, and again I cannot talk.

The afternoon is declining toward evening; it's getting chilly and empty in the park. We ate the sandwiches Matthew had brought for us and are now watching the ducks fight raucously over the crumbs and talking about the future. It all seems easy and logical. We'll get married in four and a half years, during Matthew's last semester. I will be at the Kirov—hopefully—and he'll be settled in Leningrad, married and registered at my address, so he'll be entitled to a teaching job here, and we'll be a family of two working adults, plus, of course, Babby.

"You remember that I'm not going to have children till my major dancing is done, when I'm, like, thirty-five, right?" I throw a piece of crust into the river and almost hit a fat drake on the head. He quacks indignantly, flaps his wings, and immediately grabs the crust in his bill and goes to work on it.

"People have children after thirty all the time these days. It's no big deal."

Another handful of crumbs flies into the water; another explosion of quacking.

"So when are we going to Tallinn?" I ask.

He hesitates. "We've got time."

"Yeah, but...I haven't even met your parents yet. What if they hate me?"

"Don't worry about it," he says.

That was brusque. Is this the end of the topic?

"At least Babby will be happy," I say.

"I assume she knows, then?"

"About you? Of course she knows. You've eaten her dumplings a hundred times already."

He chuckles. "No, I mean us getting married. You said it's always been the plan. Does your grandmother know that? Because over all the dumplings, she's never mentioned it to me."

"Oh." That's a confoundingly good question. "I'm honestly not sure. Come to think of it, I don't think so. I don't think I ever mentioned it. I think I just assumed." I must look pretty goofy saying that, rolling my eyes with all the orientation of a newborn, but my Matthew stays cool.

"Shall we go tell her, then?" He gets up and stretches, planting both feet and towering over me, then sticks out an elbow. "Mademoiselle Bride?"

"Monsieur Groom!"

It's almost six. We stroll back toward the main alley, then stride, unconsciously speeding up to keep from shivering. The mist in the air is beginning to turn into fine rain. Matthew pulls a railway schedule out of his pocket: "We'll make the 18:22 if we hurry up." Without another word, we lock hands and shift gears to a run. At 18:19 we are flying out of the Park gates and climbing up to the platform with three minutes to spare. I lean against Matthew, who in turn leans against a cement roof support and wraps me in his jacket. I pant and watch the rails where our train will appear from behind a curve. Near the end of the platform, a light for the outbound traffic, which has been glowing a steady green, clicks and switches to red, and in a second, the snake of our train slinks smoothly around the turn and envelops us in a thickening low rumble.

Three hours later, I hear the elevator clang shut. It hoots taking Matthew down, and I close the door. In the kitchen, Babby is clearing the table. I roll up my sleeves and assume the position in front of the sink: "I'll wash, you dry?"

She pulls up a stool with her foot, throws a towel over her shoulder. Minutes pass, interrupted only by the splashing of water and the clanking of ceramics, and slowly her reticence begins to bother me. Matthew's and my news got the reception I expected: a bear hug, a shower of kisses, and the holiday box of chocolates out on the table, though naturally sprinkled with some hustle of the "you're so young" variety. But that lasted while Matthew was here, and now Babby looks as though the air's gone out of her. *Is she getting old? She looks tired.*

"Babby, why don't you rest? I'll finish it."

"It's fine, Dinush." More clanking of ceramics. A knife

95

falls on the floor, and Babby titters, picking it up: "A good omen for a male guest!"

"We'll have a male guest around here!" I say. "Lots of him."

"Of course, kitten."

"Babby," I finally burst. "Isn't he perfect?"

She pulls up one corner of her mouth and lingers in silence. "Nobody's perfect, deary. But Matthew is a lovely boy, and I've always liked him. He's been very good for you."

That doesn't nearly match my excitement. "There seems to be a 'but' on the end of that sentence, pray tell?"

Babby sighs, as if resolving some internal struggle, hands me the towel, and points to an empty stool, swiveling to face it. I perch while she dries her hands with her apron. It's an old apron, which I made for her years ago in sewing class— salad-green with tiny white poodles waltzing all over in sentimental pairs, a fabric I proudly picked out myself. She's never put on another apron since then, and by now it has been worn translucent and covered in patches, with one of the straps torn off and stitched back on. She wipes her hands, smooths out the cloth on her knees, and tucks a stray lock of gray hair under a pin. "I'm not against your marriage, kitten, if you both keep being reasonable about it, with the timing and your education and all that. But of course I am still worried."

"What about? I have an apartment, he'll come live here with us, and—"

"No, it's not that."

"What is it, then?"

"Dinah." She bows her head and scrutinizes me from under her eyebrows the way she did when, at seven years old, I was practicing lighting up the gas stove with a box of matches. "You must be conscious of the risk you take when you marry a gentile."

"Oh, no, Babby, not *you!*"

"Dinah."

"What? Aren't you the one who says 'don't hate until you're hated'? Don't you say 'we love the Soviet people, the Soviet people are not the enemy'? So I did! I loved. And he is *not* like that! Matthew would never do anything antisemitic. Don't you remember how we met?"

"I'm sure he wouldn't. He probably wouldn't. And he would never mean to. And I already said, kitten, that I like him. But I am much, much older than you, and I've seen many things change and civilizations come and go, yes? So sit down and listen to me."

I lower myself back onto the stool, feeling righteous and sheepish and burning everywhere, from my eyes to the pit of my stomach.

"We are more than our principles." Babby's voice is creaky, like an old boat. "More than our intentions even. We are our upbringing, too. We soak in our surroundings unwillingly, unknowingly, the way trees soak in water from their soil, and it brews and grows within us. One awful day, in the heat of an argument, your husband might say something to you he will regret, but it will be too late, and after that you cannot stay. And you will have to leave the man you love, maybe with children, and both your lives will be ruined, and both your hearts broken. There is only one way to guarantee that your husband will never call you a dirty yid, and that's to marry a Jew. Do you understand?"

"Yes." I want to stroke Babby's cheek, but she isn't crying. She only looks like she is. "But Babby, I trust him."

"Of course you do. And in the end, it's your decision. But I need you to think about it hard, and to think about one more thing."

"What?"

"Matthew is...very blond."

"Is that a separate problem?"

"Don't be sassy." She takes off her apron and throws it behind her on the counter. "It is not uncommon for halves to 'pass'—you know what that means—and it's also common for them to be the worst, most rabid antisemites. It may be a coping mechanism. I don't know. Fear of discovery? In any case, half-Jews passing for non-Jews are infamous for it. Think about that."

"Yeah, I know that. I'm not completely new. But I'm not half of anything, and neither is Matthew."

"You're not, kitten. But your children will be."

We sit across from each other in our tiny kitchen, knee to knee, and Babby is wiping her hands on the dish towel, again, and again.

CHAPTER 7
1985–1986

This year is blurry like butter on glass. I try to wipe it clear, but all I do is spread around the hazy stickiness, and I can't see. Everything is dull. Disconnected. Even the Admiralty is just a dusty yellow hand of a city-sized clock, stuck at midnight.

Every day is perpetual, hourly waiting. Matthew had been drafted in the spring, before the end of his first year at the Pedagogical, but the Army allowed students to finish their exam sessions, so he didn't leave until June, and then the world halted mid-step. Paused. Froze. Matthew left, and my life of youthful anticipations ended, and the life of waiting began, so now I wait. Nothing else happens. Nothing else matters. And the city waits with me.

The summer of '85 is scorching. I am supposed to celebrate: graduation, Scarlet Sails Night. I've been hired by the Kirov. But there's something wrong about the heat, the shimmering air over the asphalt that unsteadies that great Northern firmament and threatens to melt it, ruin it, rain it down upon us in shards and droplets of molten glass. And there'll be no more spark in the sky and no more protection. There's already dust in the air. It covers the benches on the boulevards and stifles the shine of linden trees and chokes the breathing beings and gets in my eyes.

All things are in beige. Tired outlines. Matthew writes from the training camp. He's in Siberia, assigned to the border troops. His letters are jokes and pet names, but I can tell he's miserable. There's hazing. They say the first six months are the hardest. He writes hurriedly, a sentence at a time while standing watch. *Don't send money, it won't get to me. They take the rubles right out of the envelopes. Send some cookies instead. I love you.*

Early fall. My first real performance on the Kirov stage: *Giselle*, I am a wili. It's a small part, basic moves, but we're onstage almost the entire second act, and the pressure is in this geometric, unified choreography. Rehearsals. The coach shouts nonstop over the piano: "Find your person! Check the line, you're one breath, one body! Stop looking down—what are you looking for on the floor? Dead bodies? And three, and four, arrive on five, six! Don't panic. Arabesque, hold it, knee back, and lift from the core, ribs down! Don't arrive too soon: It takes two counts to come in! Bourrée, bourrée, proud chins, long necks, and push to the wings, there you go!" I keep hearing her voice in my head as we line up for our entrance.

We're all in white, full bell-shaped skirts, ghostly, haunting—the wilis are the vengeful spirits of the maidens whose hearts had been broken by men. We run on pointe across the stage; we hop, pouring through each other's lines; we bend and sway and bow like murderous weeping willows, and we kneel for the solo: I'm stage right, third in the second row. This is the corps de ballet at its most powerful. The music is smooth, singsongy, an elegy of movement— and we circle the stage in a hypnotic, continuous stream as Giselle's unfaithful lover dances himself to death under our magic. She forgives him for his betrayal because, even from beyond the grave, she cannot help but love him, and as we avert our gaze, a line in croisé derriere framing their treacly pas de deux, I think to myself: *What a wuss, that girl.*

It finally rains. A tranquil Leningrad drizzle that permeates every space between the cloud cover and the earth: bus stops, streetlamps, the innards of shoes and bags and lungs. I walk to the theatre and breathe in the rain, as though it could wash out the dust. Pastel-colored buildings on the embankment are reflected in the shiny pavement—tentative, grainy, and black-and-white, like an old photograph. Is this day a reprieve? Yesterday's letter from Matthew said he was finished with training and attached to a post. He didn't know which one, but he was on a train to Kazakhstan as he was writing it. Kazakhstan could be all right—a border with China. It's far, but it doesn't border Afghanistan.

The dome of the Kirov rises on my right as I step onto Theatre Square, and the familiar dizzying sensation whooshes through my head. My whole life I've been a dancer—nothing but a dancer, to the deep squishy center of my bone marrow—and still, every day on my way to work, I feel momentarily shocked that it is true: this miracle, this magic, my childhood dream and me, together forever. The walls of the Kirov are teal and cream, as if a foam-crested sea wave had broken through the earth in the middle of Leningrad and frozen, out of time, to listen to the music.

My theatre is over two hundred years old. It is here that Glinka premiered his first opera, and here that the young choreographer Petipa created his entirely new, modern style of ballet and produced *La Bayadére*—"the dance that was music." Now we just call it "ballet." For this stage, for Petipa, Tchaikovsky wrote *Sleeping Beauty*, *Nutcracker*, and *Swan Lake*. So many legendary feet had touched this stage that it turned into holy ground. The *Giselle* we're doing is Petipa's version, too.

I take my usual pause before going inside. I'm in the thick of Old Petersburg here. The city is mildly imperial today, imposing, and demanding in its gloomy wetness. Behind me is the ornate building of the Conservatory and the monument to Glinka by its side. He's got one hand on his hip and the facial expression of a concerned teacher: "Don't you let me down, Dinah!"

I wave him off—"Harass the opera singers, old man!"—and hurry to my morning class.

For *Giselle*'s cast, today is a rehearsal day. We come a bit early to stretch and warm up and start the morning class at 10 a.m., first at the barre, then on the floor to keep our basic moves in shape. Then we break into small rehearsals with the coaches: production-specific group numbers, couples, solos, until about six o'clock.

On my way to the dressing rooms I stop in the wings to see the crew set up for this evening's *Don Quixote.* This is one of my favorite diversions. I love the sets, the way these flat, unconnected wooden panels are angled and overlapped and moved around—and there's a whole depth of a meadow, or a dungeon, or a strategic network of passages for us to pour in and out of. It's startling how the rough designs, almost garish up close, look heavenly and captivating from the house, under the bleaching floodlights. I think, if I weren't a dancer, I'd be a set designer.

It is, of course, the same for us, the way we apply our awful, exaggerated makeup; the way we bend and reach in a manner a human body was not intended to do: too much, too far, to the tearing of tendons, to the breaking of bones, and the whole corps de ballet in a synchronized motion like a breath. It's so you can see it all, appreciate it from a safe distance. Up close it looks painful and unnatural and reeks so much of savage effort that we have to shower during intermission.

I am watching the crew assemble a gigantic windmill

when I feel two warm arms wrap around my shoulders from behind. "Doing your favorite peeping thing?" It's Lisa, and next to her is Andy Triukh. He was two years ahead of us at the Vaganova. I think he likes her.

For a minute we watch the windmill's wings balance precariously on the edge of the stage, then Andy says, "Did you know they had to bring the curtain down once during *Don Quixote*? A few years ago."

"What do you mean, 'down?' In the middle of the act? Nu-huh!"

"I'm telling you! They usually had this horse and this donkey for Quixote and Sancho Pansa to ride on, right? Well trained. Then the horse got sick and they rented a different horse, except it was a mare, and nobody noticed, so right onstage the donkey goes, 'Oh, cute mare!' And he throws Sancho right off and mounts the horse, with Quixote still on it! Can you imagine that picture? Pansa is crawling off the stage, Quixote is holding on for dear life, the animal handler is trying to pull the donkey off the horse by the tail, but the donkey won't have any of that, he's just humping away, and the orchestra screeched to an ugly stop because they're rolling in the aisles, the sensitive dames in the audience are fainting, the conductor is screaming 'Bring down the curtain! Bring down the curtain!' It was some scandal."

"That's a myth, and you know it," I say.

"Yeah, Andy, come on. That's got to be bull." Lisa is trying to keep a straight face, but neither of us can. It's just too tempting to imagine tonight's Quixote, clutching in horror to a horse's neck with his behind bobbing gracelessly up and down to the accompaniment of roof-collapsing merriment from the house.

I don't like tonight's Quixote. He showed me his cards

on my first day at the Kirov, as soon as I introduced myself at the start-of-season mixer.

"Ash," he repeated after me. I stood before him trying not to stare at a faded spit-up spot on his lapel. Hushed rumor is a thing ubiquitous as a virus, so even somebody as new and reluctant as me couldn't escape hearing that the man had three children with three different women, two of them dancers, whose careers this had brought to an abrupt halt. He appeared to roll my name in his mouth for taste. "Ash. Is that short from Ashkenazi?"

There is no such thing as a safe Jewish turn in a conversation. "I really don't know," I said.

"Oh, you should know these things. The root of your name is the history of your people," he said and patted me on the back, then rolled his eyes up to the heavens. "I love the Jewish people."

I didn't know what to do with that. He was like a serial killer who calls you a good girl while he pulls out your fingernails. I extricated myself that time, feeling slimy all over and half suffocated, and managed to steer clear ever since, but if my career goes in the right direction, sooner or later I'll have to partner with him. I'll have to let him touch me and trust him to hold me, rehearse with him for weeks, and return his friendly banter. That's a creepy thought.

I bring myself back to the present just as we near the dressing rooms. Andy is still cracking jokes about the donkey and the mare; Lisa is tee-heeing into the palm of her hand.

"I wouldn't mind him falling on his ass," I say.

Andy chuckles. "Oh, no, don't you know? They stopped using the animals after that screwup. Now Quixote and Pansa roam around the stage on foot like two idiots."

That's a small consolation. Lisa and I duck into our dressing room, which we share with three other girls—lace up each other's costumes, pin each other's hair back into tight buns, pound new pointe shoes into compliance, apply foundation to each other's backs. Every inch of skin not covered by the leotard must be matted, or we become mini-spotlights as we begin to sweat.

Our roommates are already there, changing and gossiping about yet another institutional romance I'm grateful to have missed, and we join them at locomotive speed. We only have fifteen minutes left to stretch before class.

There are no more letters for weeks. I wait, scratch with my nails inside the mailbox every evening twice, three times. What if an envelope got stuck? I lock the box, unlock it, and scratch one more time.

Cleo's show at the People's Culture Institute is an enchanted kingdom: worlds birthed from creatures' talons, swirling in the eyes of myths. It's her first professional show, and for the past week her condition has been so nearing hysterical that I've brought Lisa along for support. Just in case we need to scrape her off the walls. Professors survey the artscape, whisper to each other, and nod, and Cleo slides into me, a heap of clammy limbs and blissfulness. Lisa rolls her eyes and titters. Ballet dancers are not allowed performance anxiety.

Three letters at once from Matthew, written a week apart, the last of them a month ago, in August. He is not in Kazakhstan. They changed trains and went on to Dushanbe, then a border base in Tajikistan, he's not allowed to say where. *Don't worry, Dandelion. I am healthy, and the guys here are friendly and work together as a team, not like the training camp. I look forward to serving at a border crossing, it's what I've been training for. Send more cookies. Those weird-shaped ones are the best.* I stare at the word on the page, but it's blurry. Butter on glass. *Please, no…* What am I praying to? Tajikistan. That means Afghanistan. That means war.

The fall surges through the city unusually fast. Like a forest fire, it sweeps in from the Gulf of Finland, lights all growing things aflame in days, and leaves them burned to blackness, shaking cracked, dry branches over rugs of dead flesh. By October, leaf-fall is done, but after a rain and a warm spell there are still mushrooms, still time to pitch a tent, play a word game around a fire, bake potatoes in the reddish coals and toss them with fried late chanterelles. The Kirov's younger Vaganovians plan to take a suburban train to Komarovo and hike out into the woods in whatever direction our eyes will lead us for as long as our legs can carry us, then set up camp for two days. An '84 alum from corps de ballet will sing bard songs and strum his seven-string guitar while Lisa Ushevich sings Russian romance. She is a lyrical, heartbreaking soprano.

I am not convinced I'd have been invited if not for Lisa. She's quickly become well-loved at the Kirov, and I come with her, an inextricable part of the package. It's not that I am actively disliked, but I've brought my reputation with me from the Vaganova: aloof, arrogant, obsessive, and I *am* aloof, I suppose, though what they think to be arrogance is really caution.

It just doesn't pay for a Jew to be gregarious, or worse— obsequious. Some cope that way, ingratiate themselves to the crowd, but I decided years ago it was not a strategy for me. Believe me: When push comes to shove, your having been everybody's little friend won't make a Nazi hate you any less, won't make a coward come to your defense. All it'll do is strip you of dignity and give you false hope, because when you're in a fight, you have to learn to look for a wall to keep against your back.

Not that I walk around with a chip on my shoulder, but I imagine people can tell: There are boundaries to how fast, how close I let them come. In my whole life there've been four non-Jews I trusted completely, but one of them was Aunt Grippa back in a lowly Ukrainian village, and I only trusted her because Babby did. Aunt Grippa died three years ago of a stroke, quietly, sitting in front of the hearth with a log in her hands—just slumped against the hearth like she was resting, closed her eyes, and went to sleep. That's what they told Babby, anyway, when she made it there a week later, too late for the funeral. So if you ask me today, there are three: Matthew, Lisa, and Cleo. And people can sense it, the good people especially, they just don't know what they're sensing.

I could let myself rest easier. I could differentiate between the Nicholas Yanowskis of this world, who will kill me if I let them, and the others, the passive bigots who will stand aside and watch. Then I could make friends, because it is those others who are safe enough until they're tested.

Only I can't. I am what I am. For now.

No one's been mean to me at the Kirov, they just preserve emotional distance. Still, I don't feel like going on their outing (this isn't the time to work on my social skills), but Babby is adamant. "You will not sit sulking in your room. You're going with your friends."

"But Babby, what if—"

"If a letter comes, I will guard it with my life until you get back."

That means I won't know that a letter has come. For two days.

"If you stay behind," she says, "I will make your existence pure hell until they return. You might as well go."

In Komarovo, the sky is coral, and the forest has posted tall, decorous spruces on both sides of the red carpet. *They look a bit snooty*, I think. You know that look on very symmetrical trees, as if they were frozen in place outside Buckingham Palace? Maybe it is indeed their job to be severe standing there, guarding the entrance to the real world, so humans remember to behave.

The train clangs away, and I hear the quiet. It's been so long since I was out here that I've forgotten about the quiet. In the city there's always that subliminal level of noise, even in the deep night hours, even on the top floors of a cement, soundproof tower in the middle of a spacious residential block—that high, tiny cacophony of electrical ringings and beepings, and of a distant truck braving a pothole, and of an elevator motor responding to a late visitor's call. Those noises are fine and familiar; they are kin. But the forest has no noises, only voices, living voices. I almost forgot how much I miss them. We step into the woods, where the quiet surrounds us with the buzzing of mosquitoes and the trills of woodpeckers, with rustling and creaking and the pitter-patter of paws and feet. There's gurgling of the flowing of water, sniffing and breathing, the batting of wings, and then laughter. My human friends are laughing in the woods, and I am home again.

We spend a chilly night crowded in the tents. The morning threatens fog, though I doubt it will deliver: It's damp and fresh out, well above freezing, which keeps the foliage springy under my rain boots. The colors are all starting to run into brown now, the rot is setting in, and I can smell it. My dancers are still asleep, so I make a fire and put on a pot of creek water, then walk off on my own.

There's this birch. I saw her yesterday. She is old, gnarly, tall. She must be strong—still holding on to a few leaves here and there on the branches. I wonder how many seeds she's sent out into the wind. How many daughters she has. We passed by her yesterday, and I brushed her trunk with my hand, touched the silky white and the rough, scarred black of her skin, and I felt her. She is kind.

Trees are slow creatures. We zip past their long, anchored lives like gnats do past ours, but they barely notice. A bit of commotion now and then, a bit of quaking and smoking, and there: A war has come and gone, human devastation, and blood soaks into the ground, or cities grow on the horizon and crumble into ruins. Maybe a transitory inconvenience, maybe none at all. Yet we're not that different from them—humans, that is. We seed and grow with each other like fruit and then fall into the earth and take root there, in that spot of ground we've never chosen, and become a part of it, come floods or droughts or evil winds. We mingle branches with our neighbors and build our forests along the riverbanks. Every century they grow taller. And we send progeny across the restless waters, waving after them with pride and longing and regret. Then, spring after spring, we send more.

When I was little, I used to climb this enormous oak in Ukraine and lie in its branches, eye to the bark, watching little crawlies crawl and listening to the woodland, feeling like I belonged. For weeks I returned to it every day, years in a row, but it didn't pay attention to the tiny human till a month or more went by, and only after some years did it recognize me. I wonder if it thinks of me still.

I find the birch and stroke the bark with both my palms, press my cheek to her. I wrap my arms around her and feel her body with the length of mine. *Notice me. I'm a butterfly*

109

that landed on your finger. It's a moment you could remember. I slide down and sit leaning on her, feeling the cold of the earth through my windbreaker. The curves of her trunk contour my back. Sturdy. It will not drop me. There's a whispering of the roots around me, sleepy this time of year—*click, click-click*—and a constant sub-audible stirring: might be mushrooms growing under the fallen leaves, might be ants sealing their mounds. Might be squirrels laying down moss in the tree hollows.

The birch knows I am here. They do not sigh the way we do, but I can feel her shift, extend her awareness about me. *Daughter*, she says. A wind gust brings a whiff of smoke and canned beef from the camp. Ballet dancers are cooking breakfast.

"Are you glad you went?" Babby asks.

I am, but first things first. "Anything from Matthew?"

She hands me an envelope. It's from two weeks ago—that was fast. The return address is the same base, but something's changed. He is part of a fifty-men unit that's being "formed." To be sent where? He doesn't say. Probably can't say. Do I want to know? *We are in the Pamir mountains here, my love, a most beautiful land—snow-capped peaks and gorges. I think I can see the Mayakovsky Peak on the horizon.*

I leaf through the atlas: There, Peak Mayakovsky, Tajikistan, looks like 10 or 12 km from the Afghan border, south of Horogh. Somewhere there is my Matthew. I caress the page with a fingertip, but it's dry and waxy. Somebody help us. Birch, oak. Orion. God...

Matthew is still trying to sound upbeat, but he's beginning to fail. *I wish I could visit the Union. Miss you. The guys are mostly good, you just have to be careful who you're friends with. At the outpost we'll be serving at, we'll relieve the unit, but the officers will roll over from the previous year because they're experienced. Please send more sweets and also wool socks. My boots are kind of falling apart, and it's getting cold here. I love you.* What's an outpost? Where is an outpost? Is he going inside Afghanistan?

The November holidays wrap the country in scarlet: flags, stars, hammers and sickles everywhere. Flower kiosks by the metro stations are overflowing with red carnations. On November 7, the Great October Revolution is turning sixty-eight, and again, as every year, I muse at the lexical joke the switch to the Gregorian calendar has played on us. The wind tosses ruby banners along the streets with an uneven flapping sound that makes me want to pop my eardrums.

There's a military parade today in Moscow, in every republic capital, and in every hero city. They will fire up the Rostral Columns and draw the bridges, and the cruiser *Aurora* will lead the best of the Baltic Navy fleet into the Neva: slim, flaring Navy ships and long submarines with their crews frozen on deck in a salute. The Army will pick up the relay on the Palace Square: infantry and artillery, light and heavy, rangers, cadets, past the Party brass and city government lining the stands, past the bleachers with the cheering crowds packed into coats and hats (it's nippy), rank after perfect rank, each step a single pulse, *frrrm, frrrm, frrrm,* heads at a single angle, *frrrm, frrrm,* the might and grace and future of the Revolution. But they aren't all here. The rest are steering icebreakers and guarding nuclear silos and standing watch in the Pamir mountains, and maybe killing. And maybe dying. Dying? And they will pass.

The Square will fill with the civil parade: float after float surrounded by the best of Leningrad's industry, science, art, and education. They'll be carrying flags and balloons, children on their shoulders, enormous portraits of their heroes, and blown-up figures of their five-year plans accomplished well and early. Fireworks begin after dark. People will come out, and while they wait for the show to start, they will dance because they are merry, and dance to keep warm—the nights have been frosty. Winter is coming.

In Pamir, south of Horogh, the mercury is dropping, too. It's all shrubland, Matthew says, gorges running down to riverbeds, mostly dry. The temperatures are hovering, up and down around zero from day to night, and this turns mud into ice and back into mud, but then, that was back in October. Letters arrive in bundles: nothing for weeks, then five, six, eight together. He is writing almost twice a week. *They call us "Helipad 71": the landing pad is the main part of the outpost and our* raison d'être. *You can only see the barracks if you know to look for it, which is kind of good, safer this way. It's just a big clay hut, below grade in the front and earth-sheltered in the back, so the windows are just narrow slits under the ceiling, and it gets pretty cold and damp in here, but we fire up a little coal hearth in the middle of the room. The chopper comes twice a week, usually, and brings coal and food and mail and picks up mail. The guys from the outgoing unit said sometimes the chopper can't land due to fog, which can last for weeks, so don't worry if there aren't any letters for a while. Weather here is crazy. And don't worry about me. In case they can't bring food, we have plenty of dried bread for emergency rations. But would you send some underwear and a really warm sweater and another pair of thick socks? And that waffle cake you sent was a big hit. I'm seriously popular now. I love you so much.*

Should I be sending canned food? But when they can't deliver food, they won't be delivering mail either. He's freezing. What the hell kind of greatcoat did they give him? Or a quilted jacket? Or anything?

Mid-December brings the letters from late October and

early November, up to the 10th. I'm home with pneumonia, missing two weeks in the run of *The Golden Rooster*, where I have a short but technical solo. Lisa had taken over for me—we are the same level and studied the same part—and they just informed her that she'd be continuing in the solo after I come back. After some commiserating and calling the Kirov carefully chosen names, we turned on the TV and are now bundled under my quilt together on the couch in the living room. Lisa's got a glass of tea and made me a hot cocoa.

I'm not into movies and prefer science and travel programs, but today Lisa's favorite genre of movie is on—a murder mystery—so I am suffering through it. My thoughts have wandered, but I force myself back into the scene. Miss Marple's just zeroed in on a suspect, and Lisa waves her leg gleefully in the air, lifting up the quilt: "Ah! I told you it was her!"

"Which one is she?"

"Are you deficient or mocking me?" She pokes me in the ribs so I cough. "She was *just there*, in the kitchen, with the blackbirds!"

"Miss Marple or the criminal?"

"God, you're hopeless!" She begins to pummel me with her end of the blanket when Babby walks into the room holding envelopes.

"Letters," she says, and everything freezes. Lisa snatches the cup out of my hands, slips off the couch, and runs over to turn off the TV. Babby hands me the envelopes and sits on the edge of the sofa.

"Read aloud," Lisa says. "Can you?"

"My dearest... Dandelion—" My voice catches on the first sentence, and I go into a coughing fit. I know what will happen if I try to read it to them. "Do I have to?" My eyes are full, and the world is wavy. It spills down my cheeks, turning quickly from hot to cold, and I sniffle and feel like a child.

Babby strokes my hair. "Just give us the highlights."

It's cold and getting colder, but at least the mud is no longer such a problem. They've been issued winter gear. Thank god. *I've learned to shoot a machine gun and a grenade launcher. I'm technically a rifleman, but in this place everything is a necessity.* He's really inside Afghanistan, isn't he? Somebody help us. *I've started going on water runs. Water here is scarce. There's a small river south of us, but it's dry in the summer and it's in the middle of mujahideen territory, with several kishlaks along it, so we have to go about 3 km north to a spring. But don't worry, we have a whole armored caravan with lots of fire power: a BTR and a BMP, and we let a mine-sniffing dog run ahead.* Is the ground mined all around them? How often can they possibly do that? Are they dehydrated? It's not like I can send water. *I miss you so much, my heart. You're all I think about. Do you remember when… Do you remember…*

I give up on stifling my tears and sob right over the folds of the lined notepad paper, splattering it with wet blobs, bluish at the contours, two shades lighter than Matthew's ink. *I know you're worried, my love, but I will come back to you, I promise. Of course, you understand where I am, and it's dangerous here, but I'm careful, we are all so careful. You don't go anywhere without your weapon here, not even to chow, and we even sleep with it at the ready by our bunks, with two full magazines and two grenades clipped to the belt.* I don't think I quite understood just how frightening it was. There. All the time.

Matty… Please. Please.

New Year's Eve creeps by slowly with an unending blizzard that dims the few hours of day we are allotted and turns the night into a howling abyss. The heavens and the windowpanes are plastered with snow. I push my face to the glass and curve my hands around my eyes to catch a glimpse of Orion. He waves at me briefly and flies off into the storm.

Babby and I are alone for this one, and the table holds the bare holiday minimum: a bowl of General's salad (cabbage, carrots, apples, and mayo), a bowl of Olivier salad (everything you can find in the house and mayo), a piece of good cheese, a few precious slices of smoked salami, my favorite cream puffs from Metropolis, and a box of chocolates. She didn't even bake. We sip champagne once the Kremlin Chimes strike midnight and pull our gifts from under the tree—new warm slippers for me; a silk scarf for her, grassy-green with galloping horses on it. Then we pour some tea and turn on the Blue Light special. It's a once-a-year variety show, all things best, it cannot be missed, but I fall asleep on the couch before Babby does and wake up after three under a shaggy throw. I roll over, close my eyes, and wonder what the New Year's is like on Helipad 71.

On New Year's Day, I rise with the sun, just after ten. The blizzard has gone. It's still dawn, the sky a fragile bluish watercolor, but I can see it'll be one of those blinding winter days that are known only to the North. The city lies beneath me bundled up in the fluffiest, whitest of quilts, all folds and soft lines, and muffled sounds. Every surface is snow, which is already beginning to reflect the sparkles from the sun. Soon it'll be impossible to open our eyes without shielding them. Soon this peace will be disturbed by happy squinting crawlers and builders and skiers, and it'll turn into castles and flying snowballs, ski paths, shouting and squealing and mess, but not yet. The city is sleeping. It's a day off.

Over the grove, on the other side of my old school, I can see snow-clearing caravans laboring along the empty Glory Avenue. Watching those was a favorite childhood entertainment of mine when my greatest aspiration was to be a driver on one. I ached to get my hands on the massive wheel, to feel the beast's energy at my foot, and I imagined myself drunk with power and speed.

The clearer's mammoth pan is scraping the asphalt under the snow cover; tireless metal arms are scooping up the snow and sending it up the conveyor belt, from the top of which it falls into a dump truck in a constant stream. The truck is almost full, and an empty one pulls up behind and signals. The full truck pulls out, the empty one pulls in under the conveyor, the status quo is restored.

I don't know what makes me love this simple ritual. Maybe it's the sprightly arms that go in circles and never rest, and there: up goes the snow. Maybe it's that the truck will drive to the Neva now, back up to the waterline, and release its load onto the ice, where it will wait for the spring— and when movement resumes in nature, on the buckling, colliding floes it will travel out to sea, for which it has always been meant. Maybe it's just an assurance of this sight: When I see the snow clearer rolling along the road, I know the world still works.

The doctor finally comes over on the third and discharges me from sick list. I'm free to go back to work.

"Don't even think of going without a scarf!" she admonishes. She has the idea that I caught this pneumonia because I wasn't dressing right. "It's minus twenty degrees out there, not a joke. I know you young people, you run around with your necks out and no mittens, all pretty-pretty, and then pneumonia. And contrary to what you might think, eating ice cream outside doesn't keep a cold away."

Dr. Pulsky is the physician we're assigned to at our district polyclinic. She's a grumpy grandmotherly sort, on the elderly side and so feels entitled to scold her patients. She's all right, but I still miss my pediatrician. Dr. Shpeller got me through all those streps and a full complement of childhood diseases, the Vaganova physicals, and a proper number of dance injuries—sprains, strains, a tendonitis, and two fractures. Despite a fully staffed orthopedic mini-clinic at the school, I ran everything by her. Sometimes, as she was doing the morning house calls around her sector, if she passed by our building, she just stopped by, even if Babby hadn't called for a doctor. Just to check on me.

I keep reminding myself to go visit her at the kids' clinic, but I'll never make it. Dr. Shpeller will emigrate to Israel in 1989, after the borders open, and there she will keep treating children, mostly in Russian-speaking families, until the remarkable age of ninety-three. Dr. Pulsky will die on the day Dr. Shpeller leaves the country: a heart attack at the funeral of her son, who has been drinking himself to death for years.

But on this January day in 1986, I'm not thinking of why Olga Pulsky is irritable or overprotective, and if I did, I couldn't guess. It promises to be a good day: The sun is shining, my skis are waiting—I am, after all, still seventeen years old. Tomorrow I'm back at practice, with time to spare to start learning *Swan Lake*, and I have this airy feeling, this happy premonition that letters are coming. They're already close. Dr. Pulsky can say whatever she wants, but tomorrow we are getting our ice cream the traditional way, from a street cart. In the winter, these carts are just open tubs piled with the most coveted ice cream you can rarely find anywhere but on the Nevsky: ice milk covered in dark chocolate, on a stick. I swallow. Tomorrow, Lisa and I and Andy Triukh (they finally got together last month) and a few others from the theatre get our sticks in our thick grubby mittens and eat ice cream in the frosty winter air, without worrying about it melting and dripping down our clothes. Yes, of course I'll wear a scarf. And my fur hat. And a sweater under my fur coat. And wool socks in my fur boots, and leg warmers.

"Babby," I call out. "I think I'll go skiing a little bit. Just run a few laps."

"Now that you're a coryphée of the healthy and strong?" I can almost hear her shaking her head. "Go ahead. I haven't gone for the mail yet, just so you know."

Downstairs, I lean the skis against the wall between the mailboxes and the elevator, and fidget with the key. White in the box slit: There's mail. Three creased, splattered envelopes. I kiss each of them and fumble back into the elevator.

These letters are all from November, between the thirteenth and the twenty-third. Damn it, I'm over a month behind, and every new batch reads darker than the previous. The more he tries to find and show me a silver lining, the more terrified I am. *Can you send some foot cream and some gauze wrap and some aspirin? These ulcers they don't heal and make it very hard to walk or sleep, but actually it might be a blessing in disguise, because if it gets any worse, I could get a medical pass to the base for a few days. I'd go on the chopper and get treatment, and they have better food and showers too, so even a few days will do a lot for me just to re-charge.*

What if I went there? I heard that if somebody comes to visit a soldier, they'll bring him to base, even if it's for a couple of days or a week.

You have to be careful with people here. I'm pretty sure some guys are really no good (can't tell you more right now), but I made a friend who's from Leningrad, his name's Alexei Kuznetsov—Lesha. I'm talking his face off, all about you. You'll meet him when we get back, and you'll love him. And would you send more under-

wear and socks and another sweater because they found lice in the barracks and confiscated all the wool, but I don't think wool is the problem, it's just that 50 guys are all freezing and sweating in one room and doing common wash, and you never know who was touching a dushman *and when.*

Dushman means "enemy" in Tajik. It's what they call the Afghans there, the locals. Are they all mujahideen? Then, why would our soldiers be touching them? Or are there peaceful villagers? Then, why "enemy"? Aren't we there trying to defend them?

Maybe they don't appreciate the concept.

I don't want to appreciate any of it.

Why do Soviet soldiers have nonhealing ulcers that nobody's treating?

My Matty... Jesus, Abraham, somebody hear me...

I wasn't exactly on my way here, but I've been circling this place for a month. Leningrad's Grand Choral Synagogue sits not two blocks from the Kirov, and I pass by it with the regularity that only recently has begun to register. I don't know what I want from this place, what it can give me, but more and more often I've been slowing down to peer through the lacy steel gate crowned by a Magen Dovid, at the building itself. It's old, but the Magen Dovid (the shield of David) is the only provably Jewish feature in its appearance. It carries an air of Moorish warmth about it—cream and brown stripes and corner towers—and a Byzantine central dome like a cathedral. The dome is huge and high above and sees all things; it can lift you up or crush you. That's why cathedrals have domes, isn't it?

The synagogue reigns. It intimidates. Is it even open? If anyone sees me going in or coming out, I could have an awkward conversation to look forward to with the Komso-

119

mol Committee: Young communists aren't supposed to be duped by the cult of religion. Then again, Matthew went to church almost once a month for years, and nobody cared. I slink through the gap in the double-leaf gate, tiptoe up the stairs to the front doors, but they won't budge. A side door is leaking light through the keyhole. It's creaky, but unlocked.

Inside the synagogue, it's murky and echoic. Corridors, stacked furniture, a musty savor of neglect, hallways running into gravely darkness. The light is on in a large, low-ceilinged room crowded with benches. Scrawny wooden columns along the perimeter, a lectern up in front, a menorah, Magen Dovids and some other ornaments that probably mean something. It's dim and chilly and unsteady. A woman in a black coat and headscarf is sweeping the floor while two men in black coats and hats are huddling over a railing between the pews and the lectern. If they're trying to fix it, they seem to be failing. I cannot tell what they are saying in low murmurs, but their tone suggests they're cursing. The dome is nowhere to be seen. This must not be the main hall.

"Can I help you, comrade?" one of the men inquires from the railing. His beard is gray and bushy, and he looks about sixty. The other one is younger, thin, with a long shaven face, and he and the woman both straighten up and pause what they're doing, drilling me with their eyes.

I haven't prepared anything to say. For some reason I thought it would be like it is in a church: a service, or no service, and everyone leaves you alone. "I'm...sorry, I don't know." Should I say "Rabbi"? What if he's not?

"What do you want, young lady?" The older man separates from the railing and walks toward me. *I shouldn't have come.*

"I don't know. I just... My fiancé is in Afghanistan." I can't find the right words.

He stops a pace away and folds his hands on his belly just like that priest at St. Nicholas. "And what are you looking for here? Consolation? Luck?"

"I don't know." Hope? I think, maybe, faith. It works for Matthew. *Shouldn't you know?*

He studies my face, then steps back and smiles in the way a mutilated corpse comes out smiling after an embalmer is done with it. "Are you a Komsomol member?" he asks. His voice drips with molasses.

I hesitate. "Y-yes?"

"That's excellent. We don't engage in religious propaganda here." He spreads his hands and advances at me as though he were herding sheep out the door. "You should go now, you should go."

I walk away on a crisp, snow-packed sidewalk, shaking off the stupor that had taken over me in that awful place. Disgusting. I'm regretting ever stepping foot in it. Every few steps I shudder from head to toe like a wet dog. *Ugh. What paranoid freaks.* I suppose their lives aren't easy, but that cannot be my problem, and today's "God thing" I owe Matthew will just have to come from the usual source. I turn on the Kryukov Canal and duck into St. Nicholas. By now they're used to me here, so the woman in the kiosk nods crisply when she hands me a candle. The priest, too, has quit glaring. There seems to be a measure of acceptance in his casual disregard for my presence. I don't actually know what they think of me, but I'm not asking. Sleeping dogs.

Ten minutes later I squeeze out of the heavy doors but barely make it back to the Kryukov when I hear my name: "Dinah, wait up!" Lisa is nearing me in a dancer's sliding run and waving.

121

"Lis! What are you doing here?"

She looks confronted. "I'm not on tonight, you know that, and I always take Garden Street to the metro."

You can't really hug in winter coats, so we link arms and trot down the canal. It's almost seven o'clock, and street-lights are struggling to dispel the density of the Northern nighttime, creating overlapping circles surrounded by the dark. I pull my wool scarf over my nose and mouth and feel the moisture crystallize on it with my every inhale and thaw out with every exhale. At the entrance to the Yusupov Garden, someone has sculpted out of snow a Grandfather Frost waving good-bye to Snow Girl, who is galloping away on a winged horse.

"That's gorgeous," I say.

"Hmm."

Lisa is quieter than usual.

"Is something wrong?" I ask.

"No. Yeah, it's fine."

"No, yeah? What's going on?"

She pulls me to a stop. My cheekbones are starting to freeze, but we're standing in the middle of Garden Street, jumping from foot to foot and clapping mittens together, staring each other down.

"What's up, Lis?"

"Are you Russian Orthodox?"

"What?" I burst into laughter so completely that I get a mouthful of wet scarf and spit for twenty seconds before I can talk again.

Lisa waits for me, looking hangdog. "It's all right if you are."

"You're kidding, right?" I slide one mitten off and rub my face with the warm hand. "*Those* people? I could fashion them a cross out of my own ribs, and they would use it to carve 'Yid' into my forehead."

"But I saw you coming out of St. Nicholas, and—" She lowers her voice as if betraying a confidence. "It wasn't the first time."

"Yeah, well." We link up again and start walking. "This is Matthew's church. I go once a week to put up a candle for him. He believes in candles."

"Oh! Sure, I get that." She breathes out. Her relief is so palpable that I am thinking it's prudent to shut up now, but the bushy-bearded rabbi is nagging at my memory, and still every few minutes I want to shake him off. I want to shower. If I can't tell my best friend, whom can I tell?

It takes me as much time to explain to her what happened at the synagogue as it does for us to get to the Peace Plaza metro. At the doors, heavenly hot wind in our faces; we lean into it and push through. Warm lobby. We unbutton our coats, take off the scarves and mittens, and rummage in our pockets for five-kopeck coins. The down escalator is half empty—the rush hour is almost done—so I keep gushing into Lisa's ear: "They seriously thought I was a provocateur. Do I look like KGB?"

"Nobody looks like KGB, kid, not the informants."

"I guess." That's not true, actually.

"What were you looking for in there anyway?"

There's that question again. I wish I knew, that'd be a start. But Matthew is so far and so desperate and so alone, and every day something might happen to him, and I can't know. I can't help him. I can't save him. In books, people pray.

"I was looking for something to do."

"Look, Din." She throws her arms about my neck, and the hems of her coat rise up to wrap around us. "I'm an atheist, of course. But if there's a God in all this somewhere, he's not in those stone boxes. You know?"

We step off the escalator onto the platform. I love the metro. Amid the squeeze and chaos of the daily commute, the minutes I spend in the metro stations take me away from my life. Change me. Free me from myself. Standing in this enormous, treasure-filled cavern, I am reminded that the city above me is a palace, and the metro, its hidden enfilades. Then a low rumble begins in the thick darkness of the tunnel and swells; fresh, rubber-smelling wind rushes out and pushes against all of our faces and chests, gently, safely away from the edge, tousles our hair. The train barrels past in a blur, and before it slows, for those seconds of rumble and wind, I forget to think. I simply belong.

My favorite is the Pushkin station, where soft light floods an ageless, Hellenic space. Ancient Greek patterns frame the red granite floors under the sweeping, white sculpted ceiling. White marble pylons. Crystal lanterns are done up as chalices resting on ionic columns and surrounded by black-and-gold spears, laurels, and shields. At the end of the platform, a full-height niche displays a lit-up landscape: a pond, an overhanging branch, a familiar building. It's everlasting spring in a corner of the park where young Alexander attended the famous Lyceum. Before the painting, the soul of Russian poetry himself sits gazing upon his people, who stream past him day after day, and braids his silver words.

Peace Plaza, on the other hand, is a simple station: gray granite floors; hefty square pillars of beige-and-pinkish marble along the central platform; and a tall, vaulted plaster ceiling highlighted from beneath. It is too heavy for my taste, but today, seeing it is enough comfort. The electronic tableau over our direction's rail shows "1 MIN 05 SEC" since the last train, which means we have about a minute until the next one. There's a crowd already forming by the edge of the platform. Lisa and I choose our spot and dissolve in the purring of the metro.

CHAPTER 8
1986

By the time May Day is a week away, I'm not in the mood to go to the rally. I've been feeling sluggish and carrying a dull, elusive headache that slips through the grip of any pill. The rest of my body hurts, too—old fractures and torn ligaments, and recently pulled muscles.

To be fair, I've been used to injuries since childhood, and as a ten-year-old I already knew that it was worth it: giving up my games and friends for daily pain and the never-ending, crushing grind. Worth it for that rush of air when my partner's hands whisk me up, and I can sense with every taut fiber that my body is a singular flight of grace. Worth it for that breathless moment when the audience gasps, as if released from a trance, and the fireworks of the applause explode up to the enormous ceiling and spill, filling the air like confetti, eliciting a fine, excited tremolo from all twenty-three thousand crystal pendants in the Kirov's legendary chandelier. Worth it for the sensation that my body is a feather on the wind of music. This feeling of complete control; I only get it now and again, in perfect moments when I am art itself.

My second major production at the Kirov has just finished its run—*Swan Lake,* and I'm a little swan. In spite of positive reviews, I worry that my fatigue is beginning to show onstage. Anna-Vanna came to see it three times. After the first, she hugged me without words and left an imprint on my forehead with her eternal burgundy lipstick. After the third, she waited for me backstage with her arms crossed, searched my face as she used to do after I'd messed up in class. "You're trying too hard," she said. And now I'm told the theatre administrator wants to meet with me.

There's not much office space in a theatre if you count by percentage, but it's a nice space. Besides a desk and two chairs, the administrator has a long conference table and even three armchairs around a coffee table. He does not invite me to sit in one of those. I sit in a hard chair in front of his desk, fold my hands in my lap, and listen as befits a proper employee.

Administrator situates himself behind the desk and smooths down his glossy black suit. He has slick black hair and a groomed "Joe Stalin" mustache. From head to polished black shoes, he is elegant as a grand piano. "Comrade Ash," he says. "I'll get right to business: you're not being invited to join the troupe on the international tour this year. I'm sorry."

He's done. I should thank him and walk out. Except this fast-cooking fury starts to burn in my chest—I know it, this stirring, this buzzing. It's trouble. It's when I become my own worst enemy. When I can't keep my mouth shut.

"Why?" I ask and wrap my ankles around the chair legs. I could break them.

What are you doing? You know why.

Administrator looks embarrassed, as if I just farted. Finally he drawls, "Comrade Ash, you're a smart person."

Clearly I'm not, because I swallow and press on: "What about next year? I was told I might be dancing Gulnare in *Le Corsaire*."

That's a major part. They'd *have* to take me on tour.

"Comrade Ash, don't take this as a criticism. You're very talented, and you know you're a valuable member of the team. But…" He leans in across the desk toward me. The complete openness on his face projects that we're sharing now— comrades indeed, colleagues, maybe even friends. "You do realize that dancers of your *profile* don't make prima ballerinas. We travel abroad, you understand. We have *other* departments to consider." He signals with his eyebrows that two reasonable adults needn't take this conversation any further.

Sure. Because as soon as we touch down in London, I'm running straight to MI6 to sell the gobs of secret documents I plan to steal from the KGB headquarters. Then I'll prance around my new debauched and degenerate homeland, prowling for babies' blood to mix into my matzah, littering pounds sterling, and calling Russians "vodka heads."

"So... I won't be doing Gulnare, then?"

"We believe you will be excellent in the Odalisques Trio."

Making my way back to the dressing rooms, I'm shaking. It's wrath. It's the need to smash through the wall, to bring it all down, or even just to scream, let out a blast so goddamn raging that it would leave nothing but rubble once I'm out of breath. *Calm down.* Now I have to put on makeup and stretch and smile with my friends, my actual comrades, who didn't choose to live in a world ruled by the KGB any more than I did.

I have time to think about it. Days, weeks, months. Years, in fact, because it's not just about the tour. I need to figure out how to be a Jewish ballerina—no, I'll never be a ballerina—a Jewish dancer in the USSR. A dancer with no prospects.

What's that joke about a job interview?

"Party membership?"

"No."

"Criminal convictions?"

"No."

"Ethnicity?"

"Yes."

I want to laugh, to brush off this mood, to move on, but the laughter turns into tears, and I lean against a wall and sob into my hands, trying to be quiet and thankful for the size of the Kirov's building.

The last day of April. It's that vulnerable time of a Northern spring when the white cover has begun to melt, but the threat of late snowfall is still looming. Layers of old, frozen trash and animal droppings are surfacing from under shrinking snowbanks, black and stone-hard. The waters of the Neva, viscous as mercury and deathly gray, are lapping at the edges of separating ice floes. All things feel exposed. The delicate skies are so high and thin that there's hardly any blue in them yet. The trees, thickly covered the rest of the year in greens or golds or whites, now stand naked, weightless and poised, holding on to the ground by one fragile tether, as if any gust would take them up and away in a whirlwind of confusion, leaving us in an empty space. A chilly five o'clock sunrise; I don't want to get up, but the phone rings.

Lisa calls to whine that she doesn't want to go rally without me. "Get your butt out of bed tomorrow, or it'll be seven guys and me."

"You mean about a million and seven guys and you," I point out.

"Come on, it'll be good for you. We'll walk, we'll sing, we'll wave something uplifting."

"And who is going to help Babby cook? You? She'll be on her feet all day making eggs in aspic and stuffed peppers."

"How about you cook today, and tomorrow help workers of the world unite? Then we'll all come back to your place for the holiday dinner and clean up. Babby can rest." Her voice is too peppy for an intelligent person. It's unnatural.

"I don't know," I drawl.

"And stop being a grump." She deflates audibly on the other end of the line. "Any news?"

"Don't you think I would've told you?"

"I'm sorry," she says.

The last letter I got from Matthew arrived on January 3, written November 23. It's been seventeen weeks. One hundred and seventeen days.

Five weeks ago, a thick stack of my letters and two care packages came back to me ADDRESSEE NOT IDENTIFIED. The earliest letter that came back is from mid-November. And gauze. Foot cream. Aspirin. A box of cookies. But not the sweater or the waffle cake. Cold dread fills my veins like slush.

No one will tell me what this means. Military authorities are a wall of properly worded indifference. I am not—technically—family.

"He might have been reassigned to another service post."

"Wait until your fiancé writes you a letter."

"Ask a family member to inquire."

Don't you think I've tried?

Matthew's parents in Tallinn remain a distant mystery: We never did meet, and for the whole of my time with Matthew, his persistent evasion of the topic nurtured my growing conviction that they didn't approve of me. After several approaches from my side, careful at first and then increasingly insistent, we had a blowout, in which I accused him of hiding me, of being an orphan, of possibly being an alien, and generally of not having the guts to deal with the situation. My reward was a vague promise of a trip to Tallinn, and then the draft letter came.

At the teeming platform last June, he unclasped my white-knuckled fingers from his sleeves and covered them in hurried kisses. He pulled himself up into the car's vestibule through the shutting doors and floated away, leaving me with no connection to his other life but the return address on the letters he'd written during his previous summers at home. I didn't know his parents' phone number, his Estonian friends, anything.

When my letters came back from Tajikistan, I began to write to Estonia. No answer. I went to the Vaganova and sobbed over a desk in the records office until I had a paper with his permanent phone number in my hands. Licking cold sweat off my lower lip, I called. A man picked up, but when I started to clarify breathlessly who I was, he said something in Estonian and hung up. So on a Monday (our day off) I stuffed myself, feet and all, into a window seat on an early-morning train to Tallinn. The drafty car rocked and knocked out sinus rhythm on the rail seams, and the train flew through the soggy forest, straight and fast as a bullet toward a heart.

I arrived at the Baltic Station by midday. Matthew's parents live in Kesklinn by the port. I knew the street. My first two Vaganova summers, when I was ten and eleven, were spent at a swimming camp in Kohtla-Järve, from which the coaches took us to Tallinn almost every weekend—there was nothing much else to do—so I know the city relatively well. I should have made my way right to the address on the envelope I was fingering in my pocket, but I was stalling.

I turned left from the station, walked outside the town wall, and entered Old Town by Fat Margaret. The tower was even squatter and wider than I remembered it, inappropriately genial for something so riddled with cannon embrasures. For an hour I rambled about the narrow cobblestone streets, past Gothic churches, in and out under the arched medieval gates guarded by towers in tall, pointed hats. From the Alexander Nevsky Cathedral, I could see Tall Hermann rising over the Toompea Castle, keeping its unrelieved watch, and I thought how familiar this city was. Not just to me—to this whole country. If nothing else, movies have made it so. More or less all the Soviet movies about olden Europe are shot here and in Lviv, and we recognize these places as intimately as if we'd lived in them. I stood by the town wall and saw Athos and Aramis fencing their way out of a scrape. Any minute D'Artagnan would jump out of a tower window onto a frothing pinto steed and speed away, wind in the horse's tail.

Town hall, a café with cucumber salad and kefir, and I was running out of time. Three more turns down claustrophobic passageways before I stood undeniably in front of a neatly painted yellow building. Narrow stairs to the second floor. Out of the landing window, I could see the wall across the street, so close that it could be another hallway. It felt intimate. Or suffocating. No way out and no way back. What do they know? What will they say? I rang the bell.

The man who opened the door was blond and tall and tired, and wore black ironed pants with a white undershirt. He had inflamed raspberry-red eyes like people who don't sleep, but his cheeks were carefully shaven. He held on with one hand to the door and, with the other, to the post, and looked at me without words.

"I'm here for comrades— I mean, the parents of Matthew Kivi. I'm Dinah. Ash." I thought it was him, Matthew's father. It must be him. But he kept standing there, waiting for something, or considering something. Something sad. Violent. Inhuman. I may have taken a step back. "Comrade Kivi?" I tried. "I haven't heard from Matthew..." Pause. "Do you know who I am? Do you know Comrade Kivi?"

Maybe it's not him. Maybe he doesn't speak Russian. *At all? That'd be strange.*

I summoned the terrible beginnings of Estonian that Matthew had started to teach me. *"Ma olen su poja pruut. Kas sa tead, kus ta on?"*

The man stirred, straightened, and I saw that he was taller than I'd thought. Taller than Matthew. And more tired than

I'd thought, or maybe older. He towered over me like a ghost of the Viking past. "You did this," he said. "You Russian fucks." And slammed the door shut.

I stood for a minute before the locked door, then turned to go, back to the train. Maybe I didn't want to know what he knew, after all. What it meant.

It doesn't have to mean anything.

It is bizarre, though, isn't it? Bizarre to be a Jew hated for being Russian.

May 1 is wet and miserable. A gusty southwesterly wind picked up overnight and brought a raincloud that doesn't let up all day. It's reasonably warm, however, so our Kirov crowd decides to brave the weather as, it turns out, does most of Leningrad: The Labor Day rally is as swarming and noisy as always, full of chanting and chatting and singing, and by mid-afternoon, completely soaked. We are chilled to the bone, exhausted, and so soggy—even our boots make slurping sounds with each step—that everyone decides to call off the holiday dinner and go home to dry out and rest.

I don't mind. I still have that headache pulsating in my temples, as though dreadful, clandestine thoughts were beating against my skull, trying to break out into the world and make themselves heard. It's hard to concentrate, and I'm not fun company. I haven't been fun in seventeen weeks.

The metro is bursting with people, every crossing a bottleneck, topside transport overflowing, and it takes me an hour to get to the Lomonosov station, where, after a twenty-minute wait, I am packed onto a bus with my face pressed against the back of a large man's coat. It fills my mouth with the stench of damp wool and smothers me. Airless panic, bumping, swaying. Barely breathing, I tear my way out at my stop and slog home, anticipating pajamas and hot tea.

By the door of my building, a young man in an Army uniform is loitering under the awning: buzzed chestnut hair, sharp features around a button nose, long wet stains down from the shoulders of his greatcoat. Unusual tan for this time of year. He watches me unlock the security door and comes in after me, follows me to the mailboxes. As I slide in the mail key, he speaks.

"Excuse me. Are you Dinah?"

He has a soft, raspy voice. There's something in his tone, like the way people talk to cancer patients, and this is when I know: I'm about to find out what happened to Matthew.

I'm about to know what I haven't wanted to know since the ghost of the Viking past called me a Russian fuck and slammed the door in my face.

I'm feeling—something. Sweat, space, freefall. I've forgotten there's a key in a lock. Time needs to slow down. This could be the moment that ends my waiting life.

"I am Dinah," I say.

"Forgive me, I buzzed, but nobody answered."

"No. My grandmother is...visiting a friend... Who are you?"

"My name's Alexei Kuznetsov. I served with—"

"You are Lesha." My hand falls off the key and reaches for his sleeve.

He says, "I am Lesha."

Matthew was killed on November 24, 1985.

Lesha and I are sitting at the kitchen table in my apartment. I didn't want to hear him say anything more than his name in the stairwell, in the transience between the elevator and the mailbox, so we made our way upstairs in silence and took off our shoes and coats. I poured two cups of tea, which are standing before us now, steaming and untouched. Now that he's taken off his gloves, I see that, even though his face is tan, his hands are pale. Very pale. I don't know why I'm thinking about that. They have knotted, protruding knuckles and long fingers, which are scratching back and forth on the table. When I look him in the face, he begins to talk. Eyes down, monotone voice. He frequently clears his throat.

On November 24, five months and one week ago, the captain of Helipad 71 received orders to provide reinforcements for Helipad 30, located several kilometers southeast, in order to secure the arrival of an airborne assault team. Around 1600 hours, a subunit of twenty-two soldiers left the outpost for Helipad 30. Privates Matthew Kivi and Alexei Kuznetsov were there, as well as the captain and his second-in-command.

Lesha stops and swallows and looks at the tea, as though he were thirsty for a sip, but doesn't take one. I wish he would. I don't know why I think that, if he took a sip, it could mean Matthew is still alive. In a wheelchair. In a coma. Something. The Viking ghost said, "You did this." It could mean a lot of things.

Lesha clears his throat. The captain wasn't familiar enough with the terrain, and they got lost, radioed for instructions, but by the time they crossed the river and were ready to move out of the gorge, it was dusk, and they found themselves under *dushman* fire from above.

"We walked right into it," he says. "They could see us, but we couldn't see them behind the rocks and ridges."

When the fire started, the captain ordered the unit to disperse and take cover, but they dropped down too close to each other. Inexperienced. No one except the officers had been in combat until that day.

Most soldiers were killed in the first few minutes of the battle, including Matthew and both officers. Bleeding, stifling his moans, Lesha watched the darkness descend. The enemy fighters came down the slopes and were bashing in the skulls of the wounded. He closed his eyes, hid his face, and tried not to breathe.

"I had four bullets in me, so they must have left me for dead." He is not scratching the table anymore. He is gripping the edge. White under the fingernails. If he had the strength, he'd crush the pressed particle board into powder. I think about the shape of the bites his hands would take out of the table. "Matthew was already dead," he says, and I sense he rehearsed it. "But...just shot. They didn't touch him."

It is abominable for me to take solace in this. But I do. I suppose we take solace in abomination when abomination is all there is.

In and out of consciousness, Lesha listened for the mujahideen to leave, then checked for survivors. There was one, a sergeant, in worse shape. He tied the sergeant to his back and crawled with him to Helipad 71. The rest was unconsciousness, delirium, surgeries, hospitals, physical therapy, recovery, discharge.

"I managed to get one thing," he says, and clears his throat. "Something we promised each other." He pulls an envelope from his uniform's inner pocket, pulls a picture from the envelope, and hands it to me. It's tattered, creased, and stained. Lisa snapped it on the Square of the Arts the day Matthew passed his last entrance exam at the Pedagogical. Above us on his pedestal, Pushkin was whispering poetry into the midsummer breeze, and between the sunny nonchalance of the Russian Museum and the commotion of the Philharmonic, Matthew picked me up and held me, cradled in his arms, my feet dangling. We are cheek to cheek in this picture, teenagers still, utterly blissful for a shutter's click. He took this photo with him, our favorite. He said he'd bring it back to me.

I take the paper. I don't feel my hands shaking, but the

picture is fluttering between my fingers. Something is changing. A seam is about to tear. The earth is about to give. The
picture is fluttering. I am holding. Until finally I hear a wail
rising from the deep.

CHAPTER 9
Spring 1990

In *The Everlasting Man*, G. K. Chesterton finds humanity to be unique among animals—so odd, in fact, that he calls man "a stranger on the earth." We are more akin to aliens from another land than to children of this planet, he says. Alone among animals we invent liberties and limitations; we wear clothes and make furniture with our miraculous hands; we are uncomfortable in our own skins. Alone among animals we are shaken with the beautiful madness called laughter.

I'm wrapped around a floor-to-ceiling handrail in a muddy tin can of an old-model Leningrad tramway, fingering the volume of Chesterton in my shoulder bag and having a silent argument with him. The book was a loan from one of the vets to Lesha, who passed it to me, and I like it enough to be intrigued, but as my tram is clattering past the Field of Mars, I am finding these differences between humans and animals rather superficial. Just now, I can't help feeling a deeper affinity with the natural kingdoms than with my fellow humans.

The Field of Mars is a singular space in the center of the city. Right off the Neva, it's a sort of mash-up of a park with a parade ground: a spanning, immaculately groomed plaza of lawns, carmine flowerbeds, and intersecting walkways that converge in the middle upon the Eternal Flame. It's populated normally by tourists on their way to the Summer Garden, and the two or three locals who lay bouquets at the grave of the Unknown Soldier, but today there's a crowd. I see a rally of a few hundred men and a slowdown of passers-by who are watching them gather, and I know what this is: the National-Patriotic Front "Memory." Nazis. They started rallying a couple years ago, and now they seem to be everywhere: in the streets, on TV, in the papers, in the jokes. I don't want to look, but it's like passing a wreck—you can't help but turn your head, see the gore spilling onto the melting asphalt. It tests the strength of your stomach and leaves a notch on your memory.

The tram doors open with a labored clank, and I hear shreds of a shallow, straining tenor hollering out slogans over the Field: "...God's anointed Great Russian sovereign...Zemsky sobor...judo-zionist conspiracy..." I would swear there's a whiff of digested alcohol in the air, but it can't be coming from them: too far. The audience (all men, I note with guilty satisfaction) is standing mostly still, waffling from foot to foot, holding signs with icon prints and crossed-out Magen Dovids. The doors shut thunderously, we jerk forward, and while grabbing the handrail, I realize I was hiding my face in my elbow.

Stop being a coward. They aren't even looking your way. What would Babby have said if she could see you like this?

The Field of Mars recedes, and I put my hand back on the book, but Chesterton is timorously quiet.

An old, skinny Jew in a torn coat walks into the Memory headquarters and asks the Nazi on duty: "Excuse me, is it true that Jews sold out Russia?"

"You bet your grubby paws, you dirty Jew!" says the Nazi.

"Oh, well, in that case," says the old Jew and lights up with timid hope, "do you know where I can get my share?"

—Soviet joke

*   *   *

Today is a performance day, so I'm on my way to Lesha's after the morning rehearsal, and I have to be back by five o'clock for makeup and warm-up. Curtain is at seven. We're doing *Cinderella*, where Lisa has a solo as the Summer Fairy, I'm dancing the Goofy Stepsister, and Andy is the Prince on at least three nights. As far as I know, he doesn't have any Party-brass relatives; he's just that good. Of course, none of us are still quite at our technical peak (it's been five years since Lisa and I started at the Kirov, seven years for Andy), but what Andy lacks in fine technique he makes up for in exceptional partnering talent. Strong, reliable, gentle, focused, quick. Principals love dancing with him, and, I heard, it was the great and venerable Galina Mezanova who personally brought up his candidacy as the Prince for her Cinderella.

I wonder if I'd be nursing this quiet, heart-melting pride in a danseur if he weren't my best friend's boyfriend, but honestly I adore everything about his Prince. Especially spectacular is his entrance, the choreography and the personality of it. He bursts onto the stage in a sequence of playful leaps—grand jetés and scissor-like assemblés and little hopping temps levés—and just carouses all about until it lands him on the steps leading up to the throne, reluctantly and temporarily tamed. For the length of the ballet he is this young, immature, impulsive boy who falls head over heels in love. I keep imagining that it is not for the famous, married, forty-year-old Mezanova but for my Lisa that Prince Andy soars above the stage.

My own part is a new challenge for me: It's a character role, very comic relief, very Prokofiev with the music skipping all over. The two ugly stepsisters constantly play off one another, so our rehearsal is endless choreography—ducking under each other's legs and fake-pounding each other into the ground and even fake-strangling each other at one point, when we get in each other's way trying to show off for His Highness. "Shake her more! Bigger! And mean it!" the coach yells to my partner, the Wicked Stepsister. "And Dinah—bigger head movement, or it looks like you're having a seizure. And keep your arms straight, like a doll. You're supposed to be the goofy one. There you go! That's funny."

I'm not into "funny" these days, so it's hard to get into character, to become this clownish girl dressed in sequins who flitters about and falls on her butt. That girl cannot drown in grief, she can't carry a grudge. It'll flatten her.

Out of my shoulder bag I pull cold dumplings wrapped in newspaper and pop one in my mouth. A woman in the nearby seat glares at me with disapproval. We tend to eat in bites throughout the day because a big meal makes you too heavy to dance, and there usually isn't a break long enough between rehearsals to digest anything. A lot of people think that ballet dancers subsist on air and cabbage leaves, but that's just balderdash. We burn upwards of four thousand calories a day, and while we do need to keep the waist pliable, we also need to feed all that muscle. Some girls have to watch empty carbs, chocolate, eating late at night, but that's about it, and right now I badly need a pick-me-up.

Lesha lives on the southern Petrograd Side, in one of those buildings that still have communal quarters and no elevators: *Welcome to old Petersburg, enter through the courtyard.* The irony of these apartments, though, is location. A squished, dilapidated little street opens up onto a river (there are three of them right there), and magically you are a lazy five-minute walk from the Peter-and-Paul's Fortress, just on the other side of the zoo. Here's all this space, rolled out like a tablecloth to the North Pole, and all the pastel-colored palaces you'll ever need, and the Summer Garden across the water. A half-an-hour stroll to the Palace Square. A room with peeling walls, a kitchen and a toilet shared with two neighbor families, three flights of stairs plunged on and off into a serial killer's wet dream: The bulbs always seem to be either out or stolen. This is the heart of the city.

Since perestroika began to unravel the economy, these buildings have felt it most acutely, more than the newer ones in the residential areas. These buildings and bakeries. All the stores are empty, and for the first time since after the war, the country is on rations, but in the other stores, emptiness is just visual: You come in, you see there's no meat, no cheese, no sugar. You don't expect there to be, and you've probably forgotten your what-if bag at home for the past three weeks, so you go on your way to your supper of macaroni and ketchup. But in a bakery, the breads and pastries had always filled the air with a heavenly scent, and it used to seep out the doors and hop on the wind for a ride around the block so everyone knew: Rum-bubbas were in the oven, or raisin rolls, or caraway-sprinkled rye loaves, or eclairs. A bakery wraps you in a lush aroma before it caresses your eye. Even when luxuries are all gone, the simplest of black breads will still announce itself with a warm, sour fragrance. After mother's milk, bread is the first thing of life. A nation is in serious trouble when bakeries smell like muddy floors.

"Excuse me, you don't have any meat, do you?"

"Oh, you're in the wrong store. We don't have any fish. They don't have any meat across the street."

—Soviet joke

I get to Lesha's by noon, haul up the stairs past invisible but noxious-smelling urine—feline or human, I've long been unable to distinguish in these stairwells—and frequently updated, unprintable graffiti. Three of the guys are smoking on the landing, and I see that they are high. This is the only place I've ever had to deal with drugs, but I've learned to ignore the condition as much as I can.

"Is Lesha here?" I ask the guys.

"Inside. You bring anything?"

"A couple clippings."

There used to be just a few of us at first, coming together now and then at Lesha's: the friends he'd made in Afghanistan and in the hospitals afterwards, and me. We came and drank tea and drank cheap spirits and talked about small things and sometimes about big things, too big for most people to understand. More often than not, they smoked harsh, unfiltered cigarettes and talked, and I listened. I wanted to smoke, too, but I'm a dancer. We're not allowed.

Then these few brought a few others, and those, a few more, and Lesha's place turned into a kind of Afghan vets' watering hole, with people coming and going at all hours. Somebody tacked a picture of laughing men in fatigues to an empty wall, then a photo of a chopper in flight above it, a few days later a color clipping from a magazine to its right: a spring meadow specked with wild flowers, running up to an old cabin, half ruined and submerged in the grass. No one asked who was bringing the pictures or what they meant, and we began to add and add more. We cover some images and work around others in a sort of collage that's still growing, unchecked and tentacled, now taking over the adjacent walls. There are maybe twenty guys in and out of the place and three women: a nurse from Lesha's hospital; a helicopter pilot's wife, who touches him every few minutes as though to check that he's still with her; and me, a widow.

143

I'm a widow. Matthew is dead.

In the kitchen, Lesha's neighbor from two doors down is peeking inside the oven. She's her usual self: hot-pink in the cheeks, all plump and creased like rising dough that's overfilled its dish. Over a front-button dress she's wearing her unchanging paisley apron. A silky headscarf is tied at the back of her neck, peasant style. She patiently endures the comings and goings around Lesha's room, tolerates the noise and the occasional fights that combust out of tempers and drugs and booze and hypervigilance. She ignores the splatters of blood, hollers, and dull, startling thuds into the walls; bears without complaint the late-night doorbell ringing and the off-key singing. Only a few months ago she finally asked that the smoking be taken out onto the landing.

She respects Lesha and feels for him, so she calls him "Talich"—by patronymic only, a folksy sign of esteem, the way they still do in the village where she grew up on a collective farm, south of Ryazan. And we call her Aunt Vally. And she calls me "deary," because, of everybody milling about Lesha's, I think, she truly likes only me.

"Morning, deary. Talich is inside."

"The guys told me. How are you, Aunt Vally? How are yours?"

Aunt Vally's husband is a machinist at the Electrosila factory. I always confuse him with their other neighbor (both wiry, balding men with red bulbous noses). Her daughter is a bright and wide-eyed high schooler with dimples, crooked teeth, thick glasses, and an inexhaustible curiosity about everything she touches.

"They're good," she says, and nods a little to herself. A micro-smile is pushing through her lips, more a sensation than an expression, like a light through canvas. "They went to the zoo again." She squints at the wall clock. "I'm making you kids some raisin bars, but I'll put some away for you to take home."

Since Babby died, Aunt Vally has taken it upon herself to supply me with delectables, most notably pastries filled with dried fruit, which her sister sends regularly from Ordubad, Azerbaijan's cornucopia. Every so often I catch her muttering stifled threats of moving to the Caucasus. She never will. Aunt Vally cannot yet feel the leukemia that's brewing inside her bones, but she will next year, about the same time when the Soviet Union collapses in a heap, raising walls of dust between her and her sister. For years her sister will keep trying to convince the Russian authorities that she and her husband and children belong in Russia.

Post-Soviet economy will be hard on almost everyone— not as much on the Baltics, but hard on Russia; harder on the Slavic republics and the Caucasus; hardest, maybe, on Central Asia. And wars will flare up here and there, like flames from red, scattered coals, and make things worse. Aunt Vally will never see her sister again: Borders and cancer will win this battle.

"Aunt Vally, speaking of sweets." I hoist my what-if bag onto her kitchen table. This is the first time in three weeks the bag has come in handy. "They were selling condensed milk by the Peace Plaza, six cans per person, and I got you four."

Her eyes sparkle momentarily, then she puts the flicker out and purses her lips. "Did you check where it's made?"

"Of course." *What am I, new?* I've been walking past the shelves loaded with Belarusian milk for four years now, just like everybody else. Licking my lips, averting my gaze, and plodding away. Until 1986, Belarus had been the unquestioned, ubiquitous supplier of all things dairy, but now even the rationed and half-hungry populace is too afraid to touch

145

anything from the general area. Honestly, we shouldn't be drinking our local milk either, or eating local mushrooms—but then we'd starve. "It's not Chernobyl milk," I say. "It's from Mordovia." I bring the can up to my eyes. "Saransk Conservation Factory."

"Thank you, deary." Aunt Vally pulls me in with one hot, crumb-covered hand, and plants a kiss on my temple. Her bosom is bothered by the collision with my body like a water-filled balloon. "You're a sweet girl. I'll bring the cookies in for you."

Matthew is dead, and Babby is dead. But on the bright side, I get cookies.

We didn't know Babby had lymphoma until we knew, if you'll allow me the expression. As 1988 had worn on, she'd been getting tired earlier and sitting down more, her back had been aching, but then, she was nearing eighty-one. All we thought to do was free her from cooking and dishes, from cleaning and shopping and things. Cleo would run up on Mondays (the cooking day) and help me under the pretext of learning Babby's recipes. Our tiny kitchen couldn't fit more than two people standing, so Babby was relegated to resting in the place of honor. She sat on the stool squeezed between the table and the windowsill, giving us directions and tasting for salt, harrumphing at our ineptitude when one blintz after another flipped into a heap. We tee-heed and shoved each other; I glanced at Matthew's picture above the refrigerator and thought that, though not good, maybe decent or at least survivable times might be finally coming back.

I didn't worry when she became too exhausted to go anywhere, even for a visit with Auntie Alena down the block. I didn't worry when she seemed to catch a cold and couldn't shake it: Days turned into weeks of coughs and sniffles and swollen glands.

"Are you going to see the doctor?" I asked.

"Sure, kitten," she said.

I didn't worry enough.

Then I woke up to the sound of vomiting from the living room. As I laid her back on her couch, I felt the heat coming off her in waves, and jumped from the cold when my hand touched the sheet: wet, soaked through and through.

"It's fine, Dinush," she said, her voice cracking and raspy. "I've been having this fever on and off. It's this bug I can't fight off."

Only then did I think to demand answers. What had been happening? Well, these cold symptoms, the fevers and pain in the back, in the right shoulder and flank. Sweating buckets at night, then getting cold. Nausea. She'd lost weight—a lot more than I'd noticed. What about these? Oh, those? She turned her arms, exposed by her short-sleeved nightgown, under the sleepy light of our torchiere, and examined several small bruises below her elbows. She didn't know, didn't remember bumping into things. They just kept popping up. She hiked up the hem of the nightgown, and I saw her legs, randomly speckled with dark blue spots of various sizes and shapes like two used rolls of blotting paper.

Dr. Pulsky came over in the morning, listened to the list of symptoms as she pushed and prodded Babby on every side, and her face was getting progressively stormy.

"I'll need you to do some blood work," she said. "Today, please, Freeda Isaakievna." And handed the script to me. Babby glared at me, frowned, then closed her eyes and lay back on the couch. I realize now: That's when she knew.

Patients in Russia are rarely told when things get dire.

Cancer patients. Terminal patients. It is a culture of a particular kind of compassion, which prizes peace of mind over self-determination. In this culture, in theory, of course, if you fall ill—extremely ill—the weight of decision-making falls entirely on your doctors, and the weight of worry and fear and knowledge falls entirely on your loved ones. You can save your strength and have your hope and always have your peace. All you eventually have to do will be the dying.

Out in the foyer, Dr. Pulsky was tight-lipped while putting on her coat.

"You know what this is, don't you, Doctor?" I asked. I still didn't know, but a wave of burning cold was rolling up and down my spine.

She dropped her hat on top of her medical bag. "It's... Her liver is enlarged, and she is jaundiced. You have to get her to the lab right away, then we'll do an ultrasound."

"But you know."

She pulled me down to sit on the bench under the coat-rack and clasped my fingers. "I'm almost certain there's a tumor," she said. "I'm sorry."

I remember a ringing in my ears, like a silence at high altitude. "Liver cancer?" I still wasn't getting it. "That means surgery, doesn't it? But it should be operable?"

She squeezed my hands, looking at them as if they were the subject of examination. "Liver cancer is rare," she said to my hands. "But liver metastases are common. And given your grandmother's other symptoms, how it started, how long ago, and the enlarged lymph nodes... It's probably another kind of cancer that's spread to the liver." She looked back up. "Blood tests and an ultrasound will tell us what kind and where it is. You'll go to oncology straight from there, and we can tell your grandmother she has cirrhosis or whatever you decide with the oncologist, but you have to be ready: There'll be chemotherapy. It'll be brutal, and it might give us a little more time, but even so, it probably won't be very long. You'll have to be very tough for her."

And so it was, all except my being tough. Blood work and ultrasound and something else after that diagnosed stage IV B-cell non-Hodgkin's lymphoma involving the liver and bone marrow. We told Babby she had cirrhosis of the liver, which had caused those recurring infections, but she already knew she had cancer and knew it was terminal. It often occurs to me that she may have gone through the hell that was chemo just because that's what was expected of her. Or that she did it for me. After all, nobody asked her what she wanted.

She was a good doctor, Olga Pulsky. She knew what she was talking about. I would've liked to have gone to her funeral, but that day I was at the hospital with Babby. It was the day Babby told me to stop lying to her so she could stop lying to me, and then we both knew that we both knew. I sobbed in her skinny, blotchy arms, and she consoled me. I fell asleep in her arms like that while she tried to remember an old lullaby she said they used to sing to each other when she'd been little: her parents and siblings, then she and Uncle Samuel. She'd been preoccupied by that lullaby for weeks, after Samuel had come to her in a dream. That's how she put it to me. I didn't believe in any of that nonsense, of course (neither did she, I thought), but the dream was so vivid, she couldn't deny it. I tried to ask her about it, but she didn't offer up anything rational, just smiled and said she was all right with everything, now that he'd bothered to inform her that he was waiting up for her. And every time she said that, she snickered like a girl.

Inside Lesha's room, there's not much furniture: a rectangular dining table against one wall, a couch against another, a wardrobe in the corner. The fourth wall is covered by the collage. The room's owner is lying on the couch with a towel on his chest, another folded across his forehead, his eyes closed, and tiny red splotches are caked into the checkered waffle fabric: He's been coughing up blood.

Lesha has never talked much about the particulars of his injuries, and never again, after that first day, about how he got them. He talks sparingly about other things, too, so I started out thinking he was a kind of deliberate person, choosing his words, planting them with purpose. But then he began getting tired and nauseated and achy in every joint, and he would rub his hands and feet, trying to massage pins and needles out of them, and now he's spitting up blood. I wonder if it hasn't always been painful for him to speak. I don't know what's wrong exactly, only that, out of the four bullets that had been shot into him, one is still lodged in his lung. Or maybe it's a fragment of one, in some place where it would be safer remaining than being removed. Barbos said it was too close to his pulmonary artery, but I think he's being full of it. I just mean, if my patient had a bullet grazing a major artery, I bet I would remove it. Wouldn't you?

Barbos and Kot are at the dining table playing cards and eating bread with salted cabbage. The smell of the cabbage is pungent and overwhelming and, mixing with the sweet tang of cookies from the kitchen, disorienting. At the sight of me, the men nod simultaneously at the couch, and Barbos says, "Bad day."

Nobody here knows Barbos's and Kot's real names. These are just nicknames, symbols of a cartoon dog and a cartoon cat. I suppose they do look a bit like the animals: One is scruffy, pinched, with a shaggy head of matted brown hair; the other is groomed and soft-skinned, with frameless round glasses and a bristling mustache—but unlike their referents, these two are inseparable. They even speak often in stereo.

I cannot definitely put my finger on why I dislike them, especially Kot, but I'm rather sure the feeling is mutual. We haven't ever said much to each other, yet I am sensing that I'm not welcome in the world of cats and dogs. It's a gut feeling, a kind of radar installed by Katie Pasiuk and Nicholas Yanowski and fine-tuned every day since. Of course, nothing's for sure. If it's not anti-Semitism, it's something else, but chances are it's your garden-variety anti-Semitism. They're just polite because they're afraid of Lesha.

"Lucky hunting?" Kot points with his chin at my what-if bag, which still contains two cans of Mordovian milk. He is crunching on cabbage, and the words come out "fucky funting."

"Yeah."

"Gotta know where to look, I guess."

Because we have a Zionist conspiracy of milk? "Just came across it," I say.

Maybe I'm being paranoid, after all. Maybe they're just jerks or have a phobia of names that start with "D."

I sit by Lesha on the couch and turn over the towel on his head. "Hey. How're you feeling?"

He grins without lifting his lids. "What's interesting?"

"Nothing. I finished the Chesterton."

"Told you he wasn't that good." His grin takes on a roguish curve, and I gladly take the bait. Anything is better than the thing splattered in human juice I found lying here a minute ago. He is wincing as he talks, but at least now he's a person, not a body of one.

"It's not that he is bad." I can hear chewing from the table, the clearing of two throats and the shuffling of cards, but no talking: What I say next will be a performance piece.

"It's his anthropocentrism," I say. "He seems to think that me and some Nazi have more in common—by a magnitude—than me and, say, an elephant because me and the Nazi both wear pajamas to sleep."

Lesha curves an eyebrow, which I guess because the towel on his forehead slides up on one side and down over his eye on the other. He flicks it off, and it slips onto the parquet floor with a wet splat. "To be fair, I'm not sure Chesterton said exactly this." He moves only his lips.

"No, but he is going exactly there," I press. "It's like humans are qualitatively different from everybody else—the pinnacle of creation! So we're kin with each other, then? But you know, I think I'd rather have an ability to love than pajamas! Seriously. When an elephant gets sick, the other elephants support the sick one with their heads, and I dare think I'm more like the elephants than Nazis, thank you very much!"

I've spent myself on the tirade and feel sheepish. Chesterton's world was only slightly more innocent than mine. History is not his fault, none of my problems are, and an old dead Christian cannot grasp them or explain them and absolutely cannot fix them.

Lesha has opened his eyes and is searching my face. "What happened, kid?"

"Nothing." I know this won't fly, and I do want to tell him, but the silence at the table is burrowing into my back: The Pets quit chewing and are really listening now.

Lesha covers my hand with his. It is cool and so much bigger than mine that my whole fist is lost inside his palm with knotted knuckles and long fingers. Every time I see it, I think of the first time I noticed how long these fingers were, when they were squeezing the edge of my kitchen table.

Matthew is dead.

"Not nothing," he says. "Something." And I give in to his care and his presence and his strength. Forget the Pets.

"I rode past a Memory rally on the Field of Mars."

"Well. That's interesting," he says with comic intensity.

"It's really not."

He coughs harder and sits up to push the towel against his mouth. The Pamir tan that was covering his face four years ago is gone, and he is pale now, too pale for a living person. "Ignore 'em, ugh," he gets out between hacks. "Piss scoundrels. They'll talk themselves out. Ugh." He spits out pink, frothy phlegm into the towel and sits, wheezing and hunched over, as if mustering up strength, then raises his head to look at me. "I'll go breathe in some steam. Hang around, all right? I won't be long." The stained towel goes into the bucket; he rises with a groan, pulls a fresh one out of the wardrobe, and walks out, emptying the room. I want to go with him, or at least go away, but leaving feels demonstrative, and I stay on the couch like on a bus stop bench: biding the seconds and ready to spring up.

"Don't be scared."

It's Kot. He has swiveled on his chair and leaned toward me so cozily that the dining table is looking uncomfortably close, but I'm trying to appreciate the gesture. It's unlike him to be sweet. The sleeves of his plaid shirt are rolled up, sitting right above the elbows, and their masculinity seems hyperbolic against his squishy white forearms, a blue tattoo running up from the left wrist: TRUTH OR DEATH. I may have been wrong about him. It's hard to read these guys—they've been through too much death.

"Yeah," I say. "It'll be fine, right?"

"That's right," he says. He purrs. "There's going to be a pogrom, but you don't have to be scared. We will tell you when, and then you don't be in the city."

Shit.

I knew it. I could tell what he was, and even with all my radars, I still didn't trust myself enough, didn't protect myself enough, and here, walked into this. Now I'm trapped in a room with two Nazis. *Where the hell is Lesha?*

I stand up and evaluate the distance between me and the door with a lightning glance. Kot and Barbos stand up, too.

"You're Memory." It's not a question on my part.

He rocks on his feet from heel to toe, a self-satisfied rockabye toy. "You should be grateful. If we don't warn you, you're going down with the rest of your tribe when the time comes."

My tribe. I wish I really knew what that meant.

They're planning a pogrom in Leningrad. In 1990. This is what we've come to. The piss scoundrels opt to do more than talk.

Maybe it's good he's warning me: my chance to elicit information.

Why *is* he warning me?

"Why are you warning me?" I ask.

I've inched it almost halfway to the door during our exchange, but it doesn't work. Kot stops rocking and covers the distance between us in four large, leisurely steps, looms over me, close. He isn't tall, just irregularly shaped, like an ink splotch. He blots out the light and displaces the air and drops a short, hoarse, slippery worm of a whisper down into my half-open mouth: "No problem. You're *our* yid." And I swallow.

I must answer. I must tell him I am not his yid and to fuck off with his warnings and we will beat them Russian Nazis like we beat the German ones. I must hit his soft white cheek between the mustache and the rimless glasses. I must run.

I stir, but Barbos is already behind me. His arm slips between my elbows and my spine and fastens, and he backs us both into the wall. Tight. I strain. A wet towel against my mouth. He pushes my head backwards into his shoulder. There's no screaming now. The towel's dripping down my chest—he must have picked it out of the bucket—and I catch myself thinking that it still has Lesha's blood and spit in it. There's a hint of metal in the taste of damp cloth and something else, gaggy: soap or mucus or dirt. Everything is slow. Isn't it supposed to be before you die? I hear Barbos's steady breaths in my ear, in and out through his nose.

Kot unbuttons my shirt from top to bottom with his left hand and clicks open a Swiss knife with his right. Now I know: He wants to cut out the whisper worm that he's put inside me. I know it now, and I stop being afraid. The worm is wiggling in my stomach, up my throat, making me sick. Yes, I want it gone. I close my eyes.

It is easy.

I have braced for strong pain. For a stab, for a violent tear and convulsion and agony and darkness, but it's not like that. It is a slow pour. Like the whine of a sitar string or a smooth salty trail of a sweat droplet rolling down my skin, from the breast bone to the navel. It rolls in a wave, out and in again. The pain is thin as the blade and shallow as the skin it parts. I feel the warmth of the blood spilling down my stomach, and it feels good. I didn't realize how cold I was. I am so, so cold...

Kot's face is near. My eyes are shut tight, but I can smell him—salt cabbage and smoke and bad breath—and I can feel his body becoming the world in front of me, Barbos behind in my ear, against my shoulders, around my arms, and I'm flat between them and airless and timeless, and something is coming next but I can't think. The towel is chok-

155

ing, the worm is heaving itself out, and then a new sound crashes in: a knock on the door, it opens, a shattering dish.

"Waaaaahhhh!"

The tightness collapses like scaffolding. Aunt Vally grabs my arm and jerks me out into the open air, toward the door, over spilled cookies and shards of a plate. "Taliich!" She's shrieking, shredding her throat into inhuman sounds. "Taaliiich! Call the militiaaaa!" She's pushing me out of the room, into the hallway, shielding me with her body and making some sort of sign with one arm in the direction of the two men, who are just standing there, watching us leave. Then they burst past us—speeding bullets—and are not there anymore. She keeps making the sign into their backs, into the empty space that used to hold them, over and over and over. This is something sacred or superstitious. Vaguely familiar. Something ancient, religious, from the world of the Old Believers and the old czars. A word surfaces in my thoughts: *anathema*. It's a curse.

Lesha is tearing through the corridor red-faced and wet-haired. Aunt Vally is closing my shirt around me and wrapping her arm around me and pointing inside the room, her breathing fast and syncopated: "There! Them two! Call the militia! Look what they did!" She swivels me like a thing toward the light, and they both look. For the first time I, too, look down. The fabric has soaked up the blood—there isn't much at all. Lines. Strange, dotted lines. Uneven, spreading lines as though someone had drawn with a leaking ink pen. A vertical line and a horizontal line.

He's carved a cross into my stomach.

"What in the world happened?"

"Call the militia! Don't let 'em get away!"

"Dinah, can you hear me?"

They keep talking. To me, I think. They keep asking.

I know what they're asking, what's going to happen—everything. But I've forgotten something. There's something I must do.

"Dinah, look at me." Lesha is holding my face in both hands as if I'd sink if he let go. "You're all right. You're safe now."

That's right, I remember. I must run.

I push out of his hands, and he lets me. "Dinah?" he says after me. The apartment door is where I expect it to be. The stairwell is empty. Lesha's already on the threshold. "Dinah, where're you going?"

I take the first careful step down. My legs hold. And then I run.

CHAPTER 10
Fall 1990

I don't have to be at the embassy until 11:00 a.m., but my train comes to a soft halt at the Leningradsky Station at 7:55 a.m. on the dot. Three hours to get some breakfast, walk around Moscow, and make my way to Great Deviatinsky Lane.

I've taken the Red Arrow, an overnight express whose coolness factor is second only to the Trans-Siberian. Every night two trains leave Moscow and Leningrad at exactly five minutes to midnight and streak toward each other, invariable, speedy, and burgundy. One of them carried the Olympic flame in 1980, and every time I board the Red Arrow, I wonder if I happen to be in *that* car. It always feels dizzyingly amazing to ride it. It would this time, too, if I weren't coming to Moscow for an interview at the American Embassy, asking for a refugee status in the United States. Asking for a foreign government's help to leave everything cool and familiar behind, never again to ride the Red Arrow Express.

It's the first of October, a crisp, cloudy morning that promises to turn into a chilly day. The wind isn't bad, but it breathes with the moisture of yesterday's frigid rain, and I wrap my coat tightly around my waist and clamp my bag to my side with my elbow. If a purse was the first invention in fashion, then, I bet, purse-snatching was the second, followed closely by this elbow technique. I can't afford to get robbed today: Inside the bag, in a thick envelope, are completed questionnaires, transcripts, medical clearances—the irreplaceable documents I've just spent four months gathering. It's those papers, my passport, my return ticket for tonight, and some money. I don't need anything else. I hope.

Breakfast is an easy choice: On the nearest corner, a street vendor is selling pies. Her cart is an island of heat and steam and of gurgling, heavenly savors. Baked pies on the left, flushed in their puffy cheeks, stuffed with mushrooms, potatoes, or sour cherries. The deep-fried ones, brown and sizzling, are on the right: meat, cabbage, apples. I hear Babby's voice in my head: *Don't eat fried pastries, kitten; baked is so much better for you. Especially from street carts—who knows how many times that oil's been reheated!*

Babby always baked. It was the last thing she'd done before lymphoma made her too weak to cook: little yeast pies with eggs and scallions, my favorites. She cut out round pieces of rolled-out dough with an overturned jar and spooned tiny mounds of filling onto them; I folded up the sides and pinched them shut like toy huts, then brushed them with beaten egg, so they'd be shiny out of the oven, and spaced them on the baking sheet. We were almost two-thirds through when she fell asleep with the jar half-pressed into the dough. It was fast after that. Like she got too tired to live.

"Two fried, please," I order. "One cabbage, one beef."

This is truly folk Russian ambrosia. Greek gods had nothing better on Olympus. Back in the days of Peter—even before that, Ivan the Terrible—street vendors stomped in the mud of old Moscow with heavy wooden trays, tied to the ropes slung over the shoulder and piled high with hare meat pies.

I'm in the thick of all that history now, meandering through the Tverskoy district toward the Kremlin: the Clear Ponds, the Butchers' Row, Sretenka... Moscow is an older city than Petersburg, and it's different. It's big, for one (nine million people to our five), and it feels big: noisy, pushy, and throaty, brimming with Russia's prefeudal past in its old street names and its haphazard map, its corner-church surprises protruding their gingerbread-patterned onion domes into the modern cityscape. And it brims with all other things, tourists and government and commerce. There's something here I can never put my finger on—something in its anthill activity or its big-mall mentality, or maybe its labeling itself the "Third Rome." Babby used to summarize her feelings briefly and coldly: "A merchant town."

For centuries, after the disintegration of Kievan Rus, Moscow was the hub of all things in the middle of nothing. A backwater capital. A city of czars and bazaars.

Babby didn't like Moscow. It happens a lot between Moscovites and Leningraders.

"Leningrad is not a third of anything," she used to say. "It is the first and only."

Years later I will try to explain this to Simon by comparing us to the lovers of Beatles and Elvis, and to Harvard and Yale: We can appreciate both but never love both equally. We can belong here or there.

Peter I, the defiant child ruler, grew up in Moscow stifled and threatened by the old order and abhorred it. He escaped to the enlightened progress of the German neighborhood, dressed as a German officer, and in 1703, he founded himself a new capital in the severe beauty of the North. He made it a museum fortress (to defend against the Swedes, who never attacked again) and designed it as a single work of art. In Peter's monument to the new order, golden spires pierced the skies, statues came to life along the bridges, and gardens brushed the canals with their filigreed railings. Nothing was haphazard about St. Petersburg. When you stand on the Anichkov Bridge, and the boy and his horse surround you—on this corner, wrestling wild; on this corner, tame—and the Fontanka River slowly curves away like a dancer's arm, you are embraced by the city itself, a breathing, organic whole, and it knows you.

Ever since then there've been two capital cities in Russia, competing for power and character and for the soul of the state. They say Leningrad is a European city and Moscow is Russian, that Leningrad is a city of proletariat and intelligentsia while Moscow is a city of merchants and apparatchiks, but of course nothing is so simple. There are apparatchiks in Leningrad and intellectuals in Moscow, yet one thing's for sure: We write songs and books and make movies of the one city our hearts belong to, and you can never confuse them.

To my mind, the Moscovite bards are more playful, flirty even with their city, or else they love her like a mother, and they talk of the unmined, unending surprise she brings to their lives. When we sing of Leningrad, it is without smiles, with choked breath and hazy gaze, because Leningrad itself is music and mystery, the intimate witness and definition to all our love and loss. Sometimes we sing of nostalgia. For explorers and seafarers, life is made worth living only by the return to this city, who takes them back into its arms. As it sleeps in the night, we imagine its dreams—of heavens and rivers reflected in each other—and its nightmares, which have driven mad many a hero thought up by its genius literati sons. Our city is a beloved, but not a person. To Moscovites, Moscow is a "she" and very much a woman. Leningrad—as much as Petersburg—is a masculine noun, but it isn't a man. It is what it is, our defining reality, and there is nothing else like it.

It figures that, wandering about Moscow, I still find my

thoughts drifting back to Leningrad. I'm uneasy and have barely slept. Usually I sleep well on trains, and the Red Arrow is as comfy as they get, but this time I was restless.

Can cities feel betrayed? And when they do, how do they exact revenge?

I have read that, among the first wave of Russian émigrés, who ran from the Bolshevik Revolution after 1917, there were those who died of nostalgia. They did not commit suicide, they simply wasted away, away from home. No lifeblood to the heart.

I went to Babby's grave yesterday, hers and Uncle Samuel's. Her name is now etched out under his, on the same headstone:

FREEDA ISAAKIEVNA RESNICK, 1907–1989

I planted some new flowers on the grave, the Russian way; laid a stone on top of the monument, the Jewish way; swept the borders and the bench; and I asked her what I was doing. And I asked if she would forgive me. But she didn't answer. I asked her if I was going to be all right. But she wasn't really there. There was only a cup of ash buried over an old coffin. As though enough Jewish bodies hadn't been burned.

The flowers I planted, at least, are hardy perennials—alpine asters, modest and pretty, round furry things. They will come up next spring on their own, and the spring after next, and the one after. This may be the best and last service I will ever do my grandmother.

I shake off the eerie feeling, swallow the last of the cabbage pie, and look around. I'm on the Hunters' Row, and it's only nine o'clock. I could turn left to the Red Square, see St. Basil's and the Kremlin, or drop by one of the museums: Alexsey Tolstoy's apartment is nearby, so is the Museum of History. I have time. But I know it won't help. My thoughts are unmoored, my eyes unfocused. I can't even tell quite how I got to this spot. Today I am not really here.

I hoist up my shoulder bag and turn right, toward the embassy. I guess I'm going to be early.

The U.S. embassy is as dull inside as any office building should be. Absolutely nothing is made of gold, sparkles with sequins, or is covered in huge posters of movie stars. Nobody, wrapped head to toe in ammo belts, is shooting up the place, holding a machine gun in each hand. The armed guard at the gate is the uncanny part: He smiles at me, checking papers.

My interviewer is a man not that much older than me: I'm twenty-two, and he looks twenty-five to thirty. He is touchingly blue-eyed and brown-haired, trying to be official and casual at the same time. Every several seconds he fidgets in his chair and puts his elbows on the desk only to slide them off, crosses and uncrosses his legs. Today is his first day—the first day for all of them. It's October 1, 1990, the beginning of America's Jewish refugee program in Moscow. Until today, Jews going to the United States had to leave the Union under the pretext of family reunification in Israel, then "change their minds" during the layover in Vienna and fly to Rome, where sprawling camps had been set up for them to be interviewed by the U.S. agents, and to wait, for months, for their status. My interviewer and his friends couldn't come to Moscow to do this until today because there could not have been refugees from the Soviet Union. Imagine such a travesty. There wasn't even any anti-Semitism in the USSR, remember? The Soviet government stood unshakable on that position.

For some reason it makes me feel better that the blue-eyed interviewer is as self-conscious as I am. Maybe we're more equal now, both nervous and brand-spanking-new. Plus, his name is Bill. Only Jack or Bob could be better. He has an elongated, well-discernable accent and tends to mix up noun cases. I can finally smile back.

The room is small, neat, and smells like plastic. A desk and four chairs, two now empty. He reads my questionnaire, grunts now and again, turns pages with his right hand, and writes furiously with his left. Here and there he makes notes on the margins and check marks and some marks I cannot see from where I sit across the desk. Then he raises his head and looks me in the eyes, pointed, interested, attention itself, and asks me to explain.

You say you've been called racial slurs and had altercations in school since you were a child. Can you give me some examples?

I give examples.

You don't consider those who stand around while you're getting beaten up antisemites?

I suppose. But the overwhelming majority of the nation is passively antisemitic. If I treated them on par with the Black Hundred, I'd rarely have anyone to talk to.

He writes for a while, turns the page.

What do you mean by "minor random acts of violence"?

I'll give you two examples. One time I was in a supermarket when they brought out cheese. People kind of mobbed the counter, and someone pushed me away and knocked me on the head with a shopping basket, saying that the Jews won't even let people get to the cheese. Another time on a bus, some man was passing by me to get to the door—there weren't even that many people—and he simply elbowed me in the face.

Bill looks up from his notes. His eyebrows are high, little brown pitched roofs.

And you think it's because you were Jewish.

I'm pretty sure he was Memory.

He was what?

A white supremacist.

But did he say anything?

He said, "What are you looking at, kike?"

Bill is looking at me.

How did he know you were Jewish?

Then I laugh. I don't mean to make fun of him. It's his first day. Didn't they explain things to them? Maybe, this is one reason—this question—this is how I know I really do want to go to America.

They just know, I say. In Russia, everybody can tell just by looking at your face.

Matthew used to tease me with it. On the day we met, I told him that my face made it easy for me to read people— who is good, who is not—and from time to time, on a bus or on the street, he'd poke me in the side and push his lips to my ear and whisper, "Look, that guy has seen your face! So, what's the verdict? Make friends or run away?" I could feel him smiling, tickling my earlobe with his breath. It's not funny, though, is it?

The interviewer writes. He reads more pages. He grunts.

You're a ballet dancer? The Kirov? How wonderful. I love Russian ballet. I only arrived two weeks ago, but my first order of business was an evening at the Bolshoi.

Thank you.

You say you have not been promoted because you are Jewish. What does that mean in ballet?

It means big parts, solo parts. The ultimate goal in ballet is to become prima ballerina. I was told plainly that it was not a possibility for me.

He leafs back and forth through my papers, and he's

more agitated now than when he heard that a Nazi was beating up a girl and nobody cared.

I see you were top of your class at the Vaganova School. The Kirov hired you and then told you straight out you would not be promoted?

Essentially.

Did they give a reason?

I couldn't go on tour.

You've never gone on tour with the company?

It would mean going abroad.

He reclines in his chair, pushes away from the desk with both palms, and stares at me.

In five years, you've never gone on tour with the company?

It would mean going abroad, which requires a KGB clearance. I don't see what he needs me to clarify.

He pulls himself forward and begins to write, more, faster. Page forward, another page, nod, grunt.

I am done by one o'clock. At five, I must come back for the decision. By then, I will or will not be a refugee.

Four more hours of roaming—I cannot bear the thought, but I know what to do. It's dinnertime, I'm hungry and jittery, and there is one attraction in the whole of the USSR that will fit rightly into this day: A McDonald's opened nine months ago in Moscow, the first foreign restaurant in the Union. I hear the line is three hours long, but that's about the time I have. It'll leave me some twenty minutes to get there and the same to get back.

To speed things up, I hop down the metro, one stop to Pushkin Square, and lean on the train car doors where it says DO NOT LEAN in angular crimson letters. I squash my forehead against the chilled blackness of the glass and trace the letters with my fingers: DO NOT LEAN, and below it, NO EXIT. The paint is chipping in places. I give in to temptation and peel off one flake. Then we thunder into the station, the letters are yanked away from me to the right and left, the train clears its throat and spits me out with a small blob of people onto the platform by the exit sign.

I see I'm in the right place as soon as I get aboveground: The line is not actually on the square but across the street, on Novopushkin Green. It surrounds the Green like a gargantuan millipede, snaking and inching its unending, puffy, fluid, motley body along, and slowly, perpetually stuffs its head into an elegant addition to the existing building. Two golden arches above the building create a stylized "M." The McDonald's is glass and aluminum, a mix of whimsical angles and smooth curves. It is futuristic, fantastical, foreign—all things out of phase with the muddy empire that lies vast on its sides.

I am decided: This will be my afternoon. I will become two legs of the great millipede and spend the next few hours having a purpose without having to go anywhere or do anything. I will have my first American experience.

The decision brings me immediate relief, probably because I need to shed the apprehension of the past weeks. Cogitate. Fathom this day and its consequences. I merge with the millipede's tail, stick my hands deep into my coat pockets, and settle in for the long crawl. The soundtrack in my head, appropriate, though unplanned, is Glinka's "Traveling Song": number six in a cycle called *Farewell to St. Petersburg*. It switches from a quick, light train-patter beat to a longing melody in minor, round and round, and my thoughts switch with it.

I've been on autopilot since last spring, when I resolved to apply for the refugee status and acted on my resolve the next day, like a single gulp, the way you blow your nose or jump out of an airplane. It was a week after my last ever visit to Lesha's. I was still pulling long, thin scabs off my abdomen, standing before the mirror every morning to see how a black-and-burgundy cross would turn into a bright-pink one. Or maybe not a cross—crosshairs. The word "pogrom" was still bouncing off the inside of my skull. And the whisper worm was still wiggling, somewhere so deep that I couldn't get to it or vomit it out or strangle it or starve it. *You're our yid. Our yid.* It was making me sick.

I went to the U.S. consulate then and got the papers and mailed them to the embassy and let myself coast after that: What's done is done. But the incredulity of having done it even now hasn't registered with me, I don't think. I am postponing the need to believe it until they say "yes." Because this could all turn out to be nothing. The memory of a nervous breakdown I had, once, in 1990.

Is that what I want? To have told myself I tried? And then to stay?

Am I really ready to run for my life?

It's been bad, 1990. It is worse than last year, and that was worse than the year before, and it wasn't supposed to be this way. But everything's been getting worse since the first high of perestroika splashed up in '85 and then wore off, already by '87.

When the reforms first hit, we were ecstatic. Finally! Glasnost, we thought, would be the knife to lance the old boils of secrecy and of dark, unspoken pasts. To end the Afghan war. All at once, as if by a magic incantation from a powerful wizard, we were more than a society on the path to a bright utopia but a *free* society on the path—and we were young in it. People gathered in leadership camps, in schools, in symposia, or like my folk, in smoke-filled rooms, and argued nights into dawn, to hoarseness and stupor, about the future. What is the role of the State? Should we shift to a multiparty system or stay with one party? What would have been heresy but a few months earlier now seemed a realistic prospect. The doors of psych wards were opening and letting out dissidents, woozy from fresh air, shouting out truths and insults with impunity. Ghastly declassified documents and banned books and alternative history flowed like pus, like blood, and we believed they would cleanse us and wash our wounds, and we would heal.

But nothing can cleanse an infection that's in the blood itself. And there is no magic. And there are no wizards. Chain reaction. Sepsis. Death.

Chernobyl exploded on April 26, 1986, and no one was told while radioactive rain soaked Ukraine, Belarus, and European Russia. The Party officials in Kiev, which was receiving evacuees, were ordered to bring their families to the May Day rally—an old Soviet-style cover-up, to prevent panic. In every city, millions of people filled the streets while the wind was pushing invisible poison from Gomel to Smolensk, on to Leningrad and out there, to Sweden, Norway, and the Scottish Highlands. Not many other wounds are healing either. The Afghan war petered out by 1989, yet its veterans still exist nowhere but in the subcultural, drug-perfused recesses of urban limbos.

Turns out, Mikhail Gorbachev, the peasant darling of the West, wasn't anything new. Not a new species of Soviet leader. He just *wanted* something new. He was a product of the same regime that had spit out the graveyard parade before him: Brezhnev, Andropov, Chernenko. Uneducated and unprepared, he lost control of his reforms; unsettled the delicate balance of politics, economy, and diplomacy; and as though into a returning tide, the country descended back into poverty, from which it had emerged so torturously after the war. Between the earthquake of plummeting oil prices and the cracking support of the military industry, agriculture buckled, production crumbled into dust, and store shelves hung empty and wind-swept. Lines wrapped around blocks, and one after another, foodstuffs were being rationed.

And nationalism. Rising, rabid, spreading ethno-nationalism, anti-Semitism, anti-anything-not-Russian-ism. Because when things are bad, someone must be to blame. The Black Hundred, Memory, all sorts of neo-Nazis are marching through our streets, and it boggles the mind. Swastikas on the sleeves of Russian men—while the Homeland War veterans' parade, every year on May 9, is still full of soldiers who bled to fight the swastika.

But this is what happens when things are bad.

A foreigner is walking along the street and falls down an open sewer. He climbs out banged up, covered in shit, and very angry. A mob gathers to watch.

"Don't you people mark your shitholes with red flags or cones or something?" he yells.

"Sure we do," people say. "Didn't you notice when you crossed the border?"

—Soviet joke

Lisa doesn't think things are that dire. She calls them "crappy."

"Things are crappy sometimes," she said, "and people are crappy, but how can you just leave? Are you seriously going to get on a plane to god-knows-where alone, to America, and we'll never see you again?"

This was a week ago, when I finally got up the nerve to tell her why I was taking a day off and going to Moscow. I'd looked for what I would say to her for months, how I would defend myself, and still, when the moment came, I didn't have the answer.

I was balancing my favorite round stool on two legs in my favorite spot in her kitchen, by the radiator. With my hands wrapped around a teacup, I pretended the movement was helping me think, but really all I had was the same thought that had made my decision for me back in the spring. It was the thought that had occurred to me as I was walking home from the bus stop, trying to cover blood stains on my shirt, and shivering. I'd left my jacket at Lesha's, and I was sure I'd never see it again. When Lesha showed up at my door the next day, fretful and unsteady—holding the damned jacket— for what would be our last meeting, I had to ignore a thin whine of fear to let him in, and a connection that I'd have been the first to tell you unthinkable even a year before was suddenly more than thinkable. Obvious. And demand-ed consideration.

I put down my teacup. "You ever read about German Jews in the 1930s? You know, Hitler is coming to power, and you know what's going to happen, and you're seeing them hurtle into this maw of history, and you just want to holler at the page: Get out, get out, what are you waiting for?"

Lisa slacked in the jaw and dropped her hands, let go of her salty toast, huge round eyes like water wells. "How can you compare?"

"How can I not?" I'd had five months to compare. "It's almost worse, isn't it? At least they didn't know what they were getting into, and we have neo-Nazis rallying on the Field of Mars—in the middle of Leningrad! After what Nazis have done to this city! This country." I couldn't tell if I was justifying myself, or accusing somebody of making me go, or her, of needing to ask why. "You know," I said, "Babby used to tell me, what we can do with our Jewish faces is wear them with dignity. But walking around waiting to be punched, waiting for a pogrom and doing nothing, doesn't seem dignified to me."

"And running away from home is?" She pushed away from the table to face me. "This country is your home. When things are bad, we fight, don't we? We pick up our friends, we pick up signs, we pick up weapons—whatever we must—but we don't run. Where's your citizen's loyalty?"

"My loyalty?" It was the last sentence she shouldn't have said. "My loyalty to what? My freaking motherland? This *country* has killed everyone I've ever loved!"

I saw her face then, flat and white, broken, as if I'd whipped across it with my words and torn it open. I tripped over my rage, and it escaped like steam from a pressure valve.

"Except for you," I said, and she blinked and looked away. "Of course. Except for you. And Cleo. Look, Lis." I wanted to take her hand but didn't dare. "Russia's never really wanted the Jews. It doesn't want me."

"I want you," she said. "I am Russia. I am Russia."

The line carries me into the McDonald's in perfect time, just after four. The restaurant is huge inside, extending deep into the older building, and even more science fiction than I imagined: miniature round tables on one leg attached to the floor, miniature chairs growing out of the table legs like tree branches, all plastic and aluminum, everything irreversibly ordered and shined and light, the way spaceship cafeterias should be in zero g. The menu (mounted over the counter) is equally wondrous, and everything on it is unfamiliar and undeniably American. After consulting the clerk, I order the two most American items we can identify: a weird two-in-one upside-down sandwich called "The Big Mac," and a thick dairy cocktail with strawberry syrup. There are no dishes, just a paper cup and a wrapper, like you're eating on a park bench, but this food is amazing. The sandwich is so big, it's hard to bite into, but it's hot and juicy and strange and goes oddly well with the sweet drink. I could get used to this.

It takes me twenty minutes to order and eat, so half an hour later I am back at the embassy. It's ten minutes to five. I thought I'd be more nervous, but the buoyant energy of McDonald's, the warmth, the adventure of taste and aesthetic have picked me up, and I feel unreasonably sure that everything will be all right. I walk into the embassy pretending for a second that I'm an American citizen, walking into my own sovereign territory. I try on the sensation. It's a neat one. It's a safe one.

Well...safer. Babby's voice surfaces, as always, at the most inopportune time: *The only place you can control is inside your head, kitten. That's why you have a library.*

There is no safe haven, is there?

Theoretically, I could go to Israel. Many have already gone. It is the one place in the world Jews call their own, where they can stand back to back and defend it, live or die with it, but never run. The only place where there will never, ever be a pogrom. I recall the rabbi with the hands of a sheep herder and shudder. No. I can't go to a religious state. Not where those people rule. Not where Matthew wouldn't be welcome. America is the land of immigrants. I'm doing the right thing.

The embassy doesn't keep me long the second time. Short wait. Papers. Shorter instructions on what comes next. I step out onto Great Deviatinsky Lane feeling new and intermittently dizzy, still full of my first American experience. There's a whole long evening ahead of me before the Red Arrow leaves the station, but it's all right. I could just stand here and breathe. Or I could go see a movie.

CHAPTER 11
March 1991

It's almost midnight when my taxi skids on frozen thaw in front of the Pulkovo-2 international terminal and comes to rest at a precarious angle by the curb. In a few minutes the date will be March 21, 1991, and I keep searching for some deeper meaning in traveling from this world to the next on a vernal equinox, but if there is meaning, I can't see it. Maybe because nothing feels vernal this spring.

It's been a wintry March, but I am dressed for the flight: too lightly. As soon as I step out of the car, the wind drives icy mist like a barrage from a nail gun into my arms and legs, through the thin spring jacket and jeans. The jeans are American, fancy and too expensive, so new that they've never been worn before. I came upon them at a street kiosk a couple weeks ago and stopped without fully realizing why. Something about buying them made me feel appropriate. More prepared. One sure thing out of a thousand unsure ones. Across the ocean lies the Miltonian dark continent, and I know nothing about it, except bits of myth and pages of history books. And McDonald's. And that of the people I've met who have emigrated, none have been seen again. Boarding the airplane tomorrow morning is as close a thing to death as I can fathom from this side. On the other side is the unknown. A deaf, utter lack of predictability. A crossing of the Styx, and no one can tell me what is there or what is right or what's to come. Other than the jeans. I assume it's what they wear. I slide my hand under the jacket and touch the leathery label. It is ineffably comforting, American and Jewish at once: LEVI'S.

Not that I've been told truly nothing of what is supposed to happen next. My plane will take off in the early morning and land in Shannon, Ireland, then in Newfoundland, and finally in New York. From there I'm supposed to fly on to Philadelphia and be met by somebody either from a Jewish organization that handles refugees or from the synagogue that's volunteered to sponsor me, I'm not certain. This is where my awareness of my future ends.

I haven't been told if anyone picking me up on the other side speaks Russian. The worry of it nags me periodically, because what I speak of English is limited to the phrases I've managed to learn from my "In Common" tapes over the past five months, and most of them seem pretty stupid: "Greeting people is not simple." "Kyle is a good student." "This is a parking meter." I have trouble with the meaning of the last one. Two are useful questions: "What is your name?" for identification, and "Who are you?" for profession. So it says. Our language in school was French, which is great for ballet terms but wouldn't help me, I suspect, were I to move to Paris.

I catch some raindrops on my tongue. Cleo and the driver are fidgeting with my suitcases by the curb—I have two, plus my shoulder bag. I planned to go to the airport alone, but Cleo insisted I'd need somebody to help at check-in. I suppose it's all right. Only her. I just don't want the repetition of what happened with Lisa yesterday. She had to simmer me down with valerian root, and warm milk, and water, and we sobbed into each other until we fell asleep, intertwined and puffy-eyed, on her bed. I can't afford to make a scene with Cleo by the ticketing stand. On the bright side, I don't believe I have any left in me. All cried out and dry. Chapped lips and cracking eyelids.

The roar of takeoff rolls up over the terminal, swells in seconds and overpowers and smothers all things, bends down the sparse, bundled-up crowd, distorts straight lines, disperses air and thought, then flies off, leaving behind a short whining note and tiny mobs of passengers, who keep nosing over their luggage like beetles over dung. My bags are already on the curb; Cleo is paying the driver. I check right and left. Massive projectors are spotlighting arrows and signs along the walls: ARRIVALS. DEPARTURES. PARKING FORBIDDEN. We each grab a suitcase and drag them over the bumps of hardened mud.

The past five months have been a gray, monotone dash: selling things, packing things, saying good-bye. Endless, wordless evenings over cooling tea, me and the people who had nothing to say to me. People who'd shared my life—classmates, colleagues—growing smaller and flatter, distant, shadowy blanks. Corny wishes and promises and dry hugs.

Deciding what to sell and what to pack. Books were the hardest. I moved along the shelves, sweeping the spines with my fingertips, and they felt like braille: so familiar, I knew what I was touching with my eyes closed. Books-memories. Books-adventures. Books-friends. Which ones can I not live without?

I made a stack on the floor, on a sheet spread out in a corner of my room—too many, they won't fit in the luggage. Took away everything translated from English: I'll read them in the original one day. Took away children's books. Put back three children's books, Bradbury's short stories, selected Vonnegut, *Three Men in a Boat*, all of Lilian Voynich, and a two-volume Shakespeare. Watched as acquaintances first, then strangers sauntered in to peruse my home the way they would a second-hand shop, as they carried out Chekhov and Conan Doyle and Faulkner and Lorca, cradled to their chests like adopted pets. Or like bodies of dead children. Or like inanimate objects, no longer mine. My home had been empty already, without Babby. It became deserted now without books.

"Doesn't look like your home anymore," Cleo said last week, and for the first time I thought it was better that way. There would've been trouble when the taxi arrived to take us to the airport if the apartment had still looked like home.

I've sold some of the furniture, but Cleo will finish it. She has my power of attorney to clear the place and return control to the state, which technically owns it, to deal with whatever problems arise after I leave. She's been remarkably un-Cleo-like—rational, resilient, resourceful—ever since I came downstairs with a box of éclairs and told the Ivanidis family we needed to talk. This was last October, the morning I returned from my interview at the American embassy, fresh off the overnight train, my refugee status in hand.

Mama Ivanidis poured the tea into their fine Lomonosov cups, and Cleo scooped some cream from an éclair for Grandpa Ivanidis, who no longer has teeth. The new gigantic cat, named Incubus for being spotlessly black, softly occupied his favorite stool by the stove, and I told them why I had gone to Moscow the day before. It all stopped then (chewing, breathing, blinking), and everyone turned and looked at the youngest person in the house. Cleo is younger than me by three and a half months. She's really come into her own lately: not a whimsical oddity anymore. Cleopatra Ivanidis, illustrator of children's books, designer of the Museum of Literary Fantasy. And Cleopatra set down her cup and slid over to the seat next to me, displacing Incubus and ignoring his outraged meow. She put her arm around my neck and her nose to my cheek and said, "It's about time."

She yanks the suitcase that's stuck in a pothole and swears under her breath. She's got the bigger one, which contains seven volumes of the Strugatsky Brothers and four of Yuri German, my clothes and underwear, and a terrible pair of sandals by a local factory ironically named "Fastwalker"—as rigid and ubiquitous as the demi-seasonal shoes I'm wearing. I left behind my winter gear because it takes up too much space, and I'd checked the map: Philadelphia is a minute south of the 40th parallel, the same latitude as Armenia and Azerbaijan and the smack middle of Central Asia, and the Mediterranean. I won't be needing fur.

I did pack three pairs of pointe shoes and leotards, for auditions I have no idea how or where to get (and no idea if they exist in America). My family portraits, the teacup with firebirds Babby gave me, and the silk scarf I gave her, green with galloping horses on it. There's a box of loose things I've been gathering since I was little, the keepsakes I don't have the heart to throw into the trash. It has a little calendar with a holographic dolphin I apparently brought back from the Black Sea—Babby said I'd clutched it so hard that Mama had to buy it for me. It has Matthew's letters and a few pictures of us from the Vaganova, with Lisa and our annual revue cast and all the teachers, and one with a hiking group, where the tongues of the campfire are blotting out most of the faces. It has a petrified piece of candy, misshapen and fused to its wrapper, that was handed to me at the funeral of a classmate who'd died of brain cancer in third grade. Five or six of us had shown up, and his mother walked over to us and pressed a soft, warm, viscous candy into each of our palms, whispering, "Thank you for coming to say good-bye to my Misha." I never could bring myself to eat it.

This is the suitcase that will be lost on the way to New York.

The other one has mostly books, almost to the maximum allowed weight of thirty-two kilos, and also a plate, a bowl, a small frying pan, a set of silverware wrapped in two towels, and a few audiotapes: several bards, *Boris Godunov*, and Rach-maninov's second concerto. My carry-on is the shoulder bag, which I am guarding with my arm—a practice that served me well on my trip to Moscow—because if anything happens to it, I am done for. Inside it are my ticket, my travel passport, my immigration papers sealed in clear plastic, an envelope with four hundred and ninety-four dollars I got for the con-tents of my and Babby's life, a half-size collection of David Samoilov's poems, a strip of aspirin pills, three pictures (me and Matthew on the Square of the Arts, Babby at the kitchen table, and my parents in the Ural Mountains), a Walkman, and a tape of Russian romance songs Lisa recorded for me last month in an all-nighter of singing, sobbing, and semi-sweet Georgian wine. I remember the way she wagged the bottle at me after emptying it into her glass:

"Did you know Khvanchkara was Stalin's favorite wine?"

I tried to balance my head and bring the glass of Kh-vanchkara into focus, raised my cast-iron eyelids.

"I am too drunk to know how to feel about that," I said, and she burst out laughing—broke down completely, with her whole body, the way we'd laughed ourselves into hysterics in the wings of the grand stage at the Vaganova between class-es, an unbearably long time ago. She shook and kicked up her feet in the air and spilled her drink and snorted; her hand flut-tered before her face like she was fainting and hit the guitar, which yowled indignantly and recomposed itself with an an-gry murmur. The wine splattered everywhere. On the white throw between her knees and mine, it looked blood-red.

This was the last time I'd hear Lisa Ushevich laugh.

Cleo and I are nearly by the terminal doors when I hear my name and see movement out in the parking lot. "Dinah! Wait!"

They are running. It's Lisa with the others behind her. Of course, Andy Triukh. They're still not engaged, but I bet it is coming to that. Five more, all from the Kirov. Our farewells have been such slow torture—months of farewells, bitter and sticky—that I thought I'd left them behind when I stepped across my threshold for the last time, but I'm still covered in their residue. Bitter. Sticky. I can't start crying now. They're coming like a spiderweb, like burning to my eyes, and I feel my tears spill out.

"We had to see you off. It wasn't right." Lisa drapes herself over me, limbs everywhere, thick in her winter coat around my stick figure, and the fur trim of her hood tickles my mouth and nose. It is fleetingly warm in her embrace, then she lets go. She's sniffling, too, and wiping her eyes, and I can see she's been leaking for some time—swollen face, blood-shot eyes, dried-out nostrils from constant wiping as though she had a cold. I wonder if she's ever stopped after I left yesterday.

I did this. This is my fault. My heart falters and trips against my rib cage, makes me cough—*I'm so sorry...* But I can't be looking any better than she does. Probably worse.

The others come up one by one, hug, whisper their eulogies into my ear. This isn't like kitchen and tea; it's real. Maybe it's hit them I'm leaving. Or maybe they have forgiven me. I find I am clutching their sleeves—another second of hanging on, it won't change what I've done. Time to go.

Andy hugs with one arm, steps back, and holds out a thin bunch of poplar branches, still bristling with splinters from a fresh yellow surface where they've been broken off a tree. "Here," he says. "These are Leningrad poplars. So you'll always have a bit of home with you far away." He sounds awkward and rehearsed, and I take the branches from him awkwardly and hug him again. It is a ritual.

"I love you," I say.

"We love you," they say in unison.

Lisa says, "Please write."

"I will," I say, and grip the suitcase handle with my free hand and head for the terminal. I can't look anymore.

I can hear Lisa's voice behind me—"Let me know how she got off"—and Cleo saying "I'll call you tomorrow." She catches up to me in time to pull the door open, and we step into the racket and havoc of Pulkovo-2.

Ticketing. All is in order. Customs. The officer opens my luggage, touches the top of one book, lifts another, creases an eyebrow, scans my declaration, then me. He is smooth, milky-skinned, and sleepy, with slow eyes and apathetic movements. His forage cap seems to irritate his forehead: He adjusts it every few seconds in a mechanical motion.

"What metal is that?" He points to my great-grandmother's locket, engraved with her initials: DMF. It is the only piece of jewelry—and the only pre-revolutionary object—that's ever existed in our house. Babby kept it locked in her desk drawer and took it out just once, when she told me that I was named after her mother. I put it around my neck for the trip to ensure nothing would happen to it.

I clasp my hand around the locket. "This? Silver."

"Silver not allowed."

"What do you mean?"

He pushes along my first suitcase and moves on to the second. "Silver is a precious metal not allowed to be removed from the country. If it were gold, you could take it." Without expression, he peeks into my box of worthless treasures.

"But this is my only inheritance from my grandmother," I try. "It's a family heirloom. See the initials here?"

"Please step back." He isn't scared of a girl who weighs forty-five kilos. He is just doing his job, and his tone never changes when he says, "Contraband will be confiscated. Or if you have someone who's come to see you off, you can go now and give it to them."

There's no begging, no discussion with him—no more than you'd have with an oncoming tsunami. I bet he tickles his kids when he gets home from this job and plays "Moonrover-1" with them on the living room floor.

"I have someone, but she might have left," I say. I'm crying again. What is the percentage of émigrés that he pushes to tears? Does he count?

No. She's still there. Balancing on tiptoes, I can spot Cleo's unmistakable Sputnik-size head floating on the other side of the barricades. I wave her over to the partition by an armed guard. I cannot talk for hot, violent heaves. Wet, salty, twitchy. I've given up on restraint. My task is to survive. I fold in two and wail, taking off the necklace.

Cleo accepts it in cupped hands, like water from a stone, and says, "Shit."

Passport control washes over me like a paranoid delusion. The officer is a woman, her face lined with age and disdain, and she holds my papers with two fingertips when she hands them back to me, as though they were infected with betrayal. "Go through," she orders, and I am through to the waiting hall, my first steps between my past life and my next. The terminal is long and narrow, interrupted by square pillars of faux marble, around which everything else is concentrated: people, baggage, trash cans. Only long benches in the same style are stretched along the windowless walls.

It is easy here to tell the living from the dead. Tourists from the West are bright moving spots—skinny jeans and colored jackets—spread out on benches and floors, resting against pillars, cross-legged and in odd, relaxed poses. Laughter and strange, joyful gibberish pour from their swirling groups. In the middle of the hall, two young men in ushanka hats and what I will years later recognize as Harvard varsities are attempting three-point shots with their balled-up candy wrappers into a trash can, so the floor around it is littered with screaming-red paper.

Refugees congregate along the walls in toxic clusters around motley bags, bound up with string for assurance. Some have bread and tea in thermos cups laid out on top of the bags, and vapor and gray whispers are oozing out between their dark, heavy coats. I want to pity them, then remember that I am one of them, and I move deeper into the terminal to find a place on a bench.

From this height, the Atlantic looks remarkably like a boundless sheet of crumpled tin foil. I suppose anything moving, even a thing as mightily fluid as the ocean's skin, will look frozen and dead from far enough away. We took off at dawn, in a moody half-light, and as the plane made a wide turn over Leningrad, I saw the city sink slowly and fall away. The star-shaped fortress cut into the river's black folds, the northern developments, the white sheets of the fallow fields—it all came into view like a zooming-out of a photograph and grew finer, then dimmer, and disappeared in the ripples of cirrocumulus over the Gulf of Finland. They will have better weather tomorrow.

I tried to make out my house, then the Kirov, but couldn't. For two seconds I caught a glimpse of St. Isaac's Cathedral and the Bronze Horseman beside it, reaching out his hand over the Neva from the back of his bucking stallion, and it occurred to me that he was pointing west, as if he'd commanded me "Out of here!" and I'd obeyed. And now the sun is rising in the clearing sky, blotting out the contours of Europe behind me, the traces of civilization and all familiar things, bouncing off the tin foil underneath. It seems there's nothing else left but the two firmaments and a metal cage suspended in between, with the remnant of humanity inside.

I've never asked myself before why the ancients described the world the way they did, or why we dismiss them so. They said it was a finite slice lost in the infinite abyss, and it is. They said it was a discus resting on the back of a turtle who was swimming through space, and maybe it's not, but I imagine, when they climbed the mountains and roved the seas, they experienced what I am experiencing now, bizarrely, for the first time from ten thousand meters of perspective: the devastating flatness of the earth. And through the myth they tried to convey to us their desperate knowledge: that one cannot set off on a journey and press always ahead and return home. Ahead lies an abyss. Pressing toward it without turning back, one can fall off the edge of the world.

We are an arrogant lot, humans, and we ignore the ancient myths. We think they're primitive. We are taught in school the world is round. But it's a lie.

The voice of Charon comes on the intercom and floods the cabin with muffled masculine sounds. I cannot make out a single word. Maybe we're behind schedule. Maybe there's an iceberg to look at. Maybe the plane is on fire, and we're supposed to retrieve parachutes from super-secret compartments and jump. I wouldn't know, but it's all right. What's the worst that can happen?

Today is the vernal equinox. North of the equator, the days will become longer than the nights. Light triumphs over darkness—again—and winter begins to turn into summer, cold into warmth, sleep into wakefulness. Death into life. And still none of it has to do with me except that I, too, am turning into something different, today of all days. Turning the corner. I am no longer a Soviet Jew, a Russian Jew, a Soviet citizen—any land's citizen, really. I am landless.

Still, I'm not homeless. I've been adopted. I am now a Jewish American, a refugee—that means I have found a refuge. An immigrant in the country of immigrants. I'm trying to remember something I've read in a history book: It's a verse, I think, written on the Statue of Liberty, that was put there to make new Americans feel welcome and to give them courage, back when they arrived on boats. I can't recall what it says. Instantly I wish I were arriving on a boat.

Maybe everything will be all right.

It is peculiar to realize that, if you asked me right now what I was feeling, even if I was sad or happy, I couldn't tell you. This very minute, in a cocoon above all of the water of the earth, I am becoming something I wasn't, and unbecoming something I was.

Matthew once tried to give me a glimpse into his faith by explaining the sacrament of communion. When bread and wine are transubstantiated, they become more than the molecules of their substances but the body and blood of a mystical person, fully human yet divine, long dead yet alive. Transubstantiation: the changing of the essence of a thing. Then we can experience a confluence of dimensions, aspects of reality: plant, human, and divine; past, present and future; temporal and eternal; immanent and transcendent. The boundaries are erased, and wine is blood, and long gone is now, and "how" is a mystery, never to be known.

I went with him to Mass once, not long before he left. I was nervous—the first time I'd waded into a church, I'd squeezed back out grated like a cheese—but he swore no one would dare look askance at me, and I badly wanted to frame for myself what pulled him into that realm. So we stood in the back for nearly three hours, watched the rounded spines bow and straighten, listened to the bony knees hit stone floors, the stifled groans, listened to the cantor's basso profundo mix with the choir, pour molasses of Byzantine chant. It was beautiful, of course, and long, and filled with frankincense smoke to the brim, filled with melancholy and with singsongy, incomprehensible Church Slavonic. When time came for Communion, Matthew trembled, merging into the line, and it was after the Mass, on the benches outside St. Nicholas, that he tried to explain Christianity to me.

The Sacrament, he said, is not literal, but it's real, so when we take this changed bit of bread inside us, we, too, are transubstantiated. We're focused by the mystery just enough to get a glimpse of what it means that the transcendent divinity is immanent in the world. That there's more to us than meets the eye. Because Christ lives in each of us, life triumphs over death.

His eyes were glossy as he kept casting about for the right words, tripping and running on and gulping down excitement and reticence, pulling out notions from the depth of his gut. I told him I liked it, but mostly I liked the idea that something could be fictional and yet real. In that sense, it strikes me, religion and art work the same way, through metaphor. But I remained the atheist I'd been. Swimming in a frankincense haze in the back of the church, I couldn't be expected to frame anything much. As the Communion procession brought Matthew closer and closer to the loaf, a well-upholstered priest was pinching pieces from it and shoving them into one open mouth after another. It was like watching a procession of wingless hatchlings beg for crumbs. To me, bread was still just bread. Probably stale.

A flight attendant inserts her hand into my space, unclicks my tray table, places a tray on it, and withdraws, leaving me to stare at the food. There's white noise of breakfasting rising all about: chatter and the clanking of forks, the bubbling of liquids. A baby's been unsettled in the back and is bawling for attention. The aroma of coffee. My tray is divided into compartments, each appropriately sized for its own fare: three perfect slices of cheese and as many of ham, two minirolls, some kind of glistening pink fish, a minuscule bowl of black caviar, and an unnaturally shiny round green apple. The caviar jiggles in the turbulence.

We haven't seen this kind of luxury in a long time. Caviar, ham… Even cheese has been in deficit for years. I want it all, but I can't raise my arms. The cheese is beginning to sweat, but I am fixed, spellbound before this food, for it is art, a still life, not to be consumed but comprehended. Escape, resentment, original sin. Behind and beneath me, surrounded by water and silver and soil, three hundred million people are having breakfast, having supper—not caviar. My friends are having their meals of bread and tea or macaroni with ketchup. Living the life I've fled.

Once I eat this, what do I become?

A cold drop falls splat into a spreading wet blot on my shirt; another hangs on my chin, threatening the same. This isn't crying, just oozing. Drainage from a wound. I reach down for a handkerchief—there's one in my shoulder bag that's stuffed under the seat in front of me—and scratch my cheek on the top of a poplar branch.

The dry branches are tucked between my chair and the wall. At the bottom, fresh yellow splinters still bristle out where the flesh of their mother tree used to be, and in the room temperature of the airplane they are beginning to smell like spring.

CHAPTER 12
1991

It began in the calamitous sixth century before the common era. Jerusalem had been reduced to rubble by the hordes of Babylon, the Temple stood in ruins, and those who'd survived the siege were carried off to slavery on the shores of the Euphrates. For fifty years—three generations in those times—they mourned their fate in exile, singing psalms that dripped with languid, venomous blood, having visions of their fallow land and of God's grandeur and mercy and wrath. There was only one choice back then for the worshippers of a defeated god—convert or die—but they were stubborn. They were arrogant and faithful. And they refused.

Your god is weak or indifferent, the Babylonians said to the Jews. Our god is stronger. Convert.

No, said the stubborn Jews. Our god is Lord. If he brings us low, it is only to teach us a lesson, for idolatry, and for iniquity. Our god wields your armies as his teaching tools. He is not just a god; He is God.

And so the Jews invented a new, exile-compatible Judaism. Away from the Temple, they found refuge in the Sabbath. In the Torah they found the reconciliation they could no longer offer through blood sacrifice, and they tasted every letter on their tongues as if it were raspberry-colored. They circumcised their sons with pomp and ceremony because the Ark had been lost, stolen or destroyed by the barbarians, and now they carried the Covenant in nothing but flesh—a privilege and a responsibility. From then on, it would become a display of courage, too, for the flesh doesn't lie and doesn't convert, and in the big, brutal world where Jews are slaves, you cannot hide who you are.

They didn't hide. They pulled out of their scrolls and put on display the laws of dress and laws of food and laws of speech so their children and their neighbors would know: They were Jews. They were Jews. They were Jews.

They called themselves the Remnant. Prophet Isaiah called them the Children of Exile. In Hebrew: B'nei ha-Golah.

I am reading about the Babylonian Exile in the *Encyclopedia of Jewish History* because my sponsoring synagogue here in Philadelphia is called Temple B'nei Hagola, and I made the mistake of asking Zev Alterman what it meant. I pointed at the sign by the sidewalk (stylized letters between two Magen Dovids, which they call Stars of David) and tried to form a sentence, but it took too long, and I probably said it wrong, too. Doesn't matter. He smiled, he nodded, he and his wife both gestured enthusiastically. I'm sure he was giving me a thorough answer related to something, of which I understood exactly three words: "you," "out," and "inspired." Putting together my reading and a few other words I've collected so far from the Americans, I suppose he may have been saying they were inspired by their synagogue name to get someone like me out of the hellhole that is the Soviet Union.

Or he had no idea, and my question inspired him to figure it out one day, not soon.

Or I was annoying him with stupid questions, and I should get out and take a hike to a place called Spy Red.

I often think I hear one word when they're saying another, or two words together, or several. "Can" and "can't," for instance, sound exactly the same, don't they? If Rabbi Frum asks me to recite the Torah backwards in Hebrew—and believe me, I'm constantly terrified that he will—how will he know if I can or can't? When I have to tell the two apart, I rely on accompanying body language, and when there isn't any, I gamble. Throw the coin in my head. Tend to land on the wrong side. I call that my "opposite degree of accuracy."

English to me is a soft, gooey mouthful of porridge, through which they're trying to push out some meaning. It must consist of words, at least as they intend it, but everything is slurred and swallowed and stuck together like paste. Incomprehensible. Verbal vomit. I would bet they just pretended to understand each other if I didn't see them follow commands and laugh at jokes and nod at something in unison: "Amein."

Recently I've started picking out a word here and there—one per every few sentences—yet I am still effectively mute. A week ago I tried to contribute to a post-service chat I thought I'd grasped enough of to surmise that Mrs. Alterman was complaining about congestion on Roosevelt Boulevard. I caught "road" (or "roads"), "traffic," "Roosevelt," and possibly "tire," although that could have been "tired." But by the time I formulated my pitiful three-word statement of agreement, decided to add "very," and calculated where to embed it, they'd already moved on, apparently, so I blurted it out of context, out of order. An irrelevancy.

They stared. They smiled the way they smile at me: kind and disinterested, the way you smile at a child who inserts herself into adult conversation. *It's cute when they're curious, isn't it?* They asked me something the way they talk to me: loudly. But cranking up the volume doesn't help me parse, and I still didn't know what they wanted, so I stared back at them and smiled the way I smile at them: idiotic-looking, I imagine, and lost, hiding fear and hatred under a thin veneer of gratitude. Not a child. A dog in a cage.

I really don't hate them. I really am grateful to them. They are nice people.

It's a very American word: "nice." One of the first words I've learned, right after "okay." They use it every few minutes, they use it for everything, and it means a person or a thing or a deed that offends no one, stands in the way of nothing, has no sharp corners and no hard surfaces. A plush blanket is nice, a cup of herbal tea, a picture of a kitten. A gun is not. But then, neither is a syringe. Nice won't save your life, but it'll hug you and make you feel better. Nice isn't the same as good, not the opposite of evil, but it's a value in this violent world. It has a place. Because nice is peace and warmth and consolation. A white lie when you can't take any more truth. Nice is charity.

Come to ponder it, religion is nice, isn't it? Afterlife and Heaven and the rising of the dead, the utmost white lie for the weary soul. Marx called it "the opiate of the masses": the ultimate self-delusion, self-defense, self-medicating the pain of living. Available prepackaged from a house of worship near you. The Jews of Babylon would die without the consolation of God, so they believed the nicety that would save their nation. The Jews of Philadelphia are nice enough not to have asked me if I believe it. At least I don't think they have.

But they're good people, too. The Children of Exile who wanted to help another in exile. They offered to sponsor whatever random person needed them, and they accepted me and embraced me and never required that I prove my worth or my piety, though I'm afraid they assume I have both. They are salt of the American earth, these people. Nice, good, pious, Jewish, American, generous, all-around perfect. Plush and blanket-like. No one twisted their arms to babysit a clueless, penniless refugee who is as useless as an infant in their noisy world. Their religion inspired them to.

Was it religion?

192

Zev Alterman is the one I know best. He is tall, elegantly thin, bespectacled, with shiny male pattern baldness exposing most of his head, and even at breakfast, implausibly respectable. He came to the airport the day I arrived and brought me to his house, where I stayed for the next three weeks, bleary-eyed and jet-lagged, slept on a blow-up mattress in his home office between the desk and the fax machine, shared a toy-strewn bathroom with his three kids: Benny, Naomi, and Abner. Abner is seven—he showed me on his fingers. Benny, to my eye, is eleven to thirteen. Naomi in the middle. I'd never seen a blow-up mattress before, and I kept thinking it was a pool float.

There I saw my first combined bathroom and, silently dismayed by the unhygienic setup, learned to brush my teeth standing next to the toilet. There I had my first battles with the Alterman family faucets, from which I was rescued condescendingly by Abner.

Once I tried to help Debbie Alterman in the kitchen. I loaded the dishwasher the way I'd seen her do it and poured liquid soap into the right compartment and pushed the right button, then watched helplessly as foam filled the machine and bubbled around the seals. It spilled onto the floor again and again, even after I opened the dreadful contraption, cleaned it all out, washed out the soap, and crawled around with a rag—again, and again, and again. After she came back from wherever she'd been, Mrs. Alterman showed me the label on the soap I'd used: HAND SOAP.

"HAND SOAP!" She cranked up the volume into my ear and poked her finger into the label, then into my hand.

They laughed about it later at night. I heard them laughing and moving the soap bottles on the counter. If this happened back home, I'd go downstairs and laugh with them, because it's damn funny, and would've been funnier if they could see me bouncing about with that rag. I could tell them this story with turns so hysterical they'd squeal till they cried, till they coughed and choked and begged me to stop and, please, mercy. But this isn't home. At home, they don't have dishwashers. And I'm a person, not a monkey in an elevator. And I don't live there anymore.

I went into the office and lay on my mattress—no, not mine, theirs—pulled their blanket up to my ears, and watched a light blink on the power strip in the dark corner under the fax machine. The Altermans' merriment receded when I pulled the Walkman from under the pillow and put on my headphones. At the touch of a button, Lisa's voice filled the world, as if it were poised there at half a word, always waiting for me. I closed my eyes and spilled the tears that were always waiting, too, and let myself shake silently, face into the damp pillowcase, and did what I do now: cried myself to sleep to the sound of Lisa Ushevich, drunk and sad and loving me, singing "I Remember Evenings."

On my second day, Debbie looked through my one remaining suitcase—books, kitchenware—and drove me to a sprawling, heavyset building that lay like a spider in its web in the middle of a field-sized parking lot. "DEPARTMENT STORE!" she announced, pointing to the sign: KMART. She pasted clothes onto my back, whirled me around like she was dressing a doll, and threw the items into a shopping cart with satisfied "uh-huh's." Socks, pantyhose, and underpants in crisp plastic bags, three bras, five T-shirts, three pleated sweaters, a pair of sneakers, a calf-length skirt, and a lime-colored granny dress with a ruffle across the chest. A pair of jeans from a different part of the store, under the banner that read JUNIORS.

At the cash register I handed over the envelope with every penny I had to my name (four hundred dollars and change)

and forced myself to breathe while Debbie Alterman casually counted out one bill at a time. *Why do I need five T-shirts?*
Three sweaters? There are six pairs of pantyhose in that little bag!
I'd never in my life had that many clothes. And they were all
so bright, such primary colors—yellows and reds and indi-
go, jumping out and clowning, like erector-set pieces, like
infants' rattlers.

And it's not just the clothes. Everything here is like that.
The Altermans live in the city and yet not. A three-minute
ride from the din of Bustleton Avenue with its strip malls
and office buildings, from its honking and the roaring of the
trucks that mix into the air the stink of garbage and exhaust,
there's a single-family-home paradise, surreally picturesque
and quiet. Suburban America. The relentless and merciless
pursuit of happiness. I only know the city is near because its
light pollution washes out the night sky, and I can't see Orion.

In April, it's already warm and humid in Pennsylvania.
The last of the snow fell and promptly melted in the first
days of the month, and there's no more hint of it. Daytime
is bright and toy-like: clean little houses, white or peach or
lavender, accented by fake blue or brown shutters; crunchy
sparkling driveways cutting through emerald lawns; perfectly
shaped flower beds and blossoming bushes covered with gaudy, globular blobs (I will learn later they are rhododendrons);
triangular evergreens by the front doors; and gleaming-clean
cars of every tint of the rainbow shimmering under the garish
round sun. And American flags—red, white, and deep, con-
fident blue—waving off every other porch, as if there could
be any doubt of where we are. It's cartoonish in its tidiness
and simplicity, the clarity of shapes and the sharpness of borders. My first couple of weeks I kept waiting for an animated
four-fingered mouse paw in an inflated glove to reach in from
the sky and pull the curtain down on the scene: THE END.

Then it would all be over, cue a jaunty credit tune, back to real life. I shook off the feeling and put on a new, purple sweater. It's what they wear.

Other members of the synagogue picked me up in their cars and took me to the Jewish Family and Children's Services for English classes, to Welfare and Social Security appointments. They filled out my questionnaires and talked to my social worker in their slurry-gooey-verbal-vomit English, so all I could make out was "she, she, she, she, she." I stood aside like a hunk of unfinished wood and worked on getting used to it. It must not be rude here to refer to a person by a pronoun in her presence, or they wouldn't be doing it. Because they are nice people. I don't know what I'd do in this cement jungle of gibberish without them.

On April 12, I turned twenty-three. With my head still on the pillow under Zev Alterman's desk, I sent two silent air kisses into the ether—one to Babby, the other to Matthew—and thought about my birthday six years ago. My last birthday with Matthew. The party was at Lisa's, so mobbed that we ran out of chairs. Matthew got the bright idea to construct a human pyramid of seats, and when it merrily collapsed, the thunderous clatter and laughter brought the downstairs neighbors running up to the door. They were invited to stay and couldn't be stopped from juggling the wineglasses.

I shooed away the memory and went down to the kitchen, helped Debbie pack the kids' lunches and put away their breakfast dishes. As I was drying my hands, she put a jewelry box in front of me on the counter—a compact satiny black cube.

"Happy birthday, Dinah." They must have spied the date in my passport. "Open it." She was exuding encouragement.

Inside the box, a delicate gold chain lay coiled around a

Magen Dovid. Debbie fastened it around my neck. "There,"
she said. "Much better."

Dr. Acker, the president of the synagogue, showed up a
couple of hours later and called me away from my English
homework: "Dinah, come." He was beaming all over his
chubby body, from shiny brown loafers to gray wavy hair, and
getting into the car, he winked at me. We drove south on
Bustleton and into a claustrophobic red-brick apartment complex off Welsh Road—blind, square windows cut into square
walls, glaring into other windows. We walked up to a door at
the end of a half-lit hallway, which he unlocked and gestured
me in. He waited till I turned around inside the empty room,
then raised his arms triumphantly: "Do you like it?"

I didn't understand, smiled my idiotic smile, and waited
for a clue.

"It's for you," he said. "YOUR HOME! HOME. To LIVE. Do
you LIKE?"

In the shock of the moment, "like" wasn't a concept available to my brain. How could it be for me? I had no money
to pay for it, no idea what was happening. Was I on my own
now? What had I been made responsible for? Was I having a
panic attack?

I wanted to ask it all, shriek it all, beg him to wait—
stop—explain it to me, but I had no words. How do you
scream in English "want to be grateful—no idea what I'm
doing—don't even have a job yet—please don't throw me out
alone—mercy—mercy—mercy"?

I said, "Thank you." Or whatever that sounded like: *Sank
you.*

"You like it?" he asked again.

I said, "Yes. Thank you."

I didn't like it. I do now. I also know now that Tobias
Acker would co-sign my lease, and the synagogue would loan

me, interest-free, the first and last month's rent and a security deposit on this tiny apartment, the significance of which I would not realize until later, when I find out how much I pay in rent, and how much I get in Welfare and eventually in a paycheck. I will not fully realize it until much later, when I become American enough to comprehend how reluctantly Americans mix business with pretty much anything. For now, I am gasping for breath in the deep end of the ocean—try to say the right words, the right names, find the bus stop, turn the light on, remember where I am, breathe, paddle, paddle, and I can't see an inch along the water.

Zev, the Ackers, and Zev's best friend, David Milgrom, move me to Chapel Court Apartments on Sunday. It's called a studio: one room with a bathroom. No kitchen, but I have a stove, a refrigerator, and a sink along the wall, with a sliver of counter space in between and some cabinets above and below.

At some used furniture warehouse, they get a used twin bed with a thin, sharp-cornered metal frame, which Zev and David assemble in the course of three hours amid the wax and wane of shouts, curses, and high-fives. The frame will soon become my single most hated possession, responsible for several scrapes, countless bruises, and one broken toe. After the toe, I will disassemble the thing and stick the pieces into the trash bin in Chapel Court's parking lot with the sense of triumph probably similar to the one experienced by Zev and David when they finally get it to stay together. From that day until 1998, my mattress will always lie on the floor.

While the men are working on the bed, Ruth Acker helps me distribute my belongings in the closet cut into the wall between the bathroom and the front door. The clothes take up two hangers and a shelf. When I begin to put the books out on the other shelves, she stops me and laughs, picks up her purse from the floor.

"*Gooey-gooey* shopping!" she shouts into the room and slams the door without waiting for an answer.

Rite Aid is three blocks away. As we park, Mrs. Acker taps her pink, pointy nail on the speedometer and vomits out something cheery. I hear "smile," "walker," and "problem." I smile.

"*Gooey-gooey* WALK HERE!" She points to where we came from. "ONE MILE. NO PROBLEM!"

Two bath towels in the cart, a hand towel, two washcloths, a kitchen towel, shampoo, soap, toothpaste (I already have a toothbrush), and a white plastic box I'd never used before called Johnson&Johnson. At the Altermans', one like it sat on the bathroom sink, white thread sticking out of it, but I ignored it. A shower curtain with liner and rings goes into the cart, a growing pile of small items and my dread, but she waves away my trembling hand that emerges with the creased envelope. "My treat," she says, and I roll the sound in my brain, to remember to look it up: *T-r-i-t*. Or is it *t-r-e-t*?

Over the next week, various B'nei Hagola stop by to drop off a complete bed set: a comforter, a pillow, and a set of sheets, which takes me two days to figure out because we don't have fitted sheets in Russia, but we do always fit our blankets into covers. They also bring two mismatched but sturdy chairs, a colossal enameled pot with corn husks painted on it (it's so tall, I can't see over it when I hold it), six wineglasses in a cardboard box, an electric mixer, and a large black trash bag full of assorted secondhand clothing, size small. I myself find a perfectly functional folding table, a bit on a rusty side, sitting near the parking lot trash bin, and use one of my bath towels as a tablecloth. For now.

Until I find a job, I have forty-nine dollars a month in

food stamps—that is for food. I cannot tell how much that is, but I know it's not enough. I go back to Rite Aid and buy batteries for my Walkman, and at Dollar Basket next door I buy a teapot, which to my dismay costs $2.25. I walk to Pathmark, and my eyes glaze over. There's a thousand species of vegetables, fruits, and berries from every season, every continent: things I've only seen on the *TV Travelers' Club*—watermelon and blueberries in April! Pineapples! Persimmons! Aisles and aisles of bags and boxes and freezers and piles. *Oh, Babby, I wish you could see this.*

I spend an hour just gawking, swallowing saliva, browsing and creating combinations of the cheapest and the most necessary, then buy potatoes, loose tea, and strange, presliced, very white, soft, and tasteless cotton-like bread. I get some macaroni, a round box of salt, and then I see bananas: brown, tightly packaged, with a yellow label MANAGER'S SPECIAL. Nineteen cents a pound. That's about half a kilo.

Bananas come to Leningrad once a year, like the breath of the Exotic, and they are green—baby-bird bananas that have been sleeping in their crates on the way from the Great South, waiting to be smelled. They have silky skins and faint, incubating odors. Once a year the line wraps around the block. We spend half a day inching forward, seize the one precious bunch per person, and lay it on top of the bookcase and wait for it to wake up. Twice a day we check for yellow. I remember stretching my nose up to it, tippy-toed, with Babby over my shoulder: "Not yet, kitten, but soon. See this yellow side? It's getting ripe for you." I remember the heavenly mush in my mouth. A miracle. Bananas.

I buy the manager's special bananas and eat one on the way home. It's dark, squashy, falling apart in my hands. I imagine Matthew walking next to me. He takes my hands and licks them clean, finger by finger, exceedingly serious and thorough, as if it were a chore, but little demons are dancing in his eyes as I squirm and giggle. He pauses, frowns threateningly, and commands, "Obey me, tickly!" And moves on to the pinky. A lady shakes an umbrella at us: "Children! Behave like decent people! Immediately!"

Stop. It's not happening. It happened already, a long time ago, eight time zones away. It can never happen again.

I lick my own fingers, shoo Matthew away, and keep walking.

The next day is Friday. As we spill out of the car by the synagogue, Abner is hanging on to Naomi, and Benny is furiously pinning his skullcap to slick, too-closely-cropped hair. That's when I bungle my attempt to ask Zev what it means: *B'nei Hagola.*

Zev finishes his mysterious soundfall and looks over at Debbie for approval I've never seen her withhold. She nods energetically, and we go inside surrounded by the widening stream of Rhawnhurst Jews. Friday night is the beginning of Shabbat, the inexorable time of communal prayer. I landed in Philadelphia on a Thursday afternoon, and thirty hours later I was packed into the Altermans' back seat with a seven-year-old in my lap—no matter jet lag or insanity or nausea—for the lightning-brief ride to the kingdom of God. Because *Shabbat Shalom.* No exceptions.

B'nei Hagola is a conservative synagogue, not overly traditional but not exactly progressive, a distinction I have at this stage no wherewithal to comprehend, nor do I very much care. None of the members would dare work on a Saturday (not in an office, that is), but they'll drive to the service and back, and they aren't leaving the lights on in the bathroom to avoid flipping switches the way the Orthodox do. They are split on answering phones on Sabbath, and Rabbi Frum thinks it's a matter of judgment. They don't keep a dress code, except for skullcaps for men, but they keep "rather kosher." David Milgrom will say this a few weeks later and nudge his teenage nephew under the ribs so the boy will cough.

"What is 'rather kosher'?" I will try to pronounce his phrase.

"Well... Let's just say I don't have a chicken spoon and a dairy spoon buried in the back yard because my bubbe's got cataracts."

It is too early in my American tenure for this, and the loving mockery in David Milgrom's tone will be lost on me together with the meaning of most of the words, which is unfortunate: David can be understatedly funny. In fact, he will soon leave Philadelphia for Hollywood and make a respectable living as a sitcom writer, always sharp but never mean.

The Altermans and I go inside with the crowd. The building is simple red brick like any other on Rhawn Street, not much more than a box; you wouldn't know it from a condominium if not for the sidewalk sign with golden Magen Dovids. Outside, we are a happily mixing Jewish family, but the stream separates beyond the threshold: Men one way, women the other. Men in front, women behind. Men on the floor, women in the balcony.

It is so men can concentrate on praising the Lord, they will make clear when I am verbal enough to ask the question. It is because a man cannot keep spiritual thoughts if a feminine rump is floating before him. A man is weak and dirty-minded. Upon hearing that, I will sense a splash of desire to be offended for the men I've loved, for all the noble, strong, and pure men of the world—for Matthew, my father, and Lesha. But I'm still searching madly for each word, and these people are trying to help me, and I'm an atheist anyway, so who cares how they pray. And I'll just shrug and let it go. This won't be for a while. Today, as every week since my first week, Debbie Alterman grabs me by the hand and drags me along with her to the women's section: "No-no! This way! That way is for men!"

I come to the synagogue because its people helped me for no earthly reason and called me their own, and they pick me up and wedge me into a car and bring me here. It's important to them that I come. I come because they are doing me a favor: My membership fee has been waived. I come because they let me work out in their social hall. There is no mirror and no barre, tables and chairs are stacked along the walls, but it's the largest indoor space I've seen on this continent where I can do any moves at all—stretch, at least. I haven't danced in months, and I can feel my body mummifying. A dancer cannot stop dancing and remain a dancer, but I don't think anyone here realizes that, or maybe even realizes what a dancer is. "You're so petite!" they muse, and I could swear someone has said I should have more meat on my bones. I wish I could put it into words for them and ask them where ballet classes are here. Where ballet is here. But I don't know how.

I don't know what they say in their prayers, but I like the way they sing. There's sadness and yearning and question in the Shabbat music. I don't know which way it goes between them and God, who is questioning whom, but I haven't heard any other music for a while besides what's on my Walkman. Every night I pull it out from under my pillow in a ritual move. I put on my headphones, and with the first sounds I spill the tears, and I eat a gluey, dark-skinned banana and cry myself to sleep.

This is my religion.

In late April, Rabbi Frum himself comes to my door. He sits precariously on a chair, dips a lip into the lukewarm tea I pour into a wineglass—cups are still in the planning stage—

and leaves behind a bag of crumbly oatmeal cookies and a stack of Russian books I gather have been donated via some clerical connections. The books are clearly Jewish-leaning but otherwise random. There's a Bible in Hebrew, English, and Russian; a thin booklet called the *Haggadah;* the story of the founding of modern Israel; a biography of Theodor Herzl; something called *Maimonides;* a touchingly worn collection of Sholem Aleichem's stories, which I kiss and add to my orphaned library like a long-lost son; and a three-volume *Encyclopedia of Jewish History*. It is in this encyclopedia that I look for *"b'nei hagola."*

Two days later, I am still reading the articles in a hypnotic thread when Mrs. Frum shows up with her eldest boy, Joe. Each of them is carrying a box filled with clanking dishes. I now have four of everything: cups, plates, bowls, silverware, several mugs that seem to have made their way from various members' corporate offices (except one, which says, CATCH ME IF YOU CAN!), a small and a medium sauce pans, a large frying pan, a kettle, and an assortment of utensils like a potato peeler and a spatula. Among those is an enigmatic tool that looks creepily like a cross between a syringe and an enema: a narrowing plastic tube with a rubber ball on the end. I stuff it into the back of a drawer. Mrs. Frum refuses to come in, hugs me at the door, and I return to the *Encyclopedia*.

"B'nei Hagola" is a good name for a synagogue, I think. There are two things its members have in common with the ancient Children of Exile. Two core, inalienable experiences that define them. One: Despite their relentless American perkiness, underneath even sincere "new world" optimism, they are Diaspora, and in some corner of their Semitic hearts, with every aching Shabbat song, they long for Jerusalem, which most of them have never seen. Two: In the midst of a gigantic, scurrying, assimilating, swallowing gentile universe, above all else they want to be Jews. No one writes it into their passports. No one fences them off in the ghettos. No one calls them names in the streets, here, in America. They choose to be Jews—visibly, openly, joyfully, insistently. And they pray Hebrew words and wear skullcaps in public and erect gilded Magen Dovids on their temple walls.

I wouldn't have known I was any different from any other Soviet Russian if I hadn't been told so by Katie Pasiuk, by Nicholas Yanowski, and by countless other passing scoundrels every other day of my life. Unlike the Children of Exile, I didn't choose to be what I am.

I close the *Encyclopedia* and push it away. What makes a Jew, a Jew? What makes me one? I remember Babby's finger tracing the curve of my nose, but is it really my face? My blood? My name? Is it enough? The Children of Exile— twenty-five centuries ago and now—they know what it means to them, to work at being Jewish, to see each other and to be seen. And I only know how to be afraid. How to fight. How to run. That's the difference between us: They are real Jews. And I am a yid.

"You're our *yid," he said, and I said nothing. And Babby was dead.*

Yes, I'm better off here.

I get up from the table, toppling the chair, leave it lying on the floor, and walk to the window. I breathe and stare out over the parking lot. Maybe there's something more to be learned at the synagogue. I will go. Because real Jews go, and I'll try to be one of them, though my stomach spasms the moment I cross into the women's section, and my eyes reflexively roll when they begin to curtsy and bow in fine, devout movements, and I don't believe in anything almighty except loss. I'll stand with them. I'll join their chorus. I'll push out of my mind the image of a God who burns down cities and murders children so his favorite little toy-nation would quit cheating on Him with other, imaginary, gods. I find that image appalling and comical, about half and half.

Can "alone" be a verb? As in: Can a person alone to death? I will go. I will try.

I will ask them one day about the Holocaust. If they see it the same way as the Babylonian Exile: a lesson from the God of Israel. An angry father's punishment. And how they can still want to come home, after that.

The month of May has been sultry and sweaty, and I can't shed the feeling of July. It is ludicrous to envision today's Victory Day parade in Leningrad, everyone out on the Palace Square, having just taken off their heavy fur coats, still feeling weightless in demi-season jackets. Matthew used to wear mud boots through mid-May, so every time our path was blocked by a sprawling puddle of snowmelt, he would pick me up and carry me across without slowing down. Hop on, hop off, keep going. Here no one seems to know about Victory Day, and I celebrate it, me and myself, with a toast of morning tea.

Americans have a different temperature scale, so I've learned to do a quick approximate conversion in my head from Fahrenheit to Celsius: minus 32, divide roughly by 2, a little less. It's 92 Fahrenheit today, which means it's something like 33 Celsius. Northerners don't know that 92 degrees smell. Everything churns in the air like gaseous molasses: trash and rubber and car exhaust, food wafting from open eateries. And 92 degrees is noisy. Everything buzzes and whines because every air conditioner is on, every fan and generator and machine, except mine. Electricity is expensive. I have the window open and the door cracked for a draft, and a sheet of sweat cools down my skin the way it used to after Anna-Vanna's Classical. For a moment I stop in my tracks, waiting for her hand to brush between my shoulder blades: *Good job, Dinah. Sweat it out.*

I write down a few crucial points of reference and pin them to the wall: 0C=32F (freezing); 20C=68F (room temp); 36.6C=97.9F (body temp); 38C=100.4F (worrisome fever); 100C=212F (boiling). My reference wall is by the phone, in the hallway across from the bathroom: names, appointments, weights and measures. Common phrases to say on the phone, when I'm lost and seizing and empty-brained, life or death hanging on my answer.

My worst enemy, the phone. It does not afford the aid of context or body language, only words, a shower of words, a waterfall of *gooey-gooey*, and no pause, no choice, when it could be something important—Medicaid, Immigration, a job interview—but they keep talking like I know what's happening, like I'm sentient, they don't check, and then there's a question. And a vacuum.

I dread the phone. I hate the phone. I'll never stop hating it until the day I die, even when I'm fluent and American and, once connected, chatty. This is trauma, Simon will say. It will become a phobia that will always throw me back into the black hole of my first American years: the terror, the helpless fury. The shifting earth. Any time the phone could ring, and a wave of searing cold washes over me, cheeks to tailbone—there are only seconds before I must answer. Pick up or not? Pretend you're not home. Pretend you're dead. Do that enough times, you'll have to be dead. For a second it's tempting. Decide.

The phone is ringing. Two. Three. "Hello?"

It's Zev. "Dinah, hi! Red *gooey-gooey* card *chewy-verbal-vomit* tear?"

Damn it! I scan the list of phrases. "Umm…" *Quickly, quickly! That one!* "I'm sorry, can you repeat that, please?"

"*Wrrowr* READY TO GO SEE THE CAR AND *gooey-gooey* DOWNSTAIRS?"

The car! Yes, of course.

"Thank you, I am coming!" I take my finger off the list.

Besides a cheery outlook, there are three necessities of life in America I lack: language skills, a job, and a car—and none of them appears within reach without the other two. I am making excruciatingly slow progress on the language, though getting to the Jewish Family and Children's Services for English classes without a car has been difficult. Buses here don't run in the way I'm used to, every few minutes. Plus they don't go to every corner, and the metro doesn't even reach to this part of the city, so a single round trip takes me half a day, not to mention money.

I didn't think I was getting any better anyway and was almost ready to give up on the classes when, rummaging through my suitcase, I found my old "In Common" tapes. I popped one into the Walkman, just for kicks. The effect was stunning: no *gooey-gooey* at all. Those voices were crystal-clear, so slow they were boring, and I finally realized just how idiotic those sentences truly were. 'Margie has blond hair and red lips'? I've learned on my battered back that greeting people is not simple. Why didn't you teach me to buy toilet paper and pass a job interview?

I've gone on three interviews so far: a Wendy's fast-food restaurant, which is a McDonald's without the sweet sentimental feeling; a lighting store—lamps, shades, and torchieres; and a CVS, which, like Rite Aid, is called a pharmacy but is really a junior version of Kmart. All the jobs were minimum wage, neither skill nor brain required, and still nobody would hire me. Zev, as the one who'd organized the interviews, seems to have gotten back some sort of reports, and apparently the manager at Wendy's thought I didn't have enough English to follow directions on the grill, the one at the lighting store needed someone who could occasionally operate the cash register, and at CVS I was asked if I'd ever taken illicit drugs and I smiled and nodded: my moronic default when I'm drowning in the sea of English goo.

The next month's rent is soon due. Dr. Acker will have to pay if I don't. *Don't think about that.* I tried again to ask what ballet troupes they have in Philadelphia, how to contact them. The summer should be their hiring season, and I'm in terrible shape, but I have a skill, after all. More than that, I am a graduate of the best ballet school in the world, a soloist with the best classical ballet company in the world. Even after months without dancing, without classes, under stress, and on the brink of malnutrition, I should suffice some modest theatre in this provincial center, if nothing else, for corps de ballet. I tried again with Zev, with the Ackers, and with the Welfare case worker, but I must not be saying it right, or they don't get my meaning. They screw up their faces, they laugh, they explain something back, and now I don't get their meaning except "no." Something I'm assuming is here, isn't. They don't do ballet? They don't like Russians? You have to be born a citizen, like the president?

So I'm back to fast foods and drugstores. No English, no job. The first three places were within walking distance of Chapel Court. Zev says he's got some better prospect for me (some sort of idea I couldn't parse), but it requires a car, so today he's taking me to buy one before a two o'clock interview, someplace called Bubbe's Market.

Buy a car. I can't buy envelopes to write Cleo a letter. The car demands another loan, this one personally from Zev, and I do my best to shun the thought. I can't, can't think about it.

Back home, it's not really a thing to borrow money. If

a friend is in need, we pitch in, rarely, but it happens—but then, it's a gift.

Russia is not your home anymore. This is your home now.

I run down the stairs, plop into Zev's passenger seat, and we take off. It's a fleeting thought, how used to being handled I've gotten—led, driven, taken places, often without knowing reasons or destinations. They say "come," and I come, and they say "do," and I do, and they say "pay for this," and I pay the bleeding, precious dollars because they know what's what and they care, and they are the only rock under my feet. A slippery, slimy, precarious rock, but around it is raging white-water. Madness. And I stay.

The Ford dealership is an expansive lot covered with shiny metal bodies like a platter of sprats. They shimmer and add to the boiling heat—hundreds of massive stoves, pulling in the sun and radiating it toward any human foolish enough to be caught nearby. Tricolored balloons at the corners: red, white, and blue, of course. It's on my list of American mysteries, why car dealerships must display visible signs of patriotism like no other business.

We're in the "used car" section, sundry hues and shapes, and Zev is deep into a jolly chinwag with the salesman. He's a leviathan of a man, wide as he is tall and almost literally spherical, with blondish curls and hot-pink squirrel cheeks. Hoots and cackles are flying, backslaps reverberating off the melting pavement, stories pouring one after another. I'm melting, too. Sweat is dripping off my nose and soaking my only short-sleeved blouse, white with a punched-out pattern around the waist, which I'm wearing for the interview. It's one of those secondhand items B'nei Hagola brought me in a trash bag. All is as usual—Zev talking, me not—but it's almost 1:30 p.m., and I'm getting nervous.

We've "looked" at three cars so far—quotation marks because I'm not participating in the looking, just dragging myself behind these two best buds and standing off to the side while they open and close doors, caress the paint, and entertain each other. As a result, I haven't seen anything. It's fine, Zev's time should be a thousand times more valuable than mine, and I'll come back with him for a car another day if he'd rather, except I have this interview! That he has set up! I can't be late. What if this is the one? The one that'll make the difference between paying rent and being an Ackers' dependent? Between food and two blackish bananas a day?

Ten days ago I started discovering banana peels by my pillow in the mornings. All I can think is that I've been getting up at night, eating a banana in a somnambulant daze, and falling back to sleep with no memory of it. I can't afford this. Hiding the bananas in a kitchen cabinet didn't help. Last night I tied my feet together before bed. It helped.

I can't keep going on this way. I need a job. I'm missing an interview, and Zev is oblivious in his blithe little time bubble! I have to tell him. What do I say? *Crap. Please, look up, see my face!* The salesman shouts out some sort of punchline, and the two men explode in earsplitting laughter. What do I say? That we have to leave. Now. What's that word for "urgent"? *Matty, help me.* You start invitations with "let's," I seem to remember. Is it "let's you drive"? No, I think "drive" just applies to the car, and they use "go" for any movement, with all these prepositions I can never keep straight. Is it "let's you go," then? Or "let's you go out"? That doesn't sound right. *Oh, damn, can't I just wave at his car and point at my watch?*

It's 1:42 p.m. There's no more room for cowering, and I approach on boneless jelly legs. The heat is gone. Cold sweat, cheeks to tailbone. I catch Zev's gesticulating arm and tug him on the sleeve. He halts mid-exclamation, and an eerie silence descends on the scene: Two men, peering expectantly into a tiny girl, who is growing smaller and smaller, thimble-sized, disappearing, a puff of mortified vapor over the black parking lot tar. Curtain. The end.

"Dinah?" he says. He smiles. He cocks his head, waiting for a godly reason why I've interrupted.

I open and close my mouth. The earth refuses to swallow me. It's steaming and stubbornly solid under my feet. I say slowly, syllable by syllable, as if he were the immigrant: "PLEASE, GO A-WAY!"

Zev Alterman's unbounded conviviality will eventually collide with Debbie's jealous nature, and they'll spend years in a bitter custody battle. His second marriage, however, will be happier than the first. He will join a small practice in Bryn Mawr, go sailing on weekends, and die of Covid at the age of sixty-nine.

CHAPTER 13
1992

Who knew that watching TV was the best tool for improving listening comprehension? Better than English classes, better than futile and furious thrashing about other people's conversations. Certainly better than useless tapes. Back in September of last year, I found a television set—on the same spot as my little table, by the trash bins—but I get why this one's been put out to pasture: Something is clearly broken in there. No matter how I turn its conspicuously bent rabbit ears, it's stuck on one channel, and the picture is wavy below and grainy above a thin black strip that runs through the middle of the screen. Still, I can make out everything that's happening, and the sound is good. So before or after work I've been watching whatever is on: mostly American shows that aren't like our movies but come back day after day, for months.

I never used to be into scripted television, nor was Matthew. We didn't go to the movies much, and if we did watch TV, it tended to be the news and science programs. But now entertainment is not my main goal—learning the language is. I still don't understand news anchors or scientists when they talk straight into the camera, but in these shows the characters often repeat the same phrases and words in visible context and use conversational English. I'm even starting to recognize their favorite idioms out in the real world.

One show often on when I eat is called *The A-Team*: the adventures of vaguely military fugitives with hearts of gold

(I cannot tell why they're on the run). There's lots of fighting and macho bravado and a triumph at the end of each episode. I imagine it's classic America: cowboys and happy endings.

This sweet-natured combo of guns and misogyny is followed by a sci-fi show I've gotten to like, *Star Trek: The Next Generation*. I grew up on serious, beautiful science fiction, and this show makes me feel at home, though I still don't grasp some basics of its universe. There's clearly a crew on a spaceship and many alien races, and a noble idea at play (sometimes at conflict with itself) of learning and preserving cultures, but I cannot figure out what the ship's mission is. They look like they're just loitering around the galaxy, hoping to run into something interesting.

Yesterday's episode was fascinating. A sentient robot had to defend his right to self-determination from some scientist with a license to disassemble him for study. It's all about slavery and racism, what makes us human, about dignity and kindness and worth. I like the way they think.

Is this classic America, too?

Today is different, though. It's Saturday, *Star Trek* isn't on. I am working my evening shift at Bubbe's Market (I'm closing, done at ten), so my supper will be more of a midnight snack, and it's only 4 p.m. now. Bubbe's is a Russian store, and I've been working here eight months already, since May of last year. Tomorrow is my day off for the week, so it's six more hours in this place, then thirty-two hours away from it. I plop the last box of zucchini onto my cart and wheel it out to the floor. What's there has to be sorted, anything rotten removed, and fresh stuff added to the pile.

There are days when six hours is too long. When I just can't, can't anymore. Can't take the pain in my legs, in my back, a dancer's body rebelling against perpetual standing and daily repetitive motions. Can't take the wet vegetables, the unremitting stench of rot—even at home I smell it, as though dank discard boxes full of putrefaction had followed me to the door. The cracking, seeping calluses on my inflamed fingers. The incessant noise of low-brow Russian pop blasting from the ceiling-mounted speakers. These people. *Oh, Babby, you could never've conceived of the things I would hear. The people who would be my coworkers.* Don't ever call us "the Russian community." I can't hear any longer the ceaseless, tasteless, mindless gossip of these women; the dirtiest, unthinkable language of the men; their ubiquitous, often irrelevant racism. They are so constant and so casual about it that it dawns on me: They cannot do without, and they've never known another way.

There's a spotty drop ceiling with water damage between me and Orion. Between me and anything clean. Between me and magic.

I palpate the zucchini in the tray, pull out a slimy one, add a fresh load from my box. They're freezing, and water droplets smart the cracks in my hands. Zina and Marina behind the deli counter are discussing the size of the member of some other woman's man.

Everything is relative. Six hours is not so long.

I discovered this exercise as soon as I started here, when an hour seemed but a protracted execution, and every day I used it. I need this now. I shut my eyes and take a measured breath. For a few seconds everything disappears, and I am on a plane, on my way home, to Leningrad. Only six hours are left before I land. In six hours I will run out onto the Russian earth, solid and real and fed with the bodies that belong to me. In six hours I'll be under the pensive northern sky, weightless overhead. Only six hours, maybe seven, until I stand by the Neva, at the feet of the Bronze Horseman, holding on to Cleo's hand. Lisa will wrap her arms around me, and we'll rock a bit back and forth, inhaling the mixture of snow and granite and fur. And Peter can point west all he wants this time. I'm not going.

Let them kill me in my own home and bury me next to my grandmother. What was I thinking?

Only six hours till you undo it all. Six hours is nothing.

I open my eyes, take another breath, and push the cart back to the stockroom.

When I started here, I had two shifts a week at first, stocking shelves and keeping fruit and veggie bins filled, sweeping, dusting, and changing price tags. Then one of the workers—a nauseously perfumed Kievan with continuously clanging gaudy earrings—was fired amid a vulgar scandal laid bare in the middle of the Market floor. Mercifully, the screaming was vague enough that I don't know what she'd done. After that, Maxim assigned me another stocking shift and offered three more on the register, altogether six days of work, rotating Sundays and Mondays off. Even at the minimum wage of $4.25 an hour, that was a full-time salary, a luxury my American self hadn't yet experienced. It also meant working Saturdays. Often Friday nights.

I wasn't surprised at how easily I chose, only at how easy it was to tell Rabbi Frum, Zev Alterman, and Toby Acker. Crafting what was intended to be a formal yet eloquent mini-speech on my future inability to attend the Shabbat services due to employment requirements, a part of me felt giddy—the part that had been craving to be done with them. And so I was, to the extent I can be done until I finish paying back the apartment loan.

They all acted with the decency and sympathy I'd come to expect from them, of course, and Rabbi Frum offered to talk to my boss about religious accommodation, but I spoke enough English by then politely to decline. My boss is a Belarusian Jew from Minsk. He knows what Sabbath is. He just doesn't care any more than I do.

Bubbe's Market is not a simple store but one of three Russian supermarkets in Northeast Philly. There are a few other small shops, but they are holes in the wall, one-person counters with family-recipe kulebiakas in Tupperware containers and expired bags of buckwheat on high shelves. One major supermarket is farther north on Bustleton, the other a bit south, but the Russian population in Northeast, as it turns out, is numerous, so our store is always hopping.

We're not quite like an American supermarket: no light bulbs here, no greeting cards, just foodstuffs and some reading material at the registers—local Russian papers and outdated glossy magazines from the homeland, nothing literary. But the food is aplenty from every part of the Union, and the things I thought I'd never see again are suddenly in my trembling homesick claws. Siberian dumplings, plum juice, black bread they apparently produce in mass quantities in New York, *tvorog* (the uniquely Russian farmer's cheese, this one made in Canada), and even *riazhenka*, a kind of kefir with a baked milk base. We even sell kvass in tall plastic bottles that tastes like a reminder of the real thing. I bought it once. It was too sad to drink.

Tonight, at the end of my shift, I get a few apples, a jar of pickled Hungarian tomatoes, and half a pound of hard caramels called "goose feet." I'm making this an indulgent evening. I pay with my 15 percent employee discount, drop the bag in the passenger seat of my car, and drive home through the dark, slushy Northeast. Seven minutes without traffic. Hot shower waiting.

I hadn't appreciated the American custom of daily showering until I began working at Bubbe's. It's not just sweat;

217

it's heavy, malodorous filth, and I don't feel humanly tired until I wash—I feel oppressed. Home, to my little cave, to my shower and supper, to the beloved, crackling voices on my Walkman and rereading Lisa's letters, worn through at the creases.

On the way in, I check for mail. There's an envelope from INS, which immediately activates my fight-or-flight response triggered by phone calls, approaching strangers, and official letters: anything that potentially requires communication. I'm much more verbal now than in my first months, but the reaction of dread has become a reflex. I open the seal while standing in my apartment doorway, before I touch any of the home surfaces with my work clothes, but the letter doesn't seem bad. I am eligible to apply for status adjustment. In March, after a year of being a refugee, I will get a green card. I think that's what it says. And I think I have to go there for some paperwork. Which means I have to ask for a day off the week after next.

The Immigration and Naturalization Services office is somewhere in Center City, or so I gather from the address on the letter. I have a city atlas, and I've mapped out a route as best I could, but I'm still not fluent with the names they use for their neighborhoods. Let's just say it's in the middle of Philly.

I don't need an interview—evidently, the one I passed in Moscow in 1990 suffices to let me in and let me stay. Just lots of paperwork and a processing check, and today they will tell me if I filled the forms out correctly and take them from me. I hope. With ninety minutes to drive there and find the place, I grab my car key and my demi-seasonal jacket, the one I had on when I landed in New York ten months ago, and walk out into the dreary January chill.

I hate this winter weather, though I've liked every other season over the past year. The summer was hot and humid, different than the soft ones I'm used to, sometimes overbearing, but interesting. Irrefutable. Worthy of respect. I loved the spring, too, which exploded last April, all around, inside a week. I suppose it's because spring here is the South to my North: so extreme, so bursting at the seams, that it overwhelms every sense, fuses the scents of flowers and pine beyond recognition, blossoms into an endless parade of colors. Even in this angular urban scene, it covers every surface with a thick carpet of pollen, suffuses and suffocates you and sweeps you off your feet. It's a triumphant force of life that will not be ignored, defeated, or intimidated. If the northern spring is a bashful first kiss, the southern spring is a bash of a wedding. I wish it were spring now. I could use a little external triumph.

Pennsylvania autumn is pretty—not the exquisite artistry of Pavlovsk, but the same warm, ruminative hues. Burgundies and fawns are carried by the wind through the streets, and you get nostalgic and shivery, in need of hot tea and a blanket and of gazing out at the soggy leaf fall. It's like a scratchy throat, the way autumn ought to be.

But winter—I can't make peace with it. Gray, wilted, naked. Humdrum. Faceless. December should bring the darkness of long nights and the blinding brilliance of snow on sunny days and frost so fierce that you cannot laugh without coughing. It seemed an unquestionable law of nature on the sixtieth parallel: winters so cold that the juices freeze inside spruce trees, pushing apart their flesh, and there's crackle and groan always through the forest, a special winter sound. And the *hrrrmph* of the snow under your skis. And the dark of the firs peeking from under the white. In the North, where winter hides all the sins.

In Philadelphia, winters continuously teeter on the brink of indecision, now freezing brown liquid in potholes into twisted reliefs that rattle under the tires, now thawing back into splashy, untidy puddles. Hovering, like October in the Pamir mountains. Snowfall comes on occasion and is soon covered in soot and mud—always, mud—and melts in a day or a few, topping off the puddles.

Today is a melting day. It snowed anemically last night, and now, at 8 a.m., it's already 33 Fahrenheit: a squishy parking lot under my feet, a thin coating of slush over the windshield.

My car is a monstrous, blue, tank-like contraption I address with mild trepidation as "the Hippo." This is the '83 Oldsmobile Toronado, which Zev, it turns out, had negotiated for me in the course of his friend-making with the Ford dealer on the hottest day of last year's May, when he almost made me late for the Bubbe's Market interview. We were, however barely, on time at Bubbe's, and the next day we came back to take the car to Zev's mechanic. Zev paid two hundred and fifty dollars for this big-bodied, bigheaded atrocity that looks armored and takes up a full traffic lane from paint to paint.

To be fair, the Hippo has a solid engine and an indestructible frame. "A safe car for your friend," said our gargantuan salesman, whose name, I learned, was Grantham Smith, and whose nickname, due to the unfortunate name and a penchant for apples, was Granny. The reason we got it so cheap is that it wasn't for sale (a trade-in bound for parts), and only Zev's entrepreneurship and congeniality turned scrap into my quick salvation.

The Hippo, you see, besides its unfathomable size, is uniquely shaped due to a rear-ending accident. "Must've been hit by a pickup," Granny speculated with apparent expertise. It left the back of the frame intact but completely mutilated the trunk above the frame, folded it in toward the cabin like an accordion. And while lacking a trunk is not a terrible problem for me given the Hippo's expansive back seat, the accident also seems to have bent the fuel filler neck or some such thing in the pleats of the accordion, letting through only a trickle of gas.

Almost as soon as I manage to stick the nozzle into the precariously angled opening, press the trigger, and start to watch the numbers roll on the pump's counter, the nozzle kicks back in my hands and the numbers freeze. I press again and they roll, then the nozzle kicks back and they freeze. And so we go back and forth: press, kick, press, kick, roll, freeze, press, kick, feeding the Hippo ten drops at a time. It takes me forty-five minutes to fill the tank. Attendants used to come out to the pump when I fueled—to see if it was broken, or if I was casing the joint, or if I was crazy—but now I go to a Shell down on Academy, where they take me with a smile: The Hippo girl is here; this pump is out for an hour. It's a poorer area down there, and I must not be the only person with a freak car and no money to fix it.

I clean off the handle with my hand—numb, dripping red fingers—and yank open the massive door, pull out my scraper from the back, and push the slush off the windshield in long strokes that end with me flat on my belly on the hood. The front of my jacket is getting damp.

We are such an incongruous couple, Hippo and I...I'm ninety-nine pounds in a five-foot package, still skittish of everyone and everything—all in all, tiny and always wishing she were tinier in some darkish corner. He is four thousand pounds of polished metal, gas-guzzling, roaring and spitting, and on occasion, I fear, shoving those small-fry subcompacts out of the way. Yes, it's a he; I perceive it as a him. Maybe

221

because he protects me in this brazen, almost militaristic manner, very B. A. Baracus.

My friends don't get the picture. I've tried to explain, but every time I mention something about my car problems to Lisa or Cleo, their letters come back sprinkled with sarcasm. To them, owning a car is a luxury they cannot divine exceptions to, and they've never been able to grasp why I'd be willing to scrape for car insurance, for gas—and go hungry. In a public-transport-hopping Russian city, a car cannot get you a job, make a difference between life and death.

The Hippo will serve me faithfully for another two years, then begin to sputter and break, and the mechanic I've inherited from Zev will inform me that the rear-ending accident must have shaken the front end violently enough to shorten its life. So I will go back to Granny, this time by myself, to return my Hippo to the fate from which he got a temporary reprieve. I'll come home in a 1990 Toyota Tercel—a zippy silver girl, like me, with ninety thousand miles on her, a jagged scratch along the passenger doors, and an ineradicable bouquet of dog and ashes in the upholstery. Reminiscences and stories flying now between the two of us, Granny will make me a deal of fifteen hundred dollars, and stroking my new Tercel's flaky, droopy nose, I will feel myself a Rockefeller. She will be my second, last, and always favorite car.

Granny himself will remain the stuff of legend, a character and a caricature, so gregarious your teeth begin to itch. The mayor of every place he goes. As per stereotype, he will always be a used car salesman. Defying all stereotypes, he will remain kind, helpful, and honest. He is immortal. He will never die.

But the trip to Granny's is still years away. This January morning I finish scraping my enormous Toronado, quickly, get the back window, then brush myself off. Can't be late to the INS. Sliding into his royal driver's seat, I feel miniature and feminine, fairy-like. Beauty in the beast.

The streets of Philadelphia are clogged with sludge and morning traffic, and the Hippo is barreling through them with the bloodcurdling calm of an icebreaker. I'm still petrified of I-95, but at this rush hour it's better than pushing my way through city streets like a piston through a cylinder. At least it is more spacious.

I managed to pass the driver's exam in Leningrad, but I'd practiced in a snowed-in European city, flat as a table and sleepy. Still, I stalled on every bridge, and behind me a line of cars waited patiently, taking in the view of the Stock Exchange and farting out poison into a warm communal cloud. This thing, this riotous river of an American highway, never waits. It never stops. It disorients you, cuts you off in front and behind, carries you faster and faster and drowns you in its surge and sound, and it pulls at your face with multisyllabic, multiline exit signs you only just discern as they recede behind you.

I keep to the right and to the edge of my seat, white-knuckling the wheel as the shriek of a horn ripples the Hippo's accordion. Someone's in a hurry. *Be grateful we're alive, you lout.*

The highway veers right—why? My two right lanes just separated from the left two and turned into an exit ramp. I dart my eyes up: Immense green boards are swimming back over my head. I never have enough time to read these, but I catch a glimpse of the one above my lane: *Oh, no, crappity crap!* This isn't my exit.

I-95 is floating away, but I'm a leaf on a stray current, tunnel-like walls rising on both sides, overpasses so dense they are blocking the beginnings of daylight, creating a murky, flowing space. It's packed. I've been sucked into the Vine Street Expressway. I cannot pull out a map with my fingers clenched to the steering wheel, but one thing I know from staring at the Philly atlas all day yesterday: If I don't get off *now,* I'll be swept along from east to west, across town, over the Schuylkill, and spit out into the broad stream of I-76. Then I'll have no other choice than north or south. I'll find myself somewhere far away, outside the city, and hopelessly, irretrievably late. I have to get control.

Then I see it: an exit. I signal. I clutch the plastic harder, and into the unknown I turn.

Now I'm really lost. Philadelphia is a grid, mostly all perpendicular, and you'd think a person could easily find anything: Just turn in whatever direction you need to go. But I don't know where I am, I can't stop to look because everywhere there are signs—NO STANDING and NO STOPPING— and still the curb is thick with cars like dung with flies. All the streets are one way, and they're all the wrong way. I keep turning, but there's no place to pull over, and time is ticking away, and it's been, I'm starting to think, already too many hours to worry about the INS. I might be going insane in my mind's special labyrinth. What if it never ends?

A car pulls out right in front of me, freeing a spot. Parallel-parking the Hippo requires all of my dancer's coordination and still leaves much to be desired, but I get him in within legal limits, slam on the parking brake, and run to the corner. There's only one street sign: I'm on Cherry Street. Back to the car, grab the Greater Philadelphia Metro Area atlas from under the seat. A list of streets by name is in the back. Cherry Street... Cherry Street... Let's see.

Have you ever run, breathless, to the door after a long separation from a person you loved and swung it open, ready to jump into an embrace, to gush, to explode—and there was a stranger on your threshold? Have you ever taken a gulp of liquid expecting it to be your favorite drink—sweet, maybe, or hot, and delicious—and it was spoiled? Cold? Putrid?

There are at least a dozen Cherry Streets in the back of the Greater Philadelphia atlas. There seems to be a Cherry Street all over every corner of the blasted metro area. They must love, adore, worship cherries in Pennsylvania. I gape at the list of Cherry Streets—all different pages, different grid cells—and my last feeble hope flickers away. You can't map a route if you don't have a starting point. I'm just lost.

There's no alternative: I must talk to a stranger.

If I could choose between that and a swift execution right now, I'd seriously consider the execution.

I step out of the car, my atlas in hand. What stranger should I pick to commence mortification?

Two cars behind me, a middle-aged couple is sitting in a blue Honda Accord. I hear laughter and a staccato of conversation; he shakes a cigarette out of the driver's window. They stop talking and flash me a questioning smile when I approach on my noodle legs and stand, veiled in his smoke. Deep breath.

"I'm sorry," I start. I know this much. This is how I always start. "I must to go in INS. But I lose—I lost—I *have* lost. I drived from I-9-5 in wrong place. Where I am?" *Sigh. No, wait—English question structure!* "I'm sorry. Do you know where am I?" I poke his hand with the atlas. If he just poked back: finger on a page!

They are smiling and nodding, they are saying something. "Do you know…have to go…address?"

"This is address," I say and pull the form out of the envelope.

They smile and nod. "It's close!" The man begins to gesture—right, left—naming the streets, but the woman pulls him in with a hand on his shoulder, and they consult the way lawyers do with their clients in court, mouth to ear, serious business. He turns back to me: "We will show you." He speaks slowly now. "Follow us. FOLLOW US!" And he waves to illustrate how people follow, back to front, and watches me run to the Hippo. I look back once—to check—and he smiles and nods.

I follow the blue Accord—right, left—until I recognize the name of the street from the form letter. We're here. The Accord turns left, and the woman waves to me from her window, pointing to the right, smiling and nodding, and I smile and nod and point to the right, and she waves again and disappears into the remnants of the rush hour. It's just after 9:00. I am on time for my 9:30 appointment.

For three seconds I linger at the stop sign, looking after the blue Accord. I think I miss it a little. The road feels oddly empty in front of me. For two seconds I want to turn left and go after them, flag them down and ask them their names. Ask them if they want to be friends. My first American friends, who talked to me and made me unafraid. I turn right and navigate into a paid parking lot with a $5 FOR 2 HRS sign by the booth. It's a lot, but I might not survive a search for a curbside parking space, and relief washes over me down to the toes when the attendant takes my keys and hands me a ticket without a single word.

I hope the INS agent is like my Honda couple. I envision a twinkling face behind a window.

In two months, I'll be a permanent resident of the United States. I am an American with the basic necessities of life: I have an apartment. I drive a car from a highway onto hopping city streets—sometimes in a wrong spot, but that's correctable. I speak English. I even speak to strangers to correct any missteps I might have made driving off the highway in a wrong spot. And I have a job.

It's not a job that I should have.

I have a job that wrecks my body and shrivels my soul inside my skin and makes me ache at the mere thought of going to work.

I'm a dancer. My job should be to dance.

In two months, I'll be a permanent resident of the United States who speaks English and has an apartment and drives a car and has an income but cannot stand her job.

Maybe it's time to find out where they keep ballet in Philadelphia.

I am now armed with a green card, a spanking-new sense of confidence, and a resolve to return to ballet. I figure a few things must be the same in America as they are in Russia: Seasons run from fall to spring, so companies hire in the summer, and I have a couple of months to prepare. What I have to prepare is most likely a résumé, a body shot in first arabesque, and two audition pieces: classical and optional— something from a character part, or a modern piece, or special choreography. Lacking any guidance on the subject, I set out to obtain what I need by June, intending to deliver my papers to every ballet theatre in Philadelphia. I don't know how many there are (combing through the Yellow Pages will come later), but I reason that Leningrad usually had seven or eight stages performing around the city, and Philly is smaller, so even if they have five, out of all of them, with my credentials, I must get at least three auditions. And even my rusty, veggie-handling self can revive two glittery solos well enough to dazzle.

My first challenge is finding a place to practice. If it gave me a chance to walk out of Bubbe's Market and back on-stage, I would swallow whatever that slimy ball is in my throat and crawl to Rabbi Frum and beg. But the basement of B'nei Hagola will not do anymore. I need a dance space: a wall-wide mirror, a barre, and no tables to crash into when a coupé-jeté goes haywire. A handwritten ad for *Oksana Schnitzer's School of Russian Ballet* on Bubbe's community board catches my eye just in time—another two hours, and Zina from the deli would have covered it with her "boots for sale." Oksana Schnitzer's xeroxed page does not impress with professionalism, but it promises "daily classes ages 8 to 18" and a "beautiful studio." It's my only lead, so I call.

"Actually," she says, businesslike after my quick admission that I can't pay much, "I can let you use the place for free if you run drills for me twice a week, the afternoon classes before my date nights. I teach so late, I can never go out like a white woman, you know?" Oksana has the croaky voice of an old smoker, and when she shifts her tone to confessional, she coughs. "My boyfriend's starting to complain," she shares, and I hear her spit on the other side of the line. "Then you can stay and do your thing, and other days you can come early in the morning. How's that offer for you?"

I'm tempted to query how white women go out (a lot earlier than other women, it sounds like), but I hold my snarky tongue. Because that offer is better for me than anything I counted on, and this old, revolting, familiar expression had wormed itself into our daily Russian from the colonial times of British literature and stayed for some mind-boggling reason. People use it without thinking. Even here, in America, where "white" in fact means something real. Even Jews, who of all people should think about such things. I've heard it so much at Bubbe's, it makes my skin raw like a pass with a cheese grater. *Relax. This is a nice woman who wants to hire you.* The next day I inform Maxim that Friday and Saturday nights are off my schedule because I'm going to be teaching. And rehearsing for auditions.

Approaching Maxim, I am discomfited: Never in my first year of desperation would I have dared dictate limits to my employer, and now I might be angering him for the most precarious of chances at a dancing life—I don't even realize yet how precarious. Memories flash in my eyes: whimpering over a banana peel, inside a rumpled blanket, grieving for the breakfast I'd again have to skip; standing in the middle of a bursting supermarket as if in a desert, oscillating between envelopes and sugar; tearing in half the last piece of tasteless, textureless, cotton-like bread. If I get fired, am I going back to that existence? But Maxim's face brightens as he listens to my ultimatum and finally bursts out: "Aha! About time!"

He wraps a paternalistic arm around me. "Excellent! Our little ballerina! Oksana's good people; you'll love her. And when you're all famous on the big stage, you don't forget us with the tickets, yes? And mention us—do they give Nobels for leg-shaking?"

"No."

"Well, whatever they give, you remember Bubbe's Market!" He is positively bubbly. "You need help with anything?"

It's just been so long since this—since anyone has talked to me like I was family—that I choke. I forget how much I disdain this place and feel only his easy care, offered so immediately and taken so for granted. Before I know it, I hear myself answer: "I might."

"Tell Maxim," he says conspiratorially, raising one eyebrow, and we both laugh.

"Well...I'll need pictures," I say. "Professional shots, in a studio."

"Ah." He scratches his nose. "Hang on."

He leads me by the hand to the center of the store, the exact spot where, nine months ago, the perfumed Kievan stood sobbing under a shower of filthy names he was pouring upon her head, barking back at him through wet hiccups and smudging her mascara. We face the deli and bakery, and he proclaims in an announcer's voice, "People, people! Our Dinah needs audition pictures. Who knows a good photographer?"

There's a rise in the buzz, a wave that swells and ebbs over us. Several conversations erupt at once and cut out, only Zina and Marina furiously argue behind the deli counter. Ari, our loader, walks around the aisle holding a bottle of kvass in each hand and scratches the back of his head with one of them, smiling an apologetic smile and shrugging. Several customers dithering over produce trays stop for the announcement and are still eyeing the scene when a semi-elderly gentleman puts down his melon and approaches.

I don't call him a "gentleman" lightly. In an impeccable wool coat and a fedora, more playing than supporting himself with a cane of polished wood, he could be a character from a British novel, or from my Soviet past—a librarian, or a violinist from the orchestra pit, or a schoolmate's grandfather. He is possessed of thin features and a sharp, flawlessly clipped goatee. His round glasses have those old-fashioned flexible earpieces they wore, I think, in the last century, which accentuates the impression of an anachronism. Before he ever speaks, I like him.

"Good for you, young lady," he says. "I understand you need a headshot?" In Russian, he has a silky, nearly imperceptible accent I cannot place, but his wording is as proper and fine as you'd expect from his appearance.

"Body shot," I say. "It's for ballet."

"Oh, wonderful. I might be able to assist." He pulls out a business card from his wallet and writes something on the back. "My second cousin's brother-in-law is a photographer who does portraits, headshots, but I'm sure he can either accommodate your requirements or recommend someone. And his studio is not far."

"But will he do it for free?" Maxim interjects. "Our Dinah isn't rich, but she's going to be famous!" He winks.

"Oh, god, no, I'm sorry, please don't mind that." My face brims with horror and hot blood and mixing words, which flow over in a humiliated trickle.

The gentleman's eyebrows inch up, as do the corners of his lips. "This is a dilemma, no? Have you danced before, my dear?"

"The Kirov." I can barely breathe.

"Mmm. I think maybe we ask him together, then." He stifles a grin, more a grandfather now than a librarian, and I take a gander at the business card. It's in English:

Vladimir S. Timashevsky
Rita Reineer Professor of Anthropology
Villanova University, Villanova, PA

An address with an office suite and phone number appears underneath.

"Do you have a minute to talk?" I hear him ask.

Maxim nudges me in the back: "Yeah, go, go!"

The professor switches his cane to the left hand and sticks out his elbow. My eyes slide to my hands. They're spotted with specs of dirt and green zucchini slime.

"It's all right," Professor Timashevsky assures me. "It's only clothing. You know—" We stroll toward the exit between the beets and the jars of sauerkraut as if taking an afternoon promenade. "The eminent institution you refer to as the Kirov, to me, has always remained the Imperial Mariinsky Theatre. I was glad to find out it had become the Mariinsky again."

"Yes, I've heard." Lisa's letter arrived in mid-February, but this news couldn't deliver much of a shock after last year's referendum that had renamed Leningrad back into St. Petersburg. Obliterated the city where I was born from the map.

Outside Bubbe's doors, the strip mall's parking lot is scurrying about its business under a sunny sky: a squirming cluster of cars in front of Bubbe's, an empty space before the hardware store, a smaller cluster before the Russian bookstore with a sign board in English script: CHITATEL. I have to make an effort to turn the sound of Timashevsky back on, having missed half a sentence: "...thanks to the end of the Bolshevik terror."

Bolshevik terror? Seriously? That's the kind of expression the White Guard used in 1918.

I pull my arm out and turn to him. "Wait a minute. You're...one of *those* Timashevskys?"

"I am."

He must get this a lot, but I don't care. It's like holding a Fabergé egg. I want to poke him with a finger. "*Count* Timashevsky?"

He chuckles and tips his hat. "Count Timashevsky, at your service. Don't become too excited, my dear; noble titles don't mean much these days."

"Are you kidding? You're like the Golitsyns, or the Naryshkins! Except wasn't there a Count Timashevsky who was a socialist, during the Revolution?"

"Ah, you know your history." He resumes his constitutional into the parking lot, and I match his pace. "That was my grandfather, the Social Democrat. He was indeed an idealist in those early times, so our family stayed in Russia longer than most of the first-wave émigrés, until they saw firsthand what those ideals were turned into by the Bolsheviks. We left in 1922, first for France, then relocated to America after the Second World War. Long, hard times."

He stops by a shiny charcoal Volvo sedan that, from several cars back, I knew somehow was his. It just fits him: quiet, understated grace. I hear unconcealed pain when he adds, "I am the first generation to be born abroad and the third to be buried away from the motherland. This may change, if God have mercy." He snaps himself back to the present: "Forgive me, I have digressed."

Only then it hits me: "You didn't finish your shopping."

"It is no matter. I have an appointment, but I come to this area now and again, and then I swing by here for some indulgences: dumplings, herring, squash caviar, or a nice yellow melon, none of those cantaloupes." He opens the car and throws the cane into the passenger seat. "Why don't I arrange a meeting for Sasha, you, and me at the studio? Have you a card I can pass on?"

I can only shake my head—more hot blood, mixing words, but these are stuck in my throat. "Sorry..."

"That's quite all right. Here." He produces a spiral note-pad and a pen from his coat's inside breast pocket. "Record your information here, if you please, with name and phone number, and don't forget your schedule so we can find a mutually convenient time."

"Thank you." I try not to soil the paper as I write. "Please don't ask your relative to do anything pro bono. I can pay."

The count accepts his notepad back with a look of royal favor. "I've no doubt we shall find a dignified arrangement that will not burden anyone," he says. "And *art* will benefit."

Situating himself in the driver's seat, he lowers the window to nod good-bye.

"Thank you," I say again. "Vladimir...pardon me, your patronymic?"

"Stepanovich."

"Thank you, Vladim-Stepanych. Or do you prefer 'Your Illustrious Highness'?"

"Oh, God forbid, God forbid!"

He waves me away, laughing full throatedly and rolling his eyes, takes off sprightlier than I'd anticipate of someone his age, sneaks into the jumble of the Bustleton traffic, and is gone. I take a minute to breathe before returning to work. Count Timashevsky will call me, I'm convinced of it, and I'll be set with photos, but a thin voice in my mind whines that I'd rather he not come to my photo session. I cannot put my finger on the feeling: Meeting this man was an exceptional stroke of luck, and he himself's been perfectly charming and magnanimous. Chivalrous even. Maybe, too chivalrous. Only after he'd wheeled away did I realize that I'd been taking shallow breaths.

I sigh and feel my lungs inflate.

It occurs to me that the count's accent wasn't an accent but immaculate, deliberate Russian. Sterile Russian carried across the world seven decades ago and practiced, unchanged, in Sunday schools and at starched dinner tables. Dusted off for family gatherings. Jealously guarded from an intrusion of barbaric, proletarian, egalitarian modernity—never a native language to this generation of Russian nobility. A dead language, a museum exhibit, frozen in the past like the Russia where it belongs: the Russia of princes and high balls and serfs, and of the Pale. A curiosity, like Peter's mutant babies in the jars of the Kunstkamera.

It occurs to me he's never been to Russia. He might not have spoken to a Russian who'd been to Russia, beyond Zina and Marina's little chats over the herring, more than a handful of times in his life. Here he lives, an illustrious highness of the Russia that passed away with his grandfather's ideals, and dreams to die on Russian soil, and hates everything Russian that still lives.

Will my children be that way?

Navigating back to the Market between cars, shoppers, and shopping carts, I hesitate to put an adjective to the encounter. One thing I know: His umpteenth cousin-in-law isn't doing anything for me for free. For one head-spinning moment I have a piercing, disorienting sensation of class awareness and revolutionary zeal, and just then I can empathize with peasant mobs passing torches around the mansions of their kind masters. Their magnanimous, chivalrous, aristocratic masters.

What the hell is wrong with you? He didn't do anything, didn't say anything wrong. A nice, respectful man who's doing you a favor.

I've got to write Lisa about this. About damn time something more Russian happened to me than to her.

Spring is spent getting in shape, choosing my audition pieces, arguing about my audition pieces with Oksana, buying the attire and soft pointe shoes (*from* Oksana, who supplies her students at a steep discount but will not reveal her source, which I suspect to be the back of someone's truck), rehearsing my audition pieces (with Oksana's increasing and teacherly participation), and typing out a résumé with two fingers on a real desktop computer at the Philadelphia Public Library. I get the pictures done at Sasha's studio for a rather nominal fee, and the experience turns out to be easy, professional, and less intimidating than I had feared. I'd even call it companionable. Count Timashevsky introduces us and leaves, having barely crossed the threshold. As I pose in my most excellent arabesque, straining to hold an elegant lift through the barrage of shutter clicks, I pretend that Matthew is behind the camera. I'm posing for him.

Do you like it, Matty?

You know you're gorgeous, he says and winks.

What astounds me in June, when I finally consider my solos in good enough shape to open every nearby county's Yellow Pages to BALLET, is the dearth of entries I intend to make into a list. There is, to be precise, one relevant entry: PENNSYLVANIA BALLET. After it, the next category begins: BALLET SCHOOLS.

I bring my confusion to Oksana, who watches my dis-combobulation, then blows a hoarse cackle in my face. I am putting on my street clothes over the leotard after a morning workout; she's just walked in, smelling of her first cigarette, and leans on the barre—gaunt, pale, with her taut cheeks and deeply lined neck in such contrast that they always star-tle me anew. Her gray roots are showing beneath an aging blond dye job; locks of a pinned-up do are tousled by the wind.

"How many did you expect to find, sweetums?" She drops her duffel on the floor with a soft thud. "You're not in Petersburg anymore, Dorothy. Not even in Kiev. Oh, I guess I should've had a talk with you when we started this thing, shouldn't I? C'mon. Tomorrow you show me your résumé."

The talk is devastating and produces several sobering realizations:

One. I am still a clueless immigrant who understands nothing about her culture of residence.

Two. American cities, except maybe New York, treat their high arts the way they treat their architecture: a single sky-scraping clump in the middle and nothing but faceless, one-storied sprawl around for miles.

Three. There are so few ballet companies in the United States and so little funding that getting *hired* by one is akin to a miracle and certainly necessitates applying to every identifiable troupe with a vacancy—that is, every troupe around the country. To make matters worse, the hiring process here tends to require written or telephonic references from previous employers, and mine are not exactly easy to obtain.

Four. Ballet dancers, other than well-known principals, do not get paid all that much more than I make at Bubbe's Market, and the kind of job search Oksana describes means a willingness to relocate by fall to yet another unknown frontier, which I can't afford to do because I renewed my yearly lease back in April. While I now earn enough to live on, it's not enough to pay a penalty for breaking the lease, to rent a new place, and for moving expenses. I'm still repaying B'nei Hagola's loan.

Five. This all adds up to rather bleak prospects. I envision mailing my résumé to the few companies in any conceivably reachable distance, all of which are smaller than what I counted on, none of which might be hiring. Then waiting. Then being stuck sorting zucchini for at least another year. Probably for the rest of my life.

"Don't be blue, sweetums." Oksana bends herself into a pretzel on a plastic chair. "I think you're great. I've been toying with the idea of expanding this operation—we have a waiting list, you know. You could come teach for me full time, what do you think?"

Pennsylvania Ballet auditions me and is brutally honest: My strength lies too much in classical technique, but they're a "Balanchine company," looking for versatile dancers.

"What's a 'Balanchine company'?" I demand of Oksana the second she steps foot in the studio the next morning.

"Bastards," she says and yanks at her zipper. "Are you damn kidding?"

"What? What?"

"Well, Balanchine was the choreographer who developed this style, 'neoclassical' they call it. He's a Russian import, of course, but the style is faster and looser and sort of asymmetrical, deep pliés and odd arm placements. They do arabesque with their hips open—haven't you seen? It's sloppy but modern, very American. Supposed to be *the* American ballet technique, actually, and most companies here are Balanchine companies. Barely anybody dances Vaganova style." She shrugs, tying up a shoe. "But with your classical training you can go loose easy. It'd be a lot harder for some Balanchine-method schmuck to learn the proper form."

"Apparently, they have enough schmucks already loose the way they like."

"Idiots. I'm sorry, sweetums." She gives me a quick, swaying hug. "Mmm, there, all better. We got new *kinder* coming in soon—that'll be fun, won't it? Then you can stop punching the register, at least."

The summer passes slowly. I am mailing my thick envelopes one by one as far as I've decided I can possibly drive from home: two hours. That would make life hell, but it'd be worth it, and anything less would leave me with the "classical no" from Pennsylvania Ballet.

Soon the "new *kinder*" file in for one of the open classes we hold before auditions. It's really more for us than for them, to evaluate the prospects, but Oksana has found it gives the parents the impression they're "getting something for nothing," which attracts more customers. Most of the kids are awkward and angular, some pigeon-toed or overweight, tall girls, comically unsuited for ballet, and they slide on the smooth floor in their multicolored socks. Through the glass office door, I survey the motley crew for petite, nimble bodies. Four or five, maybe six.

Oksana watches over my shoulder. "How do they find me?" she mutters. "I don't advertise in Black neighborhoods."

"Who?"

"The Black ones! I don't get it." She turns me by the forearm away from the door. "It's okay, here's what you do: During the audition you give those *kinder* something more advanced to do, that they can't do, right? Make sure it looks ploppy, so their parents don't start up on you. Right?" She waits for confirmation.

"Oksana, what are you talking about?"

"Those two colored *kinder*, didn't you see them?"

"Uh...yeah." Out of fifteen girls and four boys who've shown up for the open class, two girls are African-American. They seem to be sisters or friends, between ten and twelve, and are dancing, hand in hand, in the middle of the studio. "They look good to me," I say. "Especially the little one, in pink socks. She's limber."

Oksana clasps my head in both hands. "Oh, deary, trust me, you don't want to deal with those people. They're cute now, but the parents! I've had experience, believe me. They'll be late paying, and they won't drill the girls, and then you watch those *kinder* pick up all the bad habits from the families and get lazy and fat and get foul mouths, it's just terrible!"

"Oksana! You don't know this family!" I feel the old, dreadfully recognizable heat spreading through my gut. The fast-cooking fury.

"I do, sweetums, I do. You're still green, honey, but you'll learn. It's okay." She turns me to the door again and points over my shoulder. "We got some good ones here. See those American girls? And that Russian family there, and that boy—very Jewish. Very nice, good form, good families. Those are *our kinder*, we'll have fun."

No problem, he said. You're our *yid. And I said nothing.*

I take Oksana's hands off me and face her. I want to wipe my fingers. "And what...what do you think *you* are, white?" It's hard to formulate, and I see her open her mouth, but I rush in, and she shuts it. "Tell that to a white supremacist!"

She steps back, and I could swear she's wounded. "I'm not being racist, hon, I'm just telling you like it is, and that's because I like you. Because we're going to be partners, and business doesn't work if you fool yourself."

"You're trying to keep children out of school because they're Black! How is it different than what's been done to us? I ran across the ocean from that!" The heat reaches my lungs, my heart is knocking into my ribs—every beat, every beat. The leotard is binding my chest.

"Oh, hush, found a comparison! Now I'm Stalin, tomorrow I'm Hitler?" She is truly hurt. Have I gone overboard? "Those *kinder* won't be comfortable here, that's all," she says. "It's a fucking Russian school of ballet, everybody's white, half the parents don't speak English. They got schools in their own neighborhoods—let 'em go there."

No. I haven't gone overboard. Haven't gone far enough.

"It's not a Russian school of ballet, Oksana. It's a school of Russian ballet. Forgot your own ad?"

"What's the difference?" she asks.

"What's the difference." I take a second. My tenure at the studio is coming to an end. "The difference is that I've devoted my life to the latter. And I wouldn't be allowed in the former. Nor would you."

"You're making big Caucasus out of tiny poopy mounds," she says and arranges her face into a saccharine smile. It is jarring on her. "Let's not fight, sweetums. We've got a class to teach, huh? And an early class tomorrow. We can even keep the Black girl you like."

"Thanks, Oksana." I suck in a long breath and listen to it leave me with a hiss. Am I really going to do this? *Dinah Ash, you've always been your own worst enemy.* "I'm sorry," I say. "I think I'm going to be busy tomorrow."

"Oh?" The saccharine smile dissolves in acid. "Doing what, pray tell?"

"Asking Maxim for my old shifts back. I hope I'm not leaving you hanging."

Looking at Oksana Schnitzer's poised, toxic figure at this moment, it's impossible to imagine she has ever smiled before. "Hey, don't worry about me. Been just fine before your noble highness, will be just fine after. But if you think they're all Blackie-lovers over at Bubbe's, you're going to be badly disappointed."

"I don't," I say. "Oh, I don't think that. I've been working there long enough. But at least they serve all their customers. And they don't proselytize."

Walking out, I hear the clicking of the lighter in my back and muse at her ability to dance with those lungs full of gunk. *How does she manage not to feel it?*

She does feel it. Oksana Schnitzer has no children and no surviving family; beyond all other things she fears growing old and lonely, and the possibility of lung cancer doesn't seem to her a categorical negative. In any case, as all of us who dare make plans, she will find hers frustrated and never get cancer. Instead, she will die of liver failure, alone in a hospital bed, waiting for an organ donor.

My limit of a two-hour commute, with a wink and a nudge, just reaches to New York City, and I apply rather haphazardly to the NYC companies I can identify. I hold out particular hope for the American Ballet Theatre after learning how big the troupe is and that they'd been under Mikhail Baryshnikov for ten years. I just missed him. Predictably, I suppose, though they bother to explain themselves, their wording eerily mirrors that of Pennsylvania Ballet: They appreciate my strong background in classical style and especially the training I've gotten at the Kirov, but the company is blazing in a direction toward the future of dance—more modern, more versatile—and looking for dancers with unconventional skills alongside rigid form.

The Washington Ballet does not reply at all, nor do any others from NYC except a small company that sounds excited to meet me. I almost let my guard down and rejoice, even though they appear willing to skip the audition and move on straight to casting. Only when a meeting with the artistic director and the ballet master is scheduled at a Brooklyn bar do I suspect something amiss. It turns out the Brooklyn Balletiers are a bunch of unemployed twenty-somethings who throw some money together to rent rehearsal and performance space and put on productions, which do not raise enough to cover their expenditures, so they throw together a bit more money and do it again. They call themselves "volunteers from the arts." They cannot pay me. I'd have to pay them. They teach me about tequila (it appears I hate it), and I teach them about cranberry infusion (it appears they love it but can't afford it) before we part ways.

The only other ballet in Pennsylvania is in Pittsburgh, but that's the other end of the state: a five-hour trip. Delaware has nothing. My last chance is New Jersey, where an extensive search of multiple areas' Yellow Pages reveals two functioning professional troupes: one almost a hundred miles away, north of New York City; the other right across the Delaware River in Cherry Hill. It's called Southern New

Jersey Ballet, and its modest ad in the Yellow Pages boasts performances "in classical tradition." It would be half an hour from home. It would truly be a miracle.

I've sent my papers, but three nights later I cannot sleep. This is do or die. Last resort. Final grasp. It deserves something radical. I slide out of bed and bring a paper and pen to my rusty table, recently upgraded with a tablecloth, climb on the chair. I will call and leave a message—prewritten, thought-out, beautiful, and proper, which I can read into their machine with no pressure. Then they will know how good I am, how much I long to be one of them. It must be harder to dismiss a person's plea than to throw out a piece of mail.

By the time I finish composing the message, it's eleven on the dot. I imagine the phone ringing in a dark, silent office and my voice filling the room. Tomorrow someone important will push a button and hear me and think, *She belongs here.* And look for an envelope with my name in the pile of fresh post. I dial.

"Cerelyn Scribe speaking."

What? That's not an answering machine! Oh, God, I made it worse!

"Southern New Jersey Ballet. Hello?" The woman's voice in the receiver is a tender, melodic contralto. Tired. "Anybody there?"

Lord help me. Baruch atah Adonai. Eloheinu...Where'd that come from?

"I'm sorry," I say. "I thinked there is machine."

The woman chortles. "No, there's just me, but I am better. I'm the artistic director. Can I help you?"

God. If I screw up with her, this is it. It dawns on me that I understood every word she just said. She wasn't shouting, she was just slow, and calm.

"Hello." I look at my message. No. It's not right to read to a living person. Turn it over. *Matty, are you with me?* "My name is Dinah Ash. I sent you résumé. I want to know you look...do you look for dancers this season." *Do better. Say something powerful.* "I very want to dance...with you. I am living...so to dance." *That sounds stupid. And I forgot her name!*

I can hear the woman breathing—minutes, hours. Should I say something else?

"Dinah Ash. Yes, I have your mailing." She rustles with something on her end. "Your arabesque has excellent form. But you did not attach any references."

This is it. The end of conversation. But she isn't hanging up. Was this a question?

I say, "I worked in Kirov Theatre."

"Yes, I can see. But we do ask for a letter of reference."

"I...uh...emigrated. I was refugee. I do not have a letter."

She is still not hanging up. She's lingering, listening. *Go for broke.*

"And I do not dance...did not dance last seventeen months."

"That was my next question."

"But I practice after March, and I have solos, they good! If you can see my solos..."

I've got nothing else. Broke. Another pause. More minutes, or hours. *Eloheinu, Melech ha-Olam... Matty, do something!*

"Why don't you come and meet with me? Show me what you have."

Though I walk through the valley of the shadow of death... Thank you.

"Thank you."

"How is Monday at ten?"

245

"Thank you. I am coming. Uh, I will come."

"Good. You have the address. You have a car?"

"Yes."

"So I'm the artistic director, and my name is Cerelyn Scribe. C-E-R..."

I record frantically on the back of my unused message.

"Good night, Ms. Ash," she says—the first and last time she'll address me so formally.

"Good night."

Drenched in sweat, I hang up the phone and slide down to the floor. *Thank you, my love.* The clock shows 11:04 p.m.—four minutes! It lasted only four minutes.

This could be nothing. Or everything. *Slow down. Take one minute to be happy, then get your wits about you.* I close my eyes and inhale as slowly as I can. The sweet smell of fresh milk, still warm from the cow's body, and the savory and sour of dark bread, rye and wheat, just now out of the oven. Babby's hands, stained by mashing blueberries with sugar. She strokes my head and leans it against her scratchy wool cardigan, which tickles my nose. Happiness wafts through and dissolves, and I'm back to the odors of carpet and urban heat, but everything's changed now. Now, there is hope.

I've saturated my pajamas all the way through. Anna-Vanna would've been proud.

It's early March, and the Atlantic along the Jersey Shore is lonesome and aloof. That's what we Philadelphians call the beaches of New Jersey: "Jersey Shore." In the summer, we consider them ours for the crowding, for the littering and seeding and the classic American hot-weather pastime: promenading along the boardwalks complete with funnel cakes, rickety wooden rides, and sunburn. The Jersey Shore is Philly's local beach from Memorial to Labor Day, but now is the off-season, and it's mostly empty. The tag-checking booth is wintering by the high-tide line. It is beautiful in the way of any seashore but lacking in wildness.

I catch myself on the thought: *I'm a Philadelphian now.* It's weird. But maybe it's good. It's how it's supposed to be.

This morning is overcast and feels autumnal. Moisture in the air gets to the bone. I'd never been to Avalon before and expected a more rugged landscape on the ocean, but I like it. There's severity here without bleakness and a quietude without a graveyard silence. I stand facing the water while, to my left, fifteen lissome figures are doing soundless pantomime. I watch them out of the corner of my eye: dark, spidery silhouettes on the beige background, a cacophony of styles and tempos, graceful turns, contorted limbs, cartwheels and pirouettes. Someone's been frozen with upraised arms like a burned-down tree husk, for several minutes now. This is improv, the creative equivalent of a good bath—or a thorough spring cleaning, shaking out the rugs and airing out the rooms. In improv, all is allowed. Nobody else can see us. The boardwalks will be unused until the summer, and the beaches belong to the smattering of locals, an occasional melancholy artist in search of a sad muse, and now and then groups like ours, out on a retreat—from colleges, convents, corporations, theatres.

The guys tell me that Cerelyn's been bringing the troupe here once a season since she started the Southern New Jersey Ballet forty-six years ago. Every year they take three days off, Monday through Wednesday, and come to Avalon in November or March—when the air is crisp and the sand tamped down, heavy but not icy. They put on whatever clothes they want, gym shorts or sweats or leotards, what befits the mood and the weather, and they dance on the beach without music, to the rhythm of the waves and the melodies in their minds. And Cerelyn Scribe stands at the high point like a sentry, with her arms crossed as they are in rehearsal, strands of salt-and-pepper hair flying. She gazes over their heads—our heads—into the distance, too far for anyone to know what's there. Except for me. I know.

It occurs to me that Cerelyn knows, too. There, on the east side of the Atlantic, is her husband. He volunteered in World War II and was killed on D-Day. I haven't heard more than that, only that she started SNJB as soon as the war ended, and it became her life, and she's had no other since.

Fifteen dancers dance on the sand while she and the sixteenth peer across the ocean, trying to see the other shore. She isn't telling me to join the rest, letting me stand.

Matthew is dead, and I'm a Philadelphian. And Leningrad is no more. And Peter is pointing west.

Oni Abiola skips around, spider-squats in front of me, and jazz-shakes her hands and braids, scowling and doing the worm with her eyebrows. Her eyes and teeth are very white against matte brown skin. I giggle, she joins in and unfolds herself. "You know..." She surveys the horizon. "Every time we come here, I keep waiting for a boat to glide out of the mist with, like, King Arthur in it holding Excalibur. Hey, do you know about King Arthur?"

"I do."

"Of course you do." She giggles again and bumps my elbow with hers. "What are you looking for so intently?"

"I am...looking on the river."

"You mean, the ocean?"

I appreciate the way my colleagues talk to me: They don't shout and don't hurry, repeat when I need it, and give me time to put my words together. I still make mistakes sometimes, but they correct me without mockery or annoyance, and nobody seems to think that I am stupid. It wasn't always like that. When I just started back in the fall, their rattling was as overwhelming as I feared it would be, then it quickly changed. I suspect Cerelyn had a talk with them. By now, of course, my English has gotten better, too. But this is not an English issue.

"No," I say. "All oceans are rivers. All..." Oni waits for me to formulate my thought. "Everything flows. Yes?"

"Okay," she says politely. I recognize this now, this "okay." They use it when I say something too foreign or too sad, when they want to respond but don't know how. She stands with me for several sympathetic seconds, then bumps me in the same spot. "You want to come dance?"

I nod. "Thank you. I am coming."

"Cool." She cartwheels away into the living forest of pantomime, and it's me and the big water again. It's deserted and steely. Hard to believe there are creatures swimming and breathing under the surface, being warm. I try to envision a vessel emerging from the haze—maybe. But there wouldn't be Arthur on it. I am thinking of a different legend.

In the myths of ancient Greece, the world of the living was separated from the world of the dead by five mighty rivers. Only dead souls could cross their terrible waters upon Charon's boat, and the most horrid of the five was the Cocytus, the River of Lamentation. So says the myth that some of the dead cannot let go of the past. They yearn for the loved ones they've left behind, for the cares and joys of the realm that lies across the water, and they pine for it and grieve for it and cry. These are the souls doomed to wander the shore of the Cocytus on the side of the dead, cherishing their memories and weeping bitter tears into the river's poisonous current. It is addictive, too. Gods save you from drinking the River of Lamentation. If you do, you will never turn away. You will never begin your afterlife.

I turn on my heels with all the purpose I can muster, screwing a small pit into the sand. Enough rumination. Time to dance.

Cerelyn Scribe is walking across the beach and, seeing my motion, flags me down. At seventy-seven, she still has the body of a ballerina, but not the gait. Arthritis hobbled her years ago—clumsy, ungainly step. I forget until she moves. I hurry toward her, to shorten her walk.

"Dinah." She runs her hands from my shoulders down my arms to the elbows. It's a unique habit of hers, which every time, for a split second, makes me want to cry. It's such a simple gesture, unasked for, unexpected, and so much more than anyone has done for me since 1991. Babby comes to life around my shoulders and dissipates. "Dinah," Cerelyn repeats. "Is this your first time at the ocean?"

"This side of the ocean," I say.

"How do you like it?"

"It is good." I want to tell her I like its infinity and soft, malleable calm. I like that with every wave it settles back into itself and that you can't see the currents or the other shores, or anything but permeable horizontality. I like that it's not actually a river. But I don't yet have the words for that. I say, "It's very big."

She smiles. "Come walk with me. I want to talk to you about your future. I want to talk about the next season. You understand?"

I do. Dancers get contracts one season at a time, October through May, then you are renewed or not. March is early to talk about it, so this is either very good news or very bad. Exceptionally bad.

I am prepared for anything, or so I'm trying to convince myself. Cerelyn took a chance on me—a year and a half of lying fallow and three weeks without Oksana's studio space had to have been showing when she watched my audition back in August. But she saw something in me, and I'd love to believe it was my gift or my passion or my potential, not simmering desperation, that moved her to run her hands down my arms (then, for the first time) and say, "I would like to hire you, Dinah, but with a caveat. You understand 'caveat'?"

I did not but didn't dare admit it and nodded. We were sitting in the third row orchestra, where I'd joined her after stepping offstage.

"We are a very small company," she said, "and don't have official casting divisions. Everyone does some corps de ballet work. But if you dance for us this season, I'd like to keep you, probably, exclusively in corps de ballet. For which you're certainly overqualified. You understand 'overqualified'? I can see you're a terrific dancer, but you are a little rusty, and also you are locked into a strictly classical style— which is a great asset, of course, but we venture out to do some fun and modern things, too, and you'll need coaching for that. You understand?"

I heard the echoes of Pennsylvania Ballet and the American Ballet Theatre. "Yes," I said. "I understand."

"If you're willing to learn, I think you'll find a home here, but you must start with the beginners." She peered into my eyes as if to tease out something I was hiding. "It'll be good for you."

And it has been. Everybody's season began in October, but mine, right away—not the salary, only the training. From that day in August I started coming to Cherry Hill twice a week for rehearsals with Cerelyn, before the ballet mistress and the repertory coaches ever returned to work. Dancing in early mornings, then back to Bubbe's shelves and crates. For seven months I've been driving over the Betsy Ross Bridge, the route that's now so automatic, I don't notice how I get home underneath the daily thoughts. For five months I've been starting my day with a class, then rehearsals. My routine from the past life, it was all but lost in the fog over the Cocytus, all but forgotten, but I fit back into it easily, like a hand into an old glove.

For four months I've been back onstage, since our first production of the season in early November. *Cinderella* in its full glory, classical, costumed, romantic, akin to a déjà vu. The prince soaring about the stage, the fairies' scintillating solos, two crazy step-sisters for comic relief, and me in corps de ballet: a grasshopper, a courtier, a guest at the ball.

After *Cinderella* we did a December of *The Nutcracker*, not nearly as classical but clearly as familiar to everyone as a toothache; then an "evening of legendary characters" (famous numbers like sugar plum fairies and little swans); then, new to me, a revival of Frederick Ashton's *A Tragedy of Fashion*, which is running now: a tongue-in-cheek romp about a courtier who commits suicide with scissors when his work displeases. April still awaits with *Romeo and Juliet*, and rehearsals will begin soon for it. Reruns in May, and that's it. If Cerelyn's pulled me aside to tell me it's over—that I'm an old dog fumbling new tricks—then this will be my last hoorah. My last ballet. I'd better savor it.

"How are you feeling in corps de ballet?" she asks.

"Well."

"You've done well."

"Thank you."

We walk by the surf, and she leans on my arm, then stops, jerking me back, grips my hand. "I want to do *La Esmeralda* next season."

Don't get excited. Slow. Slow.

"I know it," I say. "We did it at the Kirov. I…was not a principal, but—"

"Nobody does it here," Cerelyn interrupts. "They only do scenes. I want to do the whole thing. The Vaganova version." That's my version, the ballet Vaganova revived for the Kirov in 1935. Cerelyn takes my other hand. "And I want you to dance the Diana and Actéon pas de deux.'"

My stomach jumps. No old dog, then. "Thank you, Cerelyn."

"Enough thanking. You're ready." She resumes her limp along the shore, and I hurry to catch her elbow. She's just a tad shorter than me, and side by side as we are, her unruly mane slaps against my cheek. She turns her face to me; her eyes are sparkling. "You know what else I want to do, before I'm too decrepit to care? The full-length *Sleeping Beauty*."

I nod. "I know it, too."

Did you hear that, my love? We did it.

Cerelyn shivers and stretches her shawl around her shoulders. It's too chilly a day not to be dancing.

"I'm afraid it's going to snow," she says. "There's a Nor'easter coming up the coast. And smells like it. We could lose the whole weekend."

"Much snow may be here in March?" I ask. I gave up on winter two years ago, when on March 21, I'd stepped into Pulkovo-2 covered in ice rain, and not twenty hours later, Zev Alterman fished me out of the crowd at Philadelphia International. He packed me into his car and drove me, dazed and senseless, out of the garage—and the first thing I saw was a blossoming flower bed.

"Much snow may even be here in April!" She snorts at what seems to be a fun memory (or maybe at me), then grows serious. "We could get a foot or two this weekend."

"I'd like that," I say, and she laughs.

CHAPTER 15
1996–1997

It only took three years, but we're finally doing *The Sleeping Beauty*. When I told Cerelyn I knew this ballet because the Kirov had done it twice during my tenure, I understated the matter. I'd known it by heart before I ever got to the Kirov. I grew up listening to it on vinyl during my never-ending strep throats: They'd created a version narrated for children. I watched it in theatres, I learned techniques to its music at the Vaganova. It's in my mind and muscle and mitochondrial DNA.

In my junior year, I got into my head that Matthew and I might pair off one day as leads: he the prince, I the princess. When I gushed about it, he nodded. "Oh, absolutely we will. When hell freezes over," and shrugged with detached resignation: "You know I'm not good enough to be a principal. I'd rather watch you, dandelion. From the best seat in the house!"

I still courted the fantasy of getting the part at the Kirov. Until my conversation with the theatre administrator, that is. And now I got it. I'm Princess Aurora—every ballerina's dream—center stage in my white tutu, weightless and soaring, barely touching, rising and falling in Desiré's arms, the vision of beauty, the epitome of grace. Fairy tale and Tchaikovsky and me, together a spell upon a weary soul.

And yet, I cannot lose myself in the grand put-on the way I ought to. It is this season. It's been shaping into a strange time, morose and jagged, unsettling. Our February production is a world premiere, a new ballet by Leila Kahn. Rehearsals are underway already because she wants to "*potschke* with it," and it's different than anything I've ever seen. Different than anything. It's called *The Eighth Day*, and it's about the Holocaust.

Kahn sits in her wheelchair in the aisle next to Cerelyn in their invariable third row orchestra; A.J. and Gavi Haddad perch behind the women's shoulders. A.J. started last year as assistant artistic director, and Gavi is choreographing this thing. He came with Leila Kahn from Seattle to do it.

She jots down notes and shuffles staff paper, then freezes sphinxlike—hoary, lumpy, with a huge, curving beak of a nose jutting out over pursed lips. She's tightly buttoned into a wool suit jacket, old-fashioned, impossibly Jewish, and all around impossible here, in our mundane reality. A legend, like the Queen or the Dalai Lama: someone who you know exists, who emanates the mythos of your life along with Vonnegut and Bernstein and Nelson Mandela, but whom you never expect to meet in the flesh. You don't expect to see the drooping eyelid and the faded blue tattooed number protruding from under her sleeve. To hear the gurgle in her voice as it breaks. But a blanket that covers her knees is always meticulously folded. She looks fragile in the way of an unearthed relic. She is ninety-two.

"Too fast," she says to Cerelyn, scratches something out in her papers, and mutters to herself, "*Er drayt sich arum vie a fortz in russel.*"

Gavi chokes on a snigger and whispers to A.J., who runs down to the pit. I am craving to be let in on the joke (it must be about the number currently onstage) and want to ask but don't dare. I've been called up after my own solo.

"Is it too fast for you, *ziskeit?*" Kahn asks. She rolls the *r* in "for." A Yiddish accent. Russians roll their *r*'s, too, although mine has begun to soften.

"No, Ms. Kahn," I say. "I can do it better."

I'm having trouble. It's not the modern technique—I've picked up enough over the past four years. It's not the speed. It's...

There are no leads in *The Eighth Day*, only solos, group numbers, and mass scenes. No tutus or pointe work, and no white at all. Just gray and black and red, and tortured, broken lines, and stupefying tempo jumps from a bone-crushing tornado to a ghastly crawl. And we really do crawl across the stage, on flat hands and feet, like lizards, or devils, or death. My elbows hurt, and so does my dancer's sensibility. It's ugly.

This isn't a story, not of one person, not of survival or love or even of murder—the music is an ocean gone mad, a tsunami. There is no time flow, no single face to focus on, no overture. It assaults with the first quake of the curtain, and nothing feels finished: Melodies cut out in the middle, harmonies screech into silence before resolution. Above the stage, the crew is measuring a stencil that reads, AND THERE WAS EVENING...

"Will that be in blood?" I ask A.J. on the way to the sit-down meeting.

"We were thinking fire," he says. "But more like coals, I guess. Smoldering. We'll see how it looks."

When we rehearse, we dance. We don't have sit-down meetings—and when we do, we bunch around Cerelyn or A.J. for the few seconds it takes them to yell at us or praise us or deliver a bit of news or explain something particularly nuanced, then we go back to the stage. Gavi does the same: hollers from the chair, runs up onstage. But Leila Kahn wants to see faces. She wants to hear our voices, and for us to recognize what it is we are embodying in the ninety-six minutes she has conjured.

I don't know that it's possible to recognize. I see her pull her sleeve down in a habitual gesture while we gather cross-legged around her chair on the studio floor like metal shavings around a magnet. Cerelyn and A.J. are on her right, Gavi just behind—he is her shadow. Young, svelte, he could be a danseur at the height of his career, and there's an air of mystery surrounding the two of them: He doesn't leave her side. He always wheels in her chair and always wheels it out, and seems to know her wishes before she vocalizes them. And his choreography is exactly like her music. The same.

"You are *sheyne kinderlech*," she says. "Beautiful. But for this, you forget what you are, *yah?* Like it was then, people forgot what they were. It is *genem, yah?* Gehenna. Too dark to be people. Too dark to be beautiful. In *der genem*, life is like death—maybe? You crawl to a death. Maybe death is *gut*, or better. Or no? Too dark to see. Too dark to know right and wrong. And *Gott* made the world and fell asleep, *yah*, and it's *nacht*, and it's *nacht*, won't wake up. Nothing holy in the world."

She speaks, asks something, somebody answers and asks, she speaks again, and I'm having trouble. Classical ballet is the happy heir of courtly entertainments, romantic lavishness, and let's face it, universal human escapism. It is light itself, a wingless creature come to flight, the fluffiest of comedies and the featheriest of melodramas. Yet none of it has mattered until now in the vastness of its art. The story isn't the point in ballet. When the music swells, genius and tragic and high as the firmament, and the bodies arch and soar and fall—the demise of a swan, the resurrection of love— you weep the clearest fresh-water tears, free of salt, free of

sting, free of words. It is catharsis without pain. The kindest
of the muses. The greatest of the arts.

I've always known this—and now, I don't know. This
weekend's *Sleeping Beauty* will be all these marvelous things,
but I can't find my old reverence for the fairy tale where loss
has no permanence and love has no substance. You might say
there's a real catastrophe there, a dead child, but the happy
ending comes unearned, by magic and chance, and erases all
grief. No trauma. No bad dreams. I've loved this ballet my
whole life, never questioned it, but today it all seems frivo-
lous. So much filler, so much nothing. Why do I care all of
a sudden?

Leila Kahn is doing in ballet what I look for in literature: going down into the depths. There is freedom in this,
exploration and meaning, and she is right, of course: Hell
knows no beauty. But her depth comes at the cost of grace.
Isn't there enough hell outside these walls?

"*Tzores, bubeleh?*" Dry, birdlike fingers wrap around my
wrist. "You have troubles."

Am I that obvious or that bad? "I'm sorry, Ms. Kahn."

"You don't like my ballet, I think. It is ugly, *yah?*"

She has caught me near the door. Everyone's filing out of
the studio; Cerelyn scuttles past, pats me on the back, and
it's quiet but for the receding footfalls. End of the day. Leila
Kahn nods to Gavi, and we begin to move down the hallway
back to the stage, down the ramp and up the aisle, where she
makes a slight gesture: stop. He brakes her chair and walks
discreetly away to the upper rows.

"*Zitsn,*" she says, and points at the nearest seat, so close
that our legs are almost touching. "Now. I know you have di
questions inside your head. You can tell me."

Face-to-face like this, she looks even more brittle, like
she's really in pieces, and the suit jacket is what's keeping

them person-shaped. I can hear crackling when she breathes. What am I going to tell this icon of neoclassicism? She is destroying my faith in ballet? She'd been a dancer herself, with some grand troupe in Berlin until 1935, and became a composer after American troops pulled her out of Mauthausen paralyzed. She hadn't written a single ballet until now.

"I...don't dislike it," I say. "This one theme, the one that goes up, like that, it's my favorite."

"Ah." She cracks a smile I'd call impish if I had the disrespect. "That is the leitmotif of *Gott* awake. Of course you like it, *yah?* It is our dream, our prayer."

So our only light in the darkness is an impotent hope that God will awake and set the world right? Here He comes: Good morning, what'd I miss? Oh, extinction-level events, slavery, Genghis Khan, the crusades, millennia of torture and warfare, inquisition, blood libel, lynchings, chemical weapons, death camps, the nuclear bomb, Stalinism, Hitlerism, Khmer Rouge... Geez, why didn't you pray louder?

I interrupt my mental diatribe and sing the melody that's been shredding my nerves. "What about this one?"

"Your ear, it is *zaier gut.* That is the leitmotif of *Gott* asleep. It is not favorite, *yah? Nischt* mine either. It should not be."

"Ms. Kahn." It is funny that she said I could "tell" her my questions, not "ask." English is not a native tongue for either of us, but I notice, and for some reason it's easier. I've been waiting to tell this question since it first clawed itself into my brain at B'nei Hagola. "How do you...feel about God...after the Holocaust? I mean, can you—"

"*Yah.*" She bows her head, smooths out the blanket on her lap. "Don't call it Holocaust, *ziskeit.* Holocaust is 'burnt offering,' *farshtayst?* It is for *Gott.* This was not for *Gott.* We call it *Shoah.*" Her voice is monotone.

"What does *Shoah* mean?" I should know this.

"Just…Catastrophe." She lays her hand on my hand again. It is cold. "I know your question. Many people very angry with *Gott* after *Shoah*. You too, *yah?* We pray, and we pray, and it is enough to ask if *Gott* is dead."

"Isn't it enough to ask if there's any God at all?" The thought bathes me in a flash that I'm arguing with Leila Kahn about atheism.

"Oh, *bubeleh*." She lets out a brief, owlish laugh and leans back in the chair. "*Gott* is not there because there is *Gott*, somewhere up in *der volkn*. *Gott* is there because it is how you see the world, *yah?* Your heart is *Gott*, Torah is *Gott*. When *di mentshn* hide *di Yidn* from Gestapo, it is *Gott*. When you pray, it is *Gott*. You are *yiddishe maydel*—this *Gott*, it is… your history. Your inheritance, *farshtayst?*"

"I don't pray so much, Ms. Kahn," I say. I hope I'm not lying. That weird yelling I've been doing at a fictional character who is supposed to have all the answers but isn't supposed to exist, it doesn't count, does it? "I grew up an atheist. And I'm not so *yiddishe*."

She laughs and shakes her head. "Ah, but understand my Yiddish, how? It is…osmosis, I think." In a blink, she is serious. "It is not important what you say. You are *yiddishe maydeleh*. Beautiful like the moon. It is why you hate my ballet so much, *und* I tell you: I hate it, too." With as slight a gesture as before, she waves Gavi over and touches my forearm with the same hand, brush and retreat this time, then rests her hand on her knee. "You come talk to me more, *yah?* Next week, maybe. Then you will know what is your question." As her chair is rotating toward the exit, she turns her head to me, and Gavi freezes mid-motion, as if he were her very muscle. "Do not fret, *bubeleh*," she says. "These are *gezunde tzores*. Healthy troubles, *yah?*"

*   *   *

"Leila Kahn really likes you," says Oni Abiola.

"Composer's pet," adds Jamie Williams and pushes open the restaurant door with one hand, shaking out his umbrella with the other.

'Tis the season for *The Nutcracker*, in which Jamie and I are partnered for most of the ballet, and I noticed recently how much we'd grown on each other. I've always liked Oni—she is kind, smiley, easy to adore—but Jamie's got a gruff sense of humor, which I'm only starting to appreciate now that I'm getting into American jokes. Or maybe it's that he can pay a compliment and throw a curse on the same breath and mean it. With him you always know where you stand.

On Sundays, our troupe usually goes to a post-matinee brunch, but this has been the rainiest, achingly miserable December, which made people want to skulk away home to pajamas and hot cider. Today only the three of us made it out, so we've decided to try a new place in Cherry Hill called Pancakes'N'Such. A cloud of bone-chilling moisture invades the warm indoor air and dissipates in the smell of bacon and coffee and the sweet, taste-laden clanking of dishes.

"I'm not a pet," I say. "Three, please?"

"You are. She's all '*Bubeleh, maydeleh!* Let's talk our hearts out!'"

"She calls everyone '*bubeleh*.'"

"Yeah, but she doesn't have everyone over for tea and kugel."

"What kugel? I've never had kugel in my life!"

The hostess finally condescends to paying us heed—I'm curious if it was the kugel or my raised voice that did it—and pulls three menus from under her station. She measures us with her eyes, up and down, surveys the room, and turns around without signaling us to follow. We follow. She reminds me of store clerks back home, who did you a favor by selling you something. Preferred expression: "There's lots of you and only one of me!" Preferred facial expression: "Don't come any closer, I'll suck your eyes out!" Babby called it "our unobtrusive service."

"You know we're teasing, right? Chill, woman." Jamie stuffs his umbrella under his chair, Oni and I do the same with ours, unbutton, and open the menus. We're all hungry and need defrosting, and the food looks good, but I can't let it go.

"It's not because she likes me...dancing, you guys. We just have some things in common."

"Because you're Jewish?" Jamie says.

"And an immigrant," Oni inserts. She's trying to make peace. "I get it."

"Well, that. And we both lost everything we've ever loved."

I can hear an "okay" trying to get out of their throats, but they hold it in. It would sound atrocious, I suppose. The silence is stiff and tongue-tied. I should've learned by now not to say things like that. The easy atmosphere of an outing is spoiled.

Jamie stirs awkwardly, extends his long legs from under our tiny table, and a hefty man coming out of the restroom almost trips over him. We all jump up, there's an adrenaline whoosh, commotion, apologies, and we tuck ourselves back in, but now I'm irritable and nothing's right. My umbrella's made my feet wet. I still get ticked off that cloakrooms are a rarity here—my European sensibilities are revolting. In restaurants, in theatres, chairs are crowded with damp, marshmallow-shaped jackets; bags lie underfoot; soggy umbrellas leak puddles into your shoes.

"Why are we sitting by the toilets when half the restaurant is empty?" I complain into the air. "There are perfectly good tables over there. By the window even, and bigger. This is like a table for two!" No answer, but they exchange a look: I'm missing something. "What?"

"You're kidding, right?"

"What?"

"You're not this naïve, *maydeleh*. Where did you expect to sit coming in with two Black people? In the royal section?"

I am not this naïve. Except, apparently, I am.

Our server comes with coffee, swiftly measures us with her eyes, and departs to the booth by the window. Jamie smirks. Oni looks down. I hear teetering and flirting over the menus from the booth by the window. A rotund lady in a down coat passes to the restroom so close that she knocks Oni's purse off the back of her chair and walks on without noticing. Oni picks up her purse and tries to fit it over the umbrella.

"Give it to me," I say. "There's room here."

She hands it over without a word.

It happened so gradually that I didn't notice: I stopped looking for "the face." That subtle but rarely mistakable grimace, restrained aggression and contempt rippling the skin from underneath. And having seen it just now twice in fifteen minutes, I realize I hadn't seen it in years (six years, to be precise), and at some indeterminate point I simply stopped looking. I relaxed.

Our brunch arrives: strawberry pancakes for Oni, an omelet for Jamie (something stuffed with every possible meat on the planet), and French toast for me. We are all breakfast people, and French toast is one of my favorite American acquisitions. It's almost like something we make in Russia, but it's sweet, with a hint of cinnamon, just different enough. If I didn't watch my carbs, I'd live on it. Forks are clanking. It's the quietest meal we've ever had.

"You know," I say, "there's something we used to do in Russia—the Jews, I mean. When you walk into a room, you scan it for faces, you know?" They look up. "You grow up doing it, so it's second nature. You scan for 'safe' faces—that's Jewish. And for unsafe. That's anti-semites, and if they're really rabid, it could show right away. And everybody else is in between. An unknown." I nod at the hostess, loitering at her station up front. "You know?"

"Yep." Two voices in unison. They've stopped eating, and we sit around our two-top, alone in a bustling restaurant as though we were in my studio, at my little table rescued from rubbish.

"So, being Jewish in Russia is like being Black in America, huh?" Jamie says. Oni snickers.

"I guess so," I say. "But then I came here, and... It feels so strange to be—"

"White?" he assists.

"Exactly. I don't... I'm not... I don't know." How can I explain it if I don't even understand how to feel it?

Jamie asks, "When did you know it was the right thing to leave?" His fork is doing a tap around his mug.

"Funny you should ask, I can tell you exactly when: May 27, 1990. I went to the American consulate in Leningrad to get an application for a refugee status. We were supposed to fill out the papers and mail them to the U.S. embassy in Moscow: That's how you got an interview. It was really early morning—you needed to get in line at, like, 4 a.m. and wait till the consulate opened. I got out of the metro, and the whole street was filled with people waiting for the same thing. And I felt...I don't know. Unafraid. I mean, I was twenty-two years old, and I didn't even realize that I'd been walking around afraid all the time, since birth. I mean, I realized it, but I didn't; I didn't think about it unless I had to. Until I had to. And just that moment—there was this street all full of Jews, and I got taller, like some straitjacket had fallen off. I felt safe in the street for the first time in my life. That's when I knew."

"What made you decide to go? Originally?"

The whisper worm wiggles inside me, threatens to wake up, instantly turns my stomach, and coils—stop it! *You're our yid.* "I'm not sure I'm quite...ready to talk about that," I say. "It's one of those moments I try not to think about. Another time?"

For a minute we all watch Jamie's fork dance, then Oni bends over the table into a huddle, pushing her plate to the middle, pushing our plates with her plate. "You know why you feel strange?" she offers. "It's because you're passing. And nobody even asked you if you wanted to be."

It's finally February and my fourth time at Leila Kahn's house, or rather the house she's renting while she's here from Seattle to work on *The Eighth Day*.

Gavi opens the door, as always. "Leila's been worse," he says and steps aside. "But she'll be glad to see you. I'm not sure she'll eat, though." He takes the box from me and raises his eyebrows in a question.

"It's kugel. From that bakery."

"Oh, right! Let's ask."

She's been declining for weeks, and now pneumonia. She's struggling to breathe, but last time I made her laugh by describing myself as a Jew who'd never tasted kugel, and we agreed it was an oversight to be urgently fixed. When I showed up at Lipkind's Deli and Bakery in Northeast, though, I discovered that kugel was a familiar thing: a kind of egg-and-noodle casserole. Babby made it, just didn't call it that. She also made a potato version, with bits of veggies—we call it a babka. I wonder if here that'd be a kugel, too.

In the living room, black-and-white and sepia-toned pictures are strewn about the coffee table, on the sofa and armchair and Leila Kahn's knees, some fallen on the floor; a large open box stands in the corner. "Come see, *bubeleh*," she says. I can hear her wheezing through the hiss of the oxygen canula that runs under her nose.

I gather the photos from the armchair into my lap and sit next to her. "How're you feeling, Ms. Kahn?"

"*Ah, nit ahin nit aher.*" She sticks out her fingers before my face and wiggles them in a "meh" gesture. "Look. This is *alt* Berlin, *yah?* Before *di fascistn* ruined it." She hands over the pictures, one by one. They bring a fleeting whiff of nostalgia: wide avenues, plazas spanned by palatial buildings, statues, winged and domed cathedrals. There's a two-storied bus in a photo of a buzzing street, antique-shaped cars, a bicyclist weaving out of traffic holding a flat cap to his head—the air of the early '30s. "It is my city," she says, "when I was young *tentzerin*. Stupid, *yah*, and happy."

Her city is by four centuries older than mine. She hands me a photo of a Gothic church. The camera angle and the architecture stretch toward the top, as though the sky were a tent, and the church spire, the tentpole. I can appreciate this, but without affection, and even less the rest of it. It's too monumental. Too heavy. Like a frosted sadiron. It's the Berlin I recognize from documentary footage about the war and about the Cold War. I can easily imagine the endless, faceless, black-and-brown square march, arms thrown up—*Heil!*—pouring down the wide avenues. It's the Berlin I can imagine in ruins: smoking piles of stone where palatial buildings used to be, a single pillar still standing, senseless, in the middle of rubble, and blackened and burned-up Reichstag with a scarlet banner overtop. But Leila Kahn's hands are trembling when she strokes the misty image. It is *her* past life. "You like this?" she says.

"It's very nice, Ms. Kahn."

She smirks and clicks her tongue, fiddles with the photos, which rustle in her fingers like dead skin, then points at an album atop the coffee table. "Hand me that, *bubeleh*, be so good." The pages are so friable with age that every time she turns one, my toes tense in a momentary expectation that it'll crumble. "You like *this?*"

This Berlin is different. There's a house with a country feel, the flanks of two others caught in the shot: a pitched roof, crisscrossed beams over the attic, tidy open shutters, and windowsill flowerbeds. A hand-organ grinder cranks away wistfully by the front door, and a boy and a girl listen, mesmerized and holding hands—a knee-high dress and lederhosen, all as it should be at the start of an Andersen fairy tale.

"I like *this*," I admit. "Is this you and your brother, Ms. Kahn?"

"Oh, *Gott*, not my brother! That *blondeh boychik?*" The reflex to laugh throws her into a coughing fit, but she manages by the time Gavi runs into the room. They're both breathing hard, her stridor louder than the nebulizer he pushes against her mouth, but soon she squirms out of it and picks up the picture again. Gavi follows her face with the steaming medication spray, and for a few moments, I watch what must be a daily power struggle.

"Leila, you need to finish it. Please."

She pushes his arm away unflinchingly, like a metro

turnstile. Her voice is back. "It'll be finished soon enough. And I prefer friends to steroids. And you should go heat up the food, I think, *yah?* I have a dog nose for kugel, *kaddishel.*" She winks at me and taps the glossy house with her fingernail. "See these *kinder?* Very *gut*, best friends. It is me, and it is my neighbor Heinrich. We had plans, too: a street organ, a house, one monkey, and three *kinder*. He would play organ and fix the house, the monkey get money in hat, and I would raise *di kinder.*"

It bothers me that Leila Kahn is using the same word Oksana Schnitzer used: *those kinder*. Of course, I only heard Oksana say three Yiddish words—*kinder*, *putz*, and *tuchus*—but now the memory of her intrudes and sullies *this* memory. Unless I don't let it.

"What happened to Heinrich?" I ask. "No street organ?" He'd have been her age, in his thirties when the war started.

"*Fascistn*," she says.

"They killed him?"

She shrugs. "They...killed his soul. You show your pictures now, *ziskeit.*"

"My pictures?"

"I know you have them."

Gavi carries in a tray of kugel, tea, and sweets, and I hasten to clear the coffee table under his waiting arms. He pours me and himself a cup; Leila Kahn signals "no." If she is right and God's just how I see the world, He is definitely in the tea. I sip, and equilibrium begins to return to me, circulation to my limbs and order to my thoughts.

She knows I have them. Of course she knows.

"*Nu?*" She folds her hands in a gesture of infinite patience. "Show me what you have, *bubeleh*. I am getting *alt.*"

I unzip the inner pocket of my purse that holds the pictures and pull them out. I used to carry more; it's only eleven now. I pass them to her one at a time, a short, dry comment for each. I can't afford more than that. I'm busy holding upright: Stitched together on the outside. Keeping my voice level as I say words, these clinical English words about the things and people that are neither.

"This is where I grew up: my house, I lived on the top floor." I didn't take a picture of the magic tower with me. What was there to document? A tall, square cement block. And then Cleo sent me this in a letter—the camera looks up from the awning, the way I used to stand watching the clouds streak the roof—and I couldn't put it down. It's a living memory, timeless, translucent. It returns me to my first life. I always have it with me, for emergencies.

"This is Bab—my grandmother. She raised me. She's gone now." Babby is resting her chin in her hand, her elbow on our kitchen table. Her hair's a touch disheveled, and the strap of her apron with the waltzing poodles shows around her neck. She looks tired but happy, a spark in her eyes and on her lips: She's indulging the photographer. Matthew took this. He liked to photograph Babby after she baked.

"This is the Bronze Horseman. It's a statue of Peter the Great in Leningrad." Lisa sent this one—and several others.

"*Yah*," I hear an approving mutter. "*Zaier* famous."

"This is the view of Leningrad from the Palace Bridge. I mean St. Petersburg. Leningrad is gone now, too." They've all adjusted to the new name—that is, the return of the old name. Lisa first, then Cleo stopped calling the city "Leningrad" in their letters. They call it "Peter" now, abbreviated with casual familiarity, like an old friend's nickname, but every time I read it, I trip over the word. Peter is not my city. It is a memory of the gone times, the time of Revolution and civil war. The streets patrolled by the Red Guard with rifles and long, pointed bayonets; orphans begging for food on the corners. After seventy years of growing and living, after surviving the Blockade and birthing three generations of Leningraders, hasn't Leningrad earned its place in history? Don't they experience a split of personality walking down Third Soviet Street in the middle of St. Petersburg?

Snap out of it. Not now. This isn't what we are doing.

Leila Kahn takes each photo from me in both hands, holds it while I talk, and puts it down in a stack with more care than they require, then raises her eyes to me.

"This is me and my childhood friend Cleo at her first exhibit. Cleopatra Ivanidis. She's Greek and an artist and… had a cat. This is…uh…me and my fiancé in front of the statue of Pushkin. That's the Russian Museum in the back, and that place is called the Square of the Arts."

"What is his name?" Leila Kahn holds the picture close to her eyes. It's black-and-white, like her pictures, but Matthew is still visibly, unmistakably blond in it. The ghost of the Viking past. Blonder even for pressing his face to my black, unruly pouf.

"It was Matthew," I say. "He's dead now. My fiancé, not Pushkin. Well, Pushkin's dead, too." *Stop it. You're becoming hysterical.*

She puts me and Matthew atop the stack and lines up the pictures between her palms. "*Yah,*" she says. "Why is he dead?" And then I know what we are doing.

"In a war," I say.

"*Yah.*"

I have a picture of Lesha, too, but I don't carry it with me. It's at home, tucked between the pages of *The Dead Souls.* I ought to think of him more; I ought to miss him in the simple, longing way I miss my friends, but it isn't simple: Somewhere in my memory he is seeded next to Matthew's death, in the bull's-eye of the crosshairs-shaped scar on my stomach, where the whisper worm sleeps. He is intertwined with these things in the dark by the roots, and my mind pushes him deeper in. I still wonder sometimes when he died, if he died alone, and for the moment my mind lets me, I imagine Aunt Vally holding his hand on his last day. Because I wasn't there.

Leila Kahn glances at what's left in my hands, and I resume, pushing myself into action like a train from a standstill. "This is the Kirov Opera and Ballet Theatre, where I—"

"*Yah.*"

"This is—"

"Vaganova School of Ballet." She lights up with pride. "I was there for a time. Short time. *Zaier gut* time."

"This is my best friend Lisa and me at her place—that's her guitar. She sings...very well. We finished the Vaganova together. That's us graduating from the Vaganova, with some classmates. And...uh, this is my parents. They died a long time ago." In the picture, the mountains are so ancient, they've been worn into hills. They roll in the distance, covered by snow and the black stubble of a Uralian forest, and my merry and carefree parents are protruding from a laughing human heap, random as a pile of sticks, clowning and building a utopia and knowing nothing of the future.

Leila Kahn caresses my static memories as if they were hers. "*Shvertz azayan Yid, yah?*"

When she told me last year that I understood her Yiddish, she was only half wrong. It surprised me even then how much I could pick up, or infer, partly because there's a Russian streak in the language along with German and Hebrew, partly from Babby's forgotten half-comments. I know what she said just now: It's hard to be a Jew.

She lowers her head as though it's too heavy to hold.

"You are a *valgerer, yah?* Wanderer. Both of us are. No home, we keep only di remembrances." She holds up the pictures, and I accept them back. "It is a sickness that has no cure. A sickness for a gone home, *yah*. A Jewish curse, two thousand years now. But also...a *nekhuma*..." She is searching for a translation, and I can't help her this time.

"A solace," Gavi chimes from the doorway, and she nods.

I didn't see when he left, when he came back to stand in the doorway between the living room and the hallway, don't know how much he has heard of my choppy autobiography. I feel naked.

"*Zolst helfen vi a toyten bankes, yah?*" Leila Kahn coughs again, so violently that the fit contorts her body and blows Gavi toward her in a single move, and me, away and around the sofa, watching helplessly as he fusses with the nebulizer. Seconds tic and tac, and slowly the torture subsides, her breathing returns, and we wait for calm. I know she said something funny because even now, holding the mask to her face, bent over her and rigid and ready to spring into action, Gavi is tee-heeing quietly to himself, and she's oozing her roguish smile I've come to regard as the prerogative of age. Or status. Or wisdom. It must be funny, but I don't know what it means. I smile anyway.

"Ms. Kahn is probably getting tired now." Gavi inserts a pleading expression between me and her face.

"I should rest," she acquiesces into the nebulizer.

"I'll be going, then," I say, but there's something else. I hadn't decided if I'd come out with it when I knocked on the door, but I can't leave without asking. Or is it telling? Gavi turns off the machine, and I slide into a precarious I'm-only-here-for-a-second position on the sofa next to the wheelchair.

"Ms. Kahn, I am becoming a U.S. citizen." I have to swallow. I'm still not accustomed to hearing this pronounced. It's been an abstract concept for so long... "I have an oath ceremony in April. Of course, I know you'll be back in Seattle by then, or I'd be honored to invite you, but I just wanted you to know."

She lays her hand on mine, the same tender gesture I remember from the time she ordered me to "*zitsn*" in the aisle of the theatre, three months ago. Her hand is even colder now. "Seattle-shmeattle," she says. "How could I miss it? Gavi, dear, would you make us a trip for April? What is the date?"

I shut the door of the house behind me and slump against it. I'm spent. I've been tired lately. *The Eighth Day* is about to open, and I feel unraveled, as if I left everything in the rehearsal space. Anna-Vanna used to say something to us in Classical: Ballet gives you a rigid form and exaggerated, almost inhuman moves, and packages you up into a tight, idealizing costume, so to reach the hearts of the audience, you must polish your technique until you can forget about it and then forget. Then you can tear yourself open and pour out everything real and human and true, your deepest gnawing pain and the only joy that keeps you alive—and thank ballet that no one will know what it's about.

It's taken me till I am almost twenty-nine—till I'm stepping out onstage unpolished, unpackaged, stained with fake blood, hideous, dancing the *Shoah*—to appreciate the anonymity of emotion I've always loved, unawares, in classical ballet. It is because Aurora's life is so trifling that you can cry safely for yours.

Leila Kahn had better recover quickly, or she won't make it to the premiere. Her condition worries me, as does my fatigue. Am I getting old before my time, or is it dancing this soul-baring, abysmal history that's so draining?

Though I dance through the valley of the shadow of death...

Psalm 23's been floating up to the surface of my mind at uncertain, desperate times. I don't know why. I don't believe what it says, do I? God is not my shepherd. Woe to me with a shepherd like that, and I do fear the evil that fills this valley. These words are not mine, and they help, as Leila Kahn has put it, *"vi a toyten bankes"*: much as cupping helps a corpse. It's an expression I just heard but haven't yet learned. Gavi will translate it for me at her funeral, through a smile and tears, and it'll become my favorite of her expressions, cupping having been my constant childhood companion.

I hear agonized coughing from inside the house and separate myself from the door. I shouldn't be eavesdropping.

CHAPTER 16
1997

She doesn't make it to the premiere. By the time we open in mid-February, Leila Kahn is in a hospital, in and out for the next month through *The Eighth Day*'s run. She and Gavi leave for Seattle in March, for home and the familiar surroundings and the doctors who know her well.

My citizenship ceremony is April 17. I've had a few weeks to decompress and to turn twenty-nine, but I'm still worn out. My morning runs have dwindled to a mile—yes, I am counting in miles now and measuring in pounds and degrees Fahrenheit—but I arrive back to the starting point drenched and exhausted, in the shape that even a few months ago I wouldn't have reached until at least the five-mile mark.

My nights are uneasy. I wake up in blackness and sweat, tight in the chest and anxious, look for Orion in the sliver of sky I can make out through the window. He descends from his free flight and sits on the roof of the building across the parking lot, dangling his feet in shin-high Hellenic sandals. I've almost forgotten the comfort of his presence, the magic of my childhood. His encouragement. His borderless guardianship. I'm so sodden, I'm shivering, and I have to change pajamas and sheets before trying to fall asleep again.

It is surprising how many people have come to see me take the oath. I'd invited them all but didn't expect them. Something pushed me to tell everyone: to call the synagogue, to stop by Bubbe's Market, to mention it at the theatre. It isn't the importance of this day for me, I don't think, though

I'm still contemplating what exactly this day means. I think I told them all out of the same sense of obligation you'd have in Leningrad to your relatives and life-long friends—your clan, in its nearly literal meaning. People you don't choose to be yours but who are, and so you owe them the occasions of your life, the rites of passage, and whether you like them or not, they are invited to weddings and brises and birthdays. And citizenship ceremonies. The question on my mind is: Am I really forming a clan here, in America, or do I just wish to believe that I am?

If Matthew were alive, we'd be doing this together.

If Matthew were alive, we probably wouldn't be doing it at all. Or would we?

In a large, square hall in the courthouse basement, plastic chairs are in tight rows, leg to leg, one aisle in the middle, before a podium flanked by American flags and three or four others I don't recognize. The room is filling and humming, but judging by the number of future citizens, whose chairs are separated up front, my crowd will take up at least one-eighth of all guest seats. I should be proud. They've all cared enough to show up. So why do I still feel alone? And immigrant? *A Jewish curse*, Leila Kahn said. The curse of the wanderer.

Lisa's last letter came three months ago, telling me she was getting married to Andy Triukh. Two hurried paragraphs signed "kisses, the Triukhs." Nothing since. Cleo's last letter was five months ago. She is starting a business with some part-ners I've never heard of—or she *was* starting it five months ago, in the Russia I no longer know: capitalist, cutthroat, ma-fia-ruled, jungle-lawed, pandemoniac and frightening, choked by inflation. But government salaries haven't been paid in years. This loan, which comes with a protection racket from the mob, is her tenuous chance at survival. Incubus is dead—cancer—and she is done with cats. Three paragraphs.

My old threads are tearing. My new threads don't fit the pattern.

In a minute or ten, I will stand up and pledge allegiance to the country that's taken me in when my own didn't want me, to the country that adopted me, made me its own. An oath of exclusive loyalty, and I will mean it. If I have a home, it's here. I shouldn't need anything more.

There's angular awkwardness in today's parade of hugs, hellos, and chipper handshakes: These people don't know each other, an unpalatable assortment. The Altermans and the Ackers are both here, Rabbi Frum, Maxim, and—this is a shock—Ari the loader, with Zina and Marina on his arms. I continue to work summers at Bubbe's, when ballet is not in season and other dancers teach, but between September and May, they mostly see me once a week making purchases. Yet somebody from the Market pops up in the audience of the Southern New Jersey Ballet almost every production. As per my original promise to Maxim, there's always a pair of comps reserved for them at will-call.

Sasha the photographer (I've never stopped thinking of him as "the second cousin's brother-in-law") approaches with his fedora tipped and presents a card written in long hand. "Count Timashevsky sends his congratulations and hearty wishes with apologies. He is in France, unfortunately." He plants a flighty kiss on my cheek. "All the best, my dear."

Granny fills the room leaning over me, squeezes my ribs to a pitiful crack, and roars: "Saw your silver Tercel in the parking lot, eh? Looking good, looking good!" He steams over to Zev Alterman, creates merry commotion there, and knocks down chairs.

The only person not invited is Oksana Schnitzer. The only person invited who isn't here is Leila Kahn—and, of course, Gavi. I perceive him as her inextricable, intelligent body part.

"How is Leila? Have you spoken?" Cerelyn has her left knee replacement surgery scheduled for late May, to give maximum time for recovery, and in the meantime her walking's become painful to watch. She really needs both a knee and a hip replaced, but they only do one at a time. Jamie is holding her up under one arm, Cara Morikawa under the other (she is new this season, teensier than me, and sensational). Oni embraces me, one for all, and we finally sit.

"I talked to Gavi on Monday," I say. "She sent me hello and wishes, you know, but she is...too weak for a conversation."

There aren't any words for this. We just sit. We are with each other. These are the people I like.

The microphone whistles. "Please, take your seats."

It's happening. I am becoming an American, and there will be no way back.

There wasn't a way back before, but now I will owe this land more than my gratitude and taxes. I will be its muscle and blood. The vote that steers its policy, sends troops to wage war, and spends the taxes I pay. The hand that carries a blue U.S. passport, the protection and burden of being its face: Wherever I go, I answer for all that it does. I am no longer a findling, an orphan girl sheltered and fed. I am family now. I decide who is sheltered. Well. Not really.

I'm still trying to figure out what this means. All I know is that I want it. And I do mean it, these words I am speaking, right now, this second, in a shaky unison with an almost comically multicultural crowd, turbans and hijabs and screaming-bright skirts and a kaftan and suit-and-ties and two skullcaps, a floor-length dress, a mini-dress, and roaming grins, and me. ...*against all enemies, foreign and domestic, and I will bear true faith and allegiance to the same.*

We file out of the room one by one. A woman in a drab

suit stands by the door with a bucket of miniature star-and-striped flags glued to plastic sticks. She pulls out a flag, hands it to me, and says, "Congratulations, new citizen," and I say, "Thank you," and pass her, pushed by the inertia of the crowd. I can still hear as, behind me, she pulls out a flag, hands it to a Sikh man in a blue turban, and says, "Congratulations, new citizen."

Cerelyn's car is the closest, parked in the handicapped space, and we stop there to exchange good-byes while the others disperse through the lot. She lowers herself sideways into the driver's seat with the door open. "What did the doctor say?" she asks.

She suggested I go see a doctor after she'd discovered me soaked and splayed on the floor at the end of a rehearsal. Then, after I'd botched a move and another, both toward the finish of *The Eighth Day*, she insisted I go. I get out of breath, and my muscles tremble. She finally ordered me to go the day she recast the *Latin Beat* show, which is on now. I no longer have solos in it.

"He said I'm fine." I try to sound upbeat. "My blood work is fine. He said I might have had a virus or something, and it's hanging around, so that's why I'm tired. He said I should sleep more and drink orange juice and take vitamins."

"All right." Her stare is an inquisition. "You think you'll be in shape by the reruns?"

"I hope so."

God, I hope so. That's only two weeks away.

"You cannot slack off on your cardio, Dinah. Sleep, drink, take care of your body, but you have to keep working, and hard."

"Cerelyn...of course!" *Is that what she thinks of me? I'm lazy?* "I'll do better, I promise."

From inside the car, she runs her hands down my arms

where she can reach: from my elbows to my fingers. "You get some rest now," she says. "Congratulations, my dear."

My summer regime is "athlete in recovery": I discipline my body brutally while wearing kid gloves. Running, swimming at the YMCA. I get up at five on Mondays and Wednesdays for my cardio before going to work at Bubbe's. Tuesdays and Thursdays it's stretch work and ballet, just me in an empty studio, to which Cerelyn gave me the key. On Saturday afternoons I run a slow half-marathon. Endurance. The ghost of Matthew jogs next to me. Of course it's effortless for him. Memories don't get out of breath. "Come on," he chants and makes a clown face. "Move the hooves, what are you, eighty?" He floats ahead of me, running backwards. "Catch me, curly! Come on!"

On Fridays and Sundays I rest. I drink juices and take vitamins and eat medium-rare steak, and I go to bed at nine.

I splurged on a little air conditioner that fits into my window and purrs during the night: It's been a hot enough summer, often in the nineties, and on one of my expeditions into encyclopedias of healthy living, I managed to unearth a warning against sleeping in the heat. It feels true. I do a bit better at night in cooler air, but not by much. I still wake up at 3 a.m. at least twice a week in a puddle of sweat, and I still get exhausted after a half-mile run. Orion is hanging his sad, empty head and saying nothing to help me. I'm supposed to increase distances with care and determination, to build strength and energy reserves, to build speed, to build lung capacity back from whatever it was that had flattened me in the spring, but with every passing, horrifying week, I can see clearly that it's not happening.

The May reruns did not go well. I got through them barely, each performance a combat mission, discarding all freedom and flight and focusing every second on breath, technique, pacing, balance. Each day I had to pull the last of my strength from the deepest reserves, weak in the knees at the final bow, and I was soulless onstage.

They all finally noticed, approached one, two at a time, tentatively, so afraid to intrude. Chewed on their eternal American "Are you okay?"

Jamie Williams is a blunt instrument. "I almost dropped you," he said. "Are you okay? You've been dancing like crap since the Holocaust thing. Did it get to you this much?"

"I'm just tired."

"Well, get untired, would you? And get your head back on."

It isn't my head, though, is it? Cerelyn knows. At the season's closing in May, we sat together in her office, in a strained and pregnant silence, until she came out with it: My contract would not be renewed. At least not right then.

Of course, I expected it. I should have expected it. I'd just been refusing to.

"I'm worried about you." She was rapping her fingers on the desk, an intricate rhythm of her own making. "How long did the doctor say this 'post-viral fatigue' is going to last?"

"I don't know. He said it lasts for months sometimes."

"Well. We both have till mid-August to get ourselves in shape for next season." Her palm flattened with a thwack. "I'll wait to hire anyone in your place until the last moment. But you're in no condition right now."

"I know that."

"I know you do, dear. Are you seeing a doctor again?"

"August 11."

"Hmm."

I couldn't tell if she thought the appointment was too far away or if she was unhappy about the whole thing, or if

281

she was pondering something only tangentially related to the matter. She said nothing more, and we parted tight-lipped and troubled, she for her surgery and I for my months of manic and futile Sisyphean drudgery, self-condemned.

I broke the routine only once, for Leila Kahn's funeral: five days to fly to Seattle just in time for the gravesite service, to sit the first three days of shivah, and come back.

I'd never seen her Seattle house before. It was crammed, thronged with books and sheet music, photographs in boxes and albums everywhere: on shelves and desktops, under the tables, taking up chairs in every room, piled up so high in places that these things blocked lower parts of the windows, and the house was dusky from it. It was a repository of memory. The workings of her mind. As though I found myself inside her and not inside the place that had contained her. There was only one mirror to cover, by the front door, and Gavi had put her favorite shawl over it. It was a knit gray affair, traditional, the kind Babby could have had around her shoulders. She'd liked to wrap herself in it from a chill, existent or not.

Gavi was quiet, unmoored, and empty-handed. I am not sure he's going to know what to do with himself now. I brought him an invitation from Cerelyn to join SNJB as a repertory coach and consulting choreographer. He nodded, stroked the shawl on the mirror in an absentminded way, then held me in an embrace longer than people do. "I might go back to Israel," he said. "Once the house is sold. But this is... Thank you. I'll think about it."

We went into the living room together, where cushions were lined on the floor along the wall and furniture so mourners could have back support. Family clustered together. There were six of them: a cousin with a daughter and grandson, from Israel; a nephew with two children, from Canada. Gavi took a vacant cushion among them, looked up at me, and patted one next to him. I hesitated. *Those are for relatives.* Friends, who come to share the grief, sit so the relatives can see their faces. Gavi patted the cushion again, and I sat by him.

"Isn't this a place for the family?" I whispered to him.

He smiled like I told him a Leila Kahn story. "She always thought so of you. Didn't you know?" He pulled an envelope from his pocket and handed it to me. "It's for you. Your inheritance. I think you should read it tonight."

The letter was simple. Leila Kahn knew we wouldn't see each other again. *I'll see you in yeneh velt, ziskeit,* she wrote, spelling the Yiddish out in English letters for me. I read and heard her voice that was cracking from breathlessness and unfinished joke. *You are nechumah to me, you and Gavi, in my last days. Do not fret, and remember: As long as kinder bury parents and not the other way, these are gezunde tzores.* She left me three photo albums; *The Comprehensive Dictionary of Yiddish Words and Phrases*; a collection of assorted scores and books, which seemed to her particularly suited to my needs and weighed altogether about a hundred and fifty pounds (I know because I had to ship them to Pennsylvania); a magnificent portrait of herself in costume from some early '30s production on a Berlin stage; and intellectual property rights to her third symphony and to *The Desert Cycle.*

I did not quite appreciate this last gift until her attorney contacted me in late July and explained the process, including the typical amount of royalties brought by these two, her most famous, compositions. It's a couple thousand dollars a month—a fortune by my standards—and I've never had just money before, but today I am still unaware of the preciousness of its timing. I will become aware soon. This money will pay for my health insurance, deductibles, and copays for the rest of my medicine-flooded life.

*   *   *

It is August 11; I'm on my way back to the doctor's office. Next week Cerelyn has to make her last hiring decisions, but sleep and vitamins have accomplished nothing. And I no longer believe in post-viral fatigue: How long can I suffer from the flu I'd never noticed having?

Dancers grow old. You hope it won't happen to you until you're thirty-five or so. Some dance long past that (the exceptions), but it does happen earlier. Dancers grow old: Their joints give out, their backs begin to hurt too much to ignore the pain, their bones and muscles and tendons groan under the years of constant unbearable stress. Their feet are a gruesome mess. I am twenty-nine. I suppose it's possible that I'm aging out of my career, that it is time to teach, to choreograph. It's early and rather dramatic, but I did have a break of almost two years and had to retrain, which is hard on the body, and my stress wasn't limited to physical. It is part of the lore in the ballet community that unhappy dancers don't last. And I've had some unhappy years.

This may be my time.

What will I do if it is?

SNJB is as close to family as I have. Ballet is as close to the meaning of life as I've found here, in America.

The doctor I'm seeing today is different from the one I saw in April. It's a big practice, and they called me a month ago to say that "my" doctor wouldn't be in the office on my appointment date, so would I like to reschedule or see somebody else. Of course, I didn't care whom to see. I've only met "my" doctor once.

When I told Cerelyn about it on my last visit on Friday, she thought it was rather fortuitous. Her surgery had gone well, but the recovery was taking longer than she'd hoped, and between the old hip and the delicate new knee, she was leaning heavily on her walker as we ambled down her street: a block there, a block back.

"Might as well get a second opinion while you're at it," she said. Another nonbeliever in post-viral fatigue.

The practice is called Neshaminy Primary and Specialized Care, named, I imagine, after the creek that flows to the north of us into the Delaware. They have clinics all over the city with stylized letters NPSC above the front doors, and this one's a palace. Back in April I wrote to Lisa about it: "American medicine is a palace, even when it's your run-of-the-mill neighborhood polyclinic." Not a real palace, like those of Petersburg, not like the enfilades of my museums and theatres and concert halls, not like the Palace of Young Pioneers. Compared to them, this place is a cardboard cutout, a two-year-old's scratches next to Rembrandt. But next to the rooms in which I've been living for the past six years, this building is pretty grand, and I am refreshed and impressed. Faux marble pillars and a wide stone staircase with a railing of smooth polished wood, tall windows up to the ceiling create a clean, healthy feeling. It's light. I twirl about, and for the second time I begin to hope that everything will be all right—even though it didn't work before.

They have a lab, an x-ray, and some specialists on the first floor. I ascend the dignified steps. Primary Care to the right. Paperwork.

It's already prefilled; I just have to check and sign it as returning patients do. For a second I experience that old sensation that used to seize me whenever something happened for the first time. This is, unexpectedly, a very Western thing: I've never been a returning patient, a "Hello, Ms. Ash, nice to see you again" patient. So polite—this could be a Miss Marple story.

I skim the questionnaire. Name, birthdate, address. Race?

There it is again. I know I left it blank when I filled out the papers five months ago. And now, under the heading OPTION-AL and the question RACE, a little printed checkmark fits precisely into the square against the word WHITE.

I approach the window. "Excuse me. This is wrong, here."

The receptionist is an icy question mark. I clearly look white enough to her.

"I am not 'white.'" I don't know if I hate the concept or the word more, or that they presumed it on my behalf. I feel washed out by it. Erased. Nullified. How did Oni put it: *passing?*

"Okay. Um. What...would you like to put down?"

If I decline to answer, they'll probably check it again, but there isn't an answer on the list that fits. I'm not African-American or Asian or Pacific Islander. Who invented this damn thing? Why do they need this multiple choice?

"How about 'other'?"

She bends over the paper. "Okay. What should I write in here?"

I'm Jewish. It's what I know I am. But it's not a race. I don't know what a race is: something bigger than Jewish but smaller, other, more specific than "white."

"Middle Eastern," I say.

She looks up, like something is on her tongue, but she holds it and writes. I'm bothersome, sure. Or weird. Who doesn't want to be white?

"We'll be with you shortly," she says.

The old doctor was middle-aged, soft everywhere and sweet-mannered; even his hair was straw-colored and flighty as if it'd been triple-conditioned. This one is young and businesslike, but he listens even worse than the first. I make the mistake of starting my story from the beginning, from the winter and ballet and fatigue. He seems to hear and not, flipping through what I assume to be my chart, then cuts in before I get to the summer.

"Are you still feeling tired?"

"Oh, yeah. It's not getting better. Even though—"

"Do you have trouble sleeping?"

"I do."

I'm about to launch into the description of puddles of sweat, but he's on to the next thing: "How's your mood?"

"Well..." *How would your mood be?* "Pretty miserable."

"Would you say you feel hopeless? Sometimes? Often?"

"I don't know. Maybe, I guess." *You're making me hopeless right now.*

He finally puts down the binder, leans back in the chair, and crosses his ankles. "The good news is, your labs are still fine, you don't show any alarming symptoms, but I see in the notes here that you've been under a lot of stress, and I hear that's still the case. I think what's happening is you're experiencing a bit of depression. It's not uncommon in immigrant populations but underrecognized. I'm going to prescribe a medication." He jots on a pad, tears off the script, and hands it to me without pausing. "This should help your mood stabilize and help your fatigue and help your sleep as well. Take this every day at the same time, okay? If you start feeling worse or if you get a rash—or really anything unusual happens—call the office right away. But don't stop taking it without talking to me. It was nice meeting you. I hope you feel better. And I'll see you in four or five weeks, how's that?"

I have only enough time to open my mouth while he shakes my hand and blows out of the room on the wind of medical business, and I gape after him like a passenger late to a train, with the prescription in my hand fluttering in his wake.

Depression? His writing is scratches and symbols; I can't

even tell what it says until the next day, when a Rite Aid clerk shoves a baggy across the counter with a plastic bottle inside: *sertraline hcl, 25mg, 30, 1 refill.* That doesn't clarify anything.

Depression? As in, it's all in my head? I'm losing ballet—the only thing I've managed to hang on to with my last, chipping claw—because I'm sad? What he's saying is, I'm losing my mind.

No. We didn't have this in the Union, and with good reason. We...don't have this. I don't have this. Absolutely no way in hell.

We didn't have this, right? No one I ever knew back home had ever been diagnosed with depression.

I tell no one but Cerelyn about my recent "second opinion," then tell her I don't intend to take the pills. It is preposterous, isn't it? I'm not mentally ill.

She wiffles and waffles, then tells me in hesitant, slowly chosen words that I am wrong. There is no contract for me this year. Whatever is happening, I cannot dance. She loves me; she's sorry. But if I am to have any hope of coming back, I must pursue every chance that is offered. I must try everything. I must take the antidepressant.

We have the talk about acceptance and not being embarrassed—the talk reserved for those with embarrassing diseases. Except she sounds sincere when she says it's okay, and I can see she believes it. It's okay to let my mind go, to lose control. It's okay to wrap myself in a toxic cocoon of memories and fears and lie paralyzed in a fetal position, numb and deaf to the calls of alarm clocks, as life and obligations and pleas for help pass by. As all the beauty and sense and any future, which have been the point of surviving it all, pass me by. Cerelyn says it's okay to become so sad that my body breaks down and ruins my life. She believes it's okay to be crushed by the weight of the world and not die. It appears, there's a pill for that. It must be an American thing.

I take Zoloft (the brand name of my generic pill) for the next four weeks, then two at a time at the doctor's insistence that 50 mg is the "therapeutic dose," but nothing much good or bad happens. It becomes a creepy addition to my breakfast routine, a reminder of failure and dysfunction, and doesn't make me better or worse. I don't know which one I'm hoping for, but no real changes stay long enough to report. I will tell Dr. Ming the story of Zoloft when I meet her in December. She'll crane an eyebrow to that, reflexively, and stifle an expression, so that I will think she's seen it before: misdiagnosis of cancer as depression, medications thrown at patients, delay in the right diagnosis. She won't say anything of the sort— those will be my thoughts, not hers—but she'll ask me if I'd like to stay on Zoloft. Many patients of hers take an antidepressant, she'll say. In so many words, it helps them deal. I will decline, and she'll wean me off it.

But this will be in December; it's months away. I still know nothing of what's coming except that the season at SNJB has started without me, and there's emptiness in my mornings without the need to drive over the Delaware. The foliage is abrush and aflame in the Pavlovsky Park, across the world without me, but Philadelphian streets are only just touched by the yellowing breath of the fall.

My nights are still broken, often sleepless, and I while them away with Orion or playing knock-knock games with Barabashka. Barabashkas are house spirits, so they're supposed to stay in one place. Invisible, shy, and mute, they tend to the house and protect it from the families that come and go, but I suspect that mine traveled from home with me. I remember his timid, playful knocking from the magic of my childhood, and it feels the same. For many years he was dormant, but somehow I'm sure he's been here all along, and when he shows himself for the first time, I know who he is—this wimpish see-through creature that would've come up to my waist if he'd ever stopped crouching, humanoid but with floppy ears and long arms and legs so he can hide his head completely between his knees. He likes to run his fingers through the poplar branches I brought from Leningrad. They sit on top of the bookshelf, and he hugs the vase with his legs, only partially protruding from the wall.

My days are tiresome, plus sleep deprivation is taking its toll. Still, quitting Bubbe's for good and having a steady daytime schedule has been good for my mood as much as it has for my energy. Once again Cerelyn Scribe is to thank: She set me up with a job, teaching at a school that belongs to her old friends. On my way out of Cerelyn's office back in August, I ran into Oni and Cara, our latest blissful couple. I told them I wasn't coming back—every dancer's most dreaded, most inevitable conversation—and we hugged. I told them Cerelyn had set me up with the Chadaris, and Cara said, "When Scribe closes the door, she opens a window!" And they laughed. I didn't know what it meant, but I laughed with them.

Mohinder Chadari had danced for Cerelyn his whole dancing life, I understand, until he could dance no more and became a choreographer. That's when he met Laura Jones, twelve years his junior, who came at the peak of her career to the Southern New Jersey Ballet. It is as ruffled and rose-colored a story as I've ever heard. They fell in love and married and worked together until she retired, right on schedule at thirty-five, eight years ago. He retired with her from big ballet, and they opened a little studio in the heart of Philly and called it The Chadari Dancers. The business has done well, turned from a studio into a modestly sized school. They've been looking for a partner to invest and to expand, but after a phone call from Cerelyn in August, they agreed for now to take on an employee instead.

I began my Chadari tenure with the trepidation undeserved by my employers. It was a fear instilled by Oksana Schnitzer, but it dissipated by the end of my first day. Mohinder is dark, umber-skinned, with curls so black, they look oily and springy. I'd compare them to mine, but his are large and noble, streaked with a ruminant hoariness, while mine still cannot be reasoned with, and I crop my hair close to the scalp, even though it makes my beginnings of gray more visible above the temples. Laura is a sunny blonde with lacy skin so delicate, you're always concerned it'll burn from a table lamp. When they dance together—not often, either to demonstrate something to the children or, on a rare occasion, for pleasure—they braid their bodies into an astounding black-and-white hieroglyph. Our students are every tint of every human color on the spectrum between the Chadaris, a few religions (I can tell), and speak at least a dozen different languages, and I cannot imagine the Chadaris caring about that as they lead the little ones in a musical improv or drill the advanced classes in ballet moves. I thought I was comfortable at SNJB, but even there, race and color, being Black and being Jewish, was a thing. It was an issue. It wasn't *always* an issue, and it wasn't a bad thing, but I could never forget about it, just as I've lived not forgetting my whole life. Yet I have relaxed since being here, at The Chadari Dancers. I have exhaled. Here, there is no race.

The studio occupies a walk-up on a shady street in Rittenhouse Square, one of Philadelphia's old, cozy, and wealthy neighborhoods. Every building here seems to have housed somebody famous. The park was planned out by William Penn himself. There are sculptures there of lions and goats, one of which is named Billy (yes, Billy the Goat), and children always climb upon its back and press their cheeks to its stubborn bronze neck. This is so different from the sprawling, faceless Northeast that it feels like another city, one with a story to tell and a character. This city has an aura to be missed, to be recognized when you come home from afar, and surreptitiously it's come to me that I'm beginning to like Philadelphia.

I've gone out to the Delaware, too, to the Olde City with its colonial air and taverns and buckled cobblestone streets, to Penn's Landing, where the tall ships are moored. It's the only real embankment here. Looking right and left or across the river, all you can see is abandonment and a mesh of industrial shapes, but the Landing is an island out of time: Water is splashing against the granite, the masts are creaking under the weight of pulled-up sails, a couple is necking in a windless nook. Only there's trash everywhere, bags and wrappers and cigarette butts and empty paper cups with straws still in them, dancing and rolling in the breeze mixed in with fallen leaves. But trash is everywhere in Philadelphia. There's no escaping it, and I've mostly learned to ignore it.

Every so often, after work, I go walking around the Philly streets, humming to myself as I haven't in a long time—*ti-ree-ti-bum-pa-toom, ti-ree-ti-boom, doom*—and I remember the first time I thought of myself as a Philadelphian, standing on the Avalon shore almost five years ago. In truth, I wasn't a Philadelphian yet. Am I now? I wish I had someone to answer me.

I wish, too, that I could walk more than I do, but by evening, more often than not, I am too wiped to go anywhere but home to my cave. It's October now, the weather's been turning lousy off and on, with nippier nights, and I can't seem to shake a cold—not a head cold so much as a dry cough that developed a couple of weeks back, maybe three, and settled in for the long haul. It's eating at my appetite, my muscle mass and color, and my leotard is starting to hang.

This season's strangeness is different from last: I expected to be distraught mainly by being away from the stage, but the studio is a restful and creative place, a warm place for my heart. Despite everything, this could be a good fall for me if I didn't feel so unwell.

Of course, then, I would still be dancing.

I'm rather sure it was Laura who remarked to Mohinder about my being ill, and Mohinder who remarked to Cerelyn. Laura sees the most of me in the course of the day, and she's had that look on her face lately, that mix of sympathy, revulsion, and panic Americans get when they hear you cough. I can't blame them, I suppose—they don't have sick lists the way we did—but the first couple years I couldn't help being put off. I remember how one day, during one of my disastrous early months here, I showed up at the Altermans' house with a cold, and seeing my one sniffle, Debbie Alterman closed the glass screen door in my face. She had a "You-poor-thing-get-away-from-me" expression on through that whole brief conversation, while she explained to me in loud, simple phrases that it's impolite to bring my germs into her clean house.

I get it now. But I still feel like a medieval leper every time somebody wraps a scarf about their face or jerks away their hand and steps back and waves. I keep dreaming the aromas of millet porridge with milk, and buckwheat kasha with eggs, and cream of wheat. Babby called them "the sickie foods": the things that would make you better. The soft, warm things for hurting and feverish children. She would make porridge now, and it all would go away, but I turn my head, and the aroma isn't there, dissolved in another: exhaust, dust, or trash. And homesickness settles in for somebody's arms. Anybody's arms.

Because you should be wrapped in arms when you are unwell, even if they belong to a stranger.

Cerelyn calls the first week of November and pretends there is no reason but to invite me to Thanksgiving. Yet I can hear her listen to me cough—intent and prepared, like she is turning on an internal recorder on the other end of the line—and when she comes out with it, her resolve is a dam that finally bursts.

"Okay, enough of this. Dinah, we're all worried. Is it true you've been coughing for weeks?"

"It's no big deal, Cerelyn. I don't even have a fever, and doctor says I shouldn't be contagious."

"What's causing it?"

"He says my blood work is normal, so it's a virus. It'll go away."

This is the least opportune moment for Babby's voice to reach, as it is wont to do, from some corner of my subconscious like a stray sound from a distant rehearsal room: *It's fine, Dinush. It's just this bug I can't fight off.* Naturally, I've compared our symptoms more than once already. Couldn't help it. Nonsense. If I had what Babby had, I'd be dead by now, wouldn't I? Plus Chernobyl happened in 1986, and Babby's lymphoma surfaced only two years later. It's too late for me to get it now. I think. And I don't have a temperature, or nausea, or any bruising.

On the other hand, too many people are still getting cancer in Leningrad. I just got a letter from Cleo: Mama Ivanidis is in surgery. Pancreatic tumor.

I know Cerelyn is chewing her lips into the receiver—I hear the tension of the faint rustle coming from the phone, and I can see her face right then, screwed up into a writhing ball of cogitation. "Isn't that what they said seven months ago, a virus?"

"Kind of."

"Well, here's the deal." She is done cogitating. "I believe your doctor sucks, and I want you to see mine."

"Cerelyn!" I don't believe I've ever heard her use an indelicate word—and it's a shock that I only realize it now, or maybe that now it's surprising, because I don't think of her by any stretch as a delicate person. I wish I could exchange looks with somebody—Oni or Jamie or Gavi. Or Matthew. "Thanks, Cerelyn," I say. "But I doubt my insurance will pay for your doctor. He's in Jersey, right? Or she?"

"He. Dr. Santos. And if it doesn't, I'll pay for the visit. It'll be a consult," she says in the voice I know from rehearsal. It means the end to an argument. "And I'm coming with you."

She does not come with me, her knee not well enough that day to let her drive, but the week after Thanksgiving, I find myself in the office of yet another doctor. Dr. Juan Santos. And it's very different here.

There is no palace. We're in a small waiting room in a strip mall, squeezed between a hair salon and a fish store, whose odors seep through imaginary cracks in the walls and trace convoluted smoky figures in the air. Barabashka crinkles his nose in comic disgust. Orion swats at the passing wisps as if they were flies, popping some into oblivion. There's only one doctor here and so only two patients in the room, no sounds above the white noise of outside traffic, and I suppress my coughs and giggles.

I cannot tell his age. A shock of gray hair, hands like the roots of a pine tree, but his face is pasty, cheeks hanging below the jawline, brownish bags under the eyes. I think he is sick, too. Physician, heal thyself. Should I trust him? Or will he empathize with me better than those others, who can't conceive of what it's like?

He doesn't ask questions, just says, "Tell me what's going

on," and listens. Nods. Marks something in the chart. It's too thick for a new patient, and I realize the permission I gave on the phone for my "records" produced the tome in front of him. He already knows what's happened. I tell him again, tell him what the others couldn't have put into the chart because they didn't hear it.

"That's no fun," he says, and smiles, and I agree: It's no fun. How did he know?

"Hop up on the table," he asks, breathes on the stethoscope to make it warm, and slides it under my shirt. "That's an annoying cough, isn't it?" he says, and I agree completely: It's very annoying. He knows everything, this Dr. Santos, doesn't he?

His hands are warm and dry, his eyelids heavy. They make him look sleepy when he says, "I want to send you for a chest x-ray, and let's do it today, just to rule some things out."

I don't know what the "things" are, but I agree, of course, I agree. Let's rule them out. This Doctor, he knows everything.

The phone rings later that day. I almost don't pick up, but my hatred of the phone yields barely and briefly to suspicion: What if it's him? I'm not expecting Dr. Santos to call—doctors never have before, and it's too soon for results, isn't it? But still, who knows?

He's seen my x-ray, Doctor says, and it's "a little concerning." I will hear this word a lot from now on: "concerning." This is what doctors say to patients when they see death. They never say "death"; they say, "It's a little concerning," but I haven't caught on to that yet. I shouldn't panic, he says, but I should go see a specialist, whom he's already contacted. This is an excellent pulmonologist, and I have an appointment tomorrow at the University of Pennsylvania Hospital.

I must be in shock, because I say, "I have work tomorrow," and he says, "I really think it's important that you keep this appointment. We shouldn't delay your diagnosis." And I say, "Yes, Doctor," and hang up, then stand by the phone and think about the things he could have seen. The things he wanted to rule out. That he didn't rule out.

I call the Chadaris to tell them I won't be in, and Mohinder says, "Good luck" and "Keep us posted," and Laura says, "It's going to be fine," and smiles audibly into the phone. Laura says things like that, the things she doesn't know to be true. She will get into a car wreck a year from now, pounding her paper-thin Hyundai into a cow patty and cracking every bone in her body, including her skull.

Mohinder will struggle alone with the school for three more years, till he reconnects with Gavi—almost randomly, at a funeral. They'll become business partners, then more than that. In 2006, they will move to Massachusetts and get married, and for the rest of their unexpectedly long and happy lives, they will muse at the turn their lives will have taken, practically unthinkable to any of us on this December day in 1997.

The next afternoon is my first time at the U Penn medical tower. My first ascent from the 30th Street Station, my first scurry through University City. The pulmonologist is young, touchingly puffy in the cheeks, ruddy and curly-haired. He reminds me of Dennis Luzhin and our childhood war games between the birch grove and the playground. I never did lick those salty curls, such a proper girl I was. He bends over me with a stethoscope, and snarky Barabashka twirls his long, slobbery tongue near Dr. Dennis's temple. I shut my eyes tight to keep from swatting at him, but it makes the pain in my head sharper.

Dr. Dennis studies my x-ray. It is "a bit concerning." His

questions come in a measured barrage. When did the cough start? Have I noticed any blood? Have I lost weight? Am I having night sweats?

Is that what it's called?

"Yes, a lot. I make more laundry than a ballet class."

He wants to do a CT scan. No, better to do it here, at UPenn. That way he'll get the report right away and can see the films. No need to call; they'll schedule me right away, as I check out, and he'll let me know the results.

The checkout clerk looks twenty, with an artfully messy do of African braids and terrified round eyes. She flashes me quick glances while she argues with scheduling on the phone, and I hear "urgent" and "mass" and "find me one." She turns her face at an angle from me, as if it gave her privacy, and me, ignorance. Then she hangs up and moves her mouth into a customer-service grin. The CT is tomorrow, 7:30 a.m. Can I make it?

I remember the first time Babby took me to the Luna Park, which is what we call our traveling fairs with rides and games and ice cream. Americans know these, too, except, instead of cabbage pies, American fairs have funnel cake. I don't know how old I was, but little, and Babby put me on a carousel made up of different kinds of animals. I think I was riding a donkey. I remember watching her stand there, then watching her move backwards, faster and faster past me, and the world was moving faster, and then too fast, losing its shape, and I tried to fix my gaze on something, but it was all whizzing by and blending together into a single interminable smudge. The world outside like a fuzzy, permeable, nauseating wall—and me, inside some cosmic whirligig, sculpted to my donkey's neck, separated from life as I knew it by the speed of time.

I feel this way again now, like I'm on a carousel. It jerks

me on and off, an Einsteinian somersault in the pit of my stomach, and the clocks are always wrong. It spins, faster, too fast, and they won't tell me why. I should know by now, but I don't really want to know, so I'm waiting to find out for sure. I do the CT, and I wait, turn, turn. I keep asking myself what I want to hear, as though my wish could make a difference. There's a trickle of relief in the thought that the carousel might snap off the wheels and fly loose and crash to all hell, today, in a moment. What's the worst that can happen? If I'm jittery, it must just be the speed.

Dr. Dennis calls after six. I should not panic. The CT showed a mass in my left lung. It may be benign, but it should be biopsied urgently and an oncologist consulted. He has referred me to the U Penn Oncology Department and made me an appointment for Monday. Dr. Dennis's voice is soft and sticky, tickly as fresh ear wax. I should rest, and I shouldn't get too stressed out this weekend, he says. Wait until we know more. And bring a family member with you to see the doctor. Her name is Dr. Ming.

CHAPTER 17
1998

The windows in the infusion room are frosted at the bottom, which creates a curious winter effect: I don't know how much of the frosting is decorative and how much is real weather that blew into town yesterday on a passing wind from Canada. But it's cozy anyway. The winter has been snowless even for Philly, and the illusion is nice.

The oversized armchairs are cozy, too. There's a double blanket over my legs, and my gray mouse in the blanket's folds is busying herself with nesting and tickling my knees. Orion and Barabashka are under the windowsill, settled in for the next few hours like weary travelers. Dr. Ming's already been to check on me, but my chemo's just started; I know the shivers will come soon. The third blanket is waiting for when they do, and Simon is watching over the edge of the book he is reading to me out loud.

Simon Levi was the last oddity of the last year, the final gift my twisted fate had chucked at me in its dying throes as it wilted of guilt and bewilderment. Nine weeks ago I walked into his synagogue in a small town where I'd never planned to find myself, and I don't remember how long I stayed and how much I told him, I only remember crying harder than I had ever let myself before, sobbing, shaking the chair loose. He held me while I did, with manuscripts and instruments dancing over our heads because by then we were on the floor. And I remember that I slept.

When he offered to take me to my imaging appointments the next day, I just accepted with a single "thank you," as if we were friends. As if we were family. I had, after all, had my head pressed into his shirt for the past hour, soaked it with snot and tears, and he hadn't flinched. At U Penn the next morning they smiled at him, questioning, and I said, "He is my rabbi," and scared myself, but before I could apologize and take it back, they all nodded and smiled again like it was a normal thing. He nodded, too. Go figure, it's a normal thing: You're supposed to trust your rabbi.

But he is more than that now, I don't yet know what: It happened so fast that I'm not sure what happened exactly. He came with me to Dr. Ming's for the results; I came to Media for my first Reconstructionist Chanukah. He took me to my first chemo, and it didn't go well—the shivers and all—so he took me to my second, and then it simply became understood that Simon comes to pick me up. I don't know why I accepted without even an attempt at polite protestations. Maybe because he's never asked me if I am okay. Or because he's never wrapped a scarf around his mouth. Or because he rolls his *r*'s a little, with a thin, playful gargle in the back of his throat, so the way he talks reminds me of Leila Kahn.

"It's a pretty common Jewish speech impediment," he points out and shrugs the Odessan way, palms up. "Ancient Romans used to make their prisoners say: *On Ararat the grapes are red, Children of Israel are inbred.* To tell which ones were Jewish." He pulls in his upper lip, hiding a grin and bristling his mustache.

I know. I could listen to him talk for days, and read, forever. When I am edgy and flushed and sleepless, when the dry cough won't stop tearing at my lungs, I could just listen to him read out loud, or sing his long, dark, winding prayers, or chant in Hebrew from the Torah. Until I fall asleep.

301

Is it okay, Matty? Are you upset with me?

"Of course it's okay, silly." Matthew's voice is an evanescent timbre of a guitar chord. *"I'm not there, remember?"*

Sometimes I wonder what Simon feels for me. If he feels something beyond pity, beyond companionship. I wonder if this, whatever it is, has taken him by surprise, too, because I bet he wasn't looking for a romantic relationship. Simon is a widower. He knows what I know, except he knows more.

I asked him once why he was spending so much time with me—"Don't you have work to do instead of nursing a random sickie?"—and he said, "We don't choose who we... care about. It's no good to be alone. For anyone." The way he stumbled in the middle of that sentence, I wonder if he realized he was about to say "love" but stopped himself. I keep trying to convince myself it doesn't matter. Whatever his reasons for being here, I'll take them.

Today he brought a new novel. "It's about the biblical Dinah," he says, eyes sparkling with the mischief that I'm guessing refers to the novel's contents. *"The Red Tent.* Looks like it puts you right into that world, as if you lived it, but it's all 'power to the women.' Want to try it? I suppose we should see a Simon and a Levi in there, too." He breaks into laughter.

"I want to finish what I'm reading first, do you mind?"

"Oh, why would I?" He plunges his hand into my bag, no hesitation, pulls out the thin library paperback I had stuffed between my wallet and the pillbox, and I catch myself on the bitter pleasure of this moment. No one has gone into my bag without permission since Cleo paid the taxi driver at the Pulkovo airport and I left her standing there, holding my great-grandmother's locket.

You think you know how alone you are. You clench your teeth and allow yourself to be desperate and pitiable five minutes a day and accept the finality of it, and then somebody sticks a hand into your bag and you remember what you're missing. And you realize that you know, but you don't: You haven't dared admit it to yourself. You've avoided thinking about it the way you've avoided thinking about the whisper worm, and Lesha's knuckles, and a stack of books on a bedsheet, and Zev Alterman's blow-up mattress. It's just too much. Your mind protects itself, for those are the thoughts that drive people into darkness, into madness. Off the ledge.

"*Fire Next Time* by James Baldwin?" Simon's eyebrows inch up while he leafs through the pages as though airing them out. "Light reading, huh?"

"Do you know it?"

He answers slowly, "I do," then regards me anew. A thundering train of thought is running behind his eyes, and I wish I could tell where it was going. "This is what you've been reading?"

"You don't appreciate James Baldwin?"

"Ha!" Simon slaps the book against the palm of his hand. "You can't *not* appreciate this literature. It's iconic, a must-read for any American—racism, civil rights, of course, the Black American experience. It's just...pretty dark, don't you think? Just such a heavy topic for you right now. The doctor said you should be as stress-free as possible during chemo, remember?"

"Well, I don't have enough years left to spend them reading Dr. Seuss." *If he says I shouldn't be thinking such thoughts and I should be optimistic, that's it. Me and my purse again, till the grave.*

"All right," he drawls and slides his gaze off me to the book, but his voice is hoarse. "*Fire Next Time.*"

"There's a bookmark," I say. "It's the passage where he

says how after generations of abuse and disaster, people sort of get used to the bitterness of life, and they put down their hatred like it's a burden that's too heavy to carry. They just choose to, you know? So they can preserve their humanity. I'm...kind of amazed by that, but I get it, too."

"Yes..." Simon finds the bookmark and clears his throat.

"Start where he talks about the children? Something about them walking through mobs so they can go to school."

"Yes..." Simon raises his face, as though taken over by a puzzle. He looks toward some uncharted point, letting the page slip out of his fingers, then focuses on me. "Dinah. Do you like America?"

"Oh, man, not you, too!" I know why he is asking. He is trying to get at the question birthed by Baldwin's exquisitely painful reminder of his America's scarred face. But it catches me unawares and showers me in seven years of strangers' voices, syrupy and well-wishing and nice: all the random friends of random acquaintances, all the stuffed-up Children of Exile, every Southern New Jersey Ballet sponsor at every premiere after-party. Such a simple question. Much too simple. So goddamn stupid a question for something so viciously complicated. "Not you, too, Simon." And I groan.

"You hear it a lot, huh?"

"Enough to have a couple stock answers worked out."

He scratches at his beard with both hands. I've learned that it's a gesture of decision-making. Or mustering up courage. When other people take a deep breath, Simon scratches his cheeks. It's a little comical and completely his, and every time after he does it, I want to reach over and smooth out the disturbed prickly whiskers. But I don't.

"Let's hear it," he says. "Stock answer number one."

"No." I feel the need to shake something off, or maybe the shivers are starting. The gray mouse pokes her head above the blanket folds and disappears, scurries back and forth between my knees. *Breathe.* "For you," I say, "I'll try a real one. One of many real ones, if you'd like."

"I really would."

"It's...newish, though. And it's long. I'm not sure I can say it right."

"I can take it." He's all wide eyes and near me, his hand on the arm of my chair, having wandered over and stayed, and I am persuaded he can take it. It awes me that he wants to.

"Okay. I don't know if I like America. Obviously." I check Simon's reaction, but there's none, and I go on. "I adore something one minute, like this hospital, and the next minute I'll ask an American teenager about history, and I want to grab America by the neck and shake it into a vaguely Russian shape, but that's not an important thing to know. That's just a thing of life, and I suspect it's how everybody feels, Americans born here, too. What I think you're asking is if I love America."

He doesn't move, only his eyebrows twitch in a delicate rhythm, eyes still wide.

I say, "I love America. I know I love it because I'm proud of it, and I'm ashamed of it. These feelings, they come and go, and there are aspects to them, you know, but what I think about pretty often is—I love America for taking me in and giving me a home. And I hate America for making me a white person."

Now Simon stirs. "What does that mean?" I'm making him uncomfortable.

"Do you think I'm white?"

"Uhh...um..." He's dumbstruck and so squirmy, it's itching my soul. I think it's because he doesn't get what I want from him, and after four agonizing seconds, I let him off the hook.

"I didn't grow up 'white,' Simon." The pause is for me to gather words, and for him. To help it sink in. "I grew up Jewish among Russians, a minority, right? I lived trying to avoid militiamen and authorities, and every day I set out from my home expecting to be looked up and down by some dirty blond and called a kike and pushed around and told how 'us people' had sold the motherland. And I always expected to be denied something with this sticky smirk that said, 'I bet you know why you ain't gettin' it, you Zionist pig.'"

Simon's hand is still in the demilitarized zone on my armrest. He's listening.

"I didn't really think about it much," I say, "in any big-picture kind of way until I got to the U.S. My Babby did..." Her voice floats up in her usual spot in my mind: *All through human history, blood's been spilled on the altar of homogeneity...* "She tried to explain it to me, but, you know, I was too young. It's funny how reading an African-American writer from the '60s can snap your picture into place."

I'm beginning to get the chills. It's a creeping sense of illness, from skin to bone, a depth of cold that no thickness of blankets can keep away. But when I ball up instinctively in my chair, Simon covers me with the third blanket and tucks it in, and the fuzzy mass feels reassuring around me. Feels like love.

He pulls his chair closer to mine before sitting down again and leans on my armrest with his elbows. "And here?" he asks.

The "here" should be easier to explain, yet it is harder. It's where I'm really lost. In the Union, racial tensions were complicated, too: this proclaimed ideology of equality and fraternity that had been rotted out by centuries of imperialism and plain old bigotry, by politics and economics and culture gaps—but at least I understood it. And here I'm just starting to parse it all, but people look at me and see a "white person." These things I didn't know about—"white privilege," "white guilt"—they're things I do not feel, I've no reason to feel.

I'm shaking now, but I can't tell if it's the chemo or the memory of the NPSC receptionist curving an eyebrow at me, evaluating the hue of my skin: Who doesn't *want* to be white?

"You don't have to keep talking," Simon says. "Why don't you sleep awhile?" But I can't stop now—I'm spiraling down, and I have to explain. To Simon. To someone. *Does my voice sound weird?*

"Here, with this one word, 'white,' I am somebody's enemy. Somebody's oppressor. But I'm not anybody's sister. You know what I'm saying? Because here. The people who band together. For their whiteness. Will lynch you and me. Right next to the people. With brown skin. And whatever. Green polka dot skin." *Why can't I breathe?* My hands are numb, up my arms, crawling with a hundred gray mice, what an odd sensation. Simon's face is blotting out the light. He looks worried.

"Stop talking," he whispers. "I've called the nurse."

My chemo took longer than usual after they'd slowed down the drip, plus they kept me an extra hour for observation, so it's late afternoon by the time we get to the car, parked in the garage across from the Penn Tower. I'm not shaking anymore, just drained, noodle-limbed, and a slimy ball of nausea is rolling under my heart when I move. I'm not complaining. It's still a trifling thing. It'll be worse tomorrow.

Simon buckles me in, drapes a blanket over the belt, and fits a water bottle snug into my fingers and a banana in my lap. I keep wanting to tell him what it means—the banana, his hand on my armrest, and that I can close my eyes and ride and not ask for anything—but there isn't a name for this, or I can't find one. "Thank you" is flat and repetitive, not quite right. It's for the nurses and Dr. Ming. This moment is nameless, like God. Maybe all holy things are nameless.

I'm searching my brain and miss the moment: He's in the driver's seat, fussing.

"Dinah?" He is touching my cheek with the back of his hand. It's cold, or I am flushed.

"Mmm."

"You okay to go?"

"Mm-hmm."

I want to say beautiful words to him, but Simon has turned on the heat, and it's beginning to fill my feet, seep up my legs. The car is rocking softly over the bumps, through the stop-and-go traffic of Philly rush hour, and the honking and the revving of engines wash over me. My lids are cast iron, my mind is slow chaos, a churning, black river of molten thought, and I'm finally warm, and we're rocking along, we're rocking along.

"Dinah? We're home."

Simon's fingers on mine now feel warm. I open my eyes, but around us are not the red-brick boxes of Chapel Court Apartments.

"This is my place." He squeezes my hand. "You should not be alone tonight. Is it all right? I didn't want to wake you."

Simon's street is pleasant and homey. American-dream-sized houses in gingerbread shapes line up a short hill. Unobtrusive colors. Typical Media. It's grayish these days, in the bare winter months, but not cold: There are warm lights in the windows and curly-branched leafless bushes that reach over the fences, fluffy even now, waiting for the spring. I've never been here before. Simon's house is exactly as I've envisioned it: smallish but tall, with a single window under a pointed roof—there must be an attic. Deep maroon. Shutters that used to be golden, I'd wager, are beige now, weathered to a tiny web of cracks.

"It's all right," I say, "thank you." Then it hits me: "Is Mimi home?"

He smiles. "She couldn't possibly mind." And scratches his cheeks.

Mimi is fifteen. Esther Miriam Levi. Jews are supposed to name their children after dead relatives, and they did—"dutifully," Simon said with a simper when he first mentioned her to me. Esther had been his grandmother's name. But his wife had dreamed of having a daughter and calling her Mirele. Her favorite story since childhood had been of an old Yiddish lullaby, a *Shoah* song from the Vilna Ghetto, written by a twelve-year-old boy named Alek and performed for the first time by a girl named Mirele in the days when music had to hide in the shadows.

Of course, it turned out that Esther Miriam hated the nickname: Her school friends didn't get it and called her "Merely Levi." She threatened to drop her middle name entirely, and as a compromise, the family settled on "Mimi." She is in high school now, vacillating between student theatre, the Green Club, and Model UN. "All over the place," Simon said with a shrug, trying to contain a proud grin.

He told me the story on our second trip to U Penn, after Dr. Ming announced my scan results. We walked out of her office that day and went to the cafeteria, sat by the window over Styrofoam cups of tea while the words "metastatic," "inoperable," and "brain involvement" swam in my head, and we talked in spurts about death. I told him about Matthew and Babby and my parents and Lesha and Leila Kahn, and he told me about his wife. From diagnosis to grave, her breast cancer had taken seven years and most of Mimi's childhood. I thought then that he should be running, climbing, crawling away from me, and I was staggered that he did not.

I will eventually say just that to him, and he will say, "Mimi is stronger than you think."

"And you?"

"I like that verse from Isaiah, about the light." He'll smile and quote by heart: "And the light of the sun will be sevenfold, as the light of seven days, in the day that the Lord binds up the bruise of His people and heals the wound of his stroke."

"What does that mean?"

"It means every night ends in sunrise, every exile in homecoming, and the longer the night, the brighter the morning, just you wait." A deep, splendid glow will shine through his habitual serenity and emanate power—my first time seeing him like that. Simon the preacher. Simon the prophet. "We live in the valley of the shadow of death, but the light at the end of the valley... It's blinding. Disperses all shadows." He'll look down at our interlocked fingers. "Everything is finite. But we can't have love if we don't allow loss. And, you know, I keep thinking: Seven lamps of the menorah are the light of seven days, with Sabbath always burning. So...we can bear any pain as long as we know who we are. As long as we have each other. Pain is finite, too."

He will leave me speechless with this. I'll never ask again.

Simon helps me out of the car and into the living room,

which clearly doesn't see many guests: The coffee table is heaping with papers and books, bookcases crowd the walls, and he has to clear a couple of tomes from the end of the sofa before I can lie down on it. It's soft, a bit lumpy, and smells like dust. The only furniture free of reading material is the TV stand with a few videotapes underneath. Simon turns on a floor lamp and covers me with a blanket, calling out, half turned to the stairs, "Mimi, you home?"

Something stirs overhead. I hear the creaking of an old house. Mimi galumphs down from the second floor and, seeing me, freezes at the bottom of the stairs. She has disheveled gossamer hair around a delicate, birdlike face exaggerated by glasses, and she is all petite and drowning in bulky fleece pajamas, midnight blue with elves and reindeer on them. Exactly as I've envisioned her, just like the house.

"Dad?" she says.

I want to hear how Simon explains me, but sleep is like that fleece, like this bottomless sofa, like warm sand. It's wrapping me, pulling me down, and I fall in.

In my dream, Heaven looks remarkably like an assisted living cafeteria: a light-flooded, expansive hall; French doors to the ceiling; wobbly tables topped with grainy off-white laminate, the kind that makes crumbs disappear. Tiny vases with obtrusively plastic lilies of the valley decorate the tabletops. A gathering crowd of crisply ironed octogenarians is sorting itself around the tables. They're holding glasses of tomato juice and Fresca cans and chirping peacefully among themselves, all facing the same direction: behind me. It must be movie night, except it's too light for a movie. It feels like morning.

"This isn't Heaven, stupid," says Matthew.

He is sitting on my left at our square four-top, Babby

on my right, and across from me there's a man with a full, bushy beard, wearing something shapeless and snow-white that stirs in a recess of my mind the word "vestment."

I ask, "Are you Jesus?"

Matthew laughs. The man leans on the back of his chair and makes a sour face.

"Seriously?" he says.

He's too old to be Jesus, and Jesus probably wouldn't come to greet me anyway. What if it's Elijah, and I offended him? I feel gauche.

Matthew says, "This place is kind of a holding pattern. An in-between. A brief stopover. And that's my friend Steve. He's from Tulsa."

Steve from Tulsa aside, this doesn't make sense. I look at Babby. "Then, what are *you* doing here? It's been years since you died."

"Waiting for you, of course. Are you all right, kitten?" She tightens the knot of her headscarf. It's green, with galloping horses on it.

I look at Matthew. He nods. He is dressed in camouflage, and I can smell grease and sweat off him, and some sort of antiseptic. His blood type is sewn into the sleeve of his uniform: IV+. For a second I wonder if there are open wounds under that fabric, and I badly want to touch him, but then everyone stirs and quiets. I hear a mechanical whirring from behind me, and Steve from Tulsa drags his chair to the left so he can see around me and says, "Shut up, y'all. It's starting."

I twist around as a gigantic screen is descending from the ceiling, and the opening credits of some show are already playing on it, their lower edge still on the wall, faint and distorted. The theme song is slowly filling the hall. It's rather ineffable, syncopated, sad and playful at once; I'd even call it sarcastic if I dared apply such a word to music.

"What's that?" I ask no one in particular, with my back to the table.

Matthew answers. "Our favorite sitcom. It's on every day before lunch."

"A sitcom? In Heaven?" I peek back at him.

"I told you, this isn't Heaven."

"Fine." It's breathtakingly good to see him, to banter about a sitcom, to throw off casually, hiding the tension, "What's it about?"

"You," he says, and squints the way he used to when he felt sorry for me.

"What does that mean?"

Babby finally moves, puts her hand on my forearm. It's brownish and splotchy, all knots and veins, worse, I think, than it was at the end, in the hospital. "Not just you, dear," she says. "But you've had three starring episodes and two cameos already."

"What the hell are you talking about? I don't understand!" I am trying to jump up from the chair but can't, and I don't know why, and now I'm frustrated and getting scared, too.

"Stop swearing. Calm down and watch," Babby says.

On the screen, some guy steps out of a jewelry store in what looks like an American strip mall. He holds up a box with an engagement ring he's clearly just bought, opens it, gazes lovingly at it, closes it and shoves it down his breast pocket, then straddles a ten-speed and weaves into traffic. The music swells ominously.

"What's this thing called?" I ask.

"*They Plan, God Laughs*," declares Steve from Tulsa and whines, "Can you two please quit talking? It's about to happen!"

313

"Why don't you go sit somewhere else, man?" Matthew offers.

I can see where this is going and turn away from the bi- cyclist, who is steering with one hand while trying to open his ring box with the other. "All right. This is ridiculous. You can't tell me Heaven or Purgatory or the celestial way station, or whatever the crap this is supposed to be, looks like...well, looks like this! Like a freaking nursing home activities hour!"

"Hey, dandelion. It's *your* dream." Matthew shrugs.

"That sounds like a line I've heard in some bad movie," I parry. "Or several."

"I didn't say you were original."

The music shifts to a waltz in the airy minor, and I glance over my shoulder. The bicyclist is lying, as expected, on the pavement in a pool of blood, surrounded by cars and a growing mob of onlookers. At that moment I realize that I don't know what language I've been speaking all this time, Russian or English. *This is insane. I really am dreaming. But it feels so real...*

"This isn't real, is it?" I plead and drop my face on the grainy table surface. It's dark here and reeks of plastic. "It's a dream, right?"

"Does it have to be one or the other?"

"Wait." I sit up straight. "If I'm dreaming, I'm not dead."

"You're not dead yet, kitten," Babby says and taps my arm with her skeletal fingers.

Matthew echoes: "You're not dead."

We sit in silence for a minute, then I muster up the courage to ask: "Does this mean, when I am dead... You'll be here waiting for me?"

"Of course we'll be here, Dinush," Babby says, and Matthew echoes:

"We will be here."

And we sit in silence again.

"Is this really all there is?" I say. "God or whoever couldn't come up with a better idea than this place?"

Matthew laughs and snorts, throws his head back; Babby laughs into the end of her scarf, and so does Steve from Tulsa, who never did go sit somewhere else. He is cackling and hitting the edge of the table with the palms of his hands, making loud, shallow thuds.

"Of course it's not!" Matthew gathers himself and fist-bumps Steve on the shoulder, and Steve stops cackling and hitting and makes another face. "It's not all there is, dandelion," Matthew says. "It's just the cafeteria."

"So..." My eyes are pulled irresistibly to the French doors, to the light that streams through them, taking up three of the four walls. "So," I say, "what's beyond the windows?"

"Do you want to see?" Matthew asks.

CHAPTER 18
1999

Today's service was good. It's the last day of Passover, so we recited the *yizkor*, the memorial for the dead. It isn't done often, but every time we do, something churns inside me, something wakes.

After a year attending Beth Tikvah, I am still new, I still barely read Hebrew (phonetically and only at half the speed required to follow along), and I'm grateful that the rest of the service is in English. I like the prayers. They aren't so much about God as they are about the blessing that is the world, and how we are connected to it, and to each other. I like Simon's mini-sermons: shorter than Rabbi Frum's, but there's always food for thought. And I like—I love—when he pulls out his guitar, and the prayer pours and flows and flies over and covers us all with an ancient, lacy throw, sad because of how much it knows. To me, that's what really makes the service.

I felt like an impostor at first, but Simon never seemed to mind my marginal Judaism. I came right out and told him: "I'm not sure I believe in God," and he said, "I have a feeling that if you stop telling yourself that, you'll find that you do."

This was months ago, and I still don't know if I believe in God, but I am finding that maybe I don't care if I do, or at least I don't care what I call the thing I believe in. They call it "Lord" here, or more often in Hebrew: *Adonai*. Or *HaShem*, which means "the Name." But when they say that, they mean something that's...more. Something I've meant, too, since the day I made my first wish upon my first dandelion but could never define.

At B'nei Hagola I had a sense they were talking about some bearded potentate on a divan who'd fashioned the world out of clay and now played with it as with a toy, that he went through our prayers the way we do through mail: Open this one, trash the others with spam; say yes, say no. Here, it's different. Last September I was talking to Akiva Smith, one of the temple elders who volunteered to prepare me for my first High Holidays. He was telling me about the days between Rosh ha-Shanah and Yom Kippur, when we reconcile ourselves with all the human beings: those we've offended and those who've offended us in the previous year. You have to do that before you can approach God for forgiveness. I threw out the notion that the Reconstructionist movement was less about God and more about community, and he sort of smirked.

I've been mulling over this smirk, and I think I've figured it out: In this Judaism I've stumbled into, you can't separate the two. For them, God is *in* the community. God animates the community. God is tradition, history, environment, myth, social advocacy. The "bigger picture." Because God does not have a face and cannot be imagined as a guy with a beard (or even with a name), they've infused God into the world, into the nation itself and beyond it, all these tangible things. This way, the worship they do for *HaShem* can be done with their hands, healing the world and each other. They call it *Tikkun Olam*.

I like that. A lot. They still have a stone box, like everybody else, but they're not putting God in a box.

After the service, people are milling around the social hall before breaking into their groups, some for Torah study, some for Hebrew. There's a children's group and some sort of women's caucus I've managed to avoid so far. We're waiting for Simon, who is taking off his prayer shawl, so the hall is crowded and filled with din, hovering plastic cups, and Mrs. Kuntz's rugelach on half-napkins.

From the end of the snack table, a woman's voice bores into my brain: "...and after two thousand years we are still persecuted for our religion! It's almost the twenty-first century, everyone is talking interfaith dialogue, but what's really changed?"

I approach her huddle of four, and they part, making room for me. There's Akiva Smith, the Steins, and this woman, whom I don't know, with a thick layer of blood-red lipstick and an oversized Magen Dovid on a gold chain.

"Well, to be fair, some things have changed," counters Lena Stein a bit tentatively. "The Catholics haven't been trying to convert the Jews since the sixties. Officially, I mean."

"It also depends on how large a historical scale you look at," her husband inserts.

They both sound almost timid. Are they afraid of her?

"Oh, please." The woman waves them away with both hands. "If they're so interfaith, why don't they put a Jewish teacher in every Christian school to explain to their children that their Christ was an observant Jew, just like all of today's Jews and not at all like any of today's Christians?"

This is more than I can handle. I clear my throat. They all turn to me, and she screeches to a halt.

"Not all of today's Jews," I say. My finger is twitching. I don't normally do this.

"I'm sorry?" she says.

"Not all Jews are observant. Lots are secular. A billion people in the world are atheist. An ethnic distinction for the Jews is just as valid as religious."

"Um, yes, but—"

"Nearly all of us Soviet Jews were secular," I keep pressing. I've got to get this out, or I'll run out of steam. "Frankly, if I weren't told I was a Jew all the time by people who didn't like Jews, I wouldn't have known it—and yet not a single antisemite had any doubts as to my Jewishness."

I'm gearing up for an argument, I'm ready, but they're all looking behind me, and I feel Simon's hand on my shoulder. How much has he heard?

"Sounds like I missed quite a discussion," he purrs. This is Simon the diplomat. He's handling us. "Maybe we'll pick it up again? Next week? Right now Akiva has to lead the Torah study, and, Beebs, your caucus is assembling." His smile and the weight of his hand are steadying. We stand like this, side by side, while the Jews disperse from the social hall.

"Do you agree with her?" I ask.

The low sun is glaring through the windows. Shabbat is ending. We've just finished dinner and brought our drinks to the living room, where Mimi immediately rolled herself into a ball in the armchair and fell asleep. Simon and I are sitting on the opposite ends of the sofa in our favorite manner, with our legs stretched toward each other, feet at each other's hips. He has his coffee, and I have my detestable protein shake, designed to nourish people like me, who have trouble eating. The problem is, I have trouble drinking it, too, so Simon blends a banana into it for me. I can stomach almost anything that tastes like banana.

The question I've brought up is out of the blue (the huddle in the social hall was hours ago), so I'm expecting his question:

"Agree with whom, limpkin?"

"What's her name? Screechy Beebs from Beth Tikvah, with the lipstick."

"Bella O'Grady?" His eyebrows climb.

"O'Grady? Really? Did she marry an Irishman?"

You're being nasty. Stop it. I guess I didn't realize how much she got under my skin.

"She's a convert," Simon says. "And she's new. Go easy."

"No zealot like a convert, huh? Fine, I'm sorry. But do you agree with her?"

He blows into his mug, and I get a sense he's playing for time. "She has a point," he says.

How can he say that? After living with me for a year?

"How can you say that? What, atheist Jews aren't Jews? Three million Soviet Jews were run out of the country just to clear the air?"

"No," he says. He speaks slowly, deliberately. "But it's not that simple."

"Why don't you explain it to me?"

"I don't want to offend you."

"You can't do worse than vampire lips out there." *Damn. Stop it.*

"Why does this give me little assurance?" He twinkles, all aglow, trying to make peace, my peacemaker, but I'm not going for it, so he blows into his coffee again, hiding his face. "Okay, if you insist. You say you only identified as Jewish because you were oppressed as Jewish. That was your only connection to Judaism. Like you were a victim of a misunderstanding: You wouldn't be Jewish but for the blows. Am I right?"

"Pretty much. At least sometimes. I mean, what was really the difference between me and my Russian friend Lisa except for the shape of my nose and the sound of my name? They saw in me something I wasn't."

"And what I'm saying is that they saw in you something you were—you are—even if you didn't see it in yourself. Which doesn't excuse their prejudice, but it explains it. And if you understood your own Jewishness as a child, it would have given you a better context for the anti-Semitism you had to endure."

We're both cradling our mugs in our laps, neither of us drinking, staring each other down. He is actually trying to expound for me. He really agrees with her, doesn't he?

"I'm not sure I know what you mean," I tell him sincerely.

He swings his legs off and sits up, puts his mug on the coffee table. It seems we've shifted into something serious, personal. Onerous. Too much for our leisurely pose. I do the same and sit next to him.

"For two thousand years, Jewish parents have passed on their tradition to their children," he says. He doesn't look at me while he speaks but off somewhere into space, and for a second, I recall Babby doing that on the rare occasions she talked about Uncle Samuel, or the war, or the Pale. "For two thousand years, the Jews have preserved their language, their prayers, their rituals, their laws of food and attire, their myths and history and the awareness of what makes them Jewish. And they passed these things on to their children— under threat of death, during the times of mass killings, and blood libel, and exile and ghettos and pogroms and inquisitions. During *Shoah*. No matter how frightening, no matter how difficult, they passed their Judaism to their children."

"And Soviet Jews didn't. You're saying it's our own fault that we didn't know why we're getting beat up."

He sighs and finally fixes his eyes on me. "I'm saying you should have known better. As for whose fault it is, I cannot judge. Who am I to judge a mother protecting her child, caught between the state and the mob? I'm just saying, you weren't in every way like your Russian friend because you are not Russian. To her, 'Russian' came with more than a face and a name but with a whole culture, didn't it? Language and literature and history—and yes, religion, persecuted or not. And to you, 'Jewish' didn't, and it is wrong that you couldn't feel it, couldn't conceive of it. Your birthright comes with a terrible burden and an awesome responsibility and a shining honor, but all you were left with was the burden."

I ponder. I wonder if he doesn't have a point. Which means *she* has a point, the revolting woman with harlot lips and a voice that can drill holes in concrete. I am not ready to say yes. There's something wrong with his argument. Because we weren't different, Lisa and Cleo and Matthew and I, not in any way that should've mattered. And our culture wasn't just Russian, it was Soviet. And yet...what was the force that drove me to look for more, again and again, for something, not God, maybe, not even Judaism—for Leila Kahn, for answers, for Simon and his song and his Congregation Beth Tikvah? It means "the house of hope." The force that pushed me to step inside it in the bad December of '97.

"What's the responsibility?" I ask.

"Our responsibility?" He grins, wider this time. "You know. *Tikkun Olam* and Judaism. Repairing the world and staying true to ourselves."

I open my eyes and find the evening deep and velvet. The room is fuzzy-gray beyond the floor lamp's circle of light. A tiny, sharp spark is playing on the frame of the picture where Matthew holds me to his cheek in the Square of the Arts. When I moved into this house, I put the vase with my poplar branches and my little American flag from the citizenship ceremony on top of the lowest bookcase, where I could see them from the sofa, and leaned the picture against the vase. A week later I found it framed in simple, tasteful gray. Simon. I wink covertly at past Matthew and past me and concentrate on present company.

I am covered by my favorite fluffy blanket, eggshell with pink and red squares; dishes are clanking in the kitchen with distant assurance; Mimi is perched on her armchair, hugging her knees and, apparently, watching me sleep. For thirty seconds or so we contemplate each other's next move, then she says: "Dad put the wrong blanket on you. I changed it."

"Thanks," I say.

"Are you nauseous?" She makes a perfunctory move toward my throw-up basin.

"I'm okay."

She's being markedly nicer than usual. Curious.

"You know you don't feel like my mom, even 'step.'" There's no hostility in her tone. I think this may be a diplomatic meeting.

"I'm not presuming to be, kid," I say.

We study each other for a while. My main task is not to speak first.

"Are you going to die?" she asks.

This is not a diplomatic meeting. I sit up and pull the blanket around my shoulders. "They're working on it. That's what chemo and radiation are for."

"But you know, don't you? My mom knew."

I cannot discern details in the half-light, only a blob of her hands clutching her knees and black saucers of the eyes on a pale, triangular face. When Simon brought me into his house, he brought me into hers. He made the decision for her, to deal with me, a cancer patient who was probably dying—a second dying woman in her life. And I let him. I was

323

so ill and so alone, so desperately frightened that I closed my eyes and held my nose and let him. If indeed we face a reckoning on the other side, I fear one for nothing but this child.

"You know, don't you?" she says.

I wasn't planning to know this yet, but she's picking my time for me, and I have to be more honest with her than I've been with myself.

"Yeah," I say. "I'm sorry. But not yet."

She slips off the chair, soundless and catlike, comes over to the sofa, climbs on nearby but not quite next to me, and sits cross-legged, sideways. I do the same so I can face her, leaning my back on the armrest.

She says, "What's the most important thing I should do?"

"About what?"

"Like, in life?"

Is this a test?

"I don't know, Mims. Dying young doesn't make you good at life."

I regret this as soon as I say it—her mother died young—but she doesn't seem to care or hear it, picks at my blanket for a bit, then takes a noisy breath. "Dad says you have the wisdom of Israel."

"Does he now?"

I don't think she is joking.

"He says your life is the crucible of two millennia of Jewish history." She looks at me. "Actually, I don't really get it."

"You will if you look up 'crucible,'" I say, and we both giggle. Simon forever sends her to the bottom shelf of the corner bookcase, where the reference books are, to look things up, sometimes to the library, and once I heard him lecture her on the dangers of a lazy mind. It was rather comical. "When did he say that?" I ask.

"When I asked him why he married you."

I swallow. It's only been a few minutes since I woke up, yet we've both said enough to put me in a soft mini-shock. Mimi is waiting, glancing up and down.

"The most important thing is, you should find the one most important thing for you and then do it," I say. "No matter what."

"No matter *what?*" she asks. The lines on her forehead are doing a dance. A plicate leaf. Sometimes she looks so like her father, I barely keep myself from hugging her.

"You know. No matter the money or what your dad wants for you, or what society approves of, or if your girlfriend's cool with it. Like, if you have to eat your arm to do it, eat your arm."

"Ewww!" She throws the edge of the blanket in my face.

"I know, that's what I'm saying! Imagine it could demand something incredibly painful or long and difficult or disgusting, or losing everything else that you love. So it has to be worth it. The one thing that makes your presence on this planet bearable and justifiable."

She is thinking. I'm thinking watching her. I'm thinking I just gave her dangerously bad advice. But I don't have any better.

"Are you scared?" she asks, and bites her lip.

"I wasn't at first." I'm going for broke. "But now, I am a little."

"How come?"

"I guess I have something to lose."

I'm almost interested, in a kind of clinical way, what other impossible questions she's going to come up with.

"You know," she says. "You can be like a big sister."

"I can do that," I agree.

"Just don't die, though."

"Sorry, kid."

But she isn't joking.

"Seriously," she says, and touches my blanket with her fingertips. "I don't think Dad can get through it a second time."

I touch the blanket, too, and I say, "I'll try."

CHAPTER 19
2001

On the cusp of the Common Era, all hell was breaking loose in Jerusalem, one great revolt after another, until the city stood in ruins, nothing but a retaining wall left of the Temple, like a dry bone clinging to the earth. And again— exile, which would last two millennia this time. Only two kinds of Jews had remained by then: the Synagogue of the Nazarene, who called themselves Christians, and the rabbis with their flocks. The Christians, drunk on the hope for the End of Days, set out into the winds to convert and cajole, to embrace the uncircumcised. The rabbis refused. They would not cease being Jews to survive. Since the time of Babylon they'd been prepared for exile: They had the Torah; they had Shabbat. So they took their flocks and spread out around the globe, settled and assimilated, searched for safe havens. Still, they were Jews, most often Jews among Christians, and one day a safe haven always turned unsafe. When pogroms came, forced conversions or inquisitions, they grabbed their children and Torah scrolls and ran for their lives as their homes burned behind them. And they found another safe haven and loved it, and prayed and taught their children, because education is the only treasure that can never be taken away. And once a year, on Passover, they turned to each other and said, "Next year in Jerusalem."

Simon and I, we both like to look things up. When I was diagnosed forty months ago, median survival for patients like me was thirty-three weeks. I looked it up. I guess that makes me an outlier. A distant one, like a metastasis.

The chemo made me sicker than I'd ever been, so exhausted that every breath was a labor, but it gave me time. Of course, I lost my hair. They tell you this up front. I couldn't imagine myself in a wig, so Simon went out and bought me an assortment of headscarves—a cornucopia, really, a choice of at least three for every day, and I entertained myself for weeks learning to tie them, inventing new ways and new knots, getting used to this new head in the mirror. I believe, in the end, I like it better than the old one.

They blasted my brain tumor with radiation, and the first session was the third most frightening event of my life. Pinned to the table by a plastic mask, I could swear I felt the radiation boiling my brain. It was the reptilian terror of a trapped animal. I tell you: I hate that mask. I suspect that people hate people that way, and that's why people kill. Not me. I might be too tired to hate people, even Barbos and Kot. I haven't forgiven them, but I've left them behind—yet if I ever get my hands on that mask, I'll shred it.

Still, treatments work until they don't. Once a year or so, Dr. Ming can't hide an expression reading my test results. "These are a little concerning," she says. I'm on my third therapy now, and I'm grateful. These last three years, full of barfing and leaking and choking, have been the happiest I've ever had. I mean it: happier even than my life with Matthew. I was amoeba-happy then, too naïve to appreciate what I had. I'd counted one loss by then and did not remember it. I was fourteen. I was seventeen. What did I know?

Simon is not like Matthew, and that's good. I am different, too, in a different world. Matthew and I were pin-feathered chicklets itching to fly into the sun, the brighter future, and we trusted the world to get us there. I'm a dying bird now, and I trust no one but this sad man, and maybe this sad God I'm only beginning to understand: Timelessness manifest in history, in Mrs. Kuntz's rugelach, and in my Mimi.

To be fair, U Penn is not giving up on me yet. Last summer they enrolled me in a clinical trial. I qualified by being a woman and a never-smoker who'd failed two previous chemotherapies, plus my cancer has a particular gene mutation. I asked how many of us like that they could find in Philadelphia, and they told me they would have preferred I were Asian, too. There's no perfection in the world.

It's April, the new drug is working for now, but I know what's next: It works until it doesn't, and there is nothing after this. This is my last boat.

I remember the day I met Simon, what a mess I was. I'd just gotten the news I could be dying, and I thought I should be in panic, but I wasn't feeling it, or I couldn't tell what I was feeling, and it made me horrified that my life was not worth grieving over. Remember? It all sounds kind of funny now, after fighting for my life for forty months.

It'd be nice to stay awhile.

Saturday night movies had been a Levi family tradition since before I stepped on American soil, before Mimi was born even, so I tread carefully when it comes to expressing desires or changing any long-standing rituals. Mimi remembers going to Blockbuster with her mother to pick out the tapes; it's one of her dearest memories, and now she and Simon have their particular way of bickering over the selections. I tend to recede into the sofa while they do. It's comfy here, and I like to hear them banter. And I'm tired. But tonight, she turns to me.

"Let's watch something of yours. It's your birthday."

"It's July, Mims. My birthday's still in April, isn't it?"

"It's the twelfth. We're celebrating them every month now, didn't I tell you?"

She's beaming, I laugh, but Simon doesn't find this at all amusing.

"Cut it out, Mimi. You're making Dinah feel like she's dying."

I *am* dying. I've been going downhill for weeks; he just hasn't said it out loud yet.

"Come on, Simon," I whine. "I want to have a birthday."

"Yeah, Dad. Will you begrudge your sick wife a birthday?" She snuggles up to me, and we make a double-pathetic double-face at him from the sofa.

He throws up his hands. "What are we watching?"

"What about *Electronic*?"

"It's one of your Russian ones, isn't it?"

"You'll love it, I promise."

Electronic is one of my favorite childhood movies, which I bought from the *Chitatel* Russian bookstore next to Bubbe's Market. I've been doing this for years, reassembling my lost library and, while at it, creating a video library, a nostalgic shelf of old Soviet films, rather pitiful though it still may be. This one's a '70s musical for children about an android who runs away from his scientist creator because he wants to be a real boy. Of course, out in the world, our modern-day Pinocchio meets other children, risks his life with them to save the city from inevitably foreign villains, and realizes what makes a person real: courage, compassion, and friendship, not flesh and bone. Obviously, the movie is in Russian. I do some interpreting along the way, but once we establish the premise, Simon and Mimi don't need much explanation between the singing, the dancing, and the requisite adorable dog, without which no Soviet child could be expected to learn about loyalty.

I'm a little worried that the story is too simplistic and the production value is too low for my Hollywood-nurtured family, but Mimi sniggers and purrs in all the right places and even gasps a couple of times. Simon *humphs* on occasion, then sucks in his upper lip, bristling his mustache the way he does when he's hiding a grin.

It's all going pretty well, I think, until we get to the scene in which Electronic, morose and alone in the city, wanders into a toy store. Naturally having an affinity for all things mechanical, he makes himself useful and begins to fix all the broken toys. He even fixes the ones that weren't broken, so a disparate cohort of previously lifeless monkeys, robots, and dolls are belting out harmonies, turning cartwheels, and banging on a variety of drumlike objects. Watching them, children are enthralled, adults are incredulous: idyllic happy-happy. In the middle of this paradisiacal bliss, Simon picks up the remote, pauses the movie, and turns to me. His face reflects a puzzle being worked over on the inside.

"You...had toy stores?" he asks.

I look at Mimi. From under my arm, she is gazing up, echoing his question.

They're not kidding.

"No," I say. "And no hot water either. We climbed into a spaceship straight from the cave."

"What?" he says. "I'm sorry. I just thought, you had a planned economy, you know? Somebody had to sit there and plan for toys?"

"What a concept." My efforts to cut down on sarcasm have just gone down the drain. "And they planned for underwear, too, and violins, and hammers, and ice cream sticks, and pillowcases. Even toilet paper, though, I must admit, whoever was planning for toilet paper must have been sleeping on the job. Also, I was allowed to have friends. I didn't march everywhere in a gray uniform, nobody assigned me what to do for a living, and we didn't all drink a glass of vodka in the morning."

I run out of breath. They are both sitting up, at an angle from me, like a "V," and Simon is blinking noticeably. It must have been my adrenaline rush that blew them away. I haven't had an energy surge like this in months.

"I'm sorry," Simon repeats.

"I shouldn't have snapped at you," I admit.

He reaches his hand over Mimi's shoulder and strokes mine. "Do you want to stop watching? Is it upsetting you?"

"No, I'm okay." I snap my fingers in the direction of the remote, but Mimi fidgets with it without pushing "Play."

"Do you miss Russia?" she asks.

She is starting at Swarthmore this fall, says she wants to be either in environmental studies or in political science, but I think she could make a top-notch counseling psychologist. She reads people like ABCs with those round eyes of hers and slices our boils open with her questions, precision 100 percent. She just needs to learn about timing.

"Sure, Mims. I mean... I grew up there, it was my home. Friends, family. And my city... It's the most beautiful place in the world."

What the hell am I saying?

"Limpkin, do you want to go visit?" That's Simon. "We can probably arrange it."

"Yeah, that'd be *a toyten bankes!*"

Simon and Mimi speak almost no Yiddish, but by now they've gotten used to my favorite expressions, especially this one, about cupping and a corpse. Every time I say it, I can hear Leila Kahn laugh.

Simon swallows. It's not his fault I can't explain to them

about Russia. Can you imagine what it would look like, my showing up in former Leningrad with a rabbi husband in tow, a suitcase of pills, and the life expectancy of a mosquito? Sleeping in Lisa's armchair and walking the city in three-minute bursts between sit-down rests, from the Vaganova to the Winter Palace, past the screaming billboards for DHL Express and Pepsi-Cola, to the bench by the Bronze Horseman where Matthew and I first kissed, trying not to fall apart in front of Simon. Standing over Babby's grave, on which Cleo has planted new asters. Standing over the Ivanidis' graves next to Cleo, clutching on to her sleeve and finally losing it, waterfalls, nose into her neck, when she says, "Oh, I almost forgot," and pulls out my great-grandmother's locket. "I've been wearing it, I hope you don't mind."

"Thanks, Simon. Mimi." With a gargantuan effort, I reach inside myself and pull out the kind of voice they deserve to hear: Sweet. Appreciative. Nice. "I love you for offering. But it's not necessary. And I'm probably not up to traveling anyway."

But it's too late: Mimi is fired up. "You know what we could do? We could—"

"Mims," I interrupt her. If I've learned one thing with her, it's to be honest. "The Russia... My Russia... The home that I miss—it's not there anymore."

It takes her maybe eight seconds, maybe ten, then she snuggles back under my arm and hits "Play" on the remote. On the screen, a toy monkey resumes her cartwheels. Simon kicks off his slippers and lies atop Mimi so his head fits on my shoulder, and his hand, on my knee. The two of them radiate heat through my blanket; their breathing is a rhythmic rise and fall, which soon becomes a unison. It pushes into my space and recedes, ebbs and flows, but not like the ocean—gentle, barely an intrusion. A caress. Like the Neva

Bay surf. I close my eyes and begin to breathe with them. It's surprisingly easy. We ebb and flow together, no more pushing, just a faint, familiar aroma of milk and of warm, sour bread in the air.

Orion's been standing behind the back of the sofa all day today. I haven't told Simon. I know Orion is shaking his head and changing the bow from one side to the other. But I ignore him.

She comes to me on October 11. I notice the date because Simon marks it on the wall calendar, as he does every morning, and says it out loud, and when he says, "Eleven," I get the shivers, as though it were too soon even to pronounce the word. Like walking on a fresh grave.

"Hey, Dins," she says. Her kiss lands on my cheekbone, cautious not to hurt anything. "How you feeling? I haven't seen you in three days."

That's her orienting me. I want to agree, but I don't trust my brain. It's been swallowing time—hours, days—and regurgitating memories out of order, like some bloated black-hole monster. People come and sit next to me, and next thing I know, they're gone, and Simon is there, holding my head. "You've had a seizure," he says, wipes my mouth, kisses me somewhere on the cheekbone.

Cerelyn, Oni, and Jamie came like that and disappeared, then Mohinder. I think. Maxim appeared out of nowhere and, poof, vanished back into it. Gavi didn't. He stayed for a while, and we talked, but I can't recall what we were saying, only the mice—he was all covered in gray mice, scurrying in and out of sleeves and collars, a twitching tail hanging off his nose, and I could concentrate on nothing else. I kept thinking I couldn't find my mouse among them, and that she would be lost.

Mimi drags her beloved armchair closer and folds herself into it; I raise my bed so I can see her. The hospice installed an adjustable bed in the living room, where the sofa used to be, when I could no longer get up and walk. It's by the window in a strategic spot: The room is on my left, with my poplar branches on a shelf, the TV, and space enough for visitors and nurses. The kitchen is a straight shot from the foot of the bed, so Simon can keep an eye on me while he cooks or prepares a breathing treatment. The rest of the world's on my right, through the window. I watch it change colors and grow thinner and weep for itself: It's autumn. Cars are crawling up and down the hill, and there's the moon. The lazy American moon. It's been fat and round-faced lately, but last night it remembered it wanted nothing to do with us all and stuck up its nose.

Sometimes, on a clear night, I watch constellations dance and chase each other. They whip across the bushes, Canis after Corvus, a near-miss turned into a mini-tornado, wings and ears tangled in the purple bamboo that grows to the sky. Barabashka paws at the pane. I nudge him, and he goes flying after them, dizzying and disquietingly graceful.

"How's your breathing?" Mimi asks, and takes my hand in both of hers.

Naturally, it hasn't been good. Better since they started draining fluid from my lungs. Enough that I can talk.

"Fantastic," I say. "I just saw a car. That was made. I think, in eighteen. Sixty-five."

She gives a subdued laugh, as if I'd explode if she cranked up the volume. "That's nothing. I once saw a car that was made in 1265."

"You win," I say. "How is college?"

"Actually, that's what I wanted to talk about. Sort of." She glances at the kitchen, checking for her father, but I can't tell if she is waiting for him to join us or trying to keep something from him. He emerges just then, drying his hands on a towel. I know this man. He is more than familiar, he is mine somehow. I have a sense I trust him. What is his name? I remember him—something, not memories. A smell. Matthew? Not Matthew. *It's a prayer. Come, my beloved.* Simon? Not Simon. Yes!

"Simon..."

"Have you told her?" he asks.

"I was about to."

Mimi is here.

"Hey, Mims," I say. "How is college?"

They exchange a look. Have I missed something? Everything? Mice are crawling, filling Barabashka's eyes. No one dares climb up Orion's legs—he stands in the corner, a sentinel, leans on his bow, and waits. It's getting dark, a weighty, painful veil. I must go! If they draw the bridges, I'll be trapped on this shore forever.

"It's morphine time, limpkin." Simon bends over me; he is so close, I can almost feel the bristle of his beard. I can smell him—there it is. He smells of calm. "And let's get some valerian root in you, okay?"

They sit next to me, counting time, or thinking the kind of thoughts I can no longer hold together, of the past or the future; I stew in the relief spreading through my veins. Our five hands converge on the edge of my bed.

"Simon..."

He's so close, I can feel his ear with the tip of my nose. I inhale.

"What is it, love?"

"Nothing."

He smells of home.

"Mims. You wanted to tell. Me something."

Her face distorts, crumbles like a sheet of paper, lines and angles. "Are you sure you're up to it? Maybe you should rest."

"It's now. Or never. Kid."

She looks at Simon, who nods, and she pulls her hands out and stands, as if she were about to testify. *Mimi, what have you done?*

"So. You know how you said if something's really, really important, I have to do it no matter what?" She draws air in and forces it out. "I think you're right, and right now there's nothing—"

"Mimi!" Simon yelps. "Just tell her." His hands, holding mine, begin to shake, and he draws them away.

"I want to enlist. In the Army." Her voice slides down a curve. "The recruiter said they really need people in Afghanistan. I can't just watch this war on TV. You understand, don't you?"

She stands over my bed, my Esther Miriam, and waits for what I'll say. I turn my head. Simon's buried his face in his hands, and I cannot tell if he is crying or scared catatonic. Or mourning her already. Or blaming me. Or steeling himself for what's to come.

I am looking for words; they aren't there. Wheezing. Too much fluid. Too much thicket. I almost remember this. *He pulls himself into the train's vestibule through the shutting doors and floats away.* I know how it ends.

I cannot know this. Not again.

She is still talking. "You know why. You of all people should know! We have to make it safe, get rid of Al Qaeda, or it'll happen again!" She turns to Simon. "You're the one who always taught me education is like the pinnacle of life—and girls in Afghanistan can't even go to school! And I'll get mine when I come back."

"And if you don't come back?" He's nearly whispering.

Her nostrils flare. "It's the price we pay," she says to match his voice, then adds quickly: "But I will, though."

I'll bring it back to you, dandelion—and he slides the picture into his breast pocket.

They quiet down, I don't know how long. There are mice in my head. They scurry and jumble my words with their tiny feet. Everything's gone gray and heavy. I wish I could sleep.

"Dins?" Mimi says. "Are you... What do you think?"

Orion has stepped out of the corner and is standing at the foot of the bed. I believe he is ready to go. Matthew is next to him, still in camo, and there comes a gust of that odor I only now recall: grease, rubber, and antiseptic. Something else, metallic.

I try to focus on Mimi, but she's doubling and swimming before me. "You know," I say. It takes all I have to find these words, to push them out, to take the next breath. It's gurgling. *Stay awake.* "Soviet soldiers. In Afghanistan. Called local. Villagers. '*Dushman.*' It means 'enemy.' In Tajik. But in Russian. It means. 'Soul men.'"

My tongue is so heavy, it won't move. A brick in my mouth.

"Dins? What is it?"

What was I saying?

I can hear music, but it's faint. Glinka? I haven't heard this one since the millipede.

"Dinah?"

It's not Mimi. Orion is smiling and gesturing toward the window. It's bright outside now, the light is blinding, flooding through the pane.

I know this voice, but I can't name it. Too faint.

"Dinah?"

Sleep is like my fluffy blanket, like Matthew's steady arms in a high lift, like Babby's dumplings. Like a soft layer of pine needles and fine sand between my toes. Like Mimi's hair. Like Simon's voice when he sings *Shabbat Shalom*. Like a warm challah. Like Leila Kahn's laughter after she says *"a toyten bankes."* Like the bubbling of the Neva under the Palace Bridge.

ACKNOWLEDGMENTS

Writing words is a solitary endeavor, but bringing a book to life takes a lot of help. My agent, Kathy Schneider, took a chance on me, served as my first editor, and held my hand through the uncertain times of the Covid pandemic. My amazing editor, Joe Olshan, and copyeditor, Joan Matthews, saw into the heart of my creation and labored tirelessly to make this novel its best self. I am grateful for teachers, colleagues, and friends, all of whom at some point inspired, challenged, or advised me, worked on my behalf, read my drafts, and pushed me to be a better writer: Kevin Birmingham, Steve Yarbrough, Mako Yoshikawa, Fernanda Martinez, Rob McDonald, Alex Yurgenson, Jabari Asim, Jane Friedman, Laura Rosenthal, Jiyun Liu, and everyone at the Jane Rotrosen Agency and Delphinium Books. As always, I am indebted to my family for believing in me, caring for me, and doing my chores when I am buried in a manuscript.

ABOUT THE AUTHOR

Having grown up a concert pianist in Soviet Russia, River Adams (they/them) came to America as a Jewish refugee during the collapse of the USSR and began their life from scratch in their adopted homeland. Before earning an MFA in creative writing from Emerson College, they graduated from the Delaware County Community College, Rosemont College, earned an MTS degree from Harvard Divinity School, then returned to Pennsylvania to teach world religions to college students. At the same time, they worked as a certified medical interpreter for Russian-speaking patients at Philadelphia hospitals. Over the past 30 years, they have traveled to and lived in 30 states, falling in love with each. Today, River lives in Massachusetts, writing and taking care of a big, noisy family of six humans, two dogs, and a demon disguised as a cat. They are the author of many published short stories and essays and a biography of Leonard Swidler, *There Must Be YOU* (2014). *The Light of Seven Days* is their debut novel.